BRIDE
NOT
INCLUDED

Paperback first published in the United States of America in October 2025.

Cover Design by Carina Walsh

ISBN 978-1-953139-15-3 (ebook)
ISBN 978-1-953139-25-2 (paperback)

First Edition
10 9 8 7 6 5 4 3 2 1

BRIDE
NOT
INCLUDED

Carina Walsh

ALSO BY CARINA WALSH

Knot Your Average Wedding Romcom Series
Bride Not Included
Rivals Not Welcome
RSVPs Not Requried

DEDICATION

For the reader who bought this because of the cute cover...

This is smut. Very funny, giggle-while-kicking-your-feet, romcom-y smut.

There will be dick.

Too late to turn back now, sweetie.

A CALL FROM A POSSIBLE SERIAL KILLER

Chapter 1: Anica

I was elbow-deep in the bride's petticoats when the string quartet texted, "Running late lol." Because nothing says "professional musicians" like announcing your tardiness to the Wedding of the Century with an abbreviation that went out of style in 2010.

"No, I need the string quartet *now*. Tell them traffic isn't an excuse when they signed a contract that specifically mentioned their firstborn children as collateral!" I barked into my earpiece while simultaneously MacGyvering the torn hem of a twenty-thousand-dollar Vera Wang gown with dental floss and what might have been a bobby pin I found in my hair. The bride, sweet, perfect Lissa, stood trembling above me like a wedding cake topper having an existential crisis. Her gown had not only caught on her father's wheelchair exactly seven minutes before they were supposed to go down the aisle, but had also somehow attracted the venue's resident cat, who was now batting at the sequins from a suspiciously close distance.

"Mmmmph," I mumbled around the pins.

"What was that, Anica?" Devonna's voice crackled in my ear.

I secured the final pin and removed the others from my mouth. "I said, tell the quartet I'll personally ensure they never work another wedding in the tri-state area if they're not here in ten minutes. Then call the DJ and have him ready with the processional music as backup. And get someone to remove the cat before it turns this dress into a five-figure scratching post."

"Already on all three," my assistant replied. I could hear her fingers flying across her tablet. "Also, the best man just threw up in the koi pond."

Of course he did. Probably the same best man who thought seven tequila shots at the rehearsal dinner was "getting a head start on the celebration."

"Is he visible from the ceremony site?" I asked, standing to inspect my handiwork on the dress. The repair was invisible unless you were specifically looking for it, which no one would be, because I've developed ninja-level stealth techniques for emergency dress repair after nine years in the business.

"No, but the venue manager is freaking out about the fish."

"Tell him I'll pay for any casualties. And get the best man some mouthwash, activated charcoal, and coffee strong enough to raise the dead. If he ruins this wedding with alcohol breath, I'll personally ensure his dating profile specifies 'vomits at formal occasions.'"

I looked up at Lissa, whose mascara was starting to run. Raccoon eyes were not part of her carefully curated bridal vision board. I reached for the emergency makeup kit I kept strapped to my thigh like a weapon. After the Great Bridesmaid Mascara Flood of 2022, I never went to a wedding without waterproof everything.

"You're perfect," I assured her, dabbing at her under-eyes. "And your dress looks flawless. No one will ever know. Least of all your future husband, who is currently so love-drunk he wouldn't notice if you walked down the aisle in a potato sack."

That got a wobbly smile, which was all I needed. Happy bride, happy hide—mine, specifically, which remained intact for another wedding day.

The door burst open with the force of a SWAT team raid, and Mari swept in with an open bottle of champagne and three flutes dangling between her fingers. My business partner and best friend had an almost supernatural sense for when alcohol was required, like a sommelier with ESP.

"Emergency bubbles!" she announced, pouring generous servings. "Bride gets double. Wedding planner gets triple, but has to pretend it's water."

"Mari, you're a goddess," Lissa whispered, accepting the glass with shaking hands.

"Just doing my job as second-in-command to the Wedding Wizard here." Mari shot me a wink while handing me a glass. "Drink up, boss. The quartet just pulled up looking like they escaped a hostage situation, the best man is getting hosed down by two very annoyed groomsmen, and I've dispatched the ring bearer's mother to confiscate his Nintendo Switch and the slingshot I caught him making out of rubber bands and corsage pins."

I knocked back the champagne in one gulp. "That child is a terrorist disguised as a seven-year-old."

"That's why I slipped the wedding photographer an extra hundred to get action shots when the kid inevitably tries to dive-bomb the cake," Mari replied. "We can sell them to his future prom date in ten years."

Lissa laughed despite her nerves, which was exactly Mari's intention. Good cop, bad cop. Our signature dynamic. I kept things running; Mari kept everyone smiling through the chaos.

Devonna appeared in the doorway, tablet clutched to her chest. My assistant wore her usual expression of contained panic, which somehow never affected her efficiency. That woman could plan an evacuation during an alien invasion and still manage to make it to afternoon tea.

"The officiant is in position, the groom has stopped hyperventilating, and the quartet is setting up now," she reported. "Also, I've confiscated all pens from the flower girls after finding them drawing tattoos on each other."

"Smart." Last month we'd had flower girls who arrived at the altar looking like tiny convicts on leave. "We're back on schedule?"

"We're three minutes and forty-seven seconds behind, but we can make it up if the father of the bride doesn't stop for his emotional speech in the middle of the aisle like he threatened to during rehearsal."

"I cut the brake lines on his wheelchair," Mari whispered to me.

My eyes widened in horror.

"Kidding! But I did promise him an open bar tab for life if he saves the waterworks for the reception."

I turned to Lissa, who had stopped trembling and now looked radiant. The transformation I lived for. "Ready to get married?"

Her eyes welled with tears that, thankfully, didn't fall and ruin my emergency mascara application. "More than anything."

A familiar pang throbbed in my chest, one I'd gotten good at ignoring over the past two years. The same pang that had first appeared when I discovered my own fiancé and a client fucking on the mattress I'd had since college only two days before our wedding. The same client whose beach ceremony I'd orchestrated down to the custom-dyed sand that matched her bridesmaids' dresses.

I shoved the memory away.

"Then let's make it happen," I said, my professional smile sliding back into place.

Forty minutes later, I stood at the back of the venue as Lissa and her new husband shared their first dance. The ceremony had gone off without a single visible hitch. The best man had delivered his toast without vomiting again. The ring bearer had remained mysteriously well-behaved (I spotted a suspicious bulge in Devonna's purse that looked exactly like a confiscated Nintendo Switch).

Mari sidled up beside me, two flutes of champagne in hand. "Another wedding wizarded to perfection."

"Don't call me that," I muttered, but accepted the drink. "And don't jinx it. We still have cake cutting and four more hours to go. Remember the Donaldson's wedding?"

"How could I forget? That's the only time I've seen a mother-in-law try to perform an exorcism on a wedding cake."

"She claimed the raspberry filling looked 'suspiciously like the blood of the innocent.'"

Mari clinked her glass against mine. "Admit it. You pulled off another miracle."

I allowed myself a small smile as I watched the newlyweds. They looked at each other like they'd just discovered the answer to every important question in the universe.

"It's a nice moment," I admitted.

"Almost makes you believe in true love, doesn't it?" Mari waggled her eyebrows.

"I've always believed in true love. Apparently just not for me," I corrected her. My heart gave a traitorous little squeeze watching the couple.

"Way to be a Debbie-downer," Mari said, nudging me with her shoulder. "Nice job with the dress back there, by the way."

"First rule of wedding planning: Always be prepared for disaster. Second rule: Never say the word 'disaster' where the bride can hear you."

"And the third rule?"

"Don't sleep with the groom. Or in my case, don't let your fiancé sleep with the bride."

Mari winced. "Two years, and you're still carrying that around like it's part of your emergency kit."

"I learned exactly what not to do, which is mix business with pleasure."

"Or men with pulses," Mari muttered into her champagne.

"True." I clinked my glass against hers before taking a sip.

"I'm thinking about becoming a nun."

A stream of champagne bubbles erupted up my nose, and I choked, scrambling for a napkin off a nearby table. "What the hell, Mar?"

"What?" Mari asked with an obviously fake innocent expression on her face. "It's true."

"You wouldn't last two seconds. You need dick to survive."

"You're right," Mari gave me an evil grin. "You'd make a better nun. You haven't been laid in two years."

"How do you know?"

She looked me up and down. "Honey, it's kind of obvious."

I shot her a look that had made florists cry. "I date."

"The chai latte guy asking if you want an extra shot doesn't count as a date."

Before I could defend my completely adequate personal life, Devonna appeared with her tablet, now displaying what looked like a small explosion.

"The DJ just played the groom's mother's forbidden song," she reported. "She's threatening to do an interpretive dance to it."

"On it," I said, already moving toward the dance floor. "Tell him to transition to 'YMCA' immediately. No one can resist group choreography, not even vengeful mothers-in-law."

5

"I REFUSE TO be the wedding planner who can't pay her rent." I slumped in my office chair later that night, staring at our books. The McMurty wedding had been a triumph, but its payment would barely cover next month's expenses.

Our office, a converted loft in Chelsea with exposed brick walls and windows that leaked both air and street noise, was the perfect metaphor for our business: stylish on the surface with structural issues we pretended not to notice. Kind of like my dating history, but with better furniture.

"We're not that bad off," Mari argued, feet propped on my desk as she scrolled through Instagram, posting carefully selected shots from today's wedding. "The Fisher-Lu wedding next month is a big one."

"And after that, we've got nothing but small ceremonies until next year." I rubbed my temples. "We need a whale, Mari. A client big enough to float us through the rest of the winter slump."

"What about the couple who wanted their dogs as ring bearers?" Devonna suggested, looking up from her meticulous organization of our emergency supplies. She was restocking my thigh holster with extra bobby pins and what appeared to be mini bottles of tequila.

"The Great Danes with anxiety issues? Hard pass. I still have nightmares about what happened during the consultation. That, and there's still a giant brown stain on the rug by your foot."

"Ew," Devonna wrinkled her nose and stepped to the side. "How do I keep forgetting about that? Anyways, what about that socialite who called yesterday? The one planning the Christmas wedding for next year? A deposit from her might help."

"She's a bridezilla with a budget too small for her expectations," I sighed. "She wants ice sculptures of herself and the groom riding matching unicorns. The unicorns need to cry actual tears that fill champagne glasses."

"Classy," Mari snorted.

"I told her we were booked. Right after I checked whether our insurance covers 'death by falling mythical ice creature.'"

"You turned down business?" Mari dropped her feet to the floor. "Since when do we turn down paying clients?"

"Since this one would cost us more in therapy bills than we'd make on the contract." I began packing up my laptop. After fourteen hours in four-inch heels, my body was screaming for a hot bath and the leftover pad thai waiting in my fridge. "What about the politician's daughter?"

"Wants to get married on a glacier to make a statement about climate change," Mari said. "I told her nothing says 'environmental consciousness' like flying two hundred guests to the Arctic Circle."

"The Pekchov-Winstein wedding?"

"Groom's mother called six times today," Devonna reported. "She's now requesting we provide emotional support alpacas for guests who find the ceremony overwhelming."

"What the hell? That's... creative," I admitted.

"She also wants them in tuxedos that match the groomsmen."

"Of course she does." I sighed. "Anyone else promising actual money instead of exotic livestock and therapy bills?"

The office phone rang, and we all stared at it.

"Nobody answer that," I warned. "It's after nine. Whoever it is can leave a voicemail like a normal person."

Mari's eyes gleamed. Her rebellious streak had both created and nearly destroyed our friendship multiple times since college. "Could be a whale," she sang, reaching for the phone.

"If it's the unicorn bride, I will end you," I threatened. "And I know how to make it look like an accident. I've worked with enough murder mystery themed weddings."

"Knot Your Average Wedding," Mari chirped into the receiver. She listened for a moment, then frowned. "Yes, she's here, but we generally don't do consultations this late—"

She paused, eyes widening. "I see. May I ask what this is regarding?" Another pause. "Of course. One moment."

She held the phone out to me, covering the mouthpiece. "This guy's assistant says he'll only speak to you personally. Mentioned triple our normal consultation rate if you meet him tonight."

"Tonight? It's almost ten." I narrowed my eyes. "What's the catch?"

"No idea. But the assistant says he's got the cash. And she made him sound desperate. My favorite combination in a client." She wiggled the phone at me. "Plus, he apparently asked for you specifically. Said he's heard you're the best."

"Flattery and money. A dangerous combination." But I was already reaching for the phone. "This is Anica Marcel."

A woman's voice responded. "Hello Ms. Marcel. My name is Erika, and I'm calling because I've been told you're the best wedding planner in the city."

"I am." No point in false modesty when it was simply true.

"Good. My boss is in need of the best. He's currently at the Apex Building, penthouse office. I'll meet you in the lobby in half an hour."

I blinked. "Ma'am, we don't typically do same-day consultations, especially after business hours—"

"Triple your rate, as I already mentioned to your colleague. Plus a five-thousand-dollar consultation fee just for showing up tonight. Cash."

My eyebrows shot up, and Mari, who could practically smell money through phone lines, leaned closer.

"May I ask what the emergency is?" I tried to keep my voice professional despite the absurdity of the situation.

"My boss is in need of a wedding. A perfect wedding. In three months."

That was possible, though it would be challenging. We'd pulled off miracles in less time.

"And the catch?"

She chuckled. "Smart woman. I'm sure he'll discuss it when we meet in person. See you soon."

"Wait, what are you—"

The woman hung up on me before I could respond. How smug did her boss have to be to assume I'd just show up after getting so little information?

Mari and Devonna were watching me with expressions ranging from glee (Mari) to quiet horror (Devonna).

"I bet her boss is a serial killer." I tossed the phone back to Mari.

"Potentially," Mari nodded cheerfully. "But a rich one. The fancy ones at least kill you in penthouses with good views."

"That's comforting."

"Who was it?" Devonna asked.

"Her name was Erika, but she didn't say who her boss was. Just that he's at the Apex Building. He wants me to show up tonight. I don't trust it."

"Fair enough," Mari said, picking at her perfect nails. "But he did offer a lot of money just to meet with him tonight."

"I'm not a sex worker."

"You'd make a great sex worker. What with the long tan legs and the tits for days and the ass that–" Mari ducked when I chucked a bouquet of fake flowers at her. "My point is, meet with the guy, take his money, and then decide if you want to work with him."

"I know what you mean when you say that, but anyone else would think you're a cheat." I rolled my eyes as I grabbed my bag.

"The Apex Building," Devonna frowned. "As in the Burkhardt Building?"

"I guess?" I shrugged. "Why?"

Devonna spun her laptop around, displaying a business magazine cover featuring a man with dark hair, annoyingly perfect bone structure, and eyes that somehow managed to look both amused and calculating. The headline read: "Callan Burkhardt: The Billionaire Bachelor."

"That's why," Devonna said. "Callan Burkhardt. Tech billionaire. Manhattan's most eligible eternal bachelor. And apparently, your next client."

I stared at the image, an uneasy feeling settling in my stomach. "A billionaire playboy wants to plan a wedding?"

"Maybe he's turning over a new leaf," Mari suggested.

"Or maybe he's a serial killer," I countered. "I bet billionaires get away with murder all the time. They just throw money at their problems."

"Well, we need money. Let's be the one he throws it at." Mari grinned.

"Now you're making us sound like strippers." I wrinkled my nose at her.

"Oh! We would be great strippers!"

Devonna ignored Mari bouncing in her chair, focusing on me. "Either way, I do agree that meeting with him is probably worth your time."

"Fine," I whined, even though all I wanted were my sweat set and my leftovers. "I'll meet with the sexy serial killer."

WANTED: A BRIDE (PREFERABLY BREATHING)

Chapter 2: Callan

I wasn't waiting for her.

Callan Burkhardt didn't wait for people. People waited for me. Investors, developers, women who hoped I might finally settle down with them despite having better odds of winning the lottery while being struck by lightning. Even my grandmother, who had raised me and whom I adored beyond reason, knew better than to expect punctuality from me. The last time she invited me for Sunday dinner at 6:00, she told me it started at 4:30. I still arrived at 6:15.

Yet, I was pacing my penthouse office like a desperate contestant on The Bachelor waiting for the final rose?

I'd already rearranged the whiskey decanters three times, adjusted my tie seven times, and practiced my "casually leaning against the window" pose twice—once with hands in pockets, once with arms crossed. I settled on hands in pockets. Arms crossed looked too defensive, according to the body language book I definitely skimmed rather than read.

"Mr. Burkhardt, Ms. Marcel has arrived downstairs," my assistant's voice announced through the intercom. "Security is escorting her."

"I told them to send her straight up," I replied, annoyed at the delay. "Not interrogate her like she's smuggling nuclear launch codes in her wedding planner binder."

"Apparently there was some... confusion about her appointment."

"Let me guess. Rick thinks she's either an escort or a corporate spy?"

"Actually, he asked if she was here about the housekeeping position."

I nearly choked. "He did not."

"She was... not amused."

I rolled my eyes so hard I probably sprained an ocular muscle. My head of security, Rick, had a tendency to treat every woman under forty who entered the building after hours as a potential threat to either my virtue or my intellectual property. His paranoia was usually an asset. Tonight, it was making me contemplate a career change for him. Perhaps as a human doorstop.

"Tell him I'll personally ensure his next performance review is conducted by my grandmother after I've told her he made her snickerdoodle recipe 'too dry.'"

"Already handled, sir. I informed him that sexual harassment lawsuits are significantly more expensive than whatever you're paying Ms. Marcel."

Of course she had. Erika had been my executive assistant for six years, ever since I'd poached her from a rival tech firm by tripling her salary and offering stock options that had since made her wealthy enough to buy a new car each month. She stayed, she claimed, because "someone has to keep you from becoming a complete megalomaniac, and the health insurance covers therapy."

I glanced at my watch. 10:48 PM. Ms. Marcel was impressively punctual for someone summoned to a penthouse by a stranger at this hour. Most people would have waited until morning, sent a proxy, or called the police.

But then, Anica Marcel wasn't most people, according to my research. Before the call, I'd had Erika compile a thorough profile. Ms. Marcel was a fashion merchandising major who'd pivoted to event planning after planning her sorority's charity galas. She'd launched her own wedding planning business five years ago with her college roommate. Now, she was one of the most sought-after planners in Manhattan, with a reputation for turning disaster weddings into magazine-worthy events.

Also apparently immune to creepy late-night penthouse invitations from billionaires, which either made her exceptionally professional or exceptionally naïve. I was betting on the former.

Exactly what I needed.

I straightened my tie in the reflection of the floor-to-ceiling windows, admiring both my perfectly tailored Tom Ford suit and the glittering Manhattan skyline behind me. I'd chosen this building for my headquarters specifically for this view. A constant reminder of how far I'd come from the cramped Queens apartment.

The elevator doors slid open, and I turned, knowing exactly how good I looked in silhouette. I'd perfected the move in my bathroom mirror at age sixteen and had been deploying it strategically ever since.

However, I nearly forgot the entire speech I'd prepared.

Anica Marcel was not what I'd expected. The wedding planners I'd encountered at friends' weddings tended to be either aggressively cheerful middle-aged women who called everyone "honey" or nervous twentysomethings with clipboards and visible stress hives.

She was neither.

She stood in my elevator like she owned it. Dark hair pulled back in a knot so tight it looked like it was holding up not just her hair but possibly her entire skeletal structure. A black pencil skirt and matching blazer that somehow managed to be both strictly professional and distractingly flattering. Killer heels that brought her to just below my eye level and looked sharp enough to double as murder weapons in a pinch. And an expression that said she'd already calculated sixteen ways to efficiently dispose of my body if necessary.

I liked it. I liked it more than I should have.

"Ms. Marcel," I said, stepping forward with my hand extended and what People magazine had once called my "devastatingly charming" smile. "Thank you for coming on such short notice."

She assessed my hand as if it might be concealing a joy buzzer before shaking it firmly. No lingering touch, no demure smile. Just business. It was like shaking hands with a particularly attractive contract lawyer.

"Mr. Burkhardt," she replied, her voice cool and composed. "Your five minutes start now."

I raised an eyebrow. "I believe I offered a consultation fee for significantly longer than five minutes."

"The fee buys you thirty minutes. But you have five to convince me this isn't a waste of both our time." She glanced pointedly at her watch, a modestly expensive timepiece that looked like it could survive a nuclear blast. "Four minutes, forty-three seconds."

God, she was refreshing. After a day of meetings where everyone nodded at my most half-baked ideas like I was announcing the cure for cancer while simultaneously solving world hunger, her unfazed demeanor was practically an aphrodisiac.

"Drink?" I asked, gesturing toward the bar cart I'd specifically positioned to catch the light in a way that made the crystal decanters look like they contained liquid gold instead of overpriced alcohol.

"No, thank you."

"Not even to make this conversation more tolerable?" I moved to the crystal decanter of thirty-year-old Macallan. "I assure you, it's excellent. Aged longer than most of my relationships."

"I don't drink with clients until after I've saved their wedding," she replied like a pre-recorded customer service message. "Water would be fine."

I poured her a Fiji water. Of course I stocked Fiji water, imported directly from Fiji on boats made of sustainable bamboo or whatever made rich people feel less guilty about bottled water, and handed it to her, deliberately letting our fingers brush. Most women would have at least blinked at the contact. She might as well have been accepting a tax form.

"Now," she said, not bothering to sit despite my gesture toward the sofa. "About this wedding."

"Right to business. I appreciate efficiency." I took a sip of my scotch, enjoying the slow burn and the knowledge that each sip cost roughly the same as a community college textbook. "I need a wedding. A perfect wedding. In three months."

She pulled a small notebook from her bag and clicked a pen. "Budget?"

"Unlimited."

Her pen paused. "Everyone has a budget, Mr. Burkhardt."

"I don't."

"Even billionaires have finite resources," she countered. "Let's say seven figures and refine from there."

I fought a smile. She wasn't impressed by money. Or at least pretended not to be. She might be the first person in Manhattan who didn't immediately calculate my net worth upon meeting me and adjust their behavior accordingly. Another point in her favor.

"Fine. Initial budget of nine million, with flexibility for the right elements."

She nodded, making a note. I tried to peek at her handwriting but couldn't see past her expertly positioned arm. For all I knew, she was writing "pretentious rich guy" with a series of exclamation points.

"Venue preferences?"

"I'm getting married at the Rhodes Estate."

"Great, so you've already booked it then."

"No."

Her brows furrowed in a cute way that made her look like a petulant child. "No?"

I held up my scotch glass and nodded. "Nope."

"Then how do you know you're getting married there?"

Shrugging, I smirked at her. "Because it's not optional. I'm getting married there; I just haven't booked the venue. Not my job." I winked at her. She returned it with a scowl.

"I'll note it here, but most venues don't book this late. Three months will be tricky."

"I'm sure you can handle it, Ms. Marcel." I swirled my glass and raised an eyebrow. "You are the best, aren't you?"

She didn't answer my question. "Guest count?"

"Two hundred. Maybe two-fifty. Depending on how many cousins I discover once the invitations go out."

"Theme or style?"

"Tasteful. Nothing garish. I'd defer to your expertise on the details." I paused. "Though I draw the line at releasing doves. After the incident at my college roommate's wedding, I can't look at white birds without flinching."

She looked up from her notebook, one perfectly arched eyebrow raised in what might have been the barest hint of curiosity. I considered it a victory. "And your bride? What's her style?"

I smiled my most charming smile. The one that had graced magazine covers and persuaded venture capitalists to hand over millions. The smile that had once caused a sommelier to drop an entire tray of champagne flutes. "That's the interesting part. I don't

14

have a bride yet."

Her pen froze mid-word. "I'm sorry?"

"I don't have a fiancée," I repeated, watching her expression shift from professional interest to confusion. "We're planning a wedding, bride not included."

"So there's another groom?"

I choked on my scotch. "No, I assure you, there will be a bride. I just haven't found her yet."

She stared at me for a long moment. Then she laughed. It was a genuine, surprised sound that transformed her face from merely attractive to outright beautiful.

"I'm sorry," she said, composing herself. "For a moment I thought you said you wanted me to plan a wedding without a bride."

"That's exactly what I said."

The laugh died. "You're serious."

"Completely."

"Is this for a movie? A reality show?" She glanced around as if looking for hidden cameras. "Because I don't do television. My contracts specifically exclude—"

"This is not for entertainment purposes," I assured her. "It's a genuine wedding. I just need to work backward from the usual timeline."

She crossed her arms, the notebook now forgotten. "You want me to plan a real wedding for you and a woman who doesn't exist yet."

"She exists," I clarified. "I just haven't met her. Or rather, I haven't selected her yet." I flashed another smile. "Though if this is your way of applying for the position, I'm certainly open to discussing—"

"Finish that sentence and I'll use this pen in ways that violate the Geneva Convention," she cut in, her voice arctic.

I held up my hands in surrender, oddly delighted by her threat. "Just testing your professional boundaries. Consider me properly chastised."

Her eyebrows shot up. "'Selected'? Are you running some sort of dystopian dating competition? The Bachelor: Billionaire Edition?"

"Nothing so dramatic." I moved to the window, gesturing for her to join me. After a moment's hesitation, she did, though she maintained a careful distance that suggested she was calculating the trajectory

15

needed to push me through the glass if necessary. "Do you see that building there? The Binx Tower?"

She nodded.

"Three of my closest friends work there. We met at Stanford, started our first businesses together, have been competing ever since." I turned to face her. "Two are married. One's engaged. And several months ago, over drinks significantly less fancy than this one, they bet me 10 million dollars each that I couldn't commit to marriage."

That wasn't the whole story, of course. The bet had actually started as a drunken argument about whether true love existed at all. Chance, happily married for five years, insisted it did. Kris, cynically married for tax purposes, argued it was a chemical delusion. Morgan, nervously engaged and second-guessing everything, had been caught in the middle.

And I had declared the entire concept a myth perpetuated by greeting card companies and jewelry stores right before betting millions of dollars that I could get married without falling victim to the delusion myself.

"So this is about a bet," she said flatly.

"This is about proving a point," I corrected. "And yes, winning a bet. I never lose bets, Ms. Marcel. It's a personal policy."

"And the bride, this theoretical woman, she's just... what? A prop in your game? A particularly expensive betting chip?"

Annoyance flickered in my chest. Most people didn't question my motives. They just nodded and took my money. "She'll be someone compatible. Someone looking for the same arrangement."

"Arrangement," she repeated, the word dripping with judgment like an ice cream cone in August.

"A mutually beneficial partnership," I explained. "I'm not looking for love, Ms. Marcel. I'm looking for a practical union with someone who understands that marriage is ultimately a business arrangement with romantic window dressing."

She set down her untouched water with a sharp click. "Marriage isn't a business transaction, Mr. Burkhardt."

"Historically, that's exactly what it was," I countered. "The modern notion of marrying for love is relatively recent. I'm simply being pragmatic. And honest. Unlike half the couples you plan weddings for who are probably already cheating or contemplating divorce before the cake is cut."

"And the woman who agrees to this arrangement, she'll know she was selected because you needed to win a bet?"

"She'll know exactly what she's getting into," I assured her. "Transparency is important in any contract."

"A contract," she echoed. "How romantic."

I smiled despite myself. "I'm not selling romance, Ms. Marcel. I'm offering honesty. Which is more than most marriages start with. Just ask my parents, who spent years in matrimonial purgatory before finally admitting they'd rather set each other on fire than spend another day together."

She tucked her notebook back into her bag with movements that suggested she was imagining it was my face. "I appreciate your candor, Mr. Burkhardt, but I'll have to decline. This isn't the kind of event my company handles."

That wasn't the response I'd expected. People didn't say no to me. Especially not when I was offering obscene amounts of money. That was like my whole thing. Rich guy offers money, people say yes. It was practically a law of physics.

"The fee would be triple your standard rate," I reminded her. "Plus bonuses for discretion and expedited timeline. That's enough to keep your cute little Chelsea office running for a little longer?"

"Money isn't the issue."

"Then what is?"

"Professional integrity," she replied. "I plan weddings for people in love, or at least people who've met each other. Not bachelor billionaires trying to win bets."

I studied her, intrigued by her refusal. Her principles were inconvenient but admittedly admirable. Like finding out your sports car doesn't have cup holders; annoying but somehow making the whole package more impressive.

"I can find ten wedding planners by morning who'd kill for this job," I said, watching for her reaction. "Possibly literally, given how cutthroat the wedding industry is."

"Then I suggest you bother *them* with your little conundrum." She extended her hand for a goodbye shake, her posture screaming 'this meeting is over' louder than if she'd brought an actual megaphone. "Thank you for the consultation opportunity, but I'm afraid I can't help you."

I took her hand, but instead of shaking it, I held it a moment longer than necessary. Her skin was warm, her grip firm, and her expression suggested she was going to reach for hand sanitizer as soon as the elevator doors closed behind her.

"The consultation fee is still yours. Five thousand, as promised."

"Keep it," she said, withdrawing her hand like she was removing it from a particularly suspicious petting zoo animal. "Consider it a goodwill gesture from Knot Your Average Wedding."

"You heard me out, so you'll take the $5k," I said, pulling out the envelope I had with the cash from the inside pocket of my jacket. I handed it to her, and she didn't take it until I stepped forward and held it in front of her face. "I keep my word, Ms. Marcel. Let me keep it now."

She narrowed her eyes at me, flicking her gaze to the envelope and back to my face twice before rolling her eyes and snatching the envelope.

"Fine."

I smirked at her. "And my offer stands. In fact, let me sweeten it: nine million for the wedding budget, with a five hundred thousand planning fee for your company. Exclusive vendor rights. And full creative control within my parameters. It'll be a wedding for you to brag about for years."

Her eyes widened almost imperceptibly. For a normal wedding planning business, that was life-changing money. The kind of money that could turn a cute Chelsea office into a Manhattan empire.

"Mr. Burkhardt—"

"Callan," I corrected.

"Mr. Burkhardt," she repeated. "No amount of money changes the fundamental problem. You're asking me to plan a wedding for a relationship that doesn't exist."

"Yet," I added. "Doesn't exist yet. Think of it as extremely proactive planning."

"Good night," she said, turning toward the elevator. "And good luck with your search."

I watched her walk away, noting with appreciation how perfectly her skirt emphasized the gentle sway of her hips.

The elevator doors closed behind her, and I smiled at the empty space where she'd stood.

Erika's voice came through the intercom. "Should I compile a list of alternative wedding planners for tomorrow?"

"No," I replied, finishing my scotch in one unnecessarily dramatic gulp. "I want her."

"She seemed quite firm in her refusal, sir."

"Everyone has a price, Erika."

"With respect, sir, some people have principles."

I set down my glass with more force than necessary. "Then I'll just have to appeal to something besides her financial interests."

"Such as?"

"I'm not sure yet." I checked my watch. Nearly midnight. "But I'll start by finding out everything there is to know about Anica Marcel and her business. Schedule a breakfast delivery to her office tomorrow. Something impressive. And have the car ready at eight."

"May I remind you that you have the Tokyo investor call at nine?"

"Reschedule it."

A pause. "They've already rescheduled twice."

"Then they're used to it," I replied. "This is more important."

"A wedding planner is more important than a hundred-million-dollar investment deal?"

I grinned at the exasperation in her voice. "The right wedding planner is. And Anica Marcel is the right one."

"Because she said no," Erika sighed, not bothering to make it a question.

"Exactly." I walked back to the window, surveying the city. "She said no to me, Erika. When was the last time that happened?"

"Tuesday, sir. When you asked if I would water your office plants while you were in Aspen."

"That doesn't count. You're practically family."

"If you say so, sir. But might I suggest that your sudden interest in Ms. Marcel has less to do with her wedding planning abilities and more to do with how she looks in that pencil skirt?"

"I'm wounded by your insinuation," I replied, not wounded in the slightest. "This is purely professional."

"Of course it is, sir. Just like that yacht you bought last year was 'purely for business meetings.'"

"It was! We closed the Singapore deal on that yacht."

"After you renamed it 'The Billion-Heir.'"

I waved dismissively. "Details. Focus on the task at hand: Operation Wedding Planner."

"We're not calling it that," she said flatly.

"Operation Bride Hunt?"

"Worse."

"Operation 'I Do' Or Die?"

"I'm hanging up now, sir."

I spent the next hour having Erika pull every article, social media post, and business review about Knot Your Average Wedding and its principal planner. The more I learned, the more convinced I became that Anica Marcel was exactly who I needed. Someone with impeccable taste, a spotless professional reputation, and a spine of steel.

The fact that she was gorgeous and looked at me like I was a problem to be solved rather than a prize to be won? That was just a bonus. A distracting, intriguing bonus that had absolutely nothing to do with my professional interest in her services.

I'd always enjoyed a challenge. And Anica Marcel had just become my favorite kind of challenge. One I fully intended to win.

After all, I hadn't built a tech empire by taking no for an answer.

And I certainly hadn't made billions by giving up after the first rejection.

Or by ignoring excellent pencil skirts.

POSSIBLE SPONTANEOUS UNDERWEAR COMBUSTION

Chapter 3: Anica

I arrived at the office at my usual time, 7:30 AM sharp, because the wedding industry waits for no one, especially not bleary-eyed planners who spent half the night having absolutely-not-sexual dreams about billionaires with jawlines that could cut glass and eyes so blue they should require a warning label from the FDA.

God, maybe Mari was right. I needed to get laid. The vibrator wasn't cutting it anymore.

Not that I'd been thinking about Callan Burkhardt. I'd been thinking about his proposal. His business proposal. The ridiculous, ethically questionable arrangement that I had absolutely, definitively rejected right before spending three hours stalking his Instagram at 2 AM. For research purposes. Professional research about a potential client who happened to look unreasonably good in swim trunks on his private island. The same private island where he'd apparently rescued an endangered sea turtle, according to the caption. Because of course even his performative social media good deeds were annoyingly attractive. So was his six-pack.

I balanced my coffee, laptop bag, and a stack of vendor catalogs as I fumbled with the office door, feeling like I was moving through quicksand after my night of definitely-not-obsessing over Manhattan's Most Eligible Jerkface.

Usually, I was the first one in, followed by Devonna at 8:15 and Mari whenever her hangover permitted, typically somewhere between

9:00 and the apocalypse. Mari once showed up so late she missed an entire consultation, then claimed she was "operating on Australian time" despite having never been to Australia.

So I wasn't prepared to find the lights already on, coffee brewing, and Devonna, my reliable, serious, perpetually anxious assistant, giggling. Not just regular giggling. The kind of high-pitched, breathless giggle usually reserved for puppies in bow ties or Ryan Gosling doing literally anything.

That giggle was directed at Callan Burkhardt, who lounged against my reception desk like he was posing for the cover of Billionaire Monthly: Trespassing Edition. He wore a charcoal suit that probably cost more than my car, with a pale blue tie that matched his eyes to the point where I suspected he'd had it custom-dyed from a swatch of his own iris.

"Good morning, Ms. Marcel," he said, flashing that magazine-cover smile that probably made most women drop their panties. I felt my own underwear consider the possibility before I mentally slapped it back into place. "Your assistant has excellent taste in almond croissants."

Devonna, who normally maintained the demeanor of a particularly anxious tax accountant during audit season, was practically glowing. She clutched a pastry in one hand and what appeared to be a monogrammed coffee cup in the other. Her usually impeccable bun had somehow come slightly undone, and she'd unbuttoned the top button of her blouse. For Devonna, this was the equivalent of showing up in a bikini.

"Mr. Burkhardt brought breakfast," she explained unnecessarily, gesturing to an elaborate spread of pastries, fruit, and what looked suspiciously like a sterling silver coffee service. "Wasn't that thoughtful? And he asked all about my system organizing the emergency vendor contacts. He said it was" — she actually fluttered her eyelashes — "revolutionary."

"Incredibly thoughtful," I replied, my tone drier than the Sahara during a drought. "Almost as thoughtful as calling ahead for an appointment or, I don't know, respecting normal business boundaries."

"I did try," he said with mock contrition. "Your voicemail is full. Something about a woman named Amelia and her mother's demand for alpaca ring bearers in sombreros?"

"Berets, actually,'" I corrected automatically, then immediately regretted giving him any information at all. "How did you get in here?

22

Did you bribe the security guard? Hack our alarm system?"

"Your building manager is a fan of my apps. Particularly DateMe, which apparently helped him meet his fiancée." Callan looked insufferably pleased with himself. "He was happy to let me in early to surprise a valued tenant. He also mentioned you're the only person in the building who's never been late on rent, and you once helped his mother plan her vow renewal for free."

"How long have you been here interrogating people about me?" I demanded, dropping my bags at my desk. "And exactly what part of 'no' last night gave you the impression that stalking me at my workplace was an appropriate follow-up strategy?"

"The part where you looked at me like you were mentally calculating whether the benefits of saying yes outweighed the headache." He offered me a coffee cup with my name inscribed in what appeared to be actual gold leaf. "I had these made specially. Seemed a shame to settle for paper cups."

I ignored the coffee despite the traitorous part of my brain that was practically foaming at the mouth for caffeine and the even more traitorous part that was stupidly flattered he'd gone to such lengths. "This is inappropriate. We don't have a meeting scheduled, and I believe I made my position clear last night."

"Crystal clear," he agreed, taking a sip from his own cup. "Which is why I'm here with a revised proposition."

"I don't—"

"One million dollars," he interrupted. "As your planning fee. Separate from the wedding budget."

I almost dropped the vendor catalogs. One million dollars. That was enough to pay off our business loans, put a deposit down on the downtown storefront location we'd been eyeing for years, hire at least two more assistants, and still have enough left over to replace the ancient copier that had been making sounds like a dying whale since 2020. We'd named it Moby Dick, partly for the whale noises and partly because it was the bane of my existence.

But I wasn't about to let him see me react. "Mr. Burkhardt—"

"Plus exclusive rights to plan my grandmother's annual charity gala, which, I should mention, is covered extensively by every major society publication and has launched the careers of multiple event planners."

Now he was just being cruel. The Burkhardt Foundation Gala was the holy grail of social events; impossible to get unless you were already established with the upper echelon of Manhattan society. It was the event planning equivalent of getting a Broadway lead role without ever having appeared in a high school musical.

"And," he continued, placing his coffee cup down on my desk, "I'm prepared to make a significant investment in your business. Silent partner. No interference in your operations."

"Why?"

"Why what?"

"Why are you so determined to hire me specifically? There are dozens of wedding planners in Manhattan who would jump at this opportunity without requiring bribery, breaking and entering, or personalized coffee cups." Dozens of planners who wouldn't spend an embarrassing amount of time staring at the way his pants fit his absurdly well-formed backside. Not that I'd been looking. Much.

He considered me for a moment, his head tilted slightly. "Because you said no."

"That's not a reason."

"It's the best reason." He stepped closer, and I caught a whiff of whatever absurdly expensive cologne he wore. Something that probably contained actual gold flakes and the tears of finance bros he'd crushed on his way to the top. It smelled like money and masculinity and made my knees momentarily consider a career change to "jelly." "Everyone says yes to me, Ms. Marcel. Always. It's refreshing to meet someone who values principles over profit."

"So you're trying to get me to abandon those principles... for profit."

He chuckled. "Interesting." Callan shrugged. "I'm asking you to consider that your principles and my proposal aren't mutually exclusive." He gestured around our modest office. "You've built something impressive here. But with the right resources, you could build an empire."

Before I could respond, Mari burst through the door in a cloud of perfume and lateness, already talking before she fully entered the room.

"Ani, you will not believe what happened with that client from the Upper East Side. She wants swans. Not just regular swans. Black swans. In Manhattan. In July. I told her unless she's planning to

24

airbrush the regular swans or host her wedding inside a meat locker, she's going to have a bunch of dead birds floating in the—holy mother of all things fuckable."

She stopped abruptly, finally registering Callan's presence. Her mouth actually dropped open, and I watched with horrified fascination as she unconsciously licked her lips like a cartoon wolf spotting a particularly juicy steak.

"You're him," she breathed, her voice dropping an octave into what I recognized as her "I'm about to make terrible decisions" range. "You're Callan Burkhardt."

"Indeed I am," Callan replied, extending his hand. "And you must be Mari Landry, the creative genius behind the business."

Mari took his hand but instead of shaking it, she just held it, staring at him with the same expression I'd seen her use when we passed a Gucci sample sale. "Creative genius, future billionaire's wife, whatever you want to call me," she purred.

"I do have an opening for that position." Callan kissed her knuckles and for a moment, I was concerned my best friend was going to collapse.

I cleared my throat a little too loudly. "Mr. Burkhardt was just leaving."

"Oh, I don't think so," Mari countered, finally releasing his hand but maintaining eye contact with the subtlety of a neon sign. "You wouldn't leave when I just arrived, would you?"

"I wouldn't dream of it." Callan seemed far too entertained by what was happening, leaning back against my desk and sipping his coffee with the world's smuggest look on his stupid handsome face.

To my horror, my assistant took Mari's side. "I think Mr. Burkhardt was just about to tell us more about his investment offer. In detail. With numbers."

"Devonna's right, but first..." Mari grabbed my arm with alarming strength. "Excuse us one tiny moment."

Before I could protest, she had dragged me into our supply closet; a generous term for what was essentially a glorified cabinet with enough room for two adults if they didn't mind violating personal space laws.

"Are you clinically insane?" she hissed once the door was closed. "That's Callan Burkhardt. *The* Callan Burkhardt. The guy who made his first billion before thirty. The guy whose dating app revolutionized how millennials hook up and whose financial app is how I manage to pay rent despite my questionable spending habits. The guy who has his own goddamn thirst account on Instagram with three million followers who just post zoomed-in photos of his–"

"I'm aware of who he is."

"Then why aren't you jumping on whatever offer he's making? Did he proposition you? Is that why he's here? Because if so, while I absolutely support your right to say no, I also support your right to consider climbing him like a tree and seeing if billionaires do it better. For science. For womankind. For me, vicariously. And multiple times. In public."

"Mari!" My face heated up to approximately the temperature of the sun. "He's not—that's not—he wants to hire us."

"Even better! We need clients!"

"To plan a wedding."

"That's literally our job description."

"For him."

"So?"

"Without a bride."

She blinked. "Come again?"

"He literally told you the position was open."

"I was too busy imagining what it'd be like for him to pin me to your desk and–"

"Ew. Stop." I smacked her in the arm.

"Ow." Mari smacked me back.

"He doesn't have a bride." I quickly explained Callan's proposition—the bet, the nonexistent bride, the obscene amount of money now on the table. With each detail, Mari's expression shifted from confusion to disbelief to calculating interest.

"So let me get this straight," she said when I finished. "He's offering us a million-dollar planning fee, exclusive rights to the Burkhardt Gala, and a business investment, just to plan a wedding for him and some woman he hasn't met yet?"

"Yes."

"And you said no."

"Of course I said no! It's morally reprehensible and completely against everything we stand for."

"What we stand for is planning spectacular weddings and making money doing it. And apparently turning down the hottest man in Manhattan when he's literally throwing cash at us. Did you see his butt in those pants? That's not a butt, Ani. That's an achievement. That's a butt that deserves its own Forbes profile."

"Can you focus, please? This isn't about his... anatomy."

"Everything is about his anatomy. Have you seen it? Because I have, extensively, on the internet. There's a photo of him coming out of the ocean in St. Barts that should be classified as a weapon of mass seduction."

"Would you stop objectifying our potential client?"

"So he *is* a potential client now?" Mari pounced on my slip with the ferocity of a sample sale shopper spotting the last discounted Prada bag. "I knew you were considering it!"

"I'm not—" I stopped, sighing. "It's morally reprehensible and completely against everything we stand for."

"Morals don't pay for that downtown storefront you've been eyeing. They don't pay Devonna's salary or the rent increase our landlord just hit us with. And they definitely don't pay for the new spring collection at Saks that I've already charged to my card." She grabbed my shoulders. "Do you know what does pay for those things? Billionaires with commitment issues and excellent bone structure."

I closed my eyes, my resolve weakening despite myself. The worst part was, she wasn't wrong. We were doing okay, but "okay" didn't build empires. It didn't secure our future or allow us to expand. It just kept us treading water in an industry where the big fish regularly swallowed the small ones.

"Look," Mari said, her voice softening. "I get it. It's weird. But maybe we could see it as... I don't know, a challenge? The ultimate wedding planning test? If we can pull this off, we can handle anything."

"It feels like selling out," I admitted.

"It's not selling out if it funds your dreams." She squeezed my arm. "Just think about it, okay? That's all I'm asking. Think about it while staring directly at his face, which was clearly sculpted by Michelangelo during a particularly inspired period."

"You're ridiculous."

When we emerged from the closet, Callan was examining our vision board; a massive collage of wedding inspiration, business goals, and the occasional motivational quote that Mari insisted kept our "entrepreneurial chakras aligned," whatever that meant.

"Fascinating," he said, pointing to a photo of the downtown storefront we'd been coveting. "This space has been vacant for nearly a year. The owner is holding out for a specific type of tenant. Someone with... prestige."

Of course he knew about the storefront. He probably had files on our favorite coffee orders and preferred brands of toilet paper too. Possibly our menstrual cycles and exact measurements. I made a mental note to sweep the office for bugs later, though I wouldn't put it past him to have developed microscopic drones disguised as dust particles.

"Mr. Burkhardt," I began, steeling myself. "Your offer is extremely generous."

"But?" he prompted, turning to face me with those unfairly blue eyes. Eyes that should come with their own warning label: CAUTION: Prolonged exposure may cause common sense failure and spontaneous underwear combustion.

"But I need to establish some terms."

Mari made a small, triumphant noise behind me that sounded disturbingly like "cha-ching."

"I'm listening," Callan said, looking intrigued rather than victorious, which somehow annoyed me more.

"First, this will be a strictly professional relationship. No inappropriate comments, no innuendos, no... whatever that was in your office last night."

"My devastating charm?" he suggested with a smirk that made something low in my abdomen do a completely unauthorized backflip.

"Your harassment-adjacent behavior," I corrected. "Second, I won't lie to vendors or clients about the nature of this arrangement, but I will be discreet. No public statements about planning a wedding without a bride."

"Agreed."

"Third, I maintain complete creative control. If you hire me for my expertise, you need to trust it."

"Within reason," he countered.

"Within the bounds of good taste and what's logistically possible," I clarified.

"Fair enough."

"Fourth, this is a limited engagement. Once the wedding is planned and executed — assuming you find someone willing to marry you despite your personality — our business relationship concludes. No ongoing obligations."

"Except for my grandmother's gala," he reminded me. "And the investment would be ongoing."

"We can negotiate those separately. I'm talking about the wedding planning contract."

"Agreed," he said again. I was annoyed for some reason at how easily he was accepting my terms. Either he was the most reasonable billionaire in history, or he was already plotting ways around them.

I was betting on the latter.

"Do we have a deal, Ms. Marcel?" He extended his hand, and I had the distinct impression I was making a deal with the devil. A very attractive, coffee-bringing devil in a suit that was clearly made to fit him like a second, sexy skin.

I glanced at Mari, who was nodding so vigorously she resembled one of those dashboard bobbleheads. Then at Devonna, who was trying to appear professional while clearly calculating how a million-dollar contract would affect her upcoming vacation plans and also blatantly staring at Callan's ass with an expression that suggested she was mentally removing his trousers. Possibly with her teeth.

"Against every ounce of better judgment I possess... yes." I shook his hand, ignoring the voice in my head screaming that this was a terrible idea, possibly the worst since that time in college when Mari convinced me that cutting my own bangs at 3 AM after four vodka sodas was "empowering." I'd ended up looking like a regretful toddler with safety scissors and a grudge against her own forehead.

"Excellent." Callan's smile was so triumphant I immediately wanted to rescind my agreement out of spite. And also because his smile did alarming things to my internal organs, things that felt distinctly unprofessional and dangerously close to attraction. Which was ridiculous. I wasn't attracted to arrogant billionaires with god complexes, no matter how well they filled out a suit or how symmetrical their facial features might be.

"When do we start?" he asked, his thumb brushing over my knuckles before releasing my hand. The touch sent an electric current up my arm that I immediately filed under "static electricity" and "definitely not sexual chemistry."

"Right now," I said, moving to my desk with more speed than dignity. I pulled out the client questionnaire I gave to all couples, a comprehensive twelve-page document that I'd refined over years of experience. "Fill this out. All of it."

He accepted the packet with raised eyebrows. "Homework on the first day?"

"Planning a wedding requires information, Mr. Burkhardt. Lots of it." I handed him a pen. "I need to understand your preferences, deal-breakers, and vision for the day."

"My vision is 'expensive and impressive,' anything that will make the guys jealous," he said, flipping through the pages with growing amusement. "Do I really need to specify whether I prefer buttercream or fondant when I don't even have a bride yet?"

"Yes. Because regardless of who your bride is, the wedding needs to reflect you as well. Unless you plan to be a silent partner in your own marriage, which, given your personality, seems unlikely."

He laughed. It was genuine and annoyingly appealing. "Fair point. I'll complete your interrogation packet."

"Thank you. And we'll need to schedule a venue visit as soon as possible. You mentioned the Rhodes Estate. It books up years in advance."

"Don't worry about that," he said dismissively. "We'll get a date."

I stared at him. "Money doesn't buy everything, Mr. Burkhardt. Especially not the most exclusive, sought-after wedding venue in the tri-state area, with a three-year waiting list and a rumored connection to actual royalty."

"You'd be surprised Ms. Marcel. If you'll make the arrangement, we'll go see the venue this week."

"Fine, I'll make the call."

"Good." He settled into a chair and began filling out the questionnaire, looking entirely too comfortable in our modest office. "By the way, what's your coffee order? This was just a guess."

I looked down at the untouched cup he'd brought me. "Why?"

"Professional curiosity. If we're going to be working closely together for the next three months, I should know how you take your coffee."

"We're not going to be working that closely," I corrected, though my traitorous brain immediately conjured an image of exactly how closely we could work, possibly on a desk, definitely with fewer clothes. I mentally forced it back into professional mode. "And my coffee preferences aren't relevant to planning your wedding."

"Humor me."

I sighed. "Oat milk latte, double shot, with a dash of cinnamon. No sugar."

He nodded, looking oddly satisfied. "I was close. I went with almond milk."

"Fascinating," I deadpanned. "Now please fill out the questionnaire while I call the Rhodes Estate to begin arrangements."

"Of course." He returned to the questionnaire, a small smile playing at the corners of his mouth. "I wouldn't dream of interfering with your process."

Somehow, I doubted that very much.

I spent the next hour trying to work on other client matters while hyper-aware of Callan's presence. He filled out the questionnaire, occasionally chuckling or raising an eyebrow at certain questions.

Mari, meanwhile, made approximately eighteen unnecessary trips to the copier, each time finding a new angle from which to ogle Callan. By trip twelve, she'd abandoned all pretense and was essentially doing a slow lap around his chair while pretending to organize file folders.

Devonna wasn't much better. She'd reapplied her lip gloss three times and somehow found reasons to ask Callan if he needed anything every four minutes. The last time, she'd actually asked if his pen was "performing satisfactorily" in a voice usually reserved for phone sex operators.

I was about to suggest they both take an early lunch—possibly in Antarctica—when Callan finally handed the questionnaire back to me.

I was almost afraid to look.

Wedding colors? "Money green and stock-option black. Though I'm open to something more traditional, like Gold Trust Fund and Platinum Merger."

First dance song? "Haven't thought about it. 'Gold Digger' maybe? Or perhaps 'Billionaire' by Travie McCoy. If I'm feeling traditional, 'Money, Money, Money' by ABBA."

Preferred cake flavor? "Whatever doesn't clash with my future bride's dress. Do cakes and dresses clash? Is that a thing wedding planners worry about? If so, chocolate. Dark, like my soul. But expensive, like my watch."

My eye twitched as I flipped through his responses. They just got more and more inappropriate as I went through them. A vein pulsed in my forehead, but I forced myself to remain professional despite wanting to strangle him with his undoubtedly custom-made tie.

"This isn't helpful," I said finally, placing the questionnaire down.

"I thought I was quite thorough." He leaned back in his chair, the picture of false innocence. "Question twenty-three was particularly thought-provoking. I've never considered whether my wedding party should coordinate their underwear with the overall color scheme."

"That's not—" I stopped, narrowing my eyes. "That question isn't on the form."

"No?" He widened his eyes in mock confusion. "Must have been my own addition. I got carried away with the spirit of planning."

Mari snorted from across the room, not even pretending not to eavesdrop. "I vote yes on coordinated underwear. And I volunteer to be on the underwear selection committee. As your wedding planner's business partner, it's practically my duty."

"Mari!" I hissed.

"What? I'm being supportive."

"You're being inappropriate."

"No, I'm being efficient," she countered. "If we're planning a wedding with a bride to be named later, someone has to think about these critical details."

"Mr. Burkhardt," I began, summoning what remained of my professionalism.

"I think we're at the 'Callan' stage now, don't you? Considering I'm about to pay you a million dollars to find me a wife."

"I'm not finding you a wife," I corrected through gritted teeth. "I'm planning a wedding. Your spouse acquisition is your own problem."

"Ah, but that's where you're wrong." He leaned forward, suddenly all business. "The wedding and the bride are a package deal. I need both, within three months, to win the bet."

"That wasn't part of our agreement."

"It was implied."

"Nothing in wedding planning is implied, Mr. Burkhardt. That's why I have a twelve-page questionnaire and contracts with more clauses than a Christmas movie marathon."

He sighed dramatically. "Fine. Let me be explicit: I need your help finding a suitable bride as well as planning the wedding. Consider it... an extension of your existing services."

"We're wedding planners, not matchmakers."

"But you have connections throughout the social scene. You know which society daughters are looking to settle down, which divorcées are back on the market, which career women might consider a strategic partnership."

I stared at him, appalled. "You're talking about women like they're companies ripe for acquisition."

"I'm talking about mutually beneficial arrangements between consenting adults. No different from the dozens of strategic marriages that happen in high society every year." He shrugged. "Just with more honesty about the underlying motivations."

"This is insane," I muttered, but my mind was already racing despite myself. I did know several women who might consider Callan's proposal, not that I'd ever admit it to him.

"Is it?" he challenged. "Or is it simply pragmatic? Marriage has been a business transaction for most of human history. I'm just removing the romantic delusions."

"Clearly you've never been in love," I shot back.

Something flickered across his face, so quickly I almost missed it. "Love is irrelevant to a successful partnership. Honestly, compatible sex partners seem to have more successful relationships than the average 'love match.'"

"Yeah, well my ex-fiancé would probably agree with you," I said before I could stop myself. "He found a more compatible 'sex partner' in a client, it would seem."

The moment the words left my mouth, I regretted them. I never discussed Austin with clients or anyone outside my immediate circle. It was unprofessional and irrelevant and exactly the kind of personal detail Callan Burkhardt would file away to use against me later. Mari's eyes were wide across the room, and she exchanged a glance with Devonna, who'd frozen as she'd been applying her fifth layer of lip gloss.

Surprise registered on Callan's face, followed by something that looked disturbingly like genuine interest. "I didn't know —"

"It doesn't matter," I cut him off, standing abruptly. "And it's not pertinent to our current situation."

"On the contrary," he said, his voice softer than I'd heard it before. "It seems highly pertinent."

"Well, it's not," I insisted, shuffling papers to avoid meeting his gaze. "Now, if you'll excuse me, I need to create a project plan for this... arrangement."

To my surprise, he stood without argument. "Of course. I've taken up enough of your morning."

I nodded, still annoyed at myself for revealing that personal detail.

"For what it's worth," he added, pausing at the door, "he was clearly an idiot."

Before I could respond, he was gone.

Mari materialized at my side almost immediately. "Well, that was interesting."

"That's one word for it," I muttered.

"He's into you," she declared with absolute certainty.

"He's into himself. And winning his bet," I corrected. "I'm just a means to an end."

"Mmm-hmm. And I'm just casually interested in that bartender at Whiskey Blue." She perched on the edge of my desk. "So, what's the plan?"

"First, you and Devonna need to take cold showers and remember you're professionals," I said, shooting her a look. "I've seen less obvious displays of lust at actual orgies."

"You've never been to an orgy," Mari scoffed.

"No, but I've planned three wedding after-parties that turned into them, and trust me, you two were worse. Devonna asked if his pen was 'performing satisfactorily.' His pen, Mari."

"Can you blame her? I'm surprised she didn't offer to be his personal pen. I would have."

"What the hell does that even mean?"

"No idea." Mari shrugged.

I took a deep breath, shifting into planning mode. "First, I need to create a comprehensive timeline. Then we'll schedule the venue visit, start researching vendors who can accommodate the expedited schedule, and draft a bride acquisition strategy."

"A what now?"

"If he wants help finding a suitable spouse, we'll approach it like any other wedding element. Systematically, efficiently, and with impeccable taste." I was already opening a new spreadsheet. "We need categories, criteria, vetting processes."

Mari stared at me. "You're creating a wife recruitment strategy presentation."

"It's a streamlined matrimonial candidate identification protocol,'" I replied, already color-coding cells. "With accompanying flowcharts."

"You're enjoying this," she accused.

"I'm approaching it professionally," I corrected, though there was a small, twisted part of me that found satisfaction in reducing romantic partnership to the same process Callan seemed to view it as. If he wanted a business transaction, I'd give him one, complete with performance metrics and quality control.

"What metrics are you using to evaluate potential wives?" Mari asked, peering at my screen. "Ooh, is that a compatibility matrix? With weighted scores? Anica Marcel, you beautiful, psychotic genius."

"It's not psychotic to be thorough," I sniffed, though I had to admit the multi-stage evaluation process might be a tad excessive. But then, so was trying to find a bride in three months for a billionaire with the emotional depth of a kiddie pool.

"Does physical attraction get a score? Because if so, you should just put yourself at the top of the list and call it a day."

"I'm not putting myself anywhere near this list," I said firmly, ignoring the tiny, traitorous part of me that had already calculated my own compatibility score with Callan. (67.4%, which was concerning given how much I disliked him. Apparently, my spreadsheet had a thing for blue eyes and financial stability.) "And before you ask, neither of you are getting on this list either."

Three hours later, I had created a comprehensive presentation, complete with timeline, potential candidate profiles (anonymized, of course), and a detailed action plan. It was possibly the most thorough, most ridiculous document I'd ever produced, and I'd once created a twenty-page contingency plan for a hurricane-threatened beach wedding that included evacuation routes and emergency raccoon removal procedures.

As I put the finishing touches on a particularly satisfying Gantt chart, I felt a strange sense of accomplishment. If Callan Burkhardt thought he could rattle me with his unorthodox request, he was sorely mistaken. I was Anica Marcel, wedding planning extraordinaire. I could plan anything, even a wedding for a man without a bride.

Now I just had to ignore the voice in my head warning me that while I might be able to plan the perfect wedding, dealing with Callan Burkhardt himself would be the real challenge.

And that was before factoring in the unwelcome flutter I'd felt when he smiled at me—a reaction I attributed entirely to sleep deprivation and possibly a mild coffee overdose, and absolutely not to the way his voice dropped slightly when he'd called my ex an idiot, or how his fingers had lingered on mine when he handed back the questionnaire, or the brief moment when I'd caught him watching me with an expression that wasn't smug or arrogant but genuinely curious.

Professional. This was strictly professional. And it would stay that way, no matter how good he looked in that suit or how intriguing his rare moments of genuine humanity might be.

After all, I'd learned my lesson about mixing business with pleasure.

I wasn't about to make that mistake again. Even for a billionaire with a smile that could power the Manhattan skyline and a butt that, as Mari so eloquently put it, deserved its own Forbes profile.

SURE, BLAME THE DUCKS

Chapter 4: Callan

I was running late on purpose.

Some people might call it childish, but I preferred to think of it as strategic. After all, I didn't become a billionaire by playing by other people's rules. And showing up exactly when expected was decidedly boring.

Besides, there was something entertaining about imagining Anica Marcel standing outside the Rhodes Estate, checking her watch every thirty seconds with increasing irritation. Her perfect posture growing more rigid by the minute, those full lips pressing into that thin line they formed when she was annoyed.

Not that I'd been cataloging her expressions.

I glanced at the dashboard clock: 6:31 AM. I was officially thirty-one minutes late. Perfect timing. Long enough to be irritating but not quite long enough for her to give up and leave. I downshifted my Aston Martin and turned onto the long, tree-lined drive that led to the estate. The familiar mix of nostalgia and discomfort I always experienced when visiting this place made me grin like I had as a little boy in the same place.

The Rhodes Estate sat on fifty acres of pristine countryside about an hour outside Manhattan; close enough for convenience but far enough to feel like an escape. The sprawling Georgian mansion with its immaculate gardens had been a wedding venue for the elite since the 1950s. My grandmother had gotten married here long before I'd made my first million, a fact she reminded me of approximately every third conversation. She liked to remind me that she did fine before I started to provide for her, but she also didn't complain about the house I'd bought her.

I spotted Anica immediately, standing by the stone fountain at the entrance. She wore a sleek navy dress that hugged curves I'd definitely been thinking about since our last meeting. Her dark hair was twisted into some complicated updo that exposed the elegant line of her neck. Even from a distance, her body language screamed "planning a homicide."

I parked directly in front of her rather than in the designated lot, watching with satisfaction as her eyebrow twitched. When the valet approached, I handed him my keys with instructions to "keep it close. We might need to make a quick getaway if the wedding planner decides to weaponize her clipboard."

"You're late," she said as I stepped out of the car, not bothering with a greeting.

"Traffic was terrible," I replied, offering her one of the coffee cups I'd had Erika arrange from that ridiculously expensive place in SoHo. Oat milk latte, double shot, with a dash of cinnamon. No sugar. The fact that I remembered her exact order fueled the smirk on my face.

"It's 6 AM," she countered, accepting the coffee with visible reluctance. "The only traffic was the ducks crossing at the park."

"Vicious creatures. Completely disregarded my right of way." I adjusted my cuffs with exaggerated seriousness. "One of them made direct eye contact while deliberately slowing down. I'm pretty sure it was personal."

A fleeting smile crossed her face before she suppressed it. "Did you challenge it to a duel at dawn?"

"I considered it, but the duck had the tactical advantage. Very low center of gravity."

She took a sip of coffee, and there it was—the slight widening of her eyes, the almost imperceptible relaxation of her shoulders. "It's cold," she lied, taking another long sip.

"Probably the ice in your veins cooling it down," I replied cheerfully. "Shall we? I believe Ms. Windsor is already calculating how many minutes of tardiness translate to years in etiquette purgatory."

Anica looked stunning in the morning light, her skin practically glowing against the dark fabric of her dress. As she turned to walk toward the entrance, I allowed myself a moment to appreciate the view. Her dress wasn't particularly revealing, but it didn't need to be. It hugged her curves with the reverence of a Renaissance sculptor discovering marble for the first time. And when she glanced back at me with narrowed eyes, I couldn't help but notice how the sunlight caught the fullness of her lips and the gentle swell of her chest as she took an irritated breath.

God, she probably rocked a bikini. I needed to find a way to get her to my island to test that theory.

"Are you coming, or would you prefer to waste more time?" she called back, clearly catching me in my appraisal.

"Just admiring the architecture," I replied, jogging a few steps to catch up.

"The building is in the opposite direction."

"I was referring to your dress. Italian design?"

She shot me a look that could have frozen lava. "Our agreement included no inappropriate comments, Mr. Burkhardt."

"Callan," I corrected. "And that was a professional observation. You have excellent taste."

"In everything except clients, apparently," she muttered, just loud enough for me to hear.

I laughed, amused by her quick wit. Most women either simpered in my presence or treated me with excessive deference. Anica Marcel did neither, and it was refreshingly... stimulating. I adjusted my trousers as I followed her.

We approached the oak doors of the main house. The Rhodes Estate represented everything I both aspired to and rejected; old money, tradition, expectations. The weight of family legacy embodied in stone and wood.

"The main house was built in 1904," I whispered as we walked inside. "The original owner was a railroad baron who wanted to impress his much younger second wife. The east wing was added in the 1920s, and the gardens were redesigned in the 1950s by some Japanese master who apparently made the Rockefellers beg for his services."

Anica glanced at me with mild surprise. "You know quite a bit about the place."

I shrugged. "My grandmother made sure I knew."

"It's beautiful," she said, her professional mask slipping as she took in the soaring ceiling of the main hall, with its intricate plasterwork and crystal chandelier. "The proportion of the windows to the wall height is perfect for photography."

"My grandmother got married here in the late 1960s," I said, though I hadn't planned to share this detail. "Said it was the happiest day of her life. Before my grandfather turned out to be a serial philanderer with a gambling problem, of course."

"Is that why you want to get married here? Family tradition?"

"God, no," I said quickly, rebuilding my walls. "It's just convenient. And it'll impress my friends, which is the whole point of winning the bet."

The softness vanished from her face. "Right. The bet. How could I forget the romantic foundation of this entire arrangement?"

Before I could respond, a sharp voice cut through the hall.

"Mr. Burkhardt. You're late."

The voice preceded the woman, who appeared from a side door. I was tall at six foot three. Judith Windsor was almost taller. Between her rigid posture and her silver hair pulled back in a bun so tight it performed double duty as a non-surgical facelift, she was terrifying. Not to me of course. Nope. I definitely didn't take a step back. She wore a tweed suit in a shade I could only describe as "disciplinarian beige," accessorized with a pearl necklace that looked like it was cutting off the blood flow to her ability to experience joy.

"Ms. Windsor," I greeted her with my most charming smile, the one that worked on everyone except my grandmother and, apparently, dragon ladies who guarded exclusive wedding venues. Well, and my wedding planner. Maybe I was losing my edge... "Lovely to see you. You haven't aged a day since my grandmother's last charity gala."

"Flattery is the refuge of the unpunctual," she replied crisply, her British accent so pronounced it sounded like she was auditioning for *Downton Abbey*. Her gaze shifted to Anica, assessing her from head to toe. "And you must be the wedding planner my assistant mentioned.

40

I'm afraid there's been some misunderstanding. Rhodes Estate doesn't arrange viewings without both parties present. Groom and bride."

"I'm sure, and I completely understand. I'm representing the couple," Anica began, slipping into professional mode.

"We don't do proxy arrangements," Ms. Windsor cut her off, holding up a hand. "Rhodes Estate isn't for just anyone. We have standards to maintain."

She pronounced "standards" the way most people might say "last line of defense against barbarian hordes."

Irritation rose in my chest. This was exactly why I avoided these old-money circles despite my wealth. The constant judgment, the unspoken rules, the assumption that new money wasn't quite good enough.

"My grandmother is Vivian Burkhardt," I reminded her. "I believe that meets your standards."

"Of course, Mr. Burkhardt. We so appreciate your grandmother's events," she conceded with a thin smile that didn't reach her eyes. "But tradition is tradition. We need to meet the bride before proceeding. Rhodes Estate is very selective about who celebrates their union here. We're not some banquet hall off the interstate that hosts six weddings a day with a karaoke machine and a chocolate fountain." She shuddered at the mere thought.

"Of course not," I grinned. "There are much better uses for chocolate in liquid form."

Anica elbowed me in the ribs, and opened her mouth, but I spoke before her.

"I can see there's been some confusion though, and I certainly apologize for that." It was obvious Ms. Windsor was about to dismiss us, and I moved before my brain could catch up, wrapping my arm around Anica and pulling her into my side. "But *she* is the bride," I said, reaching for Anica's hand and lacing our fingers together before she could react. "This is my fiancée, Anica Marcel."

The shock on Anica's face would have been comical if it weren't for the heel that immediately stomped on my Italian leather loafer. I managed to maintain my smile despite the pain that shot through my foot, squeezing her hand in a silent plea to play along.

41

Ms. Windsor's eyebrows rose so high they nearly disappeared into her hairline, creating the first wrinkles I'd ever seen on her forehead. "Your fiancée? But my understanding was that you were the wedding plan–"

"A misunderstanding," I interrupted. "We're just keeping things on the down low because of the scandal it would cause when millions of women find out I'm taken by this beautiful gem."

Anica's fingers tightened around mine with what I suspected was barely controlled rage rather than affection. "It's true," she said, her voice strained. "It's almost a secret, even to ourselves."

Ms. Windsor looked between us, skepticism written all over her face. "Well, this changes things. Perhaps we should continue this conversation in my office."

As we followed her through the main hall, Anica leaned close to me, her lips near my ear. Anyone observing would have thought it an intimate gesture, but her whispered words were pure venom.

"I am going to murder you slowly and painfully the moment we're alone."

"No, you won't," I whispered back, enjoying the floral scent of her perfume and the way her breath tickled my ear. "You need me alive to pay your fee."

"Fine, but there are worse things than death," she hissed. "I'll make sure you experience all of them. Starting with a PowerPoint presentation on wedding etiquette that's three hundred slides long. With mandatory audience participation."

Her threat shouldn't have been arousing, but there was something about the fire in her eyes and the flush across her cheekbones that sent heat straight south. I had to remind myself that this was strictly business, even if business now involved pretending to be engaged to the most infuriating and inexplicably attractive wedding planner in Manhattan.

In Ms. Windsor's office, we sat side by side across from her imposing desk. I casually draped my arm across the back of Anica's chair, earning myself another death glare and what felt like a pinch to my kidney.

"So," Ms. Windsor began, shuffling papers. A taxidermied fox watched from a shelf behind her, its glass eyes somehow conveying the same disapproval as its owner. "How long have you two been engaged?"

"Three weeks," I said, at the exact moment Anica said, "Two months."

We exchanged a look of mutual panic.

"What he means," Anica recovered smoothly, "is that we've been engaged for two months, but we've only been actively planning the wedding for three weeks."

"Exactly," I agreed. "When you know, you know."

"And how did you meet?" Ms. Windsor asked, her pen poised over a form that apparently required our complete relationship history, blood types, and possibly genetic compatibility.

"At her office," I said.

"At a charity gala," Anica said simultaneously.

Ms. Windsor's eyes narrowed to slits that could have sliced sashimi.

"Both, actually," I improvised. "We first saw each other at a charity gala but didn't speak. Then fate brought us together when I needed a... consultation at her office. It was for my grandmother's birthday celebration."

"I'm a wedding planner, yes, but I was an event planner before this and he somehow found out," Anica added, pinching my thigh under the table with enough force to leave a mark. "Callan wanted to surprise his grandmother with a special party, so he came to me."

"How thoughtful," Ms. Windsor commented, in a tone that suggested thoughtfulness was a communicable disease she'd prefer not to catch. "And how did he propose?"

I opened my mouth to fabricate something, but Anica beat me to it.

"It was quite romantic," she said, her voice suddenly soft and her expression dreamy in a way that almost made me believe her. "He took me to the top of the Empire State Building at sunset."

"It was raining," I added, unable to resist testing her improvisation skills.

"Snowing," she corrected, with a saccharine smile.

"A light drizzle," I compromised.

"A blizzard," she insisted. "I remember because my eyelashes froze together and I almost missed the proposal because I couldn't open my eyes properly."

"Yet despite the weather," I continued, "she still said yes when I got down on one knee and told her I couldn't imagine life without her."

"He had the ring hidden in a special box," Anica added, "that played our song when it opened."

"Ah yes, our song," I said, looking at her expectantly. "What was it again, darling?"

Her smile tightened. "You know very well it was 'Can't Help Falling in Love.'"

"No, sweetheart, you're confusing it with the song from our first dance. The proposal box played 'Gold Digger.'"

Ms. Windsor's pen stopped moving.

"He's such a joker," Anica said with a laugh that sounded like she was being waterboarded. "What he actually said was that he'd never met anyone who challenged him the way I do."

That part hit uncomfortably close to truth.

"And the ring?" Ms. Windsor prompted, clearly enjoying our discomfort.

"Being sized," we said in unison.

"It needed to be adjusted," Anica elaborated. "Callan initially got a ring that was much too large."

"Because I thought her fingers matched the size of her ambition," I added.

"Very funny, *darling*," she pinched me again on the thigh. "I just have narrow fingers." She wiggled her fingers to demonstrate.

I smirked. "You know what they say about women with little fingers…" I let the words trail off, but neither woman laughed. Instead, both narrowed their eyes at me, and Ms. Windsor lowered her glasses to intensify her glare.

"No, I don't know what they say about little fingers, Mr. Burkhardt. Why don't you enlighten me?" Ms. Windsor's glare darkened, and I straightened in the chair. The room was quite a bit warmer than it had been a second earlier.

"Um, they, um… They have big hearts." I clicked my tongue and pointed my finger. "Yup. That's it."

Anica rolled her eyes. "Anyways, like I was saying, the ring kept sliding off and falling into my soup at the celebration dinner," she continued, her smile now fixed in place like rigor mortis.

"The waiter was very understanding about fishing it out of the lobster bisque," I added.

Ms. Windsor sighed, setting down her pen. "Mr. Burkhardt, Ms. Marcel… I've been managing this venue for forty-seven years. I've seen every type of couple imaginable. Nervous couples, overexcited couples, couples who clearly despise each other but are proceeding for family reasons." She leaned forward, the light catching her pearl necklace in a way that made it look like a row of judgmental eyeballs. "What I've never seen is a couple who can't keep their story straight about basic details of their relationship."

Anica tensed beside me, likely preparing for the dismissal that was surely coming.

"However," Ms. Windsor continued, "your grandmother is a valued patron of this estate, Mr. Burkhardt. And despite your... unusual circumstances, I'm willing to pencil you in."

The tightness in my muscles loosened. Gram would be excited that the wedding could be here, and anything that made her happy made me happy. "Thank you, Ms. Windsor. You won't regret it."

"You mentioned wanting a date three months from now. While we often do have our venue booked this close to the date, we had a recent drop out on the last Saturday in September. Take it or leave it." She closed her leather-bound appointment book. "I must warn you that we'll require a non-refundable deposit of thirty-five thousand dollars by the end of the week."

"We'll take it," I said immediately, ignoring Anica's sharp intake of breath.

"Very well. I'll have my assistant show you the grounds and discuss the particulars. I assume you'll want the same spot where your grandmother was married?"

I nodded, finding it difficult to speak. The same spot. Where my grandmother had pledged herself to a man who would eventually break her heart so thoroughly that she'd never remarry.

Ms. Windsor stood, smoothing her already immaculate suit. "One last thing, Mr. Burkhardt. We don't allow karaoke, chocolate fountains, or those dreadful photo booths with feather boas and plastic sunglasses. Rhodes Estate is a venue for tasteful celebrations, not carnival midways."

"No inflatable bounce houses either?" I asked, giving my best puppy dog face. "I was hoping to enter my reception in formal attire via slide."

Her expression suggested I'd proposed holding the ceremony in a Chuck E. Cheese. "I'll pretend I didn't hear that."

Ms. Windsor left to fetch her assistant, and the moment the door closed, Anica turned to me, eyes blazing as she smacked me in the shoulder. It was cute.

"What the hell was that?" she demanded, keeping her voice low.

"Improvisation," I replied, trying to recover my usual nonchalance. "And it worked. We got the venue."

"You made me lie! You put me in an impossible position!"

"An impossible position would be trying to do the splits in that dress," I said, straightening my cuffs. "This was just a little creative storytelling."

"This isn't a joke, Callan." The use of my first name surprised me. "You can't just declare people your fiancée without their consent."

"Would you have preferred I told her the truth? That I'm planning a wedding for a bride I haven't met yet to win a bet?"

She sighed, running a hand over her face, careful not to smudge her makeup. "No. But there had to be another way."

"Sometimes the direct approach is best," I shrugged. "Besides, you were quite convincing as my besotted fiancée. The frozen eyelashes were a particularly poetic touch."

"If you ever pull something like that again—"

"You'll what? Force-feed me wedding cake until I explode? Force me to try on tuxedos until my will to live expires?"

"I'll let Mari take over." Her eyes glinted as she smoothed her skirt. "She's been begging me to let her take your wedding since you showed up in the office. But hey, maybe you'll marry her and your little scheme will be true. You really will marry the wedding planner. She'd love that." She pressed a finger to her cheek and tapped it twice as if she were pondering something. "In fact, that's probably a great idea. I won't have to deal with her 10am drinking, or her hangovers, and you'll never have another boring night of your life."

"Maybe I will." I stuck my hands in my pockets, tilting my head. "She seems very fun. Was showing me some of the yoga poses she's learned. Very... bendy." I enunciated the word smirking at her.

Instead of glaring at me like I thought she would, she shrugged with an evil look in her eyes. "Oh she is. You may want to pick up some chafing cream though." She crossed her arms. "Mari is insatiable. You'll never sleep again."

"Good."

"Good.

"Fine."

"Fine."

But it wasn't her best friend I was picturing hours of mind blowing sex with.

Shit.

When was the last time I got laid? Maybe I needed to take care of that before continuing to work with the ice queen wedding planner. She looked like she was considering additional methods of torture when Ms. Windsor's assistant appeared. The cheerful young woman seemed immune to her boss's stiff edge.

"I'm Missy," she introduced herself with a bright smile. "I'll be showing you the grounds and discussing package options. Don't mind Ms. Windsor.'"

The tour was actually pleasant, despite Anica maintaining a careful ten inches of space between us at all times. The Rhodes Estate was objectively stunning, with its manicured gardens, crystal-clear lake, and various reception spaces that managed to be both grand and intimate.

I watched Anica more than the venue. The way her professional mask slipped when she saw something that particularly impressed her. The quick notes she took on her tablet. The gentle slope of her neck as she tilted her head to examine architectural details.

When we reached the garden pavilion where my grandmother had exchanged her vows, a strange tightness crossed over my chest. The white marble structure overlooking the lake was exactly as she'd described it in the moments she spoke of her wedding day.

"This is it," I said quietly. "This is where my grandmother got married."

Anica looked at me, and for a moment I felt utterly transparent. "It's beautiful," she said simply.

"Yes," I agreed, not entirely sure we were talking about the pavilion.

The spell was broken when Missy launched into details about setup options and maximum capacity. By the time we finished the tour and completed the preliminary paperwork, it was nearly noon.

"Ms. Windsor will be in touch to discuss final details," Missy said as she walked us back to my car. "Congratulations again on your engagement! You two have such great chemistry. I can totally see why you fell for each other."

Anica managed a smile that only looked slightly like she was passing a kidney stone. "Thank you for your help."

The moment Missy was out of earshot, Anica turned to me, arms crossed. "That was the most unprofessional experience of my career, and I once had to wrangle a drunken groom out of a fountain while he was wearing nothing but a bow tie."

"Sounds like my kind of party," I quipped, opening the passenger door of my car. "Get in. I'll drive you back to the city."

"I have my own car, thank you."

"Which you'll need to leave here since you're now officially my fiancée and it would look suspicious if you didn't ride with me," I pointed out. "I'll have Erika arrange for someone to bring it back to your office."

She looked like she wanted to argue, but saw the logic in maintaining our charade. With reluctance, she slid into the passenger seat of my Aston Martin.

As I pulled away from the estate, I could practically feel her fury radiating across the center console. It was strangely exhilarating.

"Like I said before, you had no right to put me in that position," she said finally, breaking the tense silence.

"I can think of a couple other positions we could–Ow!"

Anica punched me in the shoulder. "You're despicable."

"It worked, didn't it? We got the venue," I said, rubbing my shoulder and driving with my knees. She hit hard for a small woman.

"That's not the point and you know it!"

"What is the point, then?" I asked, genuinely curious. "The end result is exactly what we wanted."

"The point is consent," she said, turning to face me. "You don't get to make unilateral decisions that affect me without my input."

"You're right. I apologize for not consulting you first."

She blinked, clearly thrown. "Well... good. Don't do it again."

We drove in dead silence for a few minutes, the tension gradually dissipating.

"For the record," I said as we merged onto the highway, "I would never propose in a public place. Too cliché."

She cut a quick glance in my direction, curiosity peeking through before slipping back behind her usual mask. "Where would you propose, then? Hypothetically speaking."

I considered the question more seriously than I probably should have. "Somewhere meaningful to the relationship. And private. Grand gestures are for people who need an audience to validate their feelings."

"That's... surprisingly thoughtful."

"Don't sound so shocked. I have layers, Ms. Marcel."

"Like an onion?" she asked, the corner of her mouth quirking up.

"Like a very expensive, very complex pastry," I corrected. "With excellent taste in cars and wedding planners."

She rolled her eyes, but the hostility had left her posture. As she gazed out the window, I allowed myself another glance at her profile. The elegant line of her jaw, the curve of her lips, the way her dress had ridden up slightly to reveal more of her toned legs.

This was going to be a complicated three months to say the least.

MAYBE SHE'S THE SERIAL KILLER

Chapter 5: Anica

"**I**'m not sure if this is a wedding planning office or a CIA operations center," Mari announced, gesturing to the conference room I'd commandeered for Project Find-Callan-A-Wife-Before-He-Ruins-My-Career. "Or possibly the lair of a very organized serial killer who color-codes his victims by blood type."

I looked up from the profile I was analyzing—thirty-two-year-old hedge fund manager with a penchant for charity galas and CrossFit—to survey my handiwork. The walls were covered in photos, profiles, and sticky notes. A massive whiteboard displayed a complex matrix of compatibility metrics, and the conference table was buried under printouts sorted into piles labeled "Promising," "Potential," and "Last Resort But Still Technically Breathing."

"The difference is surprisingly negligible at this point," I replied, adjusting a photo that had slipped slightly out of alignment. "Though I think serial killers typically have better work-life balance. And probably more sex."

"Speaking of sex," Mari said, making herself comfortable by sitting directly on top of my "Potential" pile, "when are you planning to climb Mount Burkhardt? I've started a betting pool with the caterers from the Jonas wedding. I've got fifty bucks on 'within two weeks but only after a screaming match.'"

"You did not start a betting pool," I said, horrified.

"You're right." She nodded solemnly. "It's actually seventy-five dollars, and Devonna's in charge of the spreadsheet."

On cue, Devonna appeared in the doorway, tablet clutched to her chest like always. But unlike her usual anxious demeanor, she had a dreamy, distant look in her eyes.

"Mr. Burkhardt's assistant called," she announced. "He'll be here in approximately forty minutes."

"He's not due for another hour," I noted, checking my watch.

"Yes, but he mentioned he's running early today, which according to my calculations, means he'll arrive twenty minutes late instead of his usual thirty to forty-five." She adjusted her glasses. Her cheeks were flushed. "I've prepared the good coffee and arranged the almond pastries he mentioned liking last time."

Mari and I exchanged looks.

"Devonna," I said carefully, "did you buy special pastries just for Callan?"

"Of course not. I simply noticed that they happened to be on sale, and they pair nicely with our Ethiopian roast, which I also happened to purchase this morning from that specialty shop seventeen blocks away that doesn't deliver."

"Uh-huh," Mari said, grinning. "And does this specialty shop happen to be directly across the street from that gym where a certain billionaire has been photographed leaving with his shirt stuck to his abs?"

Devonna's flush deepened. "I don't know what you're talking about. I'm simply maintaining appropriate client relations."

"I'd like to maintain relations with his—"

"Mari!" I cut her off. "Please remember this is a professional workplace."

"Says the woman who's turned our conference room into a vision board for her billionaire fantasy wedding," she retorted.

"It's not—that's not what this is," I spluttered, gesturing to the profiles. "I've spent the past week compiling the most comprehensive database of eligible Manhattan socialites ever assembled outside of a dating app headquarters. Each candidate has been thoroughly vetted through social media, mutual connections, and in some cases, discreet background checks courtesy of Devonna's mysterious 'boyfriend who does security work.'"

"He's not my boyfriend," Devonna muttered. "We just occasionally exchange information and bodily fluids."

Mari and I both froze, staring at her.

"What?" she asked innocently. "I'm an adult woman with needs that occasionally include having my back blown out by a former Navy SEAL who now runs background checks."

"Who are you and what have you done with my assistant?" I demanded, genuinely shocked.

Devonna adjusted her glasses again and shrugged, returning to her usual demeanor. "I've organized the candidate files as requested. The top three have been highlighted and placed on your desk, with Destiny Gitwieler as the primary recommendation. I've also taken the liberty of pressing your blue dress for tonight's dinner observation, as blue appears to be the color Mr. Burkhardt responds to most favorably based on my analysis of his past female companions."

"You've been analyzing his... Wait, how do you even know I'm wearing blue tonight?"

"You've touched every blue item in your closet at least twice this week while sighing," she replied matter-of-factly. "And you've been staring at photos of him approximately 34% longer than is strictly necessary for professional assessment."

"I have not!" I protested, heat rising to my cheeks.

"Your pupils dilate an average of 2.7 millimeters when he enters a room," she continued, as if reciting from a scientific journal. "And you've started wearing matching underwear to work despite having no logical reason to do so."

Mari howled with laughter while I stood there, mortified and impressed in equal measure.

"How do you know about my underwear?" I finally managed.

"You don't squat down like a lady. You bend over and show the world your fancy underwear," Devonna shrugged again. "La Perla doesn't manufacture practical cotton briefs, Anica."

"Have you considered that this might be slightly..." Mari searched for the right word, tilting her head at the wall of faces, "...psychotic? And I mean that as the highest compliment, because I am here for this level of unhinged dedication."

"I prefer 'methodical,'" I corrected, adding another sticky note to the hedge fund manager's profile. "This is a million-dollar contract. I'm being thorough."

"Uh-huh," Mari said skeptically, picking up a photo of a willowy blonde and pretending to make out with it. "And the fact that you've spent more time on this than you did planning the Burgis-Schmidt wedding — which, may I remind you, included a live elephant and that ice sculpture that accidentally looked phallic when it started melting — has nothing to do with your growing obsession with our favorite billionaire?"

"I am not obsessed with Callan Burkhardt," I snapped, immediately regretting the defensive tone. "I'm obsessed with winning. With proving I can pull off the impossible."

"Right. That's why you've rejected fourteen perfectly suitable women because" — she picked up my notes and read in a mocking voice — "'laugh is too high-pitched,' 'probably wears scrunchies unironically,' 'gives off clingy energy,' and my personal favorite, 'boobs too similar to mine.'"

I snatched the notes back, my face burning. "I never wrote that last one!"

"No, but you thought it," Mari said smugly. "I saw you comparing chest sizes yesterday."

"I was assessing overall proportions for formal wear compatibility," I insisted. It sounded ridiculous.

"Mmm-hmm. And you'd know because you've spent so much time analyzing his preferences? Or because you've spent so much time analyzing him? Don't think I didn't notice you replaying that video where he emerges from the pool at the Hamptons charity event. Eleven times, Anica. I counted."

"It was research," I said, straightening a pile of profiles. "He needs someone who can match his... intensity."

"Oh, I bet you could match his intensity," Mari waggled her eyebrows suggestively. "Preferably horizontally. Or vertically against a wall. I'm not picky about the orientation, just the action. Though personally, I'd recommend starting with a solid sixty-nine, because that man's jawline was designed by God himself for — "

"You're disgusting," I informed her, ignoring the flush creeping up my neck. "And inappropriate. And fired from this project."

"You can't fire me. I'm your business partner and emotional support animal." She hopped onto the table, scattering my carefully arranged piles. "Besides, someone needs to be here to witness the sexual tension when he arrives. It's like watching National Geographic, but instead of lions mating, it's an uptight perfectionist and a Greek god incarnate pretending they don't want to rip each other's clothes off."

Devonna cleared her throat. "Mr. Burkhardt's car just pulled up outside. He appears to be seventeen minutes early for his scheduled late arrival."

Mari and I both stared at her.

"I installed a small alert system," she explained with a shrug. "It notifies me when his vehicle is within fifty feet of our building."

"That's... definitely illegal," I said slowly.

"Only in fourteen states," she replied. "And I've calculated that the financial benefit of advanced preparation outweighs the minimal legal risk."

"Who *are* you?" Mari asked, clearly impressed.

"I appreciate efficiency and good bone structure," Devonna replied, smoothing her already-immaculate blouse. "And Mr. Burkhardt has exceptional bone structure. Among other things."

"My god, he's infected both of you," I muttered. "Is there anyone in this office who can maintain professional boundaries?"

"Professional boundaries are for people who don't have the opportunity to marry billionaires," Mari declared, sliding off the table. "Speaking of which, I need to freshen up before he arrives. I'm wearing my special occasion bra. The one with the front clasp that can be undone with teeth."

"Why would he be undoing your bra with his teeth?" I demanded.

Mari's grin was positively feline. "He wouldn't be. But a girl can dream. And prepare. And possibly accidentally bump into him in a way that requires him to steady me with his enormous hands on my ass. God, do you think his hands are any indication of his dick? Or is that feet? Devonna, what size shoe does he wear?"

"Size 13 in US sizes. In European sizes that's–"

"Out," I ordered, pointing to the door. "Both of you. I need five minutes of sanity before he arrives."

"Fine, but remember—" Mari paused at the doorway, "—if you don't climb that man like a tree soon, I will. And I'll take detailed notes for posterity."

I glanced at Devonna, expecting her to be horrified by Mari's crassness, but she was nodding thoughtfully. "I've already prepared a mood board," she admitted. "With categories for technique, duration, and... creativity."

"Out!" I repeated, nearly shrieking.

Once alone, I surveyed the room with a critical eye. Was it too much? Probably. But Callan had made it clear he wanted results, and this was how I delivered results, with meticulous research, careful analysis, and an attention to detail that bordered on pathological.

The fact that the process had given me an encyclopedic knowledge of his preferences, habits, and history was purely professional. The fact that I now knew he preferred brunettes who challenged him intellectually, donated to education-focused charities, and could hold their own in any social situation was simply due diligence. The fact that I'd watched eighteen interviews with him to analyze his conversation patterns and humor style was thorough research.

And the fact that I'd caught myself wondering more than once what it would be like to be the woman who actually captured his interest? That was... a professional hazard. Nothing more.

I was adjusting the last profile when the conference room door swung open, revealing the man himself an hour early, defying even Devonna's calculations.

Callan leaned against the doorframe, taking in the scene with raised eyebrows. He wore dark jeans and a navy cashmere sweater, his hair slightly rumpled as if he'd been running his hands through it. He looked like he'd just walked off a "Billionaires at Leisure" photoshoot and directly into my increasingly complicated fantasy life.

"Should I be flattered or terrified?" he asked, gesturing to the walls. "This is either the most thorough dating service I've ever seen or the beginnings of a true crime documentary. 'The Wedding Planner: From Bouquets to Body Bags.'"

"That seems to be the consensus," I replied, refusing to show how his sudden appearance had flustered me. "Though I was hoping for 'impressed.'"

"Oh, I'm definitely impressed," he said, stepping fully into the room and closing the door behind him. "This is next-level organization. I'm pretty sure my security team doesn't have this much intel on potential threats."

"Some might say a wife is the ultimate security threat," I quipped, immediately regretting the joke when his eyes crinkled with amusement.

"Speaking from experience, Ms. Marcel?" He approached the wall, studying the photos and notes with genuine interest. "Or is this a warning?"

"Neither. Just an observation based on the dozens of mother-in-law horror stories I've collected over the years." I moved to stand beside him, careful to maintain a professional distance. "I've narrowed it down to thirty candidates who meet your basic criteria, with a top ten I'd recommend for initial meetings."

He studied the wall in silence for a moment, his expression unreadable. Then he turned to me with that infuriating half-smile. "You've categorized these women all wrong."

I blinked. "Excuse me?"

"Your categories," he gestured to my organized wall. "They're all wrong."

After a week of sixteen-hour days, background checks, and enough coffee to give a rhino heart palpitations, that was not what I wanted to hear.

"Well, you categorized your 'non-negotiables' as — and I quote — 'nice rack' and 'doesn't talk during sports,'" I replied, crossing my arms. "So forgive me if I took some interpretive liberties."

To my surprise, he laughed. "Fair point. My initial criteria were... superficial."

"Superficial is putting it kindly. Neanderthalic would be more accurate. Though I notice you haven't actually disagreed with those particular requirements."

"Would it help if I said I've evolved since then?" He moved closer to the board, examining the details I'd compiled. "Though evolution apparently means being matched with Manhattan's most polished gold-diggers."

"These women are accomplished professionals," I corrected. "CEOs, attorneys, philanthropists—"

"Who are conveniently single and open to marrying a billionaire on short notice," he finished. "Come on, Anica. You're smarter than this."

The casual use of my first name sent an unwelcome tingle down my spine. "It's Ms. Marcel. And given your parameters, these are the most suitable candidates. Unless you've decided to modify your requirements?"

He turned to face me. "I'm adding a new parameter: authenticity."

"Authenticity," I repeated flatly. "That's rather vague for a man who specifically requested, and again I quote, 'ass you could bounce a quarter off of.'"

"I'm a complex man with evolving standards," he replied with that smirk that made me want to either slap him or... other things I absolutely should not have been considering. "I want someone real. Someone who sees me as more than a bank account with abs."

"So you want a unicorn," I translated. "A beautiful, accomplished woman who doesn't care about your money, is willing to enter a marriage of convenience in less than three months, and has the patience of a saint to deal with your ego."

"Precisely," he agreed cheerfully. "I knew you understood me."

I pinched the bridge of my nose, feeling a headache forming. "Mr. Burkhardt—"

"Callan," he corrected.

"Mr. Burkhardt," I repeated. "Finding someone who matches all your criteria was already like searching for a needle in a haystack. Adding 'doesn't care about your billions' is like specifying the needle must also be made of cheese."

"I love cheese. And I love challenges," he said, stepping closer. "Don't you?"

Before I could respond, his phone ran. He glanced at it and grinned. "Perfect timing. The peanut gallery wants to check in."

Without waiting for my permission, he answered the video call and propped his phone against my whiteboard.

"Gentlemen," he greeted the three faces that appeared on screen. "Meet my wedding planner and temporary fiancée, Anica Marcel."

57

I froze, equal parts mortified and furious. "Temporary what now?"

The three men on screen erupted in varying expressions of surprise and amusement.

"Holy shit, you actually found someone?" said a dark-haired man with a perpetual smirk. "Did you have to pay extra for the 'pretend to tolerate you' package?"

"Ignore Kris," said another man, this one with kind eyes and a relaxed demeanor. "He's still bitter his wife implemented a swear jar. I'm Chance. Nice to meet you, Anica."

"And I'm Morgan," added the third, who looked like he hadn't slept in weeks. "Are you actually marrying him? Blink twice if you're being held against your will. We can send an extraction team."

"She's not actually marrying me," Callan clarified, as I stood there trying to process the ambush. "She's my wedding planner who's helping me win our bet. Though we are temporarily engaged at the Rhodes Estate to secure the venue."

"Trespassing into new territory of assholery, even for you," Kris commented. "Impressive."

"It's strategic improvisation,'" Callan replied. "And it worked."

I finally found my voice. "I'm not his fiancée," I clarified. "I'm a professional who was coerced into a charade that I'm still considering legal action for."

"She's warming up to me," Callan stage-whispered.

"Clearly. The murder in her eyes must just be how she shows affection," Morgan said.

"So where are you in the process?" Chance asked, the only one who seemed actually interested in the bet rather than mocking Callan. "Found any potential brides yet?"

Callan gestured to my wall. "Anica has compiled the most comprehensive dating database in Manhattan. We're reviewing candidates today."

Kris leaned forward, squinting at the screen. "Is that... a murder wall of women? Are you sure you hired a wedding planner and not a very organized serial killer?"

"It's a strategic visualization of potential matches," I said, lifting my chin.

"Same thing," Morgan quipped. "I'm concerned and impressed."

"Just give us the stats," Chance said. "How many candidates? What's the timeline? I need to know if I should start shopping for a wedding gift or preparing my 'I told you so' speech."

"Thirty candidates, ten front-runners, first meeting tonight," Callan reported with the confidence of someone who hadn't rejected my entire methodology five minutes earlier. "And you should definitely shop for a gift. Something expensive."

"I still say it's impossible," Kris shook his head. "No sane woman would marry you knowing it's for a bet."

"You underestimate my charm," Callan replied.

"And you underestimate women's intelligence," I muttered, earning a snort of laughter from Morgan.

"I like her," he declared. "She sees through your bullshit."

"Shouldn't you be stress-vomiting about your own wedding instead of concerning yourself with mine?" Callan shot back.

Morgan's face paled. "Just because I occasionally question if marriage is a societal construct designed to torture men doesn't mean I'm not excited about my wedding."

"He threw up twice during the menu tasting," Kris informed us. "The chef thought it was a commentary on his cooking."

"As fascinating as this fraternity reunion is," I interrupted, "we have actual work to do. If you'll excuse us..."

"She's bossy," Kris observed. "No wonder you hired her."

"I hired her because she's the best," Callan said, with sincerity that momentarily caught me off guard. "And she's right. We need to prep for tonight's meeting."

"Meeting with who?" Chance asked.

"Destiny Gitwieler," I answered automatically. "Harvard Business School graduate, runs her family's foundation, speaks four languages, and has been featured in Vogue's '30 Under 30' list."

"Boring," Kris yawned. "Marry the wedding planner instead. At least she has fire."

Heat rushed to my cheeks as Callan laughed. "Don't tempt me. She's already threatened my life twice this week."

"Only twice?" Morgan seemed impressed. "You're slipping, man."

"We'll let you get back to your bride hunting," Chance said. "But weekly updates are required. Terms of the bet."

"And photographic evidence of all meetings," Kris added. "No claiming you met with someone when you were actually just getting lap dances at Scores."

"That was one time, and it was your bachelor party," Callan protested.

"Still counts," Morgan said. "Good luck, Anica. You'll need it."

The call ended before I could respond, leaving me standing there in stunned silence.

"So those are my friends," Callan said cheerfully. "Charming, aren't they?"

"That's not the word I'd use," I replied, still processing what I'd just witnessed. "Are they always like that?"

"That was them on good behavior," he assured me. "Usually there's more profanity and at least one reference to the Stanford incident, which is legally prohibited from being discussed in public."

Despite myself, I was curious. "What Stanford incident?"

"Nice try." He winked. "That information requires at least level seven friendship clearance. You're currently at level two: 'reluctant professional acquaintance with homicidal tendencies.'"

"I'm at level 'client who's testing my patience,'" I corrected, turning back to the board. "Now, about tonight. Destiny is our best option. She's smart, accomplished, socially connected, and most importantly, looking for a strategic relationship."

"How do you know that?"

"Because I actually spoke to her, unlike some people who just make snap judgments based on photographs," I replied. "She was quite candid about wanting a partnership that would benefit her foundation. I was clear about the... unusual circumstances."

"You told her about the bet?" He seemed surprised.

"I told her you were seeking a marriage of convenience on an expedited timeline. She doesn't know the specific motivation." I handed him a folder with Destiny's complete profile. "She's interested enough to meet. Dinner tonight at Le Bernardin, eight o'clock. Wear a suit."

He flipped through the folder, his expression unreadable. "She seems perfect on paper."

"She is perfect," I insisted. "Attractive, intelligent, independent, and realistic about marriage. Exactly what you claimed to want."

He closed the folder. "We'll see."

Something in his tone worried me. "Please don't sabotage this meeting."

"Would I do that?" He pressed a hand to his chest in mock offense.

"Based on my limited experience with you? Absolutely."

He grinned. "I promise to be on my best behavior."

"Somehow that's not reassuring." I gathered my notes. "I'll email you the details for tonight. I'll be at a nearby table to observe and provide feedback afterward."

"Playing chaperone?"

"Playing wedding planner who doesn't trust you not to blow this opportunity," I corrected. "Destiny is highly sought after. Don't waste her time."

"Yes, ma'am." He saluted, then wandered back to the wall of profiles, studying them. "You really did put a lot of work into this."

Something in his tone made me glance up. He sounded genuinely impressed, maybe even a little touched.

"It's my job," I said simply. "I don't do things halfway."

"Clearly," he murmured, then turned back to me with an expression I couldn't quite read. "I need your help with something else."

I raised an eyebrow. "That depends entirely on what it is and whether it involves pretending to be engaged to you in any additional venues."

"Nothing so dramatic," he assured me. "I need a tuxedo for a charity gala this weekend. The Pediatric Cancer Foundation event at the Metropolitan Museum."

That wasn't what I had been expecting. "That's not in our contract. Call a personal shopper."

"I want *your* opinion," he said. "You have excellent taste, as evidenced by this extremely thorough presentation, and a vested interest in making sure I look respectable for potential candidates who might be attending."

"Flattery and logic in the same sentence," I observed. "You must be desperate."

"I'll buy lunch," he offered. "And we can discuss candidates simultaneously."

"I can't be bought, Mr. Burkhardt."

"Everyone can be bought with the right food, Ms. Marcel. The trick is figuring out the currency." He studied me for a moment. "You strike me as a sushi person. Precise, elegant, no unnecessary components."

The accuracy of his observation was irritating. "Fine," I conceded. "Two hours. Tomorrow. And we are discussing these women."

His smile was triumphant. "Perfect. I'll pick you up at eleven."

"I'll meet you there," I countered. "Text me the address."

"Always maintaining boundaries," he noted. "Admirable but ultimately futile. I'm very good at getting past defenses, Ms. Marcel."

"And I'm very good at maintaining them, Mr. Burkhardt," I replied. "It's why I'm still in business after my ex-fiancé tried to destroy my reputation along with my heart."

His expression shifted to something more serious, the playfulness vanishing in an instant. "This Austin sounds increasingly like someone who deserves a visit from my security team," he said, his voice suddenly hard with an edge I hadn't heard before. "Maybe a long, private conversation about how to treat women properly."

I stared at him, stunned not just by the shift in his demeanor but by the information he had. "How do you know his name? I never told you his name."

Callan had the grace to look slightly abashed, though the hardness remained in his eyes. "I may have had Erika do some background research. Purely for professional purposes."

"You investigated me?" My voice rose as a complicated mix of emotions surged through me; outrage that he'd violated my privacy, a strange flutter that he'd cared enough to look into my past, and something darker and more vengeful at the thought of Austin facing consequences for what he'd done.

"I investigate everyone I work with," he said with a shrug, though his expression remained unusually solemn. "Standard procedure."

"That is absolutely not standard procedure," I shot back, suddenly furious. "My personal life is off-limits. You had no right to dig into my past."

"You're right," he admitted, surprising me again. "I overstepped. I apologize."

The simple acknowledgment took some of the wind out of my sails, but I wasn't ready to let it go. "Why would you even care about my ex?"

"Because he hurt you," Callan said simply, as if it were the most obvious thing in the world. "And anyone who would choose someone else over you clearly suffered from a traumatic brain injury. Or deserves to experience one."

"I... that's not..."

"Just an observation," he said, mercifully letting me off the hook. "For what it's worth, his loss is currently funding my found-the-perfect-wedding-planner good fortune." He turned to leave, then paused at the door. "Oh, and Anica?"

"Ms. Marcel," I corrected automatically.

"Wear something blue," he continued as if I hadn't spoken. "It's your color."

And then he was gone, leaving me standing in my ridiculous research room.

Strictly professional, I reminded myself firmly. This was strictly professional.

But as I returned to the women's profiles, I mentally reviewed my closet for something blue to wear that night, and firmly ignoring Mari's voice in my head singing "I told you so."

LE BERNARDIN WAS exactly as intimidating as its three Michelin stars suggested. All sleek surfaces, hushed conversations, and waitstaff who moved like professional ballerinas. I arrived thirty minutes early, as was my habit for all important events, and was escorted to a small table with a perfect view of where Callan and Destiny would be seated.

I wore a midnight blue dress that I told myself I'd chosen for its professional cut rather than because Callan had suggested the color. My hair was pulled back in a sleek chignon, and I'd limited my jewelry to simple pearl earrings that had been my mother's. The goal was to be invisible. Just another diner enjoying an overpriced meal while coincidentally observing the table eight feet away.

Destiny arrived exactly on time, looking every inch the polished socialite in a designer dress. Her dark hair was styled in elegant waves, her makeup flawless but understated. She was, objectively speaking, stunning.

She was also alone, because Callan was late. Again.

She checked her watch, took a small sip of water, and maintained a pleasant expression despite the passing minutes. Five minutes. Ten minutes. Fifteen minutes.

I was about to text him a strongly worded message when he finally appeared, and my irritation immediately transformed into a different kind of discomfort.

He wasn't wearing a suit.

Despite my explicit instructions, Callan had arrived at one of New York's most exclusive restaurants in dark jeans and a simple black t-shirt that molded to his shoulders and chest that gave away way too much information for the anatomy beneath. The damn man was pure muscle. The maître d' didn't even blink. Evidently billionaires operated under different dress codes than mere mortals.

What was most infuriating was that he somehow pulled it off, looking more compelling than the men in bespoke suits at neighboring tables. The casual attire highlighted his athletic build in a way that made several women openly stare as he crossed the restaurant.

Including, I realized with horror, me.

I quickly averted my gaze, pretending to study the menu as if the price of Dover sole was the most fascinating thing I'd ever encountered. When I dared look up again, he was greeting Destiny with an apologetic smile and that particular brand of charisma that made people forget they were supposed to be annoyed with him.

I couldn't hear their conversation from my position, but I could observe their body language. Destiny was clearly charmed despite his tardiness and inappropriate attire, leaning forward slightly and laughing at something he said. Callan was... harder to read. He smiled and maintained eye contact, asked questions that made her animate in response, but something about his posture suggested he wasn't fully engaged.

Their appetizers arrived, and I forced myself to at least pretend to eat my own meal while keeping an eye on their interaction. Things seemed to be going well, until suddenly Destiny's expression shifted from warm engagement to shock, then barely concealed outrage.

I couldn't hear what Callan had said, but based on Destiny's face, it was wildly inappropriate. She recovered quickly, her social training evidently kicking in, but the warmth had vanished from her expression.

The rest of the meal continued in increasingly strained politeness. By dessert, they were essentially two strangers occupying the same table, with Destiny checking her phone with increasing frequency and Callan looking completely unbothered by the deterioration of what should have been a promising match.

When they finally parted ways outside the restaurant—Destiny leaving in a black sedan with a perfunctory air kiss that didn't come within six inches of Callan's cheek—I was seething. I waited until her car had disappeared into traffic before approaching him.

"What the hell was that?" I demanded, not caring that we were standing in front of one of New York's most prestigious restaurants.

"Dinner," he replied, shrugging. "Excellent sea bass, though the wine pairing was a bit conventional."

"You know what I mean," I said, lowering my voice as a couple passed us. "You deliberately sabotaged that meeting. Destiny was perfect."

"On paper," he agreed. "In person, not so much."

"She's intelligent, accomplished, beautiful—"

"And exclusively interested in my net worth," he finished. "Did you know her first three questions were about my investment portfolio, my real estate holdings, and whether I had a prenup requirement?"

That gave me pause. "She's financially minded. It's her background."

"She's a gold digger with an MBA," he corrected. "There's a difference."

"So you decided to torpedo any chance by saying, what, exactly? What did you say that made her look like she'd swallowed a lemon?"

He glanced down, suddenly fascinated by his shoes. "I may have asked about her sexual preferences. In somewhat explicit terms."

"You what?" I nearly screeched, then lowered my voice again when a passing woman gave us a concerned look. "Please tell me you're joking."

"I needed to test her authenticity," he said, as if this were a perfectly reasonable explanation. "I wanted to see if she was interested in me as a person or just as a bank account."

"By asking about her sexual preferences? At Le Bernardin?" I was practically vibrating with fury. "That wasn't a test, it was sexual harassment."

"Technically, it was a question about personal compatibility," he argued. "An important factor in any marriage."

"What exactly did you ask her?" I demanded, morbidly curious despite myself.

He hesitated, then leaned in slightly. "I asked if she was comfortable with the fact that I like to be tied up occasionally and spanked while being called 'naughty little trust fund baby.'"

I choked on nothing but air. "You did *not*."

"I did," he confirmed, looking far too pleased with himself. "Her exact response was to inform me that she only engages in 'normal, dignified sexual activities appropriate to people of our station.'"

"Oh my god," I groaned, mortification warring with a completely inappropriate urge to laugh. "You're impossible. Absolutely impossible." I turned to walk toward the parking area where I'd left my car. "I cannot believe you."

"Well, I actually like to do the tying up. But I don't mind being spanked once in a while." He fell into step beside me. "What can I say? I'm selective. If I'm doing this ridiculous thing, I at least want someone real who cares about more than just my money."

"I spent a week trying to find the perfect candidate, who you then insulted with inappropriate questions about being a 'naughty little trust fund baby'!" I fumbled in my purse for my keys, dropping them in my agitation.

We both bent to retrieve them at the same time, our hands colliding. I jerked back as if burned, while he calmly picked them up and held them out to me, his fingers deliberately brushing against my palm as he placed them there.

"I'm sorry for not being clearer about my requirements," he said, his voice surprisingly sincere. "You did excellent work. Destiny simply wasn't right."

The genuine apology took some wind out of my sails. "Fine. But next time, just say you're not interested. Don't ask invasive sexual questions to drive them away."

"Deal," he agreed easily. "Though I maintain that sexual compatibility is a valid consideration in marriage."

"There are appropriate times and places for those discussions," I informed him. "A first meeting at a Michelin-starred restaurant is neither."

"Noted," he said, then added with a grin, "So where would be appropriate? Third date at a moderately priced bistro? Over coffee at a discreet café? During our tuxedo shopping tomorrow?"

"You're incorrigible," I sighed, but fought a reluctant smile. "And we're still going shopping tomorrow, but only because I refuse to let you sabotage any more potential matches with your questionable wardrobe choices."

"So you didn't like my outfit?" he asked innocently. "I thought I looked rather good."

The problem was, he *had* looked good. Unfairly good. The kind of good that had made it difficult to concentrate on my overpriced fish.

"You looked inappropriate for the venue," I said primly. "Le Bernardin has a dress code."

"Not for people who tip like I do," he replied with a wink. "But I promise to wear a proper suit next time. If you promise to give me candidates with more personality than their investment portfolios."

"I'll adjust my parameters," I conceded. "But you need to take this seriously. We have less than three months, and you just burned one of our best options."

"I'm taking it very seriously," he said, running a hand through his hair. "Which is why I'm not settling for someone who sees me as a transaction."

For a brief moment, I saw past the arrogant billionaire façade to something more complicated underneath.

"I'll find you someone better," I promised, unsure why I suddenly felt so determined to succeed for his sake rather than just for the contract.

"I know you will," he said with confidence. "You're the best, remember?"

"Eleven tomorrow," I reminded him, opening my car door. "Don't be late."

"I'll try to avoid duck-related traffic incidents," he replied with a grin.

UNEXPECTED REVELATIONS IN WHITE SILK

Chapter 6: Callan

I arrived at Bespoke & Co. right on time. 11:00 AM exactly. It was sure to throw Anica off her game. Punctuality: the ultimate power move when dealing with someone who expects you to be late.

The boutique occupied the entire ground floor of a historic brownstone on the Upper East Side, it was polished mahogany and hushed voices, with prices high enough to make even billionaires check their account balances. The kind of place where they didn't display price tags because if you had to ask, you couldn't afford it.

I hated it immediately.

Don't get me wrong. I appreciated quality. But places like this weren't about quality; they were about exclusivity. About making certain people feel special by making everyone else feel inadequate. A game I'd learned to play exceptionally well but never quite enjoyed.

Growing up in Queens with hand-me-down clothes and shoes patched with duct tape had left its mark, even after fifteen years of wealth. The memory of my grandmother working double shifts to afford my school uniform still made these temples of excess feel slightly obscene.

"Mr. Burkhardt!" The owner appeared as I stepped through the door. Anatoly Roskov, a trim man with silver hair. "What an unexpected pleasure. We've been hoping you might visit us."

His accent carried traces of Eastern Europe softened by years in Manhattan's elite circles, not the affected British inflection I'd half-expected from the boutique's pretentious exterior.

"Anatoly," I nodded, having never met the man before in my life but certain he would pretend otherwise. "I need a tuxedo for the Pediatric Cancer Foundation gala."

"Of course, of course. We have several exceptional pieces that would complement your frame." He gestured toward the back of the store. "If you'll follow me, we have a private viewing area where—"

"I'm waiting for someone," I interrupted, checking my watch. 11:03. Still no Anica. Maybe my punctuality play had backfired.

"Your assistant, perhaps? We can offer refreshments while—"

"My fiancée," I said, the lie rolling off my tongue. After the Rhodes Estate, it felt almost natural. "She's helping me choose."

Anatoly's eyebrows rose. "I wasn't aware you were engaged, Mr. Burkhardt. The society pages have been surprisingly quiet."

I bit back a smile. In Anatoly's world, a billionaire bachelor getting engaged without proper society announcement was like a royal abdication. The gossip value alone probably had him mentally composing texts to his most valuable clients.

"Very recent," I assured him. "We're keeping it quiet."

"Discretion is our specialty," he said, while clearly calculating how this information could be strategically leaked. "Perhaps while you wait, I could show you our new collection of—"

The door opened, and there she was in a pantsuit with a cream silk blouse, hair in a sleek ponytail. Her expression shifted from composed to surprised when she saw me.

"You're on time," she said by way of greeting.

"Don't sound so disappointed." I grinned.

Her lips twitched in what might have been a smile. "How considerate."

"Ms. Marcel, I presume?" Anatoly stepped forward. "A pleasure to welcome Mr. Burkhardt's... fiancée to our establishment."

The look Anica shot me could have flash-frozen hell. "I'm Mr. Burkhardt's wedding planner," she corrected smoothly. "Here in a strictly professional capacity to ensure he selects appropriate attire for upcoming events."

"Of course," Anatoly said, looking between us with poorly concealed curiosity. "How... modern."

"Isn't she wonderful?" I draped an arm around Anica's shoulders. She stiffened beneath my touch. "So dedicated to her work that she insists on maintaining professional boundaries in public. We're very private about our relationship."

"Mr. Burkhardt," she said through gritted teeth, "perhaps we should focus on selecting your tuxedo?"

"Whatever you say, darling."

She shrugged off my arm. "Mr. Roskov, we're looking for something classic but distinctive for the gala. Mr. Burkhardt needs to make an impression without appearing as though he's trying to make an impression."

Anatoly nodded. "A woman who understands the subtleties of men's formal wear. Refreshing."

"I understand the subtleties of many things," she replied with a cool smile. "Including the value of efficiency. Shall we?"

As Anatoly led us toward the fitting area, I leaned close to Anica. "Subtle threat. Very effective."

"I haven't begun to threaten you," she murmured back. "And if you call me 'darling' again, you'll be wearing that tuxedo in a hospital gown configuration."

"Promise?"

Her eye-roll was magnificent.

The private fitting area resembled a gentlemen's club from another century; leather chairs, crystal decanters of amber liquids, and mirrors strategically placed to flatter even the most unfortunate physiques. Anatoly gestured to two younger men who appeared with measuring tapes draped around their necks.

"Lucas and Paul will take your measurements," Anatoly explained. "While I select some options based on your... requirements."

As the assistants approached with their tapes, a familiar discomfort rose. I hated this part. The hovering, the touching, the unspoken judgment of every physical imperfection. My mind flashed back to eighth grade, being measured for a scholarship program's donated blazer while classmates snickered about my too-short pants.

"Actually," Anica interjected, surprising me, "I have some specific ideas. Navy would be preferable to black. It's more flattering with Mr. Burkhardt's coloring. Black is too harsh against his skin tone."

Anatoly looked momentarily surprised at having his expertise challenged, then thoughtful. "You have an excellent eye, Ms. Marcel. Navy is indeed more complementary to Mr. Burkhardt's particular palette."

"And I'd suggest a specific cut to accommodate his broader shoulders and athletic build. Something custom but not overly structured." She spoke with such authority that even I was impressed. "Perhaps the Savile Row silhouette you featured in last month's GQ spread? With modifications to the lapel width."

Anatoly's expression transformed from polite tolerance to genuine respect. "You follow men's fashion, Ms. Marcel?"

"I follow everything that might impact my clients' appearances at important events," she replied. "The right attire is as crucial as the right venue."

While they discussed fabrics and cuts, I studied Anica with new appreciation. She moved through this world, a world designed to intimidate, with complete confidence. No pretension, no insecurity, just expertise.

"Mr. Burkhardt?" Lucas approached cautiously. "We need to take your measurements now."

I nodded, steeling myself for the discomfort. As they fluttered around me with their tapes, I focused on maintaining my usual nonchalance, but something must have shown in my expression.

"Perhaps we could expedite this process. Mr. Burkhardt has another appointment this afternoon," Anica suggested.

"But precision requires time," Paul protested. "Each measurement must be —"

"Just the essentials," I interrupted. "It's just clothes."

Anatoly looked taken aback. "Just clothes? Mr. Burkhardt, a properly tailored tuxedo is an investment in —"

"Mr. Burkhardt appreciates quality," Anica cut in, "but prefers functionality over fashion dissertations. Perhaps we could see the fabrics while Lucas and Paul work?"

Her intervention surprised me. She'd read my discomfort and redirected without drawing attention to it; a small kindness I hadn't expected.

As Anatoly led Anica to a display of fabrics, Lucas moved in with his measuring tape. "Arms out, please."

I complied, keeping my expression neutral despite my growing irritation with the process. The tape slid across my shoulders, down my arms, around my chest. All the while, the assistants murmured numbers to each other like they were exchanging secrets.

"You have an excellent physique, Mr. Burkhardt," Lucas commented. "Many clients require... structural assistance."

"I run," I said shortly. Five miles every morning, rain or shine. A habit from when running was my only affordable exercise option. Now I had a home gym worth more than my childhood apartment building, but the pavement still called to me.

"And your waist measurement is quite impressive given your age," Paul added.

"Given my what now?" I fixed him with a stare that had made tech CEOs reconsider their life choices.

Paul blanched. "I simply meant... for someone of your... achievement level."

"He means you don't have the typical CEO paunch," Anica translated, returning with fabric swatches. "It was a compliment, albeit a poorly phrased one."

"Hmm." I wasn't convinced, but the way Paul was now sweating suggested he'd learned his lesson.

"I've selected these three options," she continued, holding up swatches in varying shades of navy. "The midnight blue has depth without being severe."

I glanced at the nearly identical squares of fabric. "They all look the same to me."

She sighed. "This one has undertones of black, this one has undertones of purple, and this one changes slightly under different lighting conditions."

"I'll take your word for it," I said, charmed by her seriousness about fabric colors. "Whatever you think is best."

"It's your tuxedo, Mr. Burkhardt. You should have an opinion."

"My opinion is that I trust yours."

She blinked. "Well. In that case, the middle one. With a subtle shawl collar and custom buttons."

"Done." I turned to Anatoly. "Whatever she said. And we need it by Saturday."

"Saturday?" Anatoly looked concerned. "Mr. Burkhardt, a proper bespoke tuxedo requires at least three fittings and —"

"I'm sure you'll figure it out," I interrupted, with the smile that conveyed I wasn't actually making a request. "Consider it a fun challenge."

Anatoly opened his mouth to respond further, but my phone rang. "Excuse me, I need to take this."

I stepped away, answering the call. "What's up, Erika?"

"I'm sorry to interrupt, Mr. Burkhardt, but there's a situation." Her normally composed voice had an edge I rarely heard. "My mother's in the hospital. They think it might be a stroke."

"Shit, Erika." My irritation with the boutique experience instantly evaporated. "Go. Now. Take whatever time you need."

"But the Tokyo investors —"

"I'll handle them. Family comes first. Always." I meant it. After growing up with a father who put business before everything, I'd sworn never to inflict that priority system on anyone else. "Which hospital?"

"Mount Sinai."

"I'll have my car take you and make sure she gets a private room. Do you need anything else? Someone to watch your cat? A place to stay near the hospital?"

"No, I — thank you, Mr. Burkhardt." The relief in her voice was obvious. "I'll keep you updated."

"Don't worry about work. Just take care of your mom." I ended the call and turned to find Anica watching me.

"Everything okay?" she asked.

"My assistant's mother is in the hospital. Possible stroke."

"I'm sorry to hear that." She seemed genuinely concerned. "Is there anything I can do?"

"No, but thank you for offering. Shall we finish up here? I need to make some calls to cover for Erika."

73

She nodded, turning back to Anatoly, who had been hovering at a respectful distance. "We'll take the midnight navy with the modifications I specified. Mr. Burkhardt will return for one fitting on Thursday, and the tuxedo must be ready by Saturday evening."

"That's... highly irregular," Anatoly protested.

"So is a twenty percent premium above your standard rate," I countered, "which I'm happy to pay for the expedited service."

Anatoly's expression shifted from resistant to accommodating. "We would be delighted to meet your timeline, Mr. Burkhardt."

"Excellent." I checked my watch. "Are we finished?"

"Almost," Anatoly assured me. "Paul just needs a few more measurements, and then we should discuss accessories, cufflinks, studs, perhaps a custom pocket square..."

I suppressed a sigh. At this rate, we'd be here until dinner.

"Maybe we could continue this discussion after lunch?" Anica suggested, once again reading my mood perfectly. "I'm sure Mr. Roskov could prepare some sketches based on what we've discussed."

"A splendid idea," Anatoly agreed. "Paul, finish the measurements quickly, please."

As Paul approached with his tape measure again, I noticed something through the archway on the other side of the boutique; a glimpse of white satin and lace. The bridal section. An idea formed in my mind, pushing aside my discomfort with a much more entertaining prospect.

"You know," I said casually as Paul measured my inseam, "since we're here, perhaps my fiancée should try on some wedding dresses."

Anica, who had been texting something on her phone, looked up sharply. "What?"

"A wedding dress, darling. The thing women wear when they get married?" I gave her my most innocent smile. "You haven't found yours yet, have you?"

Paul stared between us, a crease forming between his brows, mouth parting like a question was on the edge.

"Mr. Burkhardt has an unusual sense of humor," Anica explained.

"I'm sure Lucas could help." I nodded to the other assistant, who shrugged.

"Sure."

"No," Anica said, shaking her head. "It's not important."

"I disagree." I was enjoying this far too much. "I'd say we've already waited too long, but I'm sure these fine gentlemen can help you find the perfect dress."

"He makes an excellent point," Anatoly interjected, suddenly reappearing. "And our bridal collection is truly exceptional. Perhaps just a quick viewing?"

Anica's expression suggested she was mentally calculating how many years she'd serve for strangling me with Paul's measuring tape. "That won't be necessary."

"Please?" I employed the puppy-dog eyes that had gotten me out of trouble since childhood. "Just one dress."

"You're ridiculous," she repeated flatly.

"And you're the best."

"Damn straight," she muttered, but her resolve weakened. "Fine. One dress. Then we're discussing the next three candidates over lunch, which you're paying for."

"Deal." I grinned, victorious. "And I promise to actually give them fair consideration this time."

"As opposed to sabotaging them with inappropriate questions?" she asked, raising a brow.

"That was a legitimate test," I protested.

Anatoly was already crossing to the other side of the store. "Christina!" he called. "We need you for a special bridal consultation!"

A stylish woman in her forties appeared almost instantly. "Yes, Mr. Roskov?"

"This is Ms. Marcel, Mr. Burkhardt's fiancée. She requires a gown. Something spectacular."

"Of course." Christina assessed Anica. "You have a lovely figure, Ms. Marcel. Classic hourglass with exceptional posture."

"Doesn't she?" I beamed at Anica, who flipped me off behind her back.

"Are you thinking traditional, modern, or somewhere in between?" Christina asked.

"I'm thinking 'let's get this over with as quickly as possible,'" Anica replied with a tight smile. "One dress. Simple, elegant, nothing too fussy."

"I have just the thing," Christina assured her. "If you'll follow me?"

As Anica was led away, looking like she was marching to her execution, I couldn't help but feel smug. This was turning out to be far more entertaining than I'd anticipated. A little payback for all her rigid professionalism and boundary-setting.

"She's quite something," Anatoly commented as we watched them disappear into the bridal section. "Not your usual type."

"And what would my usual type be?" I asked, curious despite myself.

"Models, actresses, socialites." He shrugged. "Women who... complement your status rather than challenge it. The kind I've seen you with in the tabloids or on social media."

Before I could respond to that loaded observation, Paul announced he'd finished the measurements. "Excellent work," I said, grateful for the interruption. "Now, how long does it typically take to try on a wedding dress?"

"Depends on the woman," Anatoly replied. "Some try twenty before finding the right one. Others know immediately."

"Ms. Marcel strikes me as the efficient type," Paul said, standing up.

"I agree. Though even the most practical women sometimes surprise themselves when they see their reflection in a wedding gown." Anatoly gave me a knowing look. "It can be quite transformative."

I rolled my eyes at the sentimentality. "It's just a dress."

"Just a dress?" Anatoly looked genuinely offended. "Mr. Burkhardt, a wedding gown is a statement of—"

"Mr. Burkhardt?" Christina called from the archway. "We're ready for your reaction."

"My reaction?" I turned, confused.

"It's tradition," she explained. "Well, normally it's friends and family of the bride, but since you're here, and she said she didn't mind if you saw, we'll consider it the groom's first glimpse."

"Sure, I guess that sounds—" I began, but stopped mid-sentence as Anica stepped into view.

Holy. Shit.

The dress was simple. A sleek, off-shoulder design in ivory silk that followed the curves of her body before flaring subtly at the knees. No excessive beading or lace, just perfect tailoring and a small train that pooled behind her. Her hair was still in its ponytail, her makeup unchanged, but something about seeing Anica Marcel in a wedding dress had my knees forgetting that they were essential to remaining standing. I nearly tripped off the pedestal, and didn't face plant only because Anatoly caught me by the elbow.

She was stunning. Not in the obvious way of the models and actresses Anatoly had mentioned, but in a way that made it impossible to look anywhere else. The professional armor was gone, replaced by something softer yet somehow more powerful. The silk clung to the curve of her waist, highlighting the feminine figure I'd dreamt about almost every night since meeting her. The neckline revealed collarbones delicate enough to make my fingers itch to trace them, followed by my tongue.

I realized I was staring. Worse, I realized I couldn't stop.

"Well?" she prompted, a hint of vulnerability breaking through her composed expression. "Is it ridiculous enough for you? Can we move on to lunch now?"

Words failed me, which was not a common occurrence. I, who made my fortune with persuasive pitches and quick comebacks, stood there like an idiot, trying to remember how to form a coherent sentence.

"I think we've rendered Mr. Burkhardt speechless," Christina said with obvious satisfaction. "I always love seeing couples have that reaction!"

Her comment broke the spell. "We're not—" Anica started.

"It's perfect," I interrupted, finding my voice at last. "You look... incredible."

A flush crept up her neck, and for once, she seemed at a loss for words too.

"The silhouette is perfect for her figure," Christina continued, oblivious to the tension. "And the simplicity allows her natural beauty to shine through."

"Yes," I agreed, still unable to tear my gaze away from Anica. "Exactly that."

"Perhaps we should discuss veil options?" Christina suggested. "I'm thinking something cathedral length to complement the train."

"No veils," Anica said firmly, recovering her composure. "No accessories. This was just for... demonstration purposes."

"But surely for your actual wedding—"

"We haven't set a date yet," I improvised. "Still in the early planning stages."

"Ah, I see." Christina nodded. "Well, let me get your information for our file. We can hold this gown for you. It's from our new collection, not even on the floor yet."

"That won't be necessary," Anica said, wrapping her arms around herself.

"But it's perfect on you!" Christina protested. "And it requires minimal alterations."

"We're still exploring options, but we'll definitely keep this one in mind," I said.

"At least let me take your details," Christina persisted. "When are you thinking of having the wedding?"

"Three months," I replied at the exact moment Anica said, "Next year."

We exchanged looks of mutual panic.

"What he means," Anica recovered smoothly, "is that we need to decide within three months whether we're doing a winter wedding next year or waiting for spring."

"Exactly," I agreed. "So many factors to consider. Venue availability, family schedules, whether her mother will be out of prison by then..."

"Callan!" Anica gasped.

"Kidding," I grinned. "Her mother's a lovely woman. Only served eight years."

Christina's eyes widened, but her professional smile never faltered. "Family dynamics can certainly be... complex. How did you two meet?"

"Through work."

"At a charity gala."

Another exchange of panicked looks.

"Both, actually," I improvised. "We first saw each other at a charity gala but didn't speak. Then fate brought us together when I needed her professional services for my grandmother's birthday celebration."

"So romantic," Christina sighed. "And the proposal?"

"Empire State Building," Anica said quickly, rehashing the story we'd told before.

"During a blizzard," I added with a wink. "Her eyelashes froze. Actually," I continued, warming to the story, "I had planned an elaborate proposal with skywriters and a flash mob, but when the moment came, it was just the two of us in the snow, and I realized I didn't need all the theatrics."

"That's..." Anica looked at me strangely. "Not what happened."

"You were there, darling." I moved closer, placing my hand at the small of her back. The bare skin exposed by the dress was warm beneath my palm. "Don't you remember what I said?"

She stiffened at my touch but didn't pull away. "I remember you being very... persistent."

"It's my super power." I wiggled my eyebrows at her. "Anyways, I said that from the moment we met, you challenged everything I thought I wanted. That you made me want to be better than I was."

Something shifted in her expression. Surprise, maybe confusion. For a moment, it felt like we were the only two people in the room. God, she really was breathtaking in that dress. Like it'd been made just for her.

"How long have you two been together?" Christina asked, breaking the strange spell.

"Two months."

"Four weeks," Anica said at the same time.

Christina looked between us, her professional composure finally cracking. "I... see."

"Dating for two months," Anica clarified, stepping away from my touch. "Engaged for four weeks."

"Very whirlwind," I added.

"Indeed," Christina said, clearly not believing a word. "Well, I'll just... give you a moment while I check on something in the back."

As soon as she was gone, Anica turned to me, eyes flashing. "Was that really necessary?"

"What?" I asked innocently.

"The elaborations. The touching. The... whatever that was about challenging what you wanted."

I shrugged, suddenly uncomfortable with my own improvisation. "Maintaining our cover story. Making it believable."

"And the comment about my mother in prison?"

"It adds color to our narrative." I grinned, trying to recapture the lightness of the moment. "Besides, you have to admit, it was fun seeing her expression."

"Fun is not the word I would use." But there was a reluctant quirk to her lips that suggested she wasn't as angry as she pretended.

"You do look amazing in that dress," I said, stepping back to look her up and down again.

She glanced at it, as if suddenly remembering what she was wearing. "It's just a dress."

"Just a dress?" I echoed Anatoly's earlier offense. "Ms. Marcel, a wedding gown is a statement of—"

"Oh, shut up," she said, but she was almost smiling now. "I'm going to change. Meet you out front in ten minutes."

As she disappeared back into the fitting room, I replayed the moment she'd appeared in the dress. The strange breathless feeling that had overtaken me. The way time seemed to stop.

It was just the unexpectedness of it, I told myself. Seeing my uptight wedding planner in something so contrary to her usual presentation. Nothing more than a surprise.

A BILLIONAIRE WHO BAKES

Chapter 7: Anica

"Five different bakeries have offered me free wedding cakes if I tell them who Callan Burkhardt is marrying," Mari announced, lounging across my desk like a cat with a lollipop in her mouth. "One of them said they'd throw in a chocolate fountain if I can get them exclusive rights to your engagement photos."

"There is no engagement," I reminded her for the forty-third time that week. "There is no bride. And there are definitely no photos."

"Not yet," Mari said with a wink so exaggerated it was practically a facial spasm. "But I noticed you're wearing your good bra to a cake tasting. The lacy one with the—"

"For goodness' sake, why are the two of you so obsessed with my underthings? This was the only clean one I had!" I lied, adjusting my blouse for the third time. Mari had called my wedding dress try-on my "sad attempt at playing dress-up," but that hadn't stopped me from overthinking everything about my appearance today. It had been five days since the tuxedo fiasco, and I still couldn't shake the image of Callan's face when he'd seen me in that dress. The way his eyes had widened, how his usual smirk had fallen away.

It was just a momentary lapse in his annoying persona. Nothing more. Definitely not worth the approximately seventy-four hours I'd spent overthinking it since. seventy-four hours and twenty-three minutes, but who was counting? Not me. Nope.

"I need to go if I'm going to make it to the cake testing on time," I said, groaning as I pushed myself up from my chair.

"Wouldn't want him to be there first again." Mari dangled her lollipop in front of me. "Makes you look bad."

"It does not." I swiped at the lollipop, but she moved it too quickly. "Besides, his track record falls more on the side of being late, so I'll be fine."

"Whatever you say, *darling*," she imitated a man's deep voice, but choked on spit.

I flipped her off before leaving.

To my relief, I got to the bakery before Callan. It gave me time to settle and make sure things were in order without the six foot whatever distraction.

"The strawberry champagne is their signature flavor," the baker, Eloise, explained as she arranged delicate cake samples on the tasting table. "A favorite for summer weddings."

La Petite Pâtisserie was exclusive enough that they didn't advertise. Their clientele consisted entirely of Manhattan's elite, who passed the patisserie's number around like a secret handshake. Getting this tasting appointment had required three personal favors and promising Mari she could eat the leftovers. The bakery's tasting room was intimate, a generous description for what was essentially a closet, with just enough space for a small round table and two chairs.

Two very close chairs. The kind of close where you could tell what brand of cologne your companion wore without having to ask. Callan's was something expensive that probably had notes of "liquid cash" and "hostile takeover."

"Everything looks wonderful," I said, checking my watch again. Callan was only ten minutes late, which for him was practically early. Progress. "My client should be here any—"

"Sorry I'm late."

I turned to find Callan filling the doorway, dressed in dark jeans and a light blue button-down with the sleeves rolled up to expose his forearms. Why did forearms have to be so unnecessarily appealing? They're just arms. There was nothing inherently sexual about the radius and ulna bones, yet here I was, staring at them like they were performing an exotic dance with a side of "come hither" thrown in. My libido needed a serious talking-to later.

"Traffic or ducks?" I asked, managing to drag my gaze upward.

"Traffic, actually." He looked almost sheepish. "There was a group of protestors blocking Fifth Avenue. Something about tax breaks for the wealthy. I might have been one of the people they were protesting."

"How inconvenient when the peasants revolt during rush hour," I said dryly. "Next time maybe check the 'Eat The Rich' forecast before leaving home."

He grinned, unoffended. "I always keep cake-tasting appointments. Priorities. Besides, cake is the one thing Marie Antoinette and I have in common, though I'm hoping for a better outcome."

"At least your head looks good on your shoulders," I said, immediately regretting the words.

"Why, Ms. Marcel, was that almost a compliment?"

"It was an anatomical observation," I corrected. "Like noting that water is wet or that billionaires are chronically late."

Eloise's eyes widened as she recognized him. "Mr. Burkhardt! Such an honor. I didn't realize you were her groom."

"Not my groom," I corrected quickly. "Mr. Burkhardt is my client."

"I'm marrying someone else," Callan explained. "Ms. Marcel is my wedding planner."

"Oh!" Eloise looked confused. "I assumed since it was just the two of you..."

"The bride is... busy," Callan said with a casual wave of his hand.

"She's got other obligations today," I clarified. "But she trusts his judgment."

"She's a peach," Callan added cheerfully.

To Eloise's credit, her professional smile never faltered, though her eyebrows had climbed halfway up her forehead. "How... lovely. Well, shall we begin? I've prepared eight flavor combinations for you to consider."

As Callan took the seat opposite me, I realized just how small the table was. Our knees bumped, and he murmured an apology as he adjusted his long legs. The table was clearly designed for couples who enjoyed being close enough to share breath. Not for wedding planners trying to maintain professional boundaries with irritatingly attractive clients whose cologne smelled like it had been harvested from the garden of Eden and distilled with success.

"Let's approach this systematically," I said, perhaps too loudly. "Start with the vanilla baseline, then move to more complex flavors."

"An excellent strategy," Eloise agreed, placing two plates before us. "We'll begin with our classic Tahitian vanilla bean with Swiss meringue buttercream."

I reached for my cake fork at the exact moment Callan reached for his, our fingers brushing. I jerked my hand back, knocking over my water glass. Water splashed across the table, narrowly missing the cake samples but thoroughly soaking Callan's sleeve.

"I am so sorry," I blurted, grabbing napkins to mop up the spill.

"No harm done," Callan assured me, quickly helping to clean up. "Jumpy today?" he added with a raised eyebrow when I glared at him.

"Adequately caffeinated," I replied, which wasn't a lie. I'd had three espressos just to prepare myself for another hour in his presence. "Anything less than four shots of espresso and I might accidentally enjoy your company."

"I have that effect on people," he said with a wink. "Fully conscious women find me irresistible."

"Fully delusional men often think that," I shot back, finally reclaiming my composure.

Once the mess was cleaned up, we turned our attention to the cakes. I was determined to be nothing but professional, despite the way his knee kept brushing against mine under the tiny table. I took a bite of the vanilla cake, letting the subtle flavors melt on my tongue.

"Perfect proportion of frosting to cake," I noted, making a mark on my evaluation sheet. I'd created a rating system for each cake with categories for texture, flavor balance, and visual appeal. "Excellent crumb structure."

Callan took a bite, considering it thoughtfully. "It's good, but too safe. Wedding cakes should be memorable."

"Traditional choices are traditional for a reason," I countered. "Vanilla appeals to most palates."

"Most boring palates," he muttered, but his eyes twinkled. "Like missionary position for desserts. Gets the job done but nobody's writing home about it."

I choked on my cake and had to take a sip of the champagne. The bubbles didn't help much. "Please refrain from comparing cake to sexual positions in front of the baker."

"Would you prefer I compare it to other things?" he asked innocently. "Because we could move to anatomy."

"No," I said at the same time Eloise whispered "yes please," under her breath.

I rolled my eyes. "I'd prefer you focus on selecting a cake flavor rather than creating your next stand-up routine," I replied licking my fork. His gaze followed the movement.

"Whatever you say, darling."

I kicked him under the table. "Ms. Marcel."

With his focus still on my mouth, he responded, "Yes, ma'am."

Eloise brought over the next sample before I could kick him again. "Lemon cake with lavender buttercream."

I took a bite. "Interesting combination. The floral notes might be overpowering for some guests."

"The lavender is too dominant," Callan agreed. "It should complement the lemon, not overwhelm it. They need to reduce the lavender extract by about a third and increase the lemon zest."

I stared at him. When had Callan Burkhardt become a cake expert?

Eloise looked equally surprised. "That's... a very precise observation, Mr. Burkhardt."

"Try the cardamom-honey next," he suggested. "I'm curious how it pairs with the different frosting options."

Eloise brought over two more samples, and Callan sampled each.

"The cardamom-honey pairs better with the rosewater buttercream than the vanilla," he declared. "The floral notes in the rosewater enhance the honey without competing with the cardamom."

"How do you know that?" I blurted, unable to contain my confusion. This was like discovering your accountant was secretly a champion bullfighter. A complete identity crisis.

"Know what?"

"About flavor pairing and extract ratios and... all of this." I gestured to the elaborate notes he'd begun making on a napkin. "I thought your food preferences consisted entirely of 'expensive' and 'more expensive' with the occasional 'served on a supermodel's bare back.'"

85

He laughed. "There's a lot you don't know about me, Ms. Marcel."

"Apparently," I agreed, still baffled by this unexpected facet of the man that looked like just another rich playboy. "Next you'll tell me you knit or rescue orphaned kittens in your spare time."

"Only on Tuesdays," he replied with perfect seriousness. "Mondays are for overthrowing small governments." He ran a hand through his hair. "I baked with my grandmother growing up," he admitted after a moment, his voice softer. "Every Sunday. It was our thing."

"You baked?" The image of little Callan in an apron, standing on a stool to reach the counter, was almost too adorable to bear. My ovaries practically squealed.

"Still do," he said, looking almost embarrassed by the admission. "When I can find the time. I make her birthday cake every year, no matter how crazy my schedule gets."

"That's... surprisingly sweet," I said, meaning it.

"Don't tell anyone," he replied with a mock-serious expression. "Bad for my cutthroat CEO image. I'm supposed to eat the hopes and dreams of my competitors for breakfast, not homemade cinnamon rolls."

"Your secret's safe with me," I assured him, fighting a smile. "Though I might need photographic evidence. For verification purposes only."

"Verification purposes," he repeated skeptically. "Not blackmail?"

"I would never." I placed a hand over my heart. "Though I'm sure the business tabloids would pay handsomely for shots of Manhattan's Most Eligible Bachelor wearing oven mitts and covered in flour. 'Breaking News: Billionaire Burkhardt Batters Batter.'"

"I see you missed your calling as a tabloid headline writer," he said.

"It was my backup career if wedding planning fell through. 'Planner Plots Perfect Prenup' didn't have the same ring to it."

He laughed again, and I laughed with him. For a moment, we weren't client and wedding planner, just two people enjoying each other's company. It was... nice. Dangerous, but nice.

Eloise continued bringing samples, and we fell into a comfortable rhythm of tasting and discussing. Callan's expertise was genuine, and I deferred to his opinion on several flavor combinations. It was oddly refreshing to not be the expert for once. It also meant I didn't have to eat as much cake. God, I hated cake tastings. Why did everyone want cake at their receptions? Cake was inferior to well-made cookies in my expert opinion. And I'd tried *a lot* of cakes.

"So," he said as we waited for Eloise to get the final round of samples from the back kitchen, "have you narrowed down the next batch of bride candidates? After the Destiny disaster?"

And just like that, reality crashed back. Right. The bride hunt. The whole reason we were sitting here tasting wedding cakes when there wasn't even a couple to celebrate. Just a billionaire with a bet and me with a million-dollar contract to find him someone to marry who wasn't me. Not that I wanted it to be me.

"I've revised my approach," I said, shifting back into professional mode. "Focusing more on personality compatibility and less on résumé perfection."

"Good," he nodded. "Because I meant what I said. I want someone real."

"Define 'real,'" I challenged him. "Because in my experience, most men say they want 'real' women until they actually meet one who challenges them or has opinions they don't like. Then suddenly they want 'real' women who also happen to agree with everything they say."

He considered this. "Fair point. But I do want someone to challenge me. Yes men get old fast. I want someone who gets me."

"Way to be vague and a tad cliché," I muttered, saluting him with my champagne flute before downing the rest of the shimmering liquid.

He stuck his tongue out at me like a child before continuing. "I *mean*, I want someone who would still want to be with me if all this went away." He gestured vaguely, presumably indicating his empire.

"That's a pretty big ask for a marriage of convenience," I pointed out. "You're essentially describing love, which you've made clear isn't part of the equation."

"Not love," he corrected. "Love doesn't exist."

"Cynic."

"Yes. Thanks for noticing." He shook his head. "I want authenticity. Respect. My parents had an arrangement, not a marriage. It lasted twenty-three years before they divorced."

87

"Twenty-three years?" I was surprised. "That's way longer than most love matches. Those normally last maybe eight years."

"They were excellent business partners," he explained. "Terrible spouses. They maintained separate bedrooms, separate lives, only united for public appearances and financial decisions."

"Is that what you want?"

"God, no," he said with unexpected vehemence. "But I also don't buy into the fairy tale. Marriage is a practical partnership with occasional sex thrown in to keep things interesting."

The way he tossed out the word "sex" made heat crawl up my neck. I hoped he'd attribute my sudden flush to the warm room rather than the immediate mental image of what "keeping things interesting" might look like with him.

"That's... quite the romantic perspective. I can see why women are lining up. Nothing says 'marry me' like 'practical partnership with occasional sex.'"

"You'd be surprised how appealing honesty can be," he countered. "Better than promising the moon and delivering a piece of cheese."

"I thought you liked cheese."

"Love it."

"Then that's not a metaphor I'd use for marriage, but whatever works for you," I said, biting back a laugh.

"What about you?" he asked, leaning forward. "After all the weddings you've planned, what's your take on what makes marriages work?"

I hesitated, surprised by the personal question. "That's not really relevant to our professional relationship."

"Humor me," he insisted. "Consider it research for your bride hunt. I need to know what my wedding planner thinks constitutes a good marriage if she's going to find me a wife."

I sighed, considering how to answer. "The best couples I work with are best friends first," I admitted finally. "Everything else is just details. The fancy venue, the expensive dress, the perfect cake. None of it matters if there isn't genuine affection and respect. It's about the years of ups and downs afterwards, not really the big party that starts it."

"That sounds suspiciously romantic for someone who approached my bride search with compatibility matrices."

"I'm a professional. I can separate my personal views from my work. I can believe in unicorns while still recognizing they don't belong in your wedding ceremony."

"So you're secretly a romantic," he concluded, looking entirely too pleased with himself. "Interesting."

"I'm secretly someone who's witnessed 347 weddings and can tell which ones will last before the cake is cut," I corrected. "It has nothing to do with romance and everything to do with who's still looking at each other instead of their phones during the reception speeches."

"Still sounds romantic to me." His smirk was infuriating. "It's written all over your face."

"The only thing written on my face is 'regretting this conversation,'" I replied.

Before I could say anything else, his phone rang. He glanced at the screen and his expression softened.

"Sorry, I have to take this. It's my grandmother." He stepped away from the table, answering with a warm, "Hi, Gram."

I couldn't help but watch as his entire demeanor transformed. His shoulders relaxed, the perpetual hint of sarcasm left his voice, and his smile became genuine in a way I rarely saw. The Callan Burkhardt who spoke to his grandmother was a completely different man from the one who flirted with every woman and strode into my office like he owned it already.

"Yes, I'm still coming on Sunday," he assured her. "No, I haven't forgotten... I'm actually at a cake tasting right now." He glanced at me, then quickly looked away. "With the wedding planner... No, Gram, it's not... That's not..." His face reddened. "No, it's not like that at all."

I pretended to be fascinated by my cake notes, but I was straining to hear what could be making Callan Burkhardt, Manhattan's most confident man, stammer like a teenager caught sneaking in after curfew.

"She's very professional... Yes, she's helping me with the whole thing..." His blush deepened. "Gram, please don't... No, I'm not bringing her to... That's not appropriate... She's very busy..."

Whatever his grandmother was saying, it was clearly mortifying him. I bit my lip to keep from smiling, making a mental note to send his grandmother flowers. Or a fruit basket. Or possibly my firstborn child, depending on what exactly she was saying to make him so uncomfortable.

"Fine, I'll ask her, but don't get your hopes up." He sighed deeply. "Love you too. See you Sunday."

"Everything okay?" I asked innocently. "You look like someone just asked you to explain blockchain to a kindergarten class."

"So..." He ran a hand through his hair, actually looking nervous. "My grandmother is insisting you come to Sunday dinner."

I blinked. "Excuse me?"

"Sunday dinner. At her home. With me." He winced. "She's very persistent."

"That's absolutely not happening," I said firmly. "Our relationship is strictly professional."

"That's what I told her," he agreed. "But she's 82 and has heart problems."

I narrowed my eyes. "That's emotional manipulation."

"Is it working?" he asked hopefully.

"It's about as subtle as a rhinestone codpiece at a funeral."

It shouldn't have been working. I had principles. Boundaries. A very strict no-personal-involvement policy with clients that had served me well since the Austin disaster. A policy that specifically prohibited meeting family members in non-wedding contexts.

And yet...

"What time should I arrive?" I heard myself say. God, I was a pushover.

His relief was palpable. "Five o'clock? I can pick you up."

"I'll drive myself," I insisted, already regretting my decision. "And this is a professional courtesy only. Because it might help with the wedding plans to meet your family. And because I'm not a monster who gives octogenarians heart attacks."

"Of course," he agreed, though his smile suggested he didn't believe me. "Just so you know, what Gram wants, Gram gets. Always."

"I'm not intimidated by grandmothers," I informed him. "I've faced down mother-in-laws who requested live tigers at rehearsal dinners. One bride's grandmother insisted we release doves that she'd personally trained to form her granddaughter's initials in flight."

"Did it work?"

"Let's just say the city of Newark is still finding random doves with tiny sequined vests," I replied. "Your grandmother can't be worse than that."

"Vivian Burkhardt makes those women look like amateurs," he warned. "Consider yourself warned. She once made the CEO of Goldman Sachs cry during a charity auction. With just her eyebrows."

"Impressive," I admitted. "But I have a secret weapon."

"Which is?"

"I plan weddings for a living. I'm professionally trained to handle unreasonable expectations and emotional manipulation. It's basically my superpower."

"Your funeral," he said cheerfully. "Wear something nice. She judges outfits more harshly than Tim Gunn on a bad day."

Eloise returned with the final cake samples, but I was no longer thinking about frosting ratios and flavor profiles. I was wondering what exactly I'd gotten myself into by agreeing to Sunday dinner with Callan's grandmother.

The one person, apparently, who could make the unflappable Callan Burkhardt flap.

"We should try the chocolate ganache last," Callan suggested, returning to cake mode as if the grandmother invitation had never happened. "It's the richest."

"Save the best for last?" I asked, grateful for the change of subject.

"Always," he replied.

"In that case," I said, picking up my fork, "I better pace myself. Too much richness at once can be overwhelming."

"Or exactly what you need," he countered, his eyes meeting mine.

IT'S ALL ABOUT THE WRIST ACTION

Chapter 8: Callan

"**S**ir, I've taken the liberty of hiding the merman bathtub photo," Norbert announced as I entered my grandmother's house, causing me to nearly drop the bottle of wine I was carrying. "However, I should warn you that Madam has made copies. Several copies. One of which is now her phone background."

"Of course she has," I sighed, handing my coat to the butler. "Any chance of a convenient house fire before Ms. Marcel arrives?"

"I'm afraid arson would violate both my contract and several state laws," Norbert replied without missing a beat. "Though I did attempt to persuade Madam that the naked sprinkler photos were perhaps too intimate for dinner conversation."

"And?"

"She suggested I focus on polishing the silver instead of her conversational choices." Norbert's expression remained perfectly neutral, but I swore I detected a hint of sympathy in his eyes. "The chicken is roasting to your preferences. Madam is upstairs applying what she referred to as her 'matchmaking lipstick.'"

"Her what?"

"I didn't inquire further, sir. There are some questions even I know better than to ask."

I'd arrived at my grandmother's house forty-five minutes early, which was rare.

"Madam is still getting ready," Norbert observed as he accepted the wine.

"I thought I'd help with dinner," I said, heading toward the kitchen.

Norbert's eyebrow lifted approximately two millimeters, which in Norbert-speak was the equivalent of falling to the floor in shock. "Indeed, sir. The kitchen is, as always, where you last left it."

I headed straight for the kitchen, loosening my tie as I walked. The house was exactly as it had always been; immaculate, elegant, with just enough warmth to stop it feeling like a museum. Photographs of me at various ages lined the hallway, a visual timeline of my evolution from skinny kid with too-big glasses to... well, me.

"Callan Anthony Burkhardt, is that you arriving before the night has actually started?" My grandmother's voice called from upstairs. "Should I check the sky for flying pigs? Or perhaps call my doctor to ensure I haven't died and gone to an alternate dimension?"

"I'm early for important things," I called back, grinning despite myself.

"Since when is dinner with your grandmother important?" She appeared at the top of the stairs, still fastening an earring. At eighty-two, Vivian Burkhardt was five-foot-two of pure elegance and wit. Her silver hair was styled in a sleek bob, and she wore a bright blue cashmere sweater that I remembered costing a pretty penny. Not that she cared about the price anymore. Gram wore what she liked, cost be damned.

"It's always important," I replied, climbing the stairs to kiss her cheek. "But especially when you're meeting my wedding planner and will no doubt spend the evening trying to embarrass me."

"Me? Embarrass you?" She patted my cheek a bit harder than necessary. "That would require me to tell stories about how you used to take off all your clothes and run through the garden sprinklers at age four, penis flapping in the breeze, screaming 'I'm a helicopter!'" The grin on her face was pure evil. "I'd never embarrass you."

"And yet, somehow you just did." I sighed. "Please try to remember that Ms. Marcel is a professional, here in a professional capacity, and doesn't need to hear about my naked childhood exploits."

"Professional, hmm?" Gram adjusted my tie. "Is that why you're wearing the tie I gave you for Christmas and have changed your aftershave to the one that doesn't smell like, what did I call it? 'Nightclub desperation'?"

"I'm not—" I started, then caught myself. Arguing with her was like trying to negotiate with a particularly clever cat. "I'm going to check on dinner."

Her laugh followed me down the stairs. "The chicken's in the oven. I told the cook to leave early for the night off so you could show off your domesticity to your not-bride."

Of course she had. Because Gram never missed an opportunity to meddle in my life.

In the kitchen, I rolled up my sleeves and got to work. The roast chicken, my specialty, was already perfuming the air with rosemary and lemon. I began prepping the sides, chopping vegetables with perhaps more concentration than necessary.

Why was I so nervous? It was just Anica. The same Anica who'd threatened me with PowerPoint-related torture, who'd pinned pictures of potential brides to her wall like a serial killer, who'd looked at me in that wedding dress and...

No. Not thinking about the dress. Not thinking about her in the dress. Not thinking about how the silk had clung to her curves or how for a moment I'd forgotten how to breathe. Definitely not thinking about that.

I was not nervous because of my wedding planner. I was nervous because Gram had a gift for saying exactly the wrong thing at exactly the wrong time.

The doorbell rang precisely at five o'clock, and I nearly sliced my finger off with the knife I was using to julienne carrots.

"I'll get it!" Gram called from the living room. "You keep playing with your vegetables!"

"Just let Norbert. Don't—" I began, but she was already at the door.

I wiped my hands on a dish towel and hurried after her, but it was too late. Gram had the door open and was already pulling Anica into a hug like they were long-lost friends rather than complete strangers.

"You must be the wedding planner," Gram said, holding Anica at arm's length to examine her. "My grandson didn't mention you were so lovely. Though I suppose that was strategic. If he'd told me how beautiful you were, I'd have been even more suspicious about this 'professional relationship' nonsense."

"Gram," I cleared my throat, appearing behind her. "Let the poor woman breathe. And maybe save the inappropriate comments until she's at least inside the house with a glass of something stronger than wine."

"Where's the fun in that?" Gram asked innocently.

Anica looked slightly stunned by the greeting, but recovered quickly. She wore a simple blue dress that somehow managed to be both appropriate for Sunday dinner and completely distracting. Her hair was down for once, falling in soft waves past her shoulders, and I had the sudden, inexplicable urge to run my fingers through it. For experimental purposes only, of course. To determine if it was as soft as it looked.

"It's wonderful to meet you, Mrs. Burkhardt," Anica said, offering a small bouquet I hadn't noticed until now. "Thank you for inviting me."

"It's Vivian or Gram, dear. Mrs. Burkhardt was my monster-in-law." Gram accepted the flowers with a predatory smile. "These are lovely. Come in, come in. You're right on time, unlike my grandson who's either forty-five minutes early or an hour late, with no in-between."

"I've never once seen this man be that early. But late? That does seem to be the recurring pattern," Anica agreed, shooting me a look as she stepped inside. "Though, I suppose, lately he's been surprisingly punctual. I'm still deciding if it's character growth or if he's been replaced by a very convincing doppelgänger."

"Definitely the doppelgänger theory," I said, closing the door behind her. "The real Callan Burkhardt is tied up in a closet somewhere. I'm actually his evil twin, but I'm much better with scheduling."

"The evil twin would be an improvement," Gram stage-whispered to Anica. "At least he might call more often."

"I called you yesterday," I protested. "And this morning."

"Well, who else am I supposed to talk to? Norbert has a life. You don't," Gram countered, linking her arm through Anica's as if they were already co-conspirators in the 'Torment Callan Club.'

"I have a life. A very busy one," I said, fully aware of how weak the excuse sounded. "Running multiple multi-million dollar companies takes time."

"Yes, terribly difficult, having all those minions to do your bidding," Gram replied with a dismissive wave. "I'm sure Alexander the Great said the same thing about conquering Persia."

Anica pressed her lips together, clearly trying not to laugh. I watched her take in the house, curious about her reaction. The Burkhardt mansion wasn't flashy by billionaire standards. No gold toilets or tiger pits. But it was undeniably elegant and historic. It was an old money house with new money living in it.

"Your home is beautiful," she said to Gram, her gaze lingering on a particularly hideous vase that some art connoisseur had convinced Gram to buy once my first app sold. Anica's lips twitched, and I knew she was too polite to comment on its resemblance to a diseased kidney.

"It's excessive and drafty," Gram replied. "But I've lived here too long to bother moving. The bathrooms alone are bigger than the apartment Callan's grandfather and I started out in. Would you like a tour while Callan fusses over dinner?"

"I'll make sure to slip a chicken bone on your plate if you're not careful," I muttered, glaring at the woman who'd all but raised me.

"He's making his famous roast chicken. He only does that when he's trying to impress someone. Last time was when the Prince of Monaco came to dinner, and before that was that lovely supermodel. What was her name, darling? The one with the legs up to her neck and the tits the size of cantaloupes?"

"Gram!" I snapped, my gaze darting to Anica, whose eyes had widened to saucers. "I am not—" I began, then stopped and took a deep breath. "The chicken is already in the oven. Gram's cook started it and I'm just making sure it's cooked all the way."

"Sure. I didn't make sure the cook followed your explicit instructions, delivered via three separate text messages," Gram countered. "Including one about the precise temperature and another about the lemon-to-rosemary ratio."

Anica's lips curved into a smile. "So the baking expertise extends to roast chicken as well?"

"I'm a man of many talents," I said, winking at her. "Baking, roasting, grilling. I've been known to sauté once in a while. Really, I'm basically one cooking show away from being the next Gordon Ramsay, but with better hair and fewer anger management issues."

"And more modesty, clearly," Anica replied raising an eyebrow.

"Modesty is overrated," I shrugged. "Especially when you're as good as I am. At cooking," I added hastily when Gram raised an eyebrow. "I meant cooking."

"Of course you did, dear," Gram patted my arm. "Cal could have been a chef if he hadn't been so determined to make all that money," she said to Anica. "Come, I'll show you around while he finishes in the kitchen."

I watched them walk away, Gram already launching into what was undoubtedly the first of many embarrassing stories. I was so screwed.

Retreating to the kitchen, I checked the chicken. It was perfect, because I'm not an amateur. I finished the sides and poured myself a generous scotch. Gram had already made it clear that I would need help to get through the evening.

When I returned to the living room twenty minutes later, I found Anica and Gram sitting on the sofa, heads bent over what appeared to be a photo album.

Shit.

Shit.

Shit.

"—and this is him at his eighth-grade science fair," Gram was saying. "He built a program that could predict stock market patterns. The teachers thought he'd bought it until he explained the algorithm."

"That's impressive," Anica said, grinning. "Did it work?"

"Well enough that I turned it into my first app at sixteen," I said, making my presence known. "Though I believe I was wearing significantly more flattering pants at the time."

"I don't know," Anica mused, studying the photo. "The high-waters have a certain charm. Very 'floods are coming but I'm going to save the economy first.'"

"They were not high-waters," I protested. "I was growing too fast for Gram to keep up with pants that fit."

"He was a weed," Gram agreed. "All limbs and no coordination. He once tripped over his own feet and knocked over an entire display of peanuts at the store."

"I was twelve!"

"Thirteen," Gram corrected, ignoring my protest. "And it wasn't the first time."

Anica laughed. "I'm having trouble picturing Callan as anything but perfectly composed."

"Oh, he cultivated that later," Gram waved dismissively. "After the Great Science Camp Disaster."

"We don't need to discuss—"

"He tried to impress a girl by creating a small controlled explosion," Gram continued without mercy. "Set his eyebrows on fire and singed off half his hair. Had to wear a baseball cap for the rest of the summer."

"I was demonstrating a chemical reaction," I corrected. "The fire was an unintended side effect. And for the record, she was very impressed. We dated for three whole weeks after that, which is practically marriage in fourteen-year-old years."

"Until she dumped you for the boy with the skateboard," Gram reminded me.

"The douche," I muttered, wrinkling my nose. "In my defense, I couldn't skateboard because of my delicate ankles."

"You couldn't skateboard because you were terrified of falling and looking uncool," Gram corrected.

"Semantics."

"Oh, I almost forgot. Norbert!" Gram called. "Bring the swimming photo!"

Pure horror filled my chest. "Gram, no."

"Gram, yes," she replied with an innocent smile that wouldn't have fooled a toddler.

Norbert appeared too quickly, carrying a framed photograph that I'd been trying to "accidentally" break for years.

"Traitor," I muttered to him as he passed by. He gave a small shrug. "Hid the photo my ass," I growled.

"Thank you, Norbert." Gram accepted the photo. "Now, Ms. Marcel, this is my personal favorite. Callan, age six, decided he was a merman and needed to practice for his ocean life."

She handed the photo to Anica, whose eyes widened. There I was, age six, in the massive claw-foot bathtub, wearing nothing but a homemade "merman tail" fashioned from what appeared to be green garbage bags and aluminum foil. My hair was slicked back, my chest puffed out, and I was holding a plastic fork as a "trident."

"Aw, look at the little merman. So cute," Anica said with her shoulders shaking with suppressed laughter.

"The fork really sells it," I deadpanned. "Nothing says 'fear me, underwater creatures' like plastic cutlery. Though I maintain it was an avant-garde interpretation of Aquaman that was simply ahead of its time. If I'd been born a decade later, I could've been an influencer with that kind of creative vision."

That broke her restraint, and she laughed outright. "I don't know what's more impressive, the creative use of garbage bags or the fierce expression."

"I was very committed to my undersea kingdom," I admitted, smiling despite the mortification. There was something about Anica's laughter that made the embarrassment almost worth it. "I ruled with an iron fork."

"Dinner is served, madam," Norbert announced from the doorway, saving me from further merman-related humiliation.

"Saved by the butler," I said with perhaps too much enthusiasm. "Shall we?"

Gram rose with Anica's help. "I have so many more photos to show after dinner," she assured Anica, patting her hand. "Including his brief but passionate heavy metal phase. The eyeliner was... creative."

"I look forward to it," Anica replied, her gaze meeting mine with a mixture of amusement and absolutely unrestrained glee. "Though I'm not sure how I'll maintain professional composure after seeing Callan in eyeliner."

"Bold of you to assume you had professional composure to begin with," I murmured as we walked to the dining room. "I'd like to point out that you've been laughing at me for a solid twenty minutes."

"It's not at you. It's at six-year-old you. Completely different."

"The distinction is noted but not appreciated," I replied, pulling out her chair. "Though six-year-old me would be thrilled to know he's making beautiful women laugh, even if it is at his shameless merman cosplay."

A slight blush colored her cheeks as she sat down. "I'm sure six-year-old you had other priorities. Like perfecting your fork-wielding technique."

"It's all about the wrist action," I demonstrated with a dinner fork.

Dinner proceeded with more embarrassing stories, including the time I tried to bake a cake for Gram's birthday and confused salt for sugar ("It was the thought that counted, even if the execution was criminal"), my disastrous first attempt at driving her Bentley ("The rosebushes were never the same"), and my brief stint in a teenage garage band ("We were called Quantum Theory, for god's sake, how was that not a red flag?").

Throughout it all, I watched Anica. She was different here, away from the office. More relaxed, less guarded. She laughed freely, asked questions, and seemed genuinely interested in the stories of my misspent youth. I liked it more than I should have.

"So," Gram said as Norbert cleared the dinner plates, "Callan tells me you're helping him find a bride."

And just like that, the comfortable atmosphere shifted.

"I'm planning his wedding," Anica corrected. "The bride selection is... collaborative."

"Mmm," Gram hummed, in that way that meant she wasn't buying what you were selling. "And how's that going? Has he been difficult? He's usually difficult. Once refused to eat anything green for an entire year. I had to hide spinach in chocolate brownies."

"I'm sitting right here," I reminded her.

"Yes, dear, and being difficult about it," Gram replied without missing a beat. "Now hush, the adults are talking."

Anica bit her lip, clearly trying not to laugh. "Mr. Burkhardt has very specific requirements."

"Mr. Burkhardt?" Gram repeated, eyebrows raising. "So formal. He must be on his worst behavior."

"My behavior has been impeccable," I protested.

"He asked his first candidate about sexual preferences over dinner at Le Bernardin," Anica informed Gram, the traitor.

Gram's eyebrows disappeared into her hairline. "Callan Anthony!"

"It was a test!" I defended myself. "I wanted to see if she was interested in me or just my money."

"By asking about position preferences at a Michelin-starred restaurant?" Gram shook her head. "I raised you better than that."

"No you didn't." I shook my head. "You used the phrase 'tits the size of cantaloupes' not an hour ago. If anything, you're the bad influence and the reason I–"

"In his defense," Anica interrupted, surprising me, "the woman in question did start the conversation with discussing his investment portfolio and real estate holdings. She failed the test, crude as it was."

"Hmm." Gram studied Anica with new interest. "And what kind of tests are you administering to these potential brides?"

"More professional ones," Anica replied. "Background checks, compatibility assessments, personality profiles."

"Very thorough," Gram nodded. "And tell me, dear, how do you rate on these compatibility assessments with my grandson?"

I choked on my scotch. "Gram!"

"What? It's a reasonable question." Gram's expression was pure innocence. "If she's determining compatibility, she must have some metric."

"Ms. Marcel is not being evaluated as a candidate," I said firmly, wiping scotch from my chin. "She's my wedding planner."

"And a very good one, from what you've told me," Gram agreed. "Though I wonder why you haven't considered the obvious solution to your problem."

"Which is?" I asked, though I already regretted the question.

"Marrying someone you actually like spending time with, rather than a stranger with good credentials." Gram sipped her wine. "But what do I know? I'm just an old woman who's been around the block a few times."

"You've been around the block so many times they named it after you," I muttered.

"Cheeky," Gram said without heat. "Ms. Marcel —"

"Anica, please," Anica interrupted.

"Anica," Gram smiled. "What do you think of my grandson's approach to marriage?"

I braced myself for the professional, diplomatic answer. The kind of non-answer that wedding planners must practice in mirrors to avoid offending clients with terrible taste.

"I think," Anica said carefully, "that he has very sound reasons for his approach, given his family history and personal experience."

Gram's eyebrows rose again.

"But," Anica continued, "I also think his execution leaves something to be desired. Specifically, tact."

I laughed despite myself. "Brutal but fair."

"You told me once that marriage has historically been a business arrangement," Anica said, turning to me. "And you're not wrong. But even business arrangements work better when there's mutual respect and genuine affection."

The conversation was veering into territory that made me uncomfortable. I cleared my throat. "Speaking of business arrangements, Gram, how's the foundation?"

Gram shot me a look that said she knew exactly what I was doing but would allow it. For now. "Thriving, despite the board's best efforts to drown every initiative in red tape. We're funding a new after-school program in Queens."

The conversation shifted to safer ground, but I noticed Gram watching Anica with that particular look she got when she was calculating something.

After dinner, I excused myself to take a work call that was actually legitimate for once. When I returned, Anica and Gram were nowhere to be found in the dining room.

"They've adjourned to the parlor, sir," Norbert informed me with his usual telepathy. "Madam is showing Ms. Marcel the family jewelry collection."

Oh, Christ. The jewelry collection meant one thing: Gram was going full matchmaker. The family jewelry only came out when she was sizing someone up for potential daughter-in-law status.

I approached the parlor quietly, not quite willing to interrupt whatever was happening but too curious to stay away. Their voices drifted through the partially open door.

" —quite beautiful," Anica was saying. "The craftsmanship is extraordinary."

"My husband had excellent taste in jewelry," Gram replied. "It was one of his few redeeming qualities, along with his ability to make money and his spectacular backside. The latter of which, I'm pleased to say, Callan inherited."

I nearly swallowed my tongue.

"I wouldn't know," Anica said quickly. "That's not something I've... noticed."

"Of course not, dear," Gram's voice dripped with disbelief. "What do you think of him? Really?"

I froze, knowing I should walk away but unable to make my feet move.

"I think he's..." Anica paused. "More complex than he appears."

"Most people are," Gram agreed. "But Cal particularly so. He reminds me of his grandfather in some ways. Stubborn outside, marshmallow inside. But he's plenty smarter, and his heart isn't rotten like my ex's was. My Cal has a golden heart, but of course, I'm biased."

"He's certainly... surprising," Anica admitted. "The baking, the kindness to his assistant when her mother was ill, the way he talks about you..."

"He's a good boy," Gram said simply. "Too smart for his own good sometimes, and allergic to genuine emotion, but a good boy nonetheless."

Their voices dropped lower, and I retreated before I could be caught eavesdropping like some lovesick teenager. I returned to the dining room and made enough noise to announce my presence before heading to the parlor.

"There you are," I said, pushing the door open. "Plotting world domination?"

"Don't be ridiculous, darling," Gram said, closing the jewelry box. "We've moved well past plotting to the implementation phase. Your wedding planner has some excellent ideas about restructuring global finance."

"I was just admiring your grandmother's collection. She has exquisite taste."

"The emeralds would look lovely with your coloring," Gram observed casually. "Wouldn't they, Cal?"

"I'm not falling for that trap," I replied, though I couldn't help but picture the deep green stones against Anica's skin. "It's getting late, and I'm sure Ms. Marcel has had enough Burkhardt family time for one evening."

"Nonsense," Gram waved dismissively. "We've barely scratched the surface of your embarrassing childhood stories."

"At least you acknowledge that you're doing it on purpose. But that's exactly why we should leave," I said, putting my hands in my pockets and leaning against the wall. "Before you get to the high school prom incident."

"Oh, but that's one of my favorites," Gram protested.

"Another time," I promised, though I had no intention of ever allowing such a conversation. "We should let Anica get home. She has a busy day tomorrow."

"Planning your wedding to a bride who doesn't exist yet?" Gram asked innocently.

I shot her a warning look, which she ignored like she'd been ignoring my warnings for decades.

"Among other things," Anica replied diplomatically. "Thank you so much for dinner, Vivian. It was truly a pleasure."

"The pleasure was all mine, dear," Gram said, rising to hug Anica again. "You must come back soon. Next time I'll show you the videos of Callan's brief but memorable stint in the school production of 'Grease.' His Danny Zuko was... something."

"That's our cue to leave," I said hastily, guiding Anica toward the door. "Good night, Gram. Love you."

"Love you too, darling," Gram replied, then added with a wink to Anica, "He was a terrible Danny Zuko. No rhythm whatsoever. But very enthusiastic. Much like his approach to most things, I imagine."

"I'm never bringing anyone to meet you again," I informed her as I kissed her cheek goodbye.

"We'll see. Drive safely, darlings."

We stepped out into the cool night air, making our way down the cobblestone path to where Anica had parked her car in the circular driveway.

"I should apologize for Gram," I said finally, reaching to open Anica's car door for her. "She can be a bit... much."

"Don't apologize," Anica replied, turning to face me instead of getting in. "She's wonderful. Nothing like I expected."

"What did you expect?"

"I don't know. Someone more… formal? Reserved? Less likely to show me bathtub merman photos within twenty minutes of meeting me?"

I groaned, leaning against the side of her car. "God, the merman photo. I've been trying to destroy that thing for years."

"It's adorable," she said with a small smile. "You were a cute kid."

"I was a disaster," I corrected. "As Gram thoroughly documented."

"A creative disaster," she amended. "The merman tail was genuinely impressive engineering for a six-year-old."

"One of my first entrepreneurial ventures," I agreed. "Though the garbage bag market proved less lucrative than tech. Turns out you can make billions with code, but crafting merman tails remains a niche market at best."

She giggled. I liked making Anica laugh. It felt like an achievement, like closing a particularly difficult deal or perfecting a complex recipe.

"She loves you very much," Anica said after a moment.

"She's the only person who's ever seen me," I replied without thinking. "Really seen me."

"What do you mean?"

I considered deflecting with a joke but wanted to give her an honest answer. The porch light from Gram's house illuminated half her face, leaving the rest in shadow. "Most people see what they want to see. The billionaire, the playboy, the tech genius. Whatever narrative works for them. Gram just sees… me. The good, the bad, and the embarrassing."

"That must be nice," Anica said, her voice soft. "Being seen."

"It's terrifying," I admitted. "But yes, nice too. Though I could do without the merman photos being part of the 'seeing me' package."

"The merman photos are essential to the full Callan Burkhardt experience," she teased. "Now I understand why you're so successful. You've been compensating for the garbage bag tail all these years."

"Maybe," I laughed. "Though I'll have you know that in certain circles, my merman phase is considered visionary. I was cosplaying before it was cool."

We lapsed into a comfortable silence. Crickets chirped in the garden, and somewhere in the distance, an owl called. "Thank you for coming tonight. For not treating her like a client obligation. I think she gets lonely in this big house, more than she'd ever admit."

"I enjoyed myself," she said, and I could tell she meant it. "Your grandmother is a force of nature."

"That's putting it mildly."

Our eyes met, and for a moment, neither of us moved. There was something in her gaze. A question, perhaps, or a possibility. My hand reached for hers almost without my permission, our fingers brushing lightly where they rested on the edge of the car door.

The contact seemed to break whatever spell had fallen over us. She pulled her hand away, reaching for her keys.

"I should go," she said, her mask sliding back into place. "We have the florist meeting tomorrow at eleven. Try not to be late."

"I'll do my best, though I make no guarantees. I have a reputation as a chronically late billionaire to maintain."

She smiled again. "Good night, Callan."

"Good night, Anica," I replied, using her first name without the "Ms. Marcel" shield between us.

She paused, one foot already in the car, and for a second I thought she might say something else. Instead, she nodded once and slipped into the driver's seat. I closed her door gently and stepped back as she started the engine.

I stood in the driveway long after her taillights had disappeared down the winding road. This was not part of the plan. None of this was part of the plan.

I was supposed to be finding a bride for a bet, not... whatever this was. Not standing outside my grandmother's house like some lovesick teenager, replaying the way she'd smiled when Gram showed her that ridiculous merman photo.

"Get it together, Burkhardt," I muttered to myself, turning back toward the house. "You have a bet to win."

HIS STUPID PERFECT MATCH

Chapter 9: Anica

"If I have to watch her flip that perfect hair one more time, I'm going to climb over there and check for battery compartments," Mari hissed, peering through her binoculars. "No human woman's hair bounces like that. She's either an android or she's replaced her blood with salon-quality conditioner."

"Put those away," I whispered, yanking the binoculars down. "We're supposed to be inconspicuous. Professional women don't generally bring military-grade surveillance equipment to business lunches."

"I'm gathering intel," Mari protested, though she did slip the binoculars into her oversized purse. "And my intel says she's suspiciously perfect. Her posture hasn't slipped once in forty-five minutes. Does she have a titanium spine? Is she wearing some kind of Victorian corset under that Chanel suit? Or is she just physically incapable of slouching like us mere mortals?"

I glanced over at the table where Callan sat with Angelina Mercy, candidate number three after the Destiny disaster and a second who got similar treatment. Unlike the first two, Angelina was actually going well. Very well.

Too well.

"She's accomplished," I muttered, stabbing my salad with enough force to impale a small woodland creature. "Oxford MBA. Founded a successful tech incubator for women-led startups. Speaks six languages fluently and four less fluently. Donates thirty percent of her income to charity. Once saved a litter of puppies from a burning building while negotiating a multi-million dollar merger on her Bluetooth." I snorted, wrinkling my nose. "I made up that last part," I added when Mari's eyebrows shot up.

"And her ass doesn't move when she walks," Mari added. "I watched her come in. It's like watching a cyborg in Louboutins. Not a single jiggle. Meanwhile, my ass applauds itself when I go up stairs."

"Her physical attributes aren't relevant to her suitability as a match," I replied, violently spearing a cherry tomato.

Mari snorted. "Tell that to your eyes, which haven't left her table in twenty minutes. Or to that poor salad you're conducting a medieval torture session on."

I deliberately looked down at my decimated lunch. "I'm monitoring the interaction. This is my job."

"Uh-huh. And I suppose the fact that she keeps laughing and touching his arm is also being monitored 'professionally'? Because if looks could kill, her hand would be a smoldering stump by now."

I refused to look up again, though my peripheral vision had indeed registered Angelina's perfectly manicured hand resting on Callan's forearm. For the third time. Not that I was counting.

"It indicates mutual interest and engagement," I mumbled. "Which is exactly what we want."

"Is it?" Mari raised an eyebrow, looking uncannily like Vivian Burkhardt. Meeting Callan's grandmother had only made my business partner more insufferable. Now she had a role model for her meddling. It'd been one of my biggest mistakes telling Mari about the dinner.

"Yes," I insisted. "The goal is to find Callan a compatible match for his arrangement. Angelina meets every criterion on his list. Intelligent, accomplished, socially connected, not intimidated by his success, and genuinely interested in him rather than just his money." I paused, stabbing another innocent piece of lettuce. "Plus, as you pointed out, she looks like she was genetically engineered by combining a supermodel's DNA with a CEO's LinkedIn profile and a sprinkle of Disney princess thrown in for good measure."

"And that's good," Mari said, making it sound like a question.

"Of course it's good. It's perfect." I forced a smile that felt like it might crack my face. "They're perfect together. This is a professional triumph."

"Then why do you look like you're plotting her mysterious disappearance? I half expect you to start cackling and muttering 'soon, my pretty' while stirring a cauldron."

"I don't—" I began, then caught sight of my reflection in a nearby window. My expression could have curdled milk. I quickly rearranged my features into something more neutral. "I'm just concentrating."

"On imagining her drowning in that fountain?" Mari nodded toward the decorative water feature behind Callan and Angelina's table.

"Don't be ridiculous." I took a sip of water. "The fountain isn't deep enough. Besides, with her perfect bone structure, she probably floats."

Mari nearly choked on her mimosa. "Oh my god, you're jealous!"

"I am not," I hissed, glancing around to make sure no one had heard. "I'm invested in a successful outcome. She's exactly what he claimed to want, and they're clearly hitting it off. This is a win."

"This is the opposite of a win," Mari disagreed. "A win would be you admitting you have feelings for the hot billionaire who's been making heart eyes at you for weeks. A win would be you finally getting laid by someone whose net worth has more zeros than my phone number."

"He has not been making heart eyes." I rolled my actual eyes. "And even if he were, which he's not, it would be completely inappropriate. He's my client."

"A client who took you to meet his grandmother." Mari waggled her eyebrows suggestively. "A client who memorized your coffee order and has gotten it perfect every time. A man who would look tastier naked and painted with buttercream icing than that six tiered wedding cake from the Rosenburg-Titanus wedding."

"Stop," I groaned, though the mere mention of Callan naked had me clenching my thighs beneath the table. "You're objectifying our client again."

"So? You're telling me you wouldn't want to see that?" Mari bit her fork as she stared unabashedly at Callan. "Imagine licking the icing all the way down that beautiful chest towards his likely enormous—"

"Mari!" I cut her off as a waiter approached with our check.

I handed over my credit card without looking at the total. The waiter retreated, and I turned back to Mari.

"Callan is a client," I said firmly. "A client who is currently on a very successful date with a woman I selected for him. A woman who meets every requirement on his list. A woman who might very well become his wife. And I am thrilled about that, because it means I've done my job well."

"Sure," Mari muttered, taking another sip of her mimosa. "That's why you've been shredding your napkin into confetti for the past ten minutes. Because you're so thrilled."

I looked down to find a small pile of paper scraps where my napkin had been. Quickly sweeping them into my palm, I deposited them in my water glass.

"The napkin was weak."

"Uh-huh, so was that excuse." Mari glanced over my shoulder. "Heads up. Lovebirds are leaving the nest. And, oh my god, she's actually tucking her hair behind her ear in slow motion. Is she auditioning for a shampoo commercial?"

I turned, trying to appear casual, as Callan and Angelina stood from their table. He helped her with her cream cashmere coat, his hand lingering on her shoulder. She smiled up at him, saying something that made him laugh. They looked like a matched set. Both tall, both successful, both unfairly attractive.

This was what I wanted. A perfect match for my client. Yet my stomach revolted. Clearly it thought I'd swallowed a stone and not a cherry tomato. A very large, possibly radioactive stone.

"Oof," Mari said, watching my face. "That bad, huh?"

"What?" I snapped my gaze back to her.

"Your face just did the thing it does if you were to find out a bride wanted to do an interpretive dance down the aisle. Or when someone suggests releasing doves indoors. Or that time the groomsman wanted to surprise the happy couple by playing the bagpipes at the reception despite never having taken a lesson."

"I don't know what you're talking about," I said, gathering my things. "I need to get back to the office. The wedding expo is tomorrow, and we still have a million things to prepare."

As if on cue, my phone pinged with a text from Devonna.

Need final approval on expo display layout. 3 options attached. Also, Florist for Geoffries wedding called with peony crisis. Need response ASAP.

"Duty calls," I said, standing. "You coming?"

Mari sighed dramatically. "Fine. But this conversation isn't over."

"Yes, it is," I insisted, leading the way out of the restaurant. "There's nothing to discuss."

"The lady doth protest too much," Mari sang, following me.

"The lady will fire her business partner if she doesn't drop it."

"You can't fire me. I know where all the bodies are buried. Metaphorically speaking." She paused. "Mostly metaphorically."

I ignored her, focusing on replying to Devonna's text as we walked. The wedding expo was our biggest marketing opportunity of the year; a chance to showcase our services to hundreds of potential clients in one weekend. We couldn't afford any mistakes.

Thinking about the expo was good. Professional. Safe. Much better than thinking about Callan and Angelina and their perfect compatibility and what his hand looked like resting on the small of her back as they left the restaurant.

This was just protectiveness toward a client. Nothing more. I wanted him to make a good choice, to find someone who would respect the arrangement and not take advantage. That was all.

It certainly wasn't jealousy. Because jealousy would be unprofessional. And if there's one thing I always was, it was professional.

Always.

"*NO NO NO NO NO,*" I muttered, staring at my phone screen in horror. "This is not happening."

Dying.

Mari's text read.

MARI: Literally dying. Fever of 102. Can't move. Send soup and priest for last rites. If I don't make it, tell that hot barista at Starbucks I've been stalking that my ghost will still watch him shower.

I typed furiously.

ANICA: *You can't be sick TODAY. The expo starts in THREE HOURS. You were fine yesterday.*

MARI: *Tell that to my immune system. It's not taking calls. Also, I think I might be patient zero for the zombie apocalypse. If I bite anyone, shoot me in the head. Unless it's Callan. Then just let nature take its course.*

I groaned, dropping my head into my hands. The Manhattan Wedding Professionals Expo was one of the biggest events of the year. We'd been planning our booth for weeks, and now Mari was out of commission on the day we needed all hands on deck.

My phone pinged again. This time from Devonna.

DEVONNA: *Won't be in today. Food poisoning. Spent night on bathroom floor. So sorry. P.S. If you need me to drag myself in anyway, I will, but fair warning that I projectile vomited six feet across my bathroom. Twice.*

"You have got to be kidding me," I said to my empty apartment. Both Mari and Devonna out on expo day. The universe was clearly punishing me for something. Possibly for those thoughts about Angelina Mercy and the fountain. Or for mentally setting fire to her perfect bouncy hair.

I took a deep breath, trying to center myself. I could handle this. I was Anica Marcel, wedding planning extraordinaire. I'd managed a ceremony during a blackout with only the headlights from guests' cars for lighting. I'd coordinated a last-minute venue change when a hurricane flooded the original location. I could certainly manage a simple expo booth by myself.

After speed-showering and throwing on my most professional navy dress, I loaded the booth materials into my car and headed for the convention center. Everything was fine. This was fine. I was fine.

By the time I arrived, it was clear that nothing was fine. The booth next to ours—Enchanting Endings, our main competitor—had a three-person team efficiently setting up an elaborate display with a literal champagne fountain. Meanwhile, I was struggling to haul boxes from my car while balancing a tray of sample mini-cakes that were already listing dangerously to one side like the wedding cake Tower of Pisa.

"Need a hand with that?" a voice drawled from behind me.

I whirled around, nearly dropping the cake tray, to find Callan leaning against my car. He wore dark jeans and a white button-down with the sleeves rolled up, looking more like a model for a luxury watch ad than someone who belonged at a wedding expo.

"What are you doing here?" I blurted.

"Good morning to you too, darling," he replied, straightening. "And here I thought you'd be happy to see me. Most women generally are, what with all..." he gestured vaguely at himself, "...this."

"I'm—I didn't—" I took a breath. "We had to cancel our meeting. I texted you."

"You did," he agreed. "Something about being shorthanded for some expo thing. So I thought I'd stop by and see if I could help. I'm very good at helping. Also lifting heavy things, reaching high shelves, and looking decorative in a corner if needed. I make an excellent Christmas tree."

I stared at him and Mari's numerous comments about climbing him like a tree forced their way to the front of my brain until nothing useful was left except–

"You came to... help?"

"Don't look so shocked." He reached out and took the cake tray from my hands before I could protest. "In fact, I once helped an old lady cross the street. Granted, it was Gram and she threatened to disinherit me if I didn't, but still. Helpful." He nodded at the boxes in my car. "Where does this stuff go?"

"Table at the back of booth thirty-five," I said automatically, still processing his presence. "But you don't have to—"

"I know I don't have to," he interrupted. "I want to. Now, what else needs to be brought in? And please say it's something heavy so I can impress you with my manly strength."

I hesitated, weighing pride against practicality. The expo would open in less than two hours, and I still had to set up the entire booth.

"There are three more boxes in the trunk," I said finally. "And a garment rack with sample dresses."

"Consider it done. You go start setting up. I'll bring everything in. And I'll try not to flex too obviously while carrying things."

"I—thank you," I managed.

He grinned, and my traitorous heart did a little flip. "Don't thank me yet. I expect full payment in embarrassing wedding stories later. The weirder the better. I want to hear about the drunkest mother-of-the-bride, the most inappropriate best man speech, and any and all wardrobe malfunctions."

"Deal," I agreed, heading toward the booth with the cake tray.

True to his word, Callan brought in the remaining materials. By the time I'd arranged the sample photo albums and laid out the business cards, he was wheeling in the garment rack.

"Where do you want the dresses?"

"Against that wall," I replied, gesturing. "But they need to be arranged by style, and the white tulle one goes in front because it catches the light best, and —"

"I got it," he said, already rearranging the dresses. "Display 101: Put the eye-catching stuff up front."

I blinked. "Yes, exactly."

"Don't look so surprised," he said without turning around. "I've set up a tech booth or two in my day. Different product, same principles. Though wedding dresses are significantly prettier than server racks."

Working together, we had the booth nearly complete in record time. The only thing left was hanging the banner, which proved problematic due to my height limitations.

"If I could just —" I strained on tiptoes, trying to reach the hanging hook on the booth's frame. "Almost —"

"Let me," Callan offered, stepping closer.

"I can do it," I insisted, grabbing a folding chair. "I just need a little boost."

I climbed onto the chair, wobbling as I reached for the hook. My fingers brushed it, but I couldn't quite get a grip.

"Be careful," Callan warned, moving closer to the chair. "That doesn't look stable. And while I'd love to catch you if you fall, I'd prefer you not get injured."

"It's fine," I assured him, stretching further. "I just need to —"

The chair shifted beneath me. I fell. Not gracefully. Not in slow motion. And not silently either. I yelped like a kicked puppy. Before I could process what was happening, strong arms caught me. One moment I was plummeting, the next I was cradled against Callan's chest, his heart beating rapidly under my palm.

"You okay?" he asked, his voice lower than usual.

I glanced up into his face, aware of how close we were. Close enough to count his eyelashes. Close enough to notice the tiny flecks of darker blue in his eyes. "I'm — yes. Thank you."

"You're welcome." He didn't set me down immediately, and I didn't ask him to. For a suspended moment, we just looked at each other, my hand still resting on his chest, his arms secure around me.

"I should probably..." I gestured vaguely toward the ground.

"Right," he said, carefully setting me on my feet but keeping one hand on my waist until he was sure I was steady. "Maybe let me handle the high-altitude banner installation. Since I don't need artificial height assistance."

"Show off," I muttered, trying to recover my composure.

"Always," he admitted with a grin. "It's part of my charm."

"Whatever you say lightning pole," I agreed. "My insurance doesn't cover 'death by wedding expo.' Or '. embarrassment by billionaire rescue.'"

He reached up and secured the banner, not even needing the chair.

"Perfect," I said, stepping back to admire our work. The booth looked professional, inviting, and, most importantly, completely set up.

"Not bad for a billionaire and a wedding planner," Callan observed. "We make a good team."

"We do," I agreed before I could stop myself. "I mean, thank you for your help. You really didn't have to do this."

"I told you, I wanted to." He shrugged, as if helping me set up a wedding expo booth was the most natural thing in the world for a CEO to be doing at 8 AM on a Saturday. "Besides, now I get to see you in action. Should be educational."

I frowned. "You're staying?"

"Of course I'm staying," he replied, looking offended at the suggestion. "I didn't haul all this stuff in just to abandon you. I'm here for the duration. Put me to work. I'm great at selling things. I once convinced my third-grade teacher that my dog ate my homework, despite not actually owning a dog."

"This is a professional industry event," I protested. "You don't have to — "

"Anica," he interrupted gently. "Let me help. Please."

The sincerity in his voice caught me off guard. This wasn't Callan the cocky billionaire or Callan the ridiculously charming client. This was just... Callan.

"Okay," I said finally. "But you have to follow my lead. No going rogue."

"Scout's honor," he promised, raising three fingers.

"Were you even a Boy Scout?"

"For approximately three weeks," he admitted. "Until the unfortunate incident with the campfire and a marshmallow catastrophe."

"Do I want to know?"

"Probably not. There are still parts of New Jersey where I'm not welcome. The restraining order only expired last year. And marshmallows are still mentioned in hushed tones at scout meetings."

Despite myself, I laughed. "Alright then. Let me give you a crash course in wedding planning 101..."

I HAD TO admit, Callan was surprisingly good at all of it.

"So you're saying you handle everything?" the bride-to-be asked, clearly impressed as Callan outlined our services.

"Everything," he confirmed with a confident nod. "Anica and her team take care of every detail, from venue selection to the last dance. They're wizards, really. I heard she salvaged a wedding where the best man showed up drunk, the flower girl had chicken pox, and the cake collapsed. By the time she was done, you'd never know anything had gone wrong. The only casualties were the best man's dignity and the flower girl's perfect skin dreams."

The woman's eyes widened. "Really?"

"Absolutely," Callan said. "She's the best in the business. I wouldn't trust my own wedding to anyone else."

I nearly dropped the brochure I was holding. Was he implying what I thought he was implying?

"Your wedding?" the woman asked, glancing between us.

"Hypothetically speaking," Callan clarified with a wink. "But if I were getting married, Knot Your Average Wedding would be my only

116

call. In fact—" he leaned in conspiratorially, " —I've already reserved her services for my brother's wedding next year."

The man was oozing lies. I didn't have the heart to point out he was an only child. And I would've pointed out that he was an enormous pants-on-fire liar, but I sort of enjoyed hearing all of the made up stories. Plus, I knew I was a good wedding planner, even if the stories were bullshit.

"Well, that's quite an endorsement," the woman said, clearly sold. "Do you have any availability for a June wedding next year?"

"Let me check," I said, jumping in before Callan could invent any more fictional family members. I flipped through my planner. "We do."

"Perfect!" The woman beamed. "Can I put down a deposit today?"

Twenty minutes later, we'd secured not only her booking but also two of her friends who'd stopped by to see what the excitement was about. Callan's charm offensive was proving incredibly effective.

"Not bad for a rookie," I murmured as the women walked away, clutching our promotional materials.

"I told you I'm good at selling things," he replied with a grin. "It's like riding a bicycle, except the bicycle is overpriced services and the road is paved with bridal dreams and parental bank accounts."

"You made up a brother."

"Creative marketing," he countered. "Besides, who knows? Maybe I'll adopt one by next June. Or build one. I have the technology."

I shook my head, fighting a smile. "You're ridiculous."

"And yet incredibly effective," he pointed out. "Three bookings in one hour. I'm pretty sure that means I've earned at least one of those mini-cakes."

He wasn't wrong. The morning continued in the same vein, with Callan charming potential clients while I handled the technical details. We developed a natural rhythm, playing off each other's strengths. He'd draw them in with his charisma, I'd close the deal with my experience.

I couldn't help noticing the envious glances from neighboring booths, particularly Enchanting Endings, whose champagne fountain was attracting less attention than Callan's smile.

"Your boyfriend is quite the asset," the Enchanting Endings owner, Lauryn, remarked during a brief lull. "Smart move bringing him. Does he do children's parties too? Or is he just eye candy for the mothers-of-the-bride?"

"He's not my—" I began automatically, then caught myself. "Yes, he's been very helpful."

No point in explaining the complicated reality to a competitor who'd use any information as ammunition. Let her think what she wanted.

"Lucky you," Lauryn said with a tight smile. "Well, may the best planner win." She retreated to her booth, whispering urgently to her assistants.

"What was that about?" Callan asked, returning with two cups of coffee from the concession stand.

"Just friendly industry competition," I replied, accepting the coffee gratefully. "And thank you for this. I was running on fumes."

"Can't have my star planner collapsing from caffeine withdrawal." He checked his watch. "It's almost one. Have you eaten anything today?"

I tried to remember. "I had... half a protein bar in the car? All of my leftover takeout boxes had mold in them so I had to toss them."

"A protein bar is not food," he declared. "It's a sad rectangle masquerading as nutrition. Come on, we're taking a lunch break."

"We can't both leave the booth," I protested.

"Sure we can." He glanced around, then waved over a young woman from the booth across from ours. "Excuse me, would you mind watching this booth for twenty minutes? I'll pay you five hundred dollars."

The woman's eyes widened. "Um, sure!"

Before I could object, Callan had handed her the cash and was steering me toward the exit. "Twenty minutes," he said firmly. "Doctor's orders."

"You're not a doctor," I pointed out.

"I played one in my third-grade play," he replied. "Close enough. I said 'stat' and everything. Very convincing."

He led me to a quiet corner of the convention center where food vendors had set up. After procuring sandwiches and drinks, we found a relatively secluded table away from the main crowd.

"Eat," he commanded, pushing a sandwich toward me. "Before you pass out and I have to dramatically catch you again. Though I wouldn't mind," he added with a wink.

I rolled my eyes but took a bite of the sandwich, realizing how hungry I was. We ate in comfortable silence for a few minutes.

"So," Callan said finally, "this is what you do. All the time, I mean. The behind-the-scenes stuff."

"Pretty much," I nodded. "Though usually with more staff and less last-minute panic."

"You're really good at it," he observed. "At all of it. The planning, the client management, the execution."

"Thank you," I said, surprised by the compliment.

"Why not expand?" he asked. "You clearly have the skills and the reputation. You could have offices in multiple cities."

I hesitated, not used to sharing my professional dreams. "That's the plan, eventually. But expansion requires capital, and wedding planning isn't exactly venture capital's favorite industry. Most investors hear 'wedding' and think 'frivolous,' not 'scalable business opportunity.'"

"It could be," he said, leaning forward. "With the right pitch and the right numbers."

"Still wanting to invest?" I asked, half-joking.

"Maybe I am," he replied, his tone serious. "You're sitting on a goldmine, Anica. Your approach, your attention to detail, your client management. It's all scalable. With the right business plan and funding, you could be the premier wedding planning service on the East Coast."

I stared at him, caught off guard by his interest in my business. "You really think so?"

"I know so," he said confidently. "I don't back losers, and you're anything but. You've got vision, talent, and work ethic. A rare, but impressive combination."

Excitement bubbled inside me. It wasn't just the compliment, though that was nice, but the fact that he saw the business potential in what I did. So many people dismissed wedding planning as too niche. Callan didn't.

"I've actually been working on a business plan," I admitted. "For expansion into Boston and DC first, then maybe Chicago."

"Smart," he nodded. "Regional saturation before going national. Less risk, more controlled growth."

"Exactly," I agreed, surprised and pleased that he understood my strategy. "The wedding industry is all about word-of-mouth and reputation. You can't just parachute into a new market and actually expect—"

His phone buzzed, interrupting me. He glanced at the screen, and a small smile crossed his lips.

"Sorry," he said, quickly typing a response. "Just confirming plans for tomorrow."

"Oh?"

"Second date with Angie," he explained, slipping his phone back into his pocket. "She wants to try that new rooftop restaurant in Tribeca."

"Angie," I repeated. Already at the nickname stage. Peachy. The bubbles of excitement I'd had a moment earlier popped and evaporated. "That's... great. I'm glad it's going well."

"She's pretty amazing," he agreed with that smile. "Smart, funny, accomplished. We talked for hours at lunch yesterday."

"I noticed," I said, then winced internally at how that sounded. "I mean, that's excellent. She meets all your criteria. A perfect match."

"Seems that way. Thanks for finding her. You really are good at your job."

"Just doing what you're paying me for," I replied.

An awkward silence fell between us, the easy camaraderie of moments before gone.

"I should get back," I said, gathering my trash. "Can't leave the booth unattended for too long."

"Right," Callan agreed, standing. "Wouldn't want to miss any potential clients."

I walked slightly ahead of him, trying to sort through the tangle of emotions in my chest. This was good. This was what I wanted. Callan and Angelina—Angie—were hitting it off. The arrangement would proceed as planned. The contract would be fulfilled. Everything was going perfectly.

"I need to make a quick call before we head back," I said, stopping abruptly. "You go ahead."

"You sure?" he asked, studying my face.

"Positive," I forced a smile. "And Callan? Thank you again for your help today. It means a lot."

120

"Anytime," he said, his hands in his pockets. "That's what friends are for, right?"

Friends. Right. That's exactly what we were.

"Right," I agreed. "Friends."

He hesitated for a moment, then nodded and walked away. I watched him go, telling myself that the heaviness in my chest was just fatigue from the stressful morning. Nothing more.

I'd found Callan his perfect match. I should be pleased. Proud, even. It was a professional triumph.

But no.

It sucked.

A lot.

ISN'T THAT THE WEDDING PLANNER?

Chapter 10: Callan

"To the untrained eye, this might look like a man having an existential crisis over neckwear," I announced to my empty penthouse as I held two silk ties against my chest. "But what you're actually witnessing is a billionaire who can buy small countries without blinking yet somehow can't decide between two nearly identical strips of fabric. Send help. Or a personal stylist. Or just shoot me and put me out of my misery."

I was talking to myself. Again. A habit I'd developed somewhere between making my first million and losing the ability to trust anyone's opinion that wasn't being paid for.

The tie in question—a silk Hermès in a shade that definitely wasn't chosen because it reminded me of a certain wedding planner's dress yesterday—hung limply from my hand, a victim of my indecision.

Which was ridiculous. I, Callan Burkhardt, did not do indecision. I made billion-dollar deals with less contemplation than I was giving this piece of fabric. I once bought an island in the Pacific after a fifteen-minute conversation. Granted, I was slightly drunk and extremely competitive at the time. Kris had said no one could just "buy an island on a whim," and, well, I've never been good at being told what I can't do. But still. Decisions were my thing.

I tossed the blue tie aside and grabbed a burgundy one instead. Much safer. Nothing to do with anyone's eyes or dresses or the way certain people looked when they laughed at wedding expos while balancing cake samples.

Tonight was my second date with Angelina Mercy, Angie, and I was determined to focus on her. She was perfect on paper. MBA. Spoke multiple languages. Donated to all the right charities. Laughed at all my jokes, even the bad ones. Especially the bad ones. And she was drop-dead gorgeous, with hair that somehow defied both gravity and humidity.

She was exactly what I'd asked for. The perfect candidate for my arrangement.

So why was I thinking about how Anica had nearly impaled herself with a pen when I mentioned my brother at the expo? My non-existent brother. The lie had slipped out so naturally, and watching her reaction, the slight widening of her eyes, the twitch at the corner of her mouth as she fought a smile, had been satisfying. Like finding money in an old jacket pocket, but instead of money, it was the knowledge that I could make Anica Marcel laugh despite her determined professionalism.

My phone rang, interrupting my mental wandering. The screen displayed a three-way call from "The Assholes." I briefly considered ignoring it, but experience had taught me they'd just keep calling until I answered, possibly escalating to showing up at my door with alcohol and terrible advice.

"What?" I answered eloquently.

"Is that any way to greet your best friends?" Kris's voice boomed through the speaker. "The men who've stood by you through thick and thin? The brothers of your heart, if not your blood? The witnesses to your most embarrassing moments who have photographic evidence but have graciously not posted it on social media?"

"The men who are about to lose thirty million dollars to me," I corrected, putting the call on speaker as I continued getting ready. "What do you want?"

"Updates on the bride hunt," Morgan chimed in. "Chance says you've found a viable candidate."

"And we want details," Chance added. "Specifically, is she real or are you hiring an actress to play the part? Because we all remember the fake girlfriend you invented for your grandmother's Christmas party a few years ago."

"That was a misunderstanding," I protested. "The model really was supposed to show up. It's not my fault her agent double-booked her with a yacht party in Monaco."

"Uh-huh," Kris snorted. "So this new woman, she's flesh and blood? Has been observed by people other than you? Doesn't disappear when you blink?"

"She's very real," I replied, unable to keep the pride from my voice. "Angelina Mercy. Runs a tech incubator for women-led startups. Great tits. Legs for days. I'm taking her out tonight."

"Second date?" Kris asked.

"Indeed."

"And she knows about the arrangement? The bet?"

"I've been transparent," I said, which wasn't exactly a lie. I had been clear that I was looking for a partnership rather than a love match. The specific details about the bet would come later. Like, after the honeymoon later. "She's pragmatic about marriage."

"Sounds perfect," Morgan said, a note of suspicion in his voice. "Almost too perfect. What's the catch?"

"No catch," I insisted, adjusting my cufflinks. "She's exactly what I wanted."

"Bullshit," Kris declared. "There's something wrong with her. She has a third nipple. She's secretly a spy. She collects her toenail clippings in little jars labeled by date. She believes pigeons are government drones. She only communicates in haiku on Thursdays."

"Jesus, Kris," Chance muttered. "That's oddly specific. Something you want to share with the class?"

"Don't kink-shame me," Kris shot back. "My point is, no one's that perfect. What aren't you telling us?"

I hesitated, thinking of Angelina's perfectly pleasant conversation, her appropriately timed laughs, her complete lack of challenge to anything I said. The way I'd found myself checking my watch three times during our first date.

"She's just... fine," I admitted.

"Fine?" Morgan echoed. "You don't sound thrilled."

"I'm not looking for thrills," I reminded them. "I'm looking for compatibility. A strategic partnership. A business arrangement with occasional sex. Not a Disney movie."

"Still," Chance mused, "you should at least like being around her. Otherwise, what's the point? You'll be stuck with this person for years."

"Unless you get a divorce," Kris added.

"I do like being around her," I insisted, though even to my own ears, it sounded defensive. "She's gorgeous, intelligent, and successful. What's not to like?"

"But does she make you laugh?" Chance asked. "Like, really laugh? The kind where you snort a little and then pretend you didn't?"

An image of Anica's face when I caught her falling from the chair flashed through my mind. The wide-eyed surprise, the momentary vulnerability, the way she'd felt in my arms. The undignified yelp she'd let out, followed by her determined attempt to regain her composure.

"Cal?" Morgan prompted. "You still there? Or did the question short-circuit your bozo brain?"

"Yeah, sorry. Just thinking."

"About Angie?" Kris asked.

"Anica," I replied automatically, then immediately wanted to punch myself. Preferably in the throat. Hard enough to prevent further speaking.

There was a moment of stunned silence, followed by three distinct reactions: Chance's knowing "Hmm," Kris's gleeful cackle, and Morgan's confused "Isn't that the wedding planner?"

"Yup," Kris supplied helpfully. "The one he can't stop talking about. The one he's apparently thinking about while getting ready for a date with his future wife. The one he's definitely not secretly in love with. That Anica."

"I don't talk about her that much," I protested. "And love doesn't exist."

"Dude, the last time we spoke, you mentioned her twenty-eight times. I counted. I made a little tally sheet. I was going to turn it into a drinking game, but I didn't want to die of alcohol poisoning."

"Fuck off," I muttered. "She's planning my wedding."

"To a bride you're apparently mixing up with her," Morgan pointed out.

"I'm not mixing them up," I said, running a hand through my hair in frustration. "It was a slip of the tongue."

"Is that what the kids are calling it these days?" Kris snickered. "In my day, we just called it 'wanting to bang your wedding planner instead of your future wife.'"

"As I said, fuck off," I suggested in a fake pleasant tone.

"Seriously though," Chance said, his voice taking on that annoying therapist quality he'd developed since getting happily married. "Maybe there's a reason you're thinking about your wedding planner while getting ready for a date with your potential wife."

"Yeah, because I spent all day yesterday with her at a wedding expo," I explained. "It's still fresh in my mind."

"Wait, you spent the day at a wedding expo?" Morgan sounded incredulous. "Voluntarily? Not at gunpoint? Not because someone threatened your dog? Not because it was the only way to deactivate a bomb strapped to your chest?"

"Her assistant was sick. She needed help."

"And you, billionaire CEO with multiple companies to run, dropped everything to help her set up a booth at a wedding expo," Kris summarized. "Totally normal client behavior. I do that all the time. Just yesterday, I rearranged my accountant's inner filing cabinet. The day before, I gave my dentist a nice canal drilling."

"Shut up. I was being nice," I insisted. "It's a concept you might want to look into sometime."

"I'm plenty nice," Kris countered. "I just don't confuse my dates' names with my wedding planner's, then get defensive when my friends point it out."

"You're married, so A. You shouldn't be going on dates with other women, and B. I'm not defensive!"

Three skeptical silences greeted that statement.

"Look," I said finally, "Anica is my wedding planner. Angie is a potential candidate for marriage. They both have names that start with 'A' that are conveniently five letters. They're both lovely women. And they're two separate people fulfilling two separate roles in this arrangement. End of story."

"If you say so," Chance said. "Just be careful, man. Mixing business and pleasure never ends well."

"I'm not mixing anything," I insisted. "Now if you'll excuse me, I have a date to get to."

"With Anica?" Kris couldn't resist one last dig.

"Go to hell," I replied in a fake cheerful tone, ending the call to the sound of their laughter.

I tossed my phone onto the bed, annoyed at my so-called friends and even more annoyed at myself. This was ridiculous. I was not thinking about Anica Marcel. I was focused on my date with Angelina, who was perfect, accomplished, and exactly what I needed for my arrangement.

Grabbing the burgundy tie, I knotted it with perhaps more force than necessary. Anica wasn't even my type. Sure, she was beautiful in that understated way that snuck up on you. And yes, she had a sharp wit and didn't take my shit and seemed genuinely unimpressed by my wealth. And okay, when she laughed, really laughed, it did something strange to my chest and I *sometimes* got hard.

But none of that mattered. She was my wedding planner. A professional I'd hired to do a job. Nothing more.

Angelina was waiting outside her building when I pulled up, looking like she'd stepped straight out of a magazine. Her dress, a slinky black number, hugged every curve, accentuating her perfectly round tits and her even rounder ass. Both likely fake, but still very pleasing to my eyes. And my dick. Her hair was styled in perfect waves, and her makeup was flawless. She was, objectively speaking, a knockout.

"You're late," she said with a smile as I opened the car door for her. "I appreciate punctuality."

"Sorry," I replied, trying not to think about how often I had started arriving on time to meetings with Anica. That was different. That was... a thing I did.

"You look handsome," she observed as I slid into the driver's seat. "I like a man who knows how to dress."

"Thank you," I said, pulling into traffic. "You look incredible. That dress is stunning."

"Tom Ford," she confirmed, resting her hand lightly on my thigh. "I thought you'd appreciate it."

Her touch should have been exciting. Angelina was a beautiful woman who was clearly interested in me. Her hand on my thigh should've had me uncomfortably hard in my trousers. But no. Apparently my dick was broken. Instead, I was comparing it to the way Anica had gripped my arm when an elderly mother of the bride had nearly knocked over the cake display at the expo.

"I hear the view from this restaurant is spectacular," Angelina was saying, her hand inching higher on my thigh as she leaned forward, her cleavage on full display. "Though not as spectacular as the view from your penthouse, I'm sure."

There was no subtlety in the invitation. Any other time, I would have suggested we skip dinner altogether. Instead, I gently placed my hand over hers and moved it back to a more neutral position, using the excuse of needing to shift gears.

"The restaurant does have an amazing view," I agreed, keeping my tone light. "And the chef trained in Paris. Their lobster risotto is supposed to be incredible."

If she was disappointed by my redirection, she didn't show it. "I love lobster," she said. "And Paris. I spent a semester there during business school."

"Paris is beautiful. Though I prefer the Italian coast. Less crowded, better food."

"I have a villa in Positano," she mentioned casually. "Perhaps we could visit sometime. The view from the terrace is breathtaking, and the balcony wall is very sturdy for... activities." She squeezed my leg and I cleared my throat.

Again, the invitation was clear. And again, I didn't pursue it.

What the hell was wrong with me? A gorgeous, successful woman was practically propositioning me, and all I could think about was whether Anica had managed to book that couple who'd been wavering about their date at the expo. And whether she'd gotten home safely. And if she'd eaten anything besides that sandwich I'd bought her and the protein bar she'd mentioned. I wondered what flavor she liked, or if there was a certain brand.

We arrived at the restaurant, where the maître d' recognized me immediately and showed us to the best table on the terrace. The view was indeed spectacular, the lights of the city spread out before us like scattered diamonds on black velvet.

"This is lovely," Angelina said, her voice warm with appreciation. "Thank you for bringing me here, Callan."

"I'm glad you suggested the place," I said with a smile.

The conversation flowed easily enough as we ordered drinks and appetizers. Angelina was intelligent and well-spoken, with interesting insights on the tech industry and philanthropy. On paper, she was perfect. In person, she was perfectly pleasant.

And yet.

I knew I was just going through the motions, nodding and responding appropriately while part of my mind kept wandering back to someone else. To another woman. Shit. I really did live up to the playboy rep. Though, I didn't really have a desire to sleep with the woman across from me, so maybe I was developing a new reputation.

"So," Angelina said, taking a sip of her wine. "Tell me more about these wedding plans. The Rhodes Estate, was it?"

I refocused on our conversation. "Yes, it's a beautiful venue. Classic elegance with modern amenities."

"Impressive," she nodded. "My friend got married there last year. They had to book it two years in advance. How did you manage to secure it on such short notice?"

"I have connections," I replied vaguely. "And my wedding planner is quite resourceful."

"Ah yes, the wedding planner." Angelina smiled. "She must be quite talented to arrange everything so quickly. Have you settled on the cake flavor yet?"

"Cardamom-honey with rosewater buttercream," I answered automatically, remembering the tasting with Anica.

Angelina raised an eyebrow. "That's... specific. You seem quite invested in the details."

"It's my wedding," I said with a shrug. "Might as well make sure it's exactly what I want."

"Of course." She nodded. "What about the flowers? Please tell me you're not doing basic roses."

"Absolutely not," I replied, slightly offended on Anica's behalf. "We're using a seasonal mix of native blooms with some architectural elements for visual interest."

"Impressive," Angelina said, studying me. "And the wedding favors? Please tell me you've thought beyond almonds."

I hesitated. Anica and I hadn't actually discussed wedding favors yet. "That's... still being finalized."

"And the first dance song? The dinner menu? The seating arrangement?" She pressed, her eyebrow arching slightly higher with each question.

"We're working through the details systematically," I replied, trying not to sound defensive. "My planner has a very thorough process."

"Hmm." Angelina took another sip of her wine. "It seems like there's still quite a lot to arrange in a short time. You know, my friend Allison is an excellent wedding planner. She specializes in expedited timelines. Perhaps I should introduce you?"

Something in my chest tightened. "I'm very happy with my current planner, thank you."

"I'm sure she's lovely," Angelina said with a dismissive wave. "But Allison has connections with all the top vendors. She could probably get you better deals, more exclusive options."

"Anica Marcel is the best wedding planner in Manhattan," I said, my voice sharper than intended. "She has impeccable taste, unparalleled organizational skills, and a work ethic that would put most CEOs to shame. She has connections with every worthwhile vendor in the tri-state area, and she's personally saved dozens of couples from wedding disasters that would have sent lesser planners into early retirement."

I took a breath, but apparently wasn't done. "She organizes her emergency kits and can recite the contact information for every decent florist in Manhattan from memory. She can spot a poorly constructed cake from fifty paces and has a sixth sense for which bridesmaids will cause drama. She makes wedding magic happen with nothing but pure determination and possibly some kind of wedding planner superpower that mere mortals like me cannot comprehend."

Angelina blinked, clearly surprised by my vehemence. "I... see."

"And frankly," I continued, unable to stop myself, "I don't appreciate the implication that she's anything less than exceptional at her job."

A tense silence fell between us. I realized I'd overreacted spectacularly to what was probably an innocent suggestion. Angelina studied me for a long moment, then her expression softened.

"I apologize. I didn't mean to insult your planner. I was just trying to be helpful."

I took a deep breath, trying to regain my composure. "No, I'm sorry. That was an overreaction on my part. Anica—Ms. Marcel—has just been working extremely hard on this wedding, and I respect her."

Angelina nodded, though something had shifted in her demeanor. "Of course. Let's talk about something else, shall we? I read about your new AI initiative in Tech Quarterly. Very impressive."

The conversation moved to safer ground, but something had changed. The easy flow was gone, replaced by a more cautious exchange. Angelina tried to salvage the evening, even subtly running her foot up my calf under the table in what I recognized as an attempt to reestablish our earlier connection.

A month and a half ago, I would have been intrigued. I checked my watch, wondering if the expo had generated as many bookings for Anica as she'd hoped.

When Angelina excused herself to the restroom, I pulled out my phone and texted Anica before I could think better of it.

CALLAN: How many official bookings did we end up with yesterday? Did I help set any new records?

I stared at the message for a moment before hitting send, wondering if it was inappropriate to text her while on a date with a potential bride. But it was a professional question, right? Just checking in on business matters. Totally appropriate.

A few minutes passed with no response. Angelina returned, looking refreshed and even more beautiful, if that was possible. But my attention was divided, part of me still waiting for that text notification.

When my phone finally buzzed, I tried not to look too eager as I checked it. The message wasn't from Anica, but from her assistant, Devonna.

DEVONNA: This is Devonna using Anica's phone. She can't respond right now. Major emergency at a client's wedding.

Glancing at Angelina, I made sure her focus was on the view of the city before texting a quick reply.

CALLAN: Everything alright? Where's the wedding?

Devonna responded quicker than before, probably because she had the phone handy.

DEVONNA: Sprinkler system malfunction at venue in Brooklyn. Everything and everyone is soaked. Anica's trying to salvage the situation. The bride is hysterical. The DJ equipment is ruined. Only bright side is that the drunk groomsmen sobered up fast after their impromptu shower.

I stared at the text. Anica was dealing with a crisis. At least Devonna was with her. Hopefully she was over her food poisoning. I doubted Mari was there.

"Is everything alright?" Angelina asked, running a manicured finger along my arm on the table. I pulled back.

"I'm sorry," I said, already calculating the fastest route to Brooklyn. "Something's come up. A work emergency."

Angelina's perfect eyebrows drew together in concern. "Anything serious?"

"Potentially," I said, signaling for the check. "I'm really sorry to cut this short."

"I understand," she said, though her tone suggested she didn't. "Business comes first."

I paid the bill and walked her to the car, my mind already elsewhere. After a quick text to Devonna asking for the venue address, I drove Angelina home, trying to maintain polite conversation while fighting the inexplicable need to get to Anica as quickly as possible.

"I had a lovely time," Angelina said as I walked her to her door. "Despite the abrupt ending."

"Me too," I replied automatically. "I'll call you."

She leaned in for a kiss, which I awkwardly redirected to her cheek. "Work emergency," I explained. "I should really get going."

If she was offended, she hid it well. "Of course. Good luck with your... emergency."

As soon as she was safely inside, I sprinted back to my car, inputting the address Devonna had sent into my GPS. Twenty minutes away in current traffic. I could make it in fifteen if I pushed it.

As I drove, I tried to rationalize my behavior. I was just helping out a service provider. The kind of thing any decent client would do. The fact that my heart was racing had nothing to do with Anica specifically. I was just... a good person. Who happened to be abandoning a date with a perfect woman to help my wedding planner with a crisis that wasn't remotely my problem.

THE SCENE AT the venue was exactly as chaotic as I'd imagined. The hotel's grand ballroom, which should have been elegantly decorated for a wedding reception, looked like a miniature tsunami had swept through it. Water dripped from the ceiling, staff rushed around with towels and mops, and in the center of it all stood Anica, soaking wet and issuing rapid-fire instructions like a general commanding troops.

Her normally perfect hair was plastered to her head, her dress clung to her body in a way that was distractingly appealing, outlining curves that her usual professional attire only hinted at, and she had a smear of what looked like mascara under one eye. She looked like she'd been through hell.

She looked beautiful.

I made my way through the chaos, catching snippets of conversations about ruined flowers, drenched linens, and a bride who was apparently having a breakdown in the bridal suite.

"Anica," I called, navigating around a cluster of soggy centerpieces.

She turned at the sound of my voice, her eyes widening. "Callan? What are you doing here?"

"Devonna texted," I explained, reaching her side. "Said you had an emergency."

"Yes, but—" She gestured helplessly at my suit. "You were on your date!"

"This seemed more important," I said simply. "What do you need me to do?"

She stared at me as if I'd grown a second head. "But your date!" she repeated. "With Angie! The perfect match!"

"Anica," I said, placing my hands on her shoulders. "Tell me how to help."

"Well, the flowers are ruined," she said. "We need replacements. The hotel has a garden, but the manager won't let us use any of it without proper approval, which could take hours we don't have."

"Leave the manager to me," I said. "What else?"

"The linens are soaked. We need dry ones."

"Done. I'll have someone arrange an emergency delivery."

"The sound system is fried."

"I know a guy with a mobile DJ setup. He owes me a favor."

She looked at me with that mix of surprise and something else again. "Why are you doing this?"

"Because you need help," I said simply. "And I'm good at fixing problems. Almost as good as I am at creating them, which is saying something."

For a moment, she just looked at me, water dripping from her hair onto her cheeks. Then she nodded once. "Okay. Let's do this."

The next two hours were a blur of activity. I charmed (okay, I bribed) the hotel manager into letting us harvest flowers from the hotel's private garden by casually mentioning that my investment firm was looking at hotel chains for acquisition and how impressed I was with their "community spirit." I called in favors to get a sound system delivered, promising the DJ who owned it a spot at my next charity gala. I even helped rearrange the seating chart when we had to move everything to a smaller, but dry, auxiliary ballroom.

Working with Anica in crisis mode was like watching a master artist at work. She anticipated problems before they arose, delegated tasks, and somehow managed to keep the bride calm through it all. I followed her lead without question, taking orders from someone for the first time since... well, probably since my grandmother had last told me to take out the trash.

And the strangest part? I was enjoying it.

"No, the tall centerpieces need to go on the round tables, not the rectangulars," Anica instructed a flustered waiter. "The sight lines won't work otherwise."

"Yes, ma'am," the waiter replied, clearly intimidated.

"And tell the chef we need the appetizers ready in twenty minutes, not forty," she continued. "The timeline's been compressed."

"Yes, ma'am."

She turned to me, her expression all business despite her disheveled appearance. "The bride's dress has water stains on the hem. Any brilliant ideas for that?"

"Actually, yes," I replied, pulling out my phone. "My friend dated a costume designer who specializes in quick fixes. Let me make a call."

Fifteen minutes later, a harried woman arrived with a steamer and some kind of fabric solution that, according to her, would "make water stains my bitch." I didn't ask questions, just directed her to the bridal suite.

When the ceremony finally began, only thirty minutes behind schedule, with fresh flowers, dry linens, and working music, the bride was radiant with relief.

"You literally saved the most important day of my life," she told Anica, tears in her eyes. "I don't know how to thank you."

"It's my job," Anica replied with a modest smile. "And I had help." She glanced at me with a grin.

As the reception got underway, Anica and I stood alone in the empty auxiliary room, surrounded by the remnants of our frantic preparations. Anica had somehow found time to fix her makeup and dry her hair, though her dress was still damp in places, clinging to her curves in a way that made me force my eyes to stay firmly on her face.

"You left your date with the perfect woman to help with this," she said, shaking her head. "There is something seriously wrong with your brain. You should probably get that checked out. I can recommend a good neurologist."

"Seemed like the right choice," I replied, stepping closer to her. "The date was fine, but this was... an adventure."

She looked up at me, her gaze searching my face. "You didn't have to do any of this."

"I wanted to." Another step closer. I could smell her perfume now, something floral and subtle beneath the lingering scent of wet fabric. "Besides, what kind of fake fiancé would I be if I didn't show up to help my wedding planner in her hour of need?"

Her lips quirked. "A normal one?" she suggested.

"I've never been accused of being normal," I admitted.

"Why?" she asked, her voice softer than I'd ever heard it. "Why did you really come?"

I should have had a smooth answer ready. Some charming deflection or witty comeback. Instead, I told the truth. "Because you needed me."

Her lips parted, her eyes widening a fraction. We were standing close now, close enough that I could see the faint freckles across the bridge of her nose that she usually covered with makeup. Close enough that if I leaned down just a little...

"There you are!" The mother of the bride burst into the room, her voice shrill with panic. "The DJ is playing the wrong father-daughter dance song! It's supposed to be 'Butterfly Kisses,' not 'Unforgettable'!"

Anica stepped back quickly, the moment shattered. "I'll take care of it right away." She glanced back at me, her professional expression firmly back in place. "Thank you again for your help. I should go—"

"Come to my island this weekend," I blurted out, surprising myself as much as her.

She froze. "What?"

"My island. In the Caribbean. Private getaway to recover from this chaos." The words were tumbling out now, beyond my control. "No wedding talk, no bride hunting. Just... a break. White sand beaches, crystal clear water, staff that will cater to your every need. I have a jet. We could leave Friday, be back Sunday night. Completely separate bedrooms," I added hastily. "Unless—I mean, not that I'm suggesting—"

She stared at me, clearly shocked by the invitation. "Callan, I can't just—"

"Why not?" I challenged. "When was the last time you took a day off, let alone a weekend? You deserve a break, Anica. And I happen to have a very nice island with excellent break-taking facilities. Devonna and Mari can handle a week without you. Mari owns half of the company anyway, right?"

She hesitated, and I could see her weighing all the reasons to say no. I mentally prepared for her rejection. It'd been too spontaneous. I knew that. I just had hoped that maybe–

"Okay."

Now it was my turn to be shocked. "Okay?"

A small smile tugged at the corner of her mouth. "Okay. But just as friends."

"Of course," I agreed, nodding a bit too energetically. "Just friends. Taking a completely platonic, friendly trip to a private island. Friends do that all the time. I took Kris to the Maldives two months ago. Very platonic. We braided each other's hair and everything."

She rolled her eyes, but the smile remained. "I should go fix this song situation before the mother of the bride has an aneurysm."

"Go save the day," I said. "Again."

She started to walk away, then paused, turning back to me. "For the record, I'm glad you left your date to come help."

"For the record, so am I."

She hurried off to handle the music crisis, leaving me standing alone in the room, trying to process what had just happened. Shit. I'd invited my wedding planner to my private island. And she'd said yes.

The guys were going to have a field day with this.

BLUE DRINKS AND ANCIENT SHIRT LAW

Chapter 11: Anica

"**M**y suitcase looks like it's having the same existential crisis I am," I muttered, staring at the chaotic heap of clothing I'd packed, unpacked, and repacked three times already. "Half professional retreat, half 'help-I've-agreed-to-a-tropical-getaway-with-a-hot-billionaire-and-don't-know-if-I'm-supposed-to-pack-condoms.'"

"The answer is yes on the condoms," Mari declared from where she lounged across my bed, mimosa in hand at eight in the morning. "Always yes. Even for funerals. Never know when a sexy mourner might need consoling."

"Not helping," I snapped, meticulously rearranging my neatly folded clothes for the fourth time. I'd been agonizing over the appropriate wardrobe for a "just friends" weekend on a private island with a client for approximately six hours, and my sanity was hanging by a thread thinner than the lingerie Mari kept trying to sneak into my luggage.

"You know what would help?" Mari asked, sipping her drink. "This." She reached into a shopping bag beside her and pulled out what could generously be described as "dental floss masquerading as a bikini" but was actually just three triangular fabric scraps held together by wishful thinking.

"Absolutely not," I said, not even looking up. "I'm bringing my black one-piece. It's perfectly respectable."

"It's perfectly funereal," Mari corrected. "You look like you're about to officiate a burial at sea. Or audition for the role of 'professional whale trainer who's allergic to joy.'"

"It's practical," I insisted. "Appropriate for swimming laps, and it's what normal people wear at normal beaches."

"There's nothing normal about a private island owned by a hot billionaire who's clearly wants to bend you over and fuck you in his private jet." Mari flopped back on the bed. "And nobody swims laps on vacation. They lounge seductively and sip fruity drinks with little umbrellas while plotting how to accidentally-on-purpose brush against their crush's abs."

"He's not my crush," I replied automatically. "He's my client. A client who happens to own a small island where we'll be spending the weekend. In separate buildings. As business associates. Who are friends. Friendly business associates."

"Clients don't invite you to their private islands for 'no wedding talk' weekends." Mari made exaggerated air quotes. "That's not in any client services contract I've ever seen. Trust me, I've checked all of ours since he invited you, looking for the 'tropical getaway with optional sexual tension' clause."

"I agreed because he had just saved the wet wedding, and it seemed rude after his help. Help you gave none of, by the way," I explained, smoothing a non-existent wrinkle from my khaki shorts. "Anyways, it's strictly business."

"I was on my deathbed, for the record. And secondly, of course it's strictly business. You know, the classic business retreat to a romantic tropical paradise," Mari nodded sagely. "I send all my vendors to the Bahamas when they do a good job. The caterer who didn't overcook the salmon at the Thomas wedding? Took him to Paris. The florist who found peonies in December? Straight to Bali. The DJ who played 'Sweet Caroline' only once instead of seventeen times? Weekend in my private love grotto."

I threw a sock at her head, which she deftly dodged.

"Oh look," Mari said, pulling something from beneath my folded clothes. "How did this get in there?" She dangled a scrap of black lace that I recognized with horror as the lingerie set she'd given me for my birthday last year. The one I'd never worn because it was so impractical it might as well have been made of cotton candy and broken dreams.

"Give me that!" I lunged for it, but she held it out of reach.

"Why? You're just going as friends, right? So what's the harm in bringing sexy underwear that no one will see?" Her smile was pure evil. "Unless you're planning on someone seeing it..."

"I'm not planning anything," I said, snatching the lingerie and tossing it into the trash can. "I'm bringing the bride portfolios to review. It's a working trip."

"He literally said 'no wedding talk, no bride hunting,'" Mari reminded me, fishing the lingerie out of the trash and tucking it into a side pocket of my suitcase when she thought I wasn't looking. "But sure, bring work. Nothing says 'I'm maintaining professional boundaries' like ignoring your host's one request."

"The portfolios are my security blanket," I admitted. "I need something to fall back on if conversation lags or things get... weird."

"Things like uncontrollable sexual tension?" Mari suggested. "Intense eye contact over tropical drinks? His hand accidentally brushing yours while you both reach for the sunscreen? His muscles glistening with seawater as he emerges from the ocean like some kind of Greek god having a midlife crisis in the Caribbean?"

"Stop," I groaned, though my treacherous brain had already painted a vivid picture of Callan's hands applying sunscreen to my shoulders, my back, maybe even the backs of my thighs... "It's not like that."

"It's exactly like that," Mari insisted. "And you know how I know? Because you're packing khaki shorts and button-ups for a beach vacation. You're overcompensating because you're terrified of what might happen if you let yourself enjoy this. It's like watching a nun pack for spring break."

I glared at her, hating that she might be right. "I'm bringing my running shoes and workout clothes too," I added defiantly. "For morning jogs on the beach."

"Of course you are," Mari said, rolling her eyes. "Nothing says 'romantic getaway' like 6 AM cardio. Nothing gets a man hotter than seeing a woman voluntarily wake up before sunrise to punish herself with exercise on vacation."

"It's not a romantic getaway!" I protested for what felt like the hundredth time.

"Then why are you packing the secret good bra?"

I froze, staring at the navy bra in my hands; the comfortable-yet-flattering one that somehow made even my modest chest look spectacular. "It's... practical," I said weakly.

"Uh-huh." Mari took another sip of her mimosa. "Just like it's practical that I added waterproof mascara to your toiletry bag. And that little sundress you never wear because it shows too much leg."

"You what?" I dug through the bag she'd helpfully packed earlier, finding not only the mascara and sundress but also a bottle of my good perfume, three types of condoms, and a travel-sized bottle of tequila. "Mari!"

"What? You never know what you might need," she said innocently. "Better safe than sorry. The tequila is in case of snake bite. The condoms are in case of... snake bite of a different variety."

"I'm not going to need condoms," I hissed, throwing them at her. "This is a platonic trip between a wedding planner and her client."

"So you keep saying," Mari replied, catching the condoms and tucking them into a different compartment of my suitcase. "But your lady parts might have other ideas. They've been in hibernation so long they're probably desperate for attention. Like a neglected houseplant that's about to get an unexpected downpour."

"My lady parts are highly professional," I insisted. "And very discerning."

"Which is exactly why they've been on a sabbatical since Austin," Mari pointed out. "They're so discerning they've rejected everyone. But now along comes a guy who makes you laugh, challenges you, respects your work, left a hot date to help you in a crisis, and looks like he was carved by horny gods specifically to make sensible women abandon their professional ethics. Even the most discerning lady parts might make an exception."

I refused to acknowledge the accuracy of her assessment. "I'm bringing the bride portfolios," I repeated stubbornly. "And my laptop."

"Fine. Bring your work security blanket. But I'm leaving the good underwear in your suitcase, and I bet you fifty dollars you'll be glad I did."

I didn't take the bet. I wasn't entirely sure I'd win.

I'D NEVER BEEN on a private jet before. Not that I was going to admit that to Callan, who was watching me with amusement as I tried to act like this was all perfectly normal and not like I'd just stepped into an episode of "Lifestyles of the Rich and Ridiculous."

"First time on a private jet?" he asked, gesturing to a cream leather seat that looked more comfortable than my entire apartment, including my bed and that expensive pillow I splurged on during a moment of weakness.

"I usually take the subway to private islands," I replied, sliding into the seat and trying not to audibly gasp at how luxurious it felt. "Less traffic. More colorful characters. Occasionally someone plays the bongo drums."

He laughed, dropping into the seat across from me. "Let me guess. You're also going to pretend you haven't been secretly checking out every detail of this plane since you stepped onboard."

"I have no idea what you're talking about," I lied, fighting the urge to press my face against the window like an excited child. "It's just a plane with... fewer people. And nicer seats. And what looks suspiciously like a full bar. And is that... is that an actual crystal chandelier? On an airplane? That seems like a safety hazard. What happens during turbulence? Death by flying crystals?"

"It's secured very well," he assured me. "And yes, it is a full bar. And there's a bedroom in the back. And yes, the bathroom is big enough to shower in. Explore. I won't judge. Much."

"I'm perfectly comfortable right here," I said with as much dignity as I could muster, though my gaze kept darting to different features of the cabin.

"Suit yourself," he shrugged, then called to the attendant. "Josie, could you bring Ms. Marcel a glass of champagne? And I'll have my usual."

"Right away, Mr. Burkhardt," the attendant replied with a warm smile.

"You have a 'usual' on your private jet," I observed. "That's not at all obnoxiously wealthy. Next you'll tell me you have a preferred caviar for mid-flight snacks."

"Would it help if I told you my usual is just cranberry juice?" he asked, raising an eyebrow. "I don't drink alcohol when I fly. Makes me woozy."

That surprised me. "Cranberry juice? Really?"

"With a splash of seltzer," he nodded. "Gram got me hooked on it as a kid. Said it kept bladder infections at bay."

I couldn't help laughing at that. "Bladder health. Very sexy topic for a private jet. Do you discuss urinary tract infections with all your female guests, or am I just special?"

"I'm full of sexy conversation starters," he agreed. "Bladder health, tax shelters, the proper way to fold pocket squares. I'm basically a walking aphrodisiac."

I was still laughing when Josie returned with our drinks; champagne for me and, sure enough, cranberry juice with seltzer for him. The champagne was, of course, perfectly chilled.

"So," Callan said after we'd taken off, "ground rules for the weekend."

"I thought the whole point was no rules," I replied. "A break from structure and planning. A vacation from your wedding planner."

"Fair point," he conceded. "But I do have one request."

"Which is?"

"No work talk," he said firmly. "No wedding details, no bride hunting, no business expansion plans. Just... relaxation."

I shifted uncomfortably, thinking of the bride portfolios neatly packed in my carry-on. "Define 'work talk,'" I hedged.

His eyes narrowed suspiciously. "You brought work, didn't you?"

"I might have packed a few... resources," I admitted. "Just in case."

"In case of what? A sudden wedding emergency on my private island? A surprise bride candidate washing up on shore? 'Help, help, I'm a perfect match for a billionaire and I've been shipwrecked on his private island! Good thing his wedding planner brought my compatibility profile!'"

"In case of awkward silence," I said, feeling foolish now. "Or if you changed your mind about the bride search. Or if I have a panic attack about being trapped on an island with a man who looks like you and need something work-related to focus on instead of your... everything." I gestured vaguely at him, then immediately regretted it.

Callan shook his head, but he was smiling. "Anica Marcel, professional to the bitter end. Fine, you can keep your work. But it stays in your suitcase unless explicitly requested. Deal?"

"Deal. Any other rules?"

"Just one more," he said, raising his cranberry juice in a toast. "Have fun. That's an order."

I clinked my champagne glass against his. "I'll do my best, boss."

His eyes lit up. "Boss? I like that. Feel free to call me that all weekend. 'Yes, boss.' 'Whatever you say, boss.' 'Of course I'll rub sunscreen on your back, boss.'"

"Don't push it, Burkhardt," I warned, but I was smiling. "Or I'll start calling you 'bladder health guy.'"

The flight passed more pleasantly than I'd anticipated. Callan was easy company when he wasn't being deliberately provocative, and I relaxed despite my earlier anxiety. We played cards (he cheated shamelessly), watched a movie (he had terrible taste in comedies), and ate a lunch that put every first-class airline meal I'd ever had to shame.

By the time we began our descent, I'd almost forgotten to be nervous about the weekend ahead. Almost.

"Finally," Callan announced as the plane touched down on what appeared to be a private airstrip. "Welcome to my humble abode."

I peered out the window and gasped despite myself. Crystal-clear turquoise water stretched as far as I could see, surrounding a lush green island ringed with perfect white-sand beaches. It looked like a postcard come to life, or possibly a green screen background for a movie too beautiful to be real.

"This is your island?" I asked, unable to keep the awe from my voice. "The whole thing?"

"All 300 acres of it. I bought it on a whim after Kris said it couldn't be done. Not my most financially sound decision, but definitely one of my favorites. It's like the world's most expensive 'I told you so.'"

As we deplaned, the humid tropical air enveloped me. A gentle breeze carried the scent of salt and flowers, and the sun felt hotter.

"The villa is just up that path," Callan said, pointing to a winding trail through lush foliage. "Don't worry about the luggage. The staff will bring it up."

"There's staff?" I asked. "Here in the middle of nowhere?"

"Just Titus and Rhonda," he explained as we walked. "They manage the place when I'm not here, which is most of the time. They live on the other side of the island and are basically self-sufficient. They'll make our meals and keep things running, but otherwise, they'll stay out of our way. I told them we wanted privacy."

The way he said "privacy" sent a little shiver down my spine. "That's... thoughtful," I managed.

"I figured you'd appreciate not having an audience," he said. "You seem like someone who values her space."

He'd read me correctly, which was both gratifying and unsettling. I wasn't used to clients, to anyone, really, paying such close attention to my preferences.

The path opened up to reveal what Callan had described as a "villa" but what I would have called a small luxury resort designed by someone with unlimited funds and excellent taste. The main building was a stunning blend of modern architecture and natural materials, with wide windows that faced the ocean and an infinity pool that seemed to merge with the sea beyond.

"This is..." Words failed me.

"Home away from home. Though I've only been here a handful of times. Never had anyone to share it with, aside from the guys once for a weekend that none of us fully remember. Kris ended up with a tribal tattoo he can't explain and Morgan lost an eyebrow."

Something about that admission, that he'd never brought any other women here, made my stomach do a strange little flip.

"Let me show you to your quarters," he continued. "I thought you'd prefer the guest house to a room in the main villa. More privacy."

The guest house turned out to be a charming bungalow set slightly apart from the main building, with its own small patio overlooking the water. Inside was a spacious bedroom, a luxurious bathroom with a soaking tub positioned to take advantage of the ocean view, and a small living area with comfortable furniture and a fully stocked bookshelf.

"This is perfect," I said, genuinely touched by his consideration. "Thank you."

"Rhonda stocked the fridge with snacks and drinks. There's a phone by the bed if you need anything. Just dial one for the main house."

As I explored the bungalow, I noticed little touches that seemed suspiciously personalized; my favorite brand of sparkling water in the fridge, a selection of thrillers on the bookshelf (my guilty pleasure reading), and even a yoga mat rolled up in the corner, as if someone had anticipated my morning routine.

"How did you know I like these things?" I asked, holding up a book by my favorite author.

Callan grinned and rubbed the back of his neck. "I might have asked Devonna a few questions. For hospitality purposes only."

"You interrogated my assistant about my preferences?"

"Interrogated is a strong word," he protested. "I merely inquired about certain details that might make your stay more comfortable. No waterboarding was involved. Though I did have to bribe her with fancy coffee."

I should have been annoyed at the invasion of privacy, but I was oddly touched. No one had ever gone to such lengths to make me comfortable before.

"Well, thank you. It's... very thoughtful."

"Don't sound so surprised," he replied. "I can be thoughtful when properly motivated."

"And what's your motivation here?" I asked before I could stop myself.

Something flickered in his eyes. "I want you to enjoy yourself, Anica. You deserved a break even before the sprinkler incident. Now you've earned a medal of honor and possibly sainthood."

I laughed, relieved by the shift to lighter territory. "So this island is my medal?"

"Consider it a loaner medal," he corrected with a grin. "I'm still quite attached to it."

"Duly noted."

"I'll let you get settled," he said, moving toward the door. "Meet me at the main house when you're ready. No rush."

This was not normal client behavior. This was not normal anything.

BY LATE AFTERNOON, I'd changed into my sensible black one-piece (hidden beneath a cover-up that provided maximum skin coverage) and made my way to the beach. Callan was already there, stretched out on a lounge chair with a book, wearing nothing but swim trunks.

I'd seen attractive men before. I'd even seen Callan in images without a shirt on. But nothing had prepared me for the reality of Callan Burkhardt shirtless in person. His chest and abs looked like they'd been sculpted by an artist with a particular appreciation for the male form. His shoulders were broad, his waist narrow, and a tantalizing trail of dark hair disappeared into his swim trunks.

I forced my eyes upward, only to find him watching me.

"See something you like?" he asked, because of course he'd noticed me staring.

"Just making sure you're wearing sunscreen," I replied with as much dignity as I could muster. "Skin cancer is no joke, even for billionaires. Melanoma doesn't care about your bank account."

"How considerate." He patted the lounge chair beside him. "Join me? The view is spectacular."

He wasn't wrong. The beach was pristine, the water a shade of blue I'd previously only seen in heavily filtered Instagram photos. I settled onto the chair, careful to maintain my cover-up's strategic coverage.

"You're not swimming?" he asked, nodding at my outfit.

"Maybe later," I hedged. "Just enjoying the view for now."

"Fair enough." He returned to his book, seemingly content with silence.

After a few minutes of tense self-awareness on my part, I finally began to relax. There was something about the rhythm of the waves, the warmth of the sun, and the absence of phone calls, emails, and wedding emergencies that slowly unwound the knot of anxiety I perpetually carried between my shoulder blades.

"I can't remember the last time I had a day off," I admitted, breaking the companionable silence.

Callan glanced up from his book. "Seriously? Not even a weekend?"

"Weekends are the worst, actually. Wedding season is year-round when you're building a business. If I'm not at an actual wedding, I'm meeting with clients, or vendors, or working on marketing, or dealing with emergencies."

"That sounds exhausting. Don't you ever burn out?"

"Occasionally, but I love what I do. Most of the time, it doesn't feel like work."

"What about your family? Do they understand the crazy schedule?"

"My parents are actually pretty supportive," I said. "They've been married for thirty-seven years and still act like newlyweds sometimes. I think that's part of why I love weddings—I grew up seeing what a good marriage looks like."

"Thirty-seven years," Callan mused. "That's impressive. What's their secret?"

I considered the question. "They genuinely like each other. They're best friends first, partners second. And they never go to bed angry. That's their big rule."

"Never?"

"Never," I confirmed. "My dad says life's too short to waste it being mad at the person you love most in the world."

"Wise man," Callan said softly. "My parents could have used that advice. They specialized in multi-day silent treatments. The record was two weeks over a misplaced cufflink. Two entire weeks of frosty silence in a house so big they could literally avoid each other for days."

"And that's why you're so skeptical about marriage?" I asked, venturing into territory we usually avoided.

He was quiet for a moment. "Probably part of it. Hard to believe in something you've never really seen work."

"Same thing happened with your grandmother and grandfather, right?"

"My grandfather wasn't exactly a stand-up guy. Gram's amazing, but she ended up alone anyway."

"And that's why you think it's all pointless?" I couldn't keep the challenge from my voice. "Love, I mean."

He turned to face me fully. "I think it's a gamble. And I'm not convinced the potential payoff justifies the risk."

"Hence the arrangement. All the benefits, none of the messy emotions."

"Exactly." But he didn't sound as convinced as he usually did.

"And what if you're wrong?" I asked. "What if there's more to it than you think? What if love does exist?"

A shadow crossed his face. "Then I'll have missed out. But at least I won't have been hurt." He dropped his gaze down to his book before meeting mine. "I don't think I could handle that. At least not well."

"For what it's worth," I said carefully, "I think you're selling yourself short."

He raised an eyebrow. "How so?"

"You've made yourself an image of a billionaire playboy, but I see through it. You care about people. You have an incredibly adorable relationship with the strong woman who all but raised you. You left a date to help me with a wedding crisis. You brought me here to make sure I got a break. Those aren't the actions of someone incapable of genuine connection. You're not just some rich fuckboy."

He studied me for a long moment. "Or maybe I'm letting you see all of that because the smirks and cash don't work with you, and it's a more efficient way of seeing what you're hiding beneath that coverup," he suggested, but there was no conviction behind it.

"Uh huh. Sure," I said, though I didn't believe it. "Or maybe you're just a decent human being who happens to be obscenely wealthy and irritatingly attractive."

That made him laugh. "Irritatingly attractive, huh? Do tell me more about how my attractiveness irritates you. Is it the abs? The jawline? The rakish smile? I need specifics for my ego."

And just like that, we were back on safer ground. The moment of vulnerability passed, replaced by our usual banter.

"It's distracting," I said, playfully flicking sand at him. "How am I supposed to maintain professional composure when you're walking around looking like that?" I gestured vaguely at his physique.

"It's a curse. Being this handsome is actually a burden. It's like being a beautiful piece of art that no one bothers to read the little plaque next to." He sighed dramatically.

"Oh, poor baby," I mocked. "Life must be so hard for you."

"It is," he insisted. "Do you know how difficult it is to find shirts that fit both my broad shoulders and my narrow waist? It's a constant struggle. Sometimes I have to settle for shirts that only make me look like a 9.5 instead of a perfect 10. It's truly a tragedy."

I laughed, rolling my eyes. "I'm playing the world's tiniest violin for you right now. The saddest song ever composed specifically for the billionaire who can't find shirts to properly showcase his perfect body."

The rest of the afternoon passed in a similar fashion; relaxed conversation interspersed with comfortable silences. I couldn't remember the last time I'd felt so at ease with another person besides Mari.

As the sun began to set, Callan suggested we head back to the villa for dinner. "Rhonda's making her famous seafood paella," he explained. "Trust me, you don't want to miss it."

"I should probably change first," I said, suddenly self-conscious about dining in my swimwear.

"No need to get fancy. Island rules. Anything goes."

But I changed anyway, choosing a simple sundress that was more revealing than I'd normally wear but still modest by most standards. It was one of the items Mari had snuck into my suitcase, and I hated to admit she'd been right about it being perfect for the setting.

When I arrived at the main villa, I found Callan on the expansive patio, mixing drinks at an outdoor bar. He'd changed into linen pants and a loose white shirt, looking like he'd stepped out of a luxury travel advertisement. Or possibly my most inconvenient, distracting daydreams.

"Perfect timing," he said, glancing up. "I was just making us some island specialties." He gestured to the colorful concoctions he was preparing. "Don't worry, they're stronger than they look."

"Is that a warning?" I asked, accepting the vibrant blue drink he handed me.

"Yup. Careful with these. They're like the tropical version of truth serum. Two of these and you'll be telling me your deepest secrets. Three and you might start removing clothing. Not that I'm keeping track or anything. Here, take another one."

I shook my head, rejecting the second one. I took a cautious sip. It was absolutely delicious; sweet and fruity on the surface, with a definite kick of rum beneath. "Tasty," I acknowledged. "And potent."

"Just like me," he quipped, clinking his glass against mine with a wide grin.

I rolled my eyes but couldn't suppress a smile. "You're impossible."

"Part of my charm."

Rhonda served us dinner at a table overlooking the water, with the sunset painting the sky in spectacular shades of pink and orange. Her paella was indeed amazing.

As we ate, Callan kept our glasses filled with his "island specialties," which seemed to get stronger with each iteration. By the time we'd finished the main course, I was feeling pleasantly warm and significantly less inhibited than usual.

"This is amazing," I said, gesturing broadly at the setting. "All of it. The food, the view, the... everything. Even you're not so bad, for a client who's probably breaking at least sixteen professional ethics guidelines by bringing me here."

Callan smiled, seeming pleased by my enthusiasm. "I'm glad you're enjoying it. It's nice to share this place with someone who appreciates it."

"So you really haven't brought anyone else here?" I asked, frowning at my drink when the straw had no more liquid to suck up. "No supermodels? No Hollywood starlets? No tech heiresses? No one else has experienced the full Callan Burkhardt private island experience?"

"Just the guys, once," he confirmed. "And they spent most of the time seeing who could jump from the highest point into the pool without dying. Not exactly the sophisticated island experience I was going for."

"And what experience are you going for with me?" The question slipped out before I could censor it.

His gaze met mine, surprisingly serious. "Honestly? I just wanted to see you relax. You're always so... contained. Even at the wedding expo, even in crisis mode, you maintain this perfect composure. I wanted to see what Anica Marcel looks like when she's not planning someone else's perfect day."

"And?" I prompted, caught somewhere between flattered and exposed. "What's the verdict?"

"The jury's still out," he said with a small smile. "But I like what I'm seeing so far. Especially the part where you keep forgetting not to stare at my chest."

"I do not—" I began, then caught myself looking exactly where he'd claimed. "Okay, fine. You have a nice chest. Congratulations. It's very... chesty. But in my defense, you've been parading around half-naked all day. That's basically entrapment."

"Entrapment? So now I'm guilty of forcing you to appreciate my physique? Should I put on a potato sack to protect your professional virtue?"

"The potato industry doesn't deserve that kind of publicity. Your abs would probably make potato sacks the new fashion trend, and then what would potatoes be stored in? You'd cause a worldwide agricultural crisis."

He laughed, looking genuinely delighted by my nonsense. "I've never had my abs described as a potential threat to global agriculture before. I'm flattered."

"Well, keep the tropical truth serum coming, and you might see more than you bargained for," I said, holding out my empty glass.

"Is that a warning?" he asked, echoing my earlier question and refilling my cup with the magical blue liquid.

"Yup," I replied.

After dinner, we moved to a seating area closer to the beach, where Callan built a small fire in a pit. The night had brought a slight chill to the air, and the fire's warmth was welcome. Or maybe I just needed something to blame for the heat I felt whenever Callan's eyes lingered on me.

"Another drink?" he offered, holding up a bottle of something amber.

"I probably shouldn't," I said, then immediately contradicted myself by holding out my glass. "But when in Rome..."

"Or when on a private island with no responsibilities and no witnesses," he added, pouring generously.

"Speaking of no witnesses, does anyone even know we're here together? I mean, professionally speaking, this is... unconventional."

"Mari knows, obviously. And Devonna. And probably my grandmother by now, because she has an uncanny ability to know everything I do before I do it." He took a sip of his drink. "Does it matter who knows?"

"I guess not. It's just... I've worked so hard to build a reputation for professionalism. For boundaries. And here I am, on a private island with a client, drinking..." I squinted at my glass. "What is this anyway?"

"Fifteen-year-old rum. And technically, we're friends having a weekend away. The client-planner relationship is on pause."

"Is that how it works? We can just pause professional relationships when convenient?"

"Why not?" he challenged. "People are more than their jobs, Anica. Even you."

"Sometimes I wonder," I admitted, staring into the fire. "Everyone's planning their happily ever after, and I'm just... planning everyone else's."

"Do you want your own happily ever after?" he asked quietly.

"I don't know. After Austin, I'm not sure I trust my judgment anymore."

"What happened?" Callan asked. "I mean, I know the basics, but..."

"I walked in on him with a client. In our bed. Two days before our wedding."

Callan winced. "That's brutal."

"The worst part wasn't even the cheating," I continued, the words spilling out. "It was the humiliation. She was this gorgeous, wealthy socialite whose wedding I'd spent months planning down to the last detail. I knew her favorite flowers, her favorite songs, her childhood stories... I thought we were almost friends."

"And she slept with your fiancé," Callan finished.

I nodded, taking another gulp of rum. "In our apartment. While I was out picking up our custom cocktail napkins. They didn't even hear me come in, they were so loud."

"What did you do?" he asked.

"I stood there like an idiot, holding these stupid napkins with our initials intertwined, watching the man I thought I'd spend my life balls deep in another woman." I flinched. God, I could still see them. Worse, I could hear her moaning his name as he pounded her. "I just... left. Didn't say a word. Walked out, went to Mari's, and drank an entire bottle of tequila."

"You didn't confront them?"

I shook my head. "What was the point? It was pretty clear what was happening. And I guess part of me wasn't even that surprised. Austin had always been... insecure about my success. He was a struggling musician, and I think he resented that I was the breadwinner. Sleeping with a wealthy client was probably his way of feeling powerful again."

153

"He sounds like an asshole," Callan said, his voice low.

"He was. But I loved him. Or thought I did. We'd been together since college. He was my first serious relationship. I thought we were building something real."

"And after that, you swore off men?" Callan guessed.

"Not consciously. I just... haven't found anyone worth the risk of a relationship. Haven't found anyone to trust. And I've been busy building the business. It's easier to focus on work than to put myself out there again. Plus, with work, at least when people inevitably disappoint you, they're paying you for the privilege."

"I get that. It's always easier to stick with what you're good at than to risk failing at something that matters."

I looked at him, surprised by his insight. "Exactly."

For a moment, we just sat there, the fire crackling between us, the sound of waves in the background. Then I realized I'd just spilled my most painful secrets to a client. A client who was supposed to be marrying someone else in the near future.

"I should probably go to bed," I said abruptly, standing up and immediately regretting it as the world tilted. "Whoa. The island is spinning. Did you... did you buy a spinning island? Very fancy. Ver... very elaborate."

God, was I slurring my words?

Callan was on his feet instantly, his hand on my elbow to steady me. "You okay there, Bambi?"

"I'm fine," I insisted, though in truth, I was significantly more intoxicated than I'd realized. "Just stood up too fast. And possibly drank too much of your island truth... truth juice. The blue stuff. The rum. All the alcohols. You have very good alcohols, Callan. Very tasty."

"Let me walk you back to the bungalow," he offered, his hand still on my arm.

"I can manage," I insisted, taking a step and promptly stumbling over absolutely nothing. "Oops! The sand jumped up and attacked me. Very aggressive sand you have here."

"Sure it did," he said, wrapping an arm around my waist. "But humor me."

I was too dizzy to argue. The combination of sun, alcohol, and emotional confessions had left me thoroughly disoriented. I leaned into Callan more than I'd intended as we made our way down the path to the guest house.

"You know what's really sad?" I said as we walked, my filter completely dissolved by rum. "I haven't had sex since Austin. That's more than two years of cel... celi... not having sex. My vagina probably has cobwebs."

Callan made a loud choking sound. "I'm sure that's not anatomically possible."

"You don't know. It could be like an abandoned house down there. Dusty. Haunted. Full of spiders. The ghosts of orgasms past, rattling their chains and moaning sadly. A condemned building with a sign that says 'Do Not Enter' but really means 'Please, Someone, Anyone, Enter Before I Forget How This Works.'"

"This is a fascinating metaphor," he said, clearly struggling to keep a straight face.

"It's not funny," I pouted. "It's tragic. I'm a tragic figure. Like... like Jane Eyre. Or Hamlet. But with less murder and more... more sexual frustration. Sexual-Frustra-Hamlet. That's me."

"Hamlet died in the end," Callan pointed out as we reached the bungalow. "Let's aim for a less tragic comparison."

He helped me inside and guided me to the bedroom, where I immediately flopped onto the mattress with a contented sigh. "This bed is amazing," I mumbled into the pillow. "Like sleeping on a cloud made of dreams and marshmallows and... and really good mattress stuff. What's in mattresses? Clouds? Baby dreams? Rich people tears?"

"Glad you approve," he said, sounding amused. "I'll get you some water."

He disappeared into the bathroom and returned with a glass, which he set on the nightstand. "Drink this before you sleep," he instructed. "It'll help with tomorrow's headache."

"You're so nice," I said, rolling onto my back to look up at him. The ceiling seemed to be gently undulating, like waves. Very pretty waves. "Why are you so nice to me? You're s'posed to be a mean rich person. That's how it works in movies. The rich person is mean until the poor person teaches them the true meaning of Christmas."

"What if I'm Jewish," he replied, clearly amused.

"Then the true meaning of... of Hanukkah," I amended, waving my hand dismissively. "Whatever. You know what I mean. The point is... the point is... what was the point?"

"That I'm being nice to you?" he suggested.

"Yes! That. Why are you so nice to me? Even when I compare my vagina to a haunted house. A very sad, lonely haunted house that misses visitors."

"I like you," he said simply. "Even when you compare your vagina to a haunted house."

"Especially then," I suggested with a giggle. "You like me because I'm weird. Because I say the things. The things in my brain just come out of my mouth. Like right now."

"Among other reasons," he agreed. "Now get some sleep."

"Stay," I said impulsively, reaching for his hand. "Just for a little while. Please? Pretty please with sugar and cherries and whipped cream and sprinkles and... and all the other ice cream things?"

Something flickered in his eyes. "Anica, you're drunk. Like, really, really drunk. Olympic-level drunk. Gold medal in the Drunk Olympics drunk."

"Not that drunk," I protested, though the way the ceiling was gently spinning suggested otherwise. "Just drunk enough to be honest. An' honestly, I don't want to be alone right now. Too many... thinky thoughts. Brain won't shut up. Need comp'ny."

He sighed, sitting carefully on the edge of the bed. "Fine. I'll stay until you fall asleep."

"You're a gentl'man," I said, patting his arm clumsily. "A gentl'man with very nice arms. Have I mentioned your arms are nice? Because they are. Very nice. All... arm-like. Good at arm stuff. Lifting. Carrying. Arm... ing."

"I believe that's the textbook definition of arms," he agreed, chuckling under his breath.

"Don't laugh at me," I pouted. "I'm eloquent. I'm just also drunk. Very drunk. The most drunk. Never been this drunk before. Except maybe when Austin... when the napkins... y'know."

156

"I know," he said softly, his expression sobering. "I'm sorry he did that to you."

"Me too," I said, feeling suddenly melancholy. "But then I wouldn't be here with you if it hadn't. Silver linings and stuff. Cloud linings? Whatever the saying is. The good part of bad stuff."

I pushed myself up to a sitting position, which was a mistake. The room tilted, and I clutched at his shirt for stability. "Whoa. Everything's spinning. Make it stop spinning. Did you break the island? Is it s'posed to spin?"

"Lie back down," he suggested, gently trying to guide me back to the pillow.

"No, wait. I'm hot." I tugged at the neckline of my sundress. "This dress is strangling me. Like a fabric snake. A very pretty snake, but still a snake. I need to take it off before it eats me."

"That's not necessary," Callan said quickly, catching my hands as I reached for the zipper. "You can sleep in your clothes. It's fine."

"It's not fine," I insisted, trying to wiggle out of his grasp. "I can't sleep in clothes. I always sleep naked. Nakey-nakey-nakey."

His eyes widened. "You do?"

"No," I admitted with a giggle. "But I could start. New island tradition! Naked island sleeping! All the cool kids are doing it. Or just me. I'd be the cool kid."

I managed to free one hand and immediately started pulling at the thin strap of my dress, sliding it down my shoulder.

"Anica, stop," Callan said, his voice strained. "You're going to regret this in the morning."

"I regret lots of things," I said. "I regret not seeing what a jerk Austin was. I regret working so much. I regret not bringing the sexy bathing suit Mari tried to pack for me. 'S just three triangles held together by threads. Very small triangles. Tiny lil fabric triangles for covering tiny lil parts."

"You can regret all those things with your clothes on," he said firmly, capturing my hands again.

I frowned at him. "You don't want to see me naked? Am I not pretty enough? Do you not like me? You said you liked me, but maybe you were lying. Maybe you secretly think I'm ugly and my vagina really does have spiders."

"That is definitely not the issue," he assured me. "You're beautiful. But you're also drunk, and I'm trying to be a decent human being."

"So noble," I sighed, flopping back onto the pillow. "But what if I don't want you to be noble? What if I want you to be... ignoble? Is that a word? The opposite of noble. Un-noble. Dis-noble. Whatever. That's what I want. The bad thing. The good-bad thing."

"Noted," he said, clearly fighting a smile. "But right now, what you need is sleep."

"And water," I remembered, reaching for the glass he'd brought. I took a long drink, spilling about half of it down my chin and neck. "Oops. I'm all wet now. Better take off these wet clothes..."

"You're fine," he said, taking the glass away before I could make more of a mess. "It's just a little water."

"Thank you for taking care of me," I said. "Most men wouldn't. They'd be trying to get in my pants. My sad, cobwebby pants. With the spiders. Spider pants."

"I'm not most men," he said simply.

"No, you're not. You're... Callan. Callan Burkhardt. Cal-lan Burk-hardt. Funny name. Kinda fun to say. Callan Burkhardt, Callan Burkhardt, Callan Burkhardt." I sing-songed his name, clearly amusing myself.

"That is my name," he confirmed.

"A good name," I nodded solemnly. "For a good person. A good, good person. Despite what you want people to think. You're secretly nice. Like a reverse super-villain. Outside villain, inside hero. You're a sneaky good person pretending to be bad."

His expression shifted, something vulnerable flickering across his features. "I think that's the nicest thing you've ever said to me."

"I can be nice," I assured him. "When drunk."

"And what other nice things do you have to say?" he asked.

I considered the question. "Your face," I decided. "It's a nice face. The kind of face that deserves nice words. A face-words-nice situation. Very handsome."

He laughed softly. "I think that's the rum talking."

"The rum is very wise," I insisted. "It knows things. Secret things. Rum secrets. The secrets of the rum gods."

"Like what?"

158

I leaned forward conspiratorially, nearly falling into his lap in the process. "Like the fact that I think about you. When I shouldn't. Which is all the time, because you're my client, and I'm not supposed to think about clients like... that. The 'that' way. The sexy that way."

His breath caught. "Like what?"

"Like wondering what it would be like to kiss you," I whispered. "Or what you look like without a shirt. Except now I know about the shirtless part, and it's even better than I imagined, which is very unfair. Very, very unfair."

"Anica—"

"Shh," I pressed a finger against his lips, misjudging the distance and nearly poking him in the eye. "Oops. Sorry. Eye. That was your eye, not your mouth. My bad. Don't say anything. Just let me look at you for a minute. One minute of looking."

I studied his face. The strong jawline, the perfect nose, the blue eyes that seemed to see right through my carefully constructed defenses. "You really are irritatingly attractive," I concluded. "It's very inconsiderate of you. Very rude, actually. How dare you? How. Dare. You. Be. So. Pretty." I poked his chest with each word for emphasis.

"I apologize for the inconvenience," he said, gently removing my finger from his chest.

"You should. And you should also kiss me. To make up for it. Kissing as apology. Very traditional."

I leaned forward, eyes closed, lips puckered in what I was sure was a very seductive manner. Like a sexy fish. A sexy, drunk fish. Instead of his lips, I felt his hand gently pushing me back.

"Not like this," he said softly. "Not when you're drunk."

I opened my eyes, hurt and confusion warring with the alcohol-induced haze. "You don't want to kiss me? I've been un-kissed for so long. Years and years of no kisses. My lips are getting dusty, just like... y'know. The haunted house. Everything dusty. So dusty."

"That's not it, but I want you to remember it if we ever do kiss. And I want you to be sure it's what you want."

"I am sure," I insisted, though even in my drunken state, I recognized the wisdom in his restraint. "But fine. Be noble. See if I care. I don't care. I care so little. The least caring that has ever been cared."

I flopped back against the pillows, suddenly exhausted. The room was still spinning, but now it was a comforting carousel rather than a nauseating whirlwind.

"I'm going to take off your shoes," Callan said, moving to the foot of the bed. "Is that okay?"

"My shoes can stay on," I mumbled. "But the dress has to go. It's strangling me. Slowly killing me with its... its dressness. Death by dress. Dress death."

He sighed, and I heard him moving around the room. "Here," he said, returning to the bedside. "Let's try this."

He was holding one of his own button-down shirts.

"I'm going to put this on you backwards," he explained. "That way you won't be, uh, exposed."

"Clever," I approved, sitting up with effort. "But complicated. Very, very complicated."

With infinite patience and careful positioning to preserve my modesty, Callan managed to get the shirt on me. It was enormous, hanging almost to my knees.

"Now you can take your dress off inside the shirt," he instructed, turning his back to give me privacy.

I fumbled with the zipper, nearly dislocating my shoulder in the process, but eventually managed to wiggle out of my dress while keeping his shirt in place. The sensation of soft cotton against my skin was heavenly.

"Done," I announced proudly. "I am now wearing your shirt. This means I own your soul according to ancient law. Ancient shirt law. Very serious. Very binding. Like a contract but with cotton."

He turned back with a smile. "I think you're confusing shirts with fairy contracts."

"Same principle," I insisted, my eyelids growing heavy. "Very binding. Very serious. Very... magical. Shirt magic. The strongest magic."

"I'll take my chances," he said, pulling the covers up over me. "Now get some sleep."

"You'll stay?" I asked, fighting to keep my eyes open. "Just till I fall asleep? Just for a lil bit? A teeny tiny bit?"

"I'll stay," he promised, sitting back on the edge of the bed.

"Good," I murmured, already drifting. "Because I like having you here. I like you, Callan Burkhardt. Even though I shouldn't. Shouldn't like you. Bad idea."

His hand brushed a strand of hair from my face, his touch impossibly gentle. "I like you too, darling. Even though I probably shouldn't."

I wanted to respond, to explore this mutual admission, but exhaustion and alcohol were dragging me under.

TWO FOR THE HONEYMOON SUITE

Chapter 12: Callan

A haunted house. That was a new one. I could not wait to see if she remembered saying that.

The sun streaming through my bedroom windows reminded me it was morning, and morning meant facing Anica with the uncomfortable knowledge that I'd seen a side of her I doubted she ever intended to show. I'd watched her walls crumble under the influence of my admittedly too-strong island cocktails, listened to her confess her attraction to me, and then, like some kind of deranged gentleman, tucked her into bed without taking advantage of the situation.

Who even was I anymore? And could I return this evolved version of myself for the original model? The new firmware update seemed to have disabled my "billionaire playboy with no moral compass" setting.

I glared at the ceiling. Anica had stared up at me with her bright eyes, telling me she thought about me "in the that way. The sexy that way." Anica had begged me to kiss her. Anica had worn my shirt and declared it meant she owned my soul according to "ancient shirt law."

Drunk Anica was adorable. Unfiltered. Real in a way few people ever allowed themselves to be with me. I grinned like an idiot. The woman who had been nothing but organization and pencil skirts had spent twenty minutes talking to me about her absent sex life.

Shit.

She was going to be pissed.

I had a feeling she'd probably remember the mortifying details and would rather swim with sharks than acknowledge any of it. Actually, knowing Anica, she'd have a laminated action plan for swimming with sharks. The woman probably packed a shark deterrent in a secret emergency kit.

I dragged myself out of bed, showered, and instructed Rhonda to prepare a hangover-friendly breakfast. Aspirin, coffee strong enough to wake the dead, and enough carbs to soak up whatever rum remained in Anica's system. I arranged everything on a tray, trying to convince myself this was just basic hospitality, not an excuse to see her first thing in the morning with bed-head and sleepy eyes.

I spent the walk to the bungalow rehearsing casual opening lines. *"Morning, how's the head?"* No, that sounded like I was inquiring about a blowjob. *"Sleep well?"* Too loaded. *"Remember declaring your vagina has cobwebs and asking me to kiss you?"* Definitely not. *"How's the haunted house? Any ghost evictions overnight?"* Tempting, but I enjoyed having all my limbs attached to my body.

I settled on a simple "Good morning" as I knocked on her door, balancing the breakfast tray in one hand. I could've made it as a waiter. Maybe. Actually, I probably would've gotten fired for eating other people's food. The closest I'd come was serving drinks at a college party, which ended with me charging people five dollars to watch me do a handstand on a keg. Not exactly fine dining service.

After an extended pause, during which I imagined her hiding under the covers or possibly searching for an escape route through the bathroom window, the door opened to reveal Anica looking like someone who had made a series of questionable life choices, starting with accepting blue drinks from a man whose middle name might as well be "Bad Influence."

Her hair was pulled back in a messy ponytail, glasses emphasized her bloodshot eyes, and she wore a resort robe cinched tightly at the waist. My shirt from last night was clutched in her hand like evidence from a crime scene she was planning to burn.

"Is that coffee?" she asked, her voice hoarse and gravelly in a way that should not have been attractive but somehow was.

"And aspirin," I confirmed, lifting the tray slightly. "And enough carbs to construct a small fortress. Or at the very least, a modest carbohydrate bungalow with a nice view."

"You're a saint," she muttered, stepping back to let me in. "A saint who makes drinks that should be classified as weapons of mass destruction by the Geneva Convention, but a saint nonetheless."

I set the tray on the small table by the window, sneaking glances at her as she shuffled across the room like a zombie in a luxury bathrobe. Even hungover and clearly miserable, she was beautiful in that understated way that snuck up on you. The way that made you think about what she'd look like waking up next to you every morning, not just on a tropical island after too many cocktails.

Stop it, Burkhardt. Client. Wedding planner. Professional relationship. The woman who is currently planning your wedding to someone else. Get a grip, preferably not on her.

"Sleep well?" I asked casually, immediately regretting choosing the one opening line I'd explicitly rejected in my mental rehearsal. Smooth, real smooth.

"Like I was hit by a truck filled with rum," she replied, reaching for the coffee like it contained the elixir of life. "You?"

"Great. Perfect. Never better," I said, sounding about as natural as a robot attempting human conversation for the first time. "Very... sleep-like. The sleep. That I did. Sleeping."

Dear god, I sounded like someone had performed a lobotomy on my language center. Worse. I sounded like Drunk Anica. I, Callan Burkhardt, notorious smooth-talker who once convinced a venture capitalist to invest twenty million dollars during an extended elevator ride, was stammering like a teenager asking someone to prom.

"Good. That's... good." She nodded, then winced at the movement. "About last night —"

"Already forgotten," I cut in, flashing my best reassuring smile. "Island rules. What happens under the influence of tropical cocktails stays under the influence of tropical cocktails. Like Vegas, but with more sand and fewer Elvis impersonators."

164

Relief flashed across her face, followed by something that looked almost like disappointment before she masked it with another sip of coffee. "Right. Good. Thank you."

"For what?" I asked innocently.

"For..." she gestured vaguely with her coffee cup. "You know. Taking care of me. Making sure I didn't..."

"Fall into the ocean? Declare war on neighboring islands? Attempt to communicate with sea turtles using interpretive dance? Release all my exotic pets into the wild to start a new civilization?"

"Something like that." She attempted a smile that turned into a grimace. "God, my head feels like it's hosting a death metal concert. With a mosh pit. And possibly some kind of ritual sacrifice."

"The aspirin should help," I said, pushing the pills toward her. "And food. Even if you don't think you want it, trust me. It's like putting a sponge in a puddle of toxic waste. Necessary clean-up procedure."

She dutifully swallowed the pills and took a tentative bite of toast. "I'm surprised you're so chipper. You drank as much as I did."

"Superior genetics," I replied with a wink. "That, and years of practice neutralizing alcohol with late-night board meetings. Nothing sobers you up like trying to explain quarterly projections to investors in Tokyo at 3 AM while secretly being so hungover that even your eyebrows hurt."

"Sounds thrilling," she muttered.

"About as thrilling as watching paint dry on a tax form. During an audit. Conducted by the world's most monotone accountant." I agreed. "Speaking of thrilling activities, how would you feel about a boat trip today?"

She lowered her glasses enough to peer at me over the rims, her expression suggesting I'd just proposed we wrestle alligators while covered in barbecue sauce. "A boat. On water. Moving water. With my current hangover. You're joking, right?"

"The fresh air will help. And there's a neighboring island with a famous local market. Best conch fritters in the Bahamas. Plus, the boat ride is smooth. Like gliding on glass. Or sliding across a freshly waxed floor in socks, but with fewer bruises."

"Unless there are waves. Which there are. Because it's the ocean. Where waves live. Professionally. It's literally their job to be wavy and make people like me feel like their stomach is trying to escape through their esophagus."

"Minor detail. Come on, where's your sense of adventure?"

"I left it in the bottom of whatever blue monstrosity you kept refilling last night. What time would we leave?"

"After you've finished breakfast and feel human again," I promised. "No rush."

She sighed, taking another bite of toast. "Fine. But if I throw up, that's on you. Literally and figuratively."

"I accept full responsibility for any and all vomiting scenarios," I said solemnly, placing a hand over my heart. "My rum, my rules, my cleanup duty. I'll even hold your hair back. I'm very good at it. I once helped Morgan through an unfortunate tequila incident that resulted in him proposing marriage to a potted plant."

That earned me a genuine smile, small but real. "You're very strange for a billionaire, you know that?"

"I prefer 'uniquely eccentric,'" I corrected. "It sounds more expensive. Like I'm not weird, I'm a limited-edition collectible human."

"Of course it does," she replied, shaking her head but still smiling. "Give me an hour to pull myself together?"

"Take all the time you need," I said, backing toward the door. "I'll be at the main house whenever you're ready. No rush. I have several very important business calls to ignore while I stare at the ocean."

I paused at the doorway, holding up my shirt that she'd set aside. "By the way, according to ancient shirt law, I believe you now own my soul. Just wanted to confirm that's still in effect in the cold light of day. There's usually a 24-hour return policy, but you didn't keep the receipt."

Her cheeks flushed an adorable shade of pink. "I have no idea what you're talking about," she lied.

"Of course not," I agreed. "Must be thinking of someone else who claimed ownership of my soul last night. Easy mistake. I lose track of all the people who own pieces of my soul. You, my grandmother, the barista who makes my coffee exactly right. It's getting crowded in there."

I ducked out before she could throw something at me, grinning like an idiot all the way back to the main house.

TRUE TO MY word, I didn't rush her. When Anica finally appeared at the main house, she looked significantly more like herself. She'd switched out the glasses for sunglasses, and her hair was neatly styled. She'd changed into shorts and a light blouse that managed to be both modest and distractingly flattering.

"Ready for adventure?" I asked, setting aside the book I'd been pretending to read while actually watching the path from her bungalow. I hadn't actually turned a page in twenty minutes.

"Ready to prove that a human can survive on aspirin and spite," she corrected, but her tone was lighter. "Let's go before I change my mind or my stomach stages a full rebellion."

The small marina was a short walk from the main house, with several boats of varying sizes bobbing gently in the crystal-clear water. I only owned three of them, but I'd already decided we'd take the ferry.

"The ferry should be here in a minute." I slipped my hands into my pockets and stared out at the water.

"What, you can't drive one of these?" She gestured to the other boats.

"Oh I can *captain* all of those, but I want to enjoy the ride." I shrugged. "Besides, the ferry will probably be smoother, and that's what you need, right?"

It was obvious by the look on her face that I'd gotten her there. "Fair enough." She glanced at the yacht I'd used to close a couple business deals. "You even drive that one?"

"I'm an incredible captain."

"Your humility continues to inspire," she deadpanned. "You're like a walking TED Talk on self-esteem."

"I'm considering writing a self-help book. 'How to Love Yourself Almost As Much As I Love Me.'"

The ferry came soon after and it skimmed across the water, cutting through the gentle waves. The wind whipped through Anica's hair, sending strands flying around her face. She'd removed her sunglasses once we were on the water, and her eyes were bright despite her lingering hangover.

"Okay, I admit it," she called over the engine noise. "This was a good idea."

"I'm full of good ideas," I replied. "Some involving boats, some involving blue drinks that you'll probably never touch again. The quality varies, but the quantity is impressive."

"Never," she agreed with feeling. "If I so much as smell rum in the next decade, I might spontaneously combust. Or throw up. Or both simultaneously, which would be a sight to behold."

The ride to the neighboring island took about thirty minutes, during which Anica gradually relaxed, trailing her fingers in the water and asking questions about the various sea birds and boats we passed. I pointed out a pod of dolphins in the distance, and her face lit up with delight.

"They're showing off for you," I told her as the dolphins leaped and played in our wake.

"For the boat," she corrected.

"For you," I insisted. "They recognize a kindred spirit when they see one. Intelligent, graceful, occasionally makes squeaking noises when excited."

"I do not squeak!"

"You definitely squeaked when you saw the dolphins. It was adorable. Very high-pitched. Dolphin-approved. Like a tiny mouse discovering cheese for the first time."

"I made a sound of appreciation. A mature, adult sound."

"A squeak," I corrected. "Like a dog toy being stepped on. Or a rusty door hinge, but cuter."

She punched me in the shoulder.

The market was as vibrant and colorful as I'd promised, with stalls selling everything from fresh seafood to handwoven baskets to touristy trinkets. We wandered through the maze of vendors, Anica stopping occasionally to admire a piece of jewelry or artwork.

"No cell service," she noted, glancing at her phone. "I feel naked without it."

"The horror," I gasped in mock sympathy. "How will you survive without checking your email every thirty seconds? What if someone

168

has a wedding emergency? A bride might be choosing the wrong shade of ivory right now, and you wouldn't even know it. The world could be ending in a catastrophic ivory crisis."

"Very funny," she said, tucking her phone away. "But you're one to talk. Don't billionaires have some rule about always being available to make more billions? I thought that was in the handbook they give you when you reach your third comma."

"I left my copy at home. Along with my golden monocle and top hat made of hundred-dollar bills. Rookie mistake. Now how will I know the proper way to light cigars with flaming stock certificates?"

She laughed. "You'd look ridiculous in a top hat."

"I look amazing in all headwear. It's a curse, really. Hats see my face and just... elevate themselves. They sense greatness and rise to the occasion."

"Your humility is showing again," she said. A stall selling colorful scarves caught her attention. "These are beautiful."

The elderly woman manning the stall beamed at her. "All hand-dyed, miss. No two alike."

Anica ran her fingers over a scarf in shades of blue and green that reminded me of the ocean around my island. "It's gorgeous," she said.

"It would look beautiful on you," the woman said. "Matches your eyes."

Before Anica could respond, I'd already pulled out my wallet. "We'll take it." I handed over more than the asking price.

"Callan!" Anica protested. "You don't have to—"

"Consider it a souvenir," I said, taking the scarf and draping it around her shoulders. "A memory of the weekend. Much better than those tacky shot glasses or t-shirts that say 'I got wasted on a private island and all I got was this lousy t-shirt and a detailed memory of comparing my vagina to a haunted house.'"

Her eyes widened in horror as she glanced at the vendor, but the woman was counting her money and hadn't heard my comment. Anica pinched my arm hard enough to leave a mark.

"Ow! Violent," I whispered.

The woman smiled knowingly between us. "You two make a lovely couple."

"We're not—" Anica began automatically.

"Thank you," I interrupted, placing my hand at the small of Anica's back. "We're celebrating our anniversary. First time away since the wedding."

Anica's eyes widened, but to her credit, she didn't contradict me. "He's very romantic," she said instead, with just enough sarcasm that only I would catch it. "Knows exactly what to say to sweep a girl off her feet."

"Never let that fade," the woman advised, patting Anica's hand. "My Nickie and I were married sixty-two years before he passed. We never stopped celebrating each other."

"That's beautiful," Anica said softly, and I could tell she meant it.

"The secret is laughter," the woman continued. "And separate bathrooms if you can manage it."

I chuckled. "We'll keep that in mind. Though at this point I'd settle for her not plotting my murder over breakfast."

"Early days," the woman said knowingly. "You'll get there."

As we walked away, Anica adjusted the scarf around her shoulders. "Why did you tell her we were married?" she asked, but there was no real annoyance in her tone.

"People love a good love story," I shrugged. "And she seemed like the type who'd appreciate it. Besides, it's not like we haven't pretended to be engaged before. I figured we could upgrade our fake relationship status while on vacation. Next stop: fake divorce, followed by fake dramatic reconciliation. And then fake make up sex. Ow."

She punched me again, but she was chuckling.

"From fake fiancés to fake spouses," she mused. "Very progressive of us."

"I'm all about relationship growth," I agreed solemnly. "Even the imaginary kind. I'm very committed to our non-existent commitment."

We continued through the market, stopping to try the famous conch fritters (which lived up to the hype) and various other local delicacies. I bought us both fresh coconuts to drink from, complete with silly paper umbrellas and bendy straws.

"This is nothing like the coconut water they sell at Whole Foods," Anica observed, sipping from her straw. "It's so much better."

"Everything tastes better in its natural environment," I said. "Like how beer tastes better at a ballpark, or how coffee tastes better when someone else makes it."

"Or how rum tastes better until it makes you confess embarrassing personal details to your client," she added.

I decided to let her off the hook. "I have no idea what you're talking about," I said, echoing her earlier denial. "Must be thinking of someone else. Maybe one of your other clients who makes lethal blue cocktails on private islands."

She gave me a grateful smile. "Must be. I have so many of those, they all blur together."

We found a small local restaurant for lunch, a weathered wooden structure right on the beach with mismatched chairs and tables set directly in the sand. The menu was written on a chalkboard, and the only options were whatever had been caught that morning.

"This is amazing," Anica said as our food arrived; grilled fish so fresh it had probably been swimming an hour earlier, served with rice and plantains. "How did you find this place?"

"The first time I came to the island, I got spectacularly lost. Ended up here by accident. Best wrong turn I ever made. Unlike that time I accidentally walked into the women's restroom at the Met Gala. Much less charming outcome, considerably more screaming."

"Sounds like you might actually be human."

"What else would I be?"

"Well, Mari's guess is Greek god. Devonna mentioned something about an immortal vampire. I'd go for very advanced AI."

I chuckled, nudging her foot under the table. "Just Callan. Human guy from Queens."

She considered this as she took another bite of fish. "I think I like 'just Callan' better than 'Callan Burkhardt, tech billionaire.'"

"Yeah?"

"Yeah. He seems more real. Less rehearsed."

"I am quite rehearsed. You have to be, when everyone's watching. One wrong move, one bad decision, and suddenly you're not the boy genius anymore. You're the cautionary tale. The guy people reference in business school as 'what not to do with your first billion.'"

"That sounds exhausting."

"It can be. There's this constant pressure to never fail. To always have the answer. To be the smartest person in every room."

"Are you?" she asked. "The smartest person in every room?"

"Usually. Until I met you," I said with a grin, then sobered. "But that's not the point. The point is that everyone expects me to be. And when your whole identity, your whole value, is built around being the guy with the answers..."

"You can't ever admit you don't know something," she finished for me.

"Exactly."

She nodded, understanding in her eyes. "I get that, in a way. Not the billionaire part, obviously. But the pressure to always have the answer, to always be in control. To make it look effortless even when you're barely holding it together."

"Wedding planning," I guessed.

"It's not just about making pretty centerpieces," she confirmed. "It's about managing expectations, emotions, family dynamics... all while making it look easy. If I plan everything perfectly, nothing can go wrong."

"Except when it does anyway," I pointed out. "Like sprinkler systems with a vendetta against wedding dresses."

"That's what the emergency kits are for. And the backup plans for the backup plans. And the emergency contact list for when the backup to the backup fails. And sometimes, apparently, billionaires who show up at the last minute to help save the day."

"I do look dashing in a superhero cape. Though the spandex chafes in unfortunate places."

"You're very good at that," she observed.

"At chafing? I mean, I wouldn't say I'm good at it, more that I'm particularly susceptible to—"

"At deflecting. Whenever the conversation gets too real, you make a joke."

I blinked, caught off guard by her insight. "Force of habit. Vulnerability isn't exactly encouraged in board rooms."

"We're not in a board room," she pointed out, gesturing to the water.

"No," I agreed, meeting her eyes. "We're not."

A seagull dive-bombed our table, snatching a piece of fish and breaking the spell.

"Feathered menace!" I shouted, waving my hands. "Go steal from the tourists with fanny packs! They expect it!"

Anica burst out laughing, and I joined her

We finished our meal and continued exploring the island, wandering through small shops and along the beach. The afternoon slipped away without either of us noticing, lost in conversation that ranged from childhood memories to professional disasters to favorite movies (she loved old black and white films, I preferred action blockbusters with improbable explosions).

"Tell me something no one else knows about you," I said as we walked along the water's edge, shoes in hand, letting the warm water lap at our feet. "Something that would shock your clients."

She thought for a moment. "I hate cake."

"What?" I stopped walking, genuinely surprised. "But you're a wedding planner! Cake is like... 30% of your job!"

She grimaced. "I know. It's terrible. I can appreciate a well-made cake aesthetically, but I've never understood the appeal. Too sweet, too much frosting, too... cake-like."

"This is scandalous. Like finding out a sommelier secretly drinks boxed wine, or a fashion designer who wears sweatpants at home."

"I do wear sweatpants at home," she admitted. "The rattiest, most comfortable ones you can imagine. With holes in inappropriate places."

"Stop, I can only handle so many revelations in one day," I clutched my chest dramatically. "Next you'll tell me you have a secret collection of reality TV shows on your DVR."

"All the Real Housewives franchises," she confirmed. "And several baking competitions, ironically."

I laughed. "You're full of surprises, darling. What would you have at your wedding reception since you don't like cake?"

Anica shrugged. "Cookies. All different sorts."

"Favorite?"

"There's this recipe my mom and I made. It's an oatmeal chocolate chip cookie. It's amazing, but they have to be at least five hundred calories a cookie. Those have to be my favorite." She glanced sidelong at me. "Your turn," she said. "Tell me something no one knows about the great Callan Burkhardt."

"I'm afraid of jellyfish. Terrified, actually. Like, full-on panic attack, grown man crying terror."

"Jellyfish?" she repeated, clearly fighting a smile. "The billionaire tech genius with multiple homes and a private island is afraid of jellyfish?"

"Have you seen those things?" I defended myself. "They're basically floating bags of poison with tentacles. No faces, no brains, just... ghostly death sacks drifting through the water waiting to sting you. They're like nature's way of saying 'fuck you in particular.'"

She lost the battle with her smile, breaking into laughter. "Ghostly death sacks? That's your assessment?"

"I stand by it. They're an abomination. And don't get me started on the immortal ones."

"The what now?"

"There's a species of jellyfish that's technically immortal. They can revert to an earlier stage of development when injured or stressed. Basically, they're unkillable poison ghosts of the sea."

"How do you know so much about something you're terrified of?" she asked, still laughing.

"Know thy enemy," I replied gravely. "I have a Google alert set up for jellyfish scientific advancements. I need to be prepared for the inevitable jellyfish uprising. When they evolve arms and develop political aspirations, I'll be ready."

The sun was beginning its descent toward the horizon, painting the sky in brilliant shades of orange and pink. I checked my watch and realized we'd been wandering for hours.

"We should probably head back soon. Before it gets dark."

Anica checked her watch and looked surprised. "I had no idea it was so late. Where did the day go?"

"Time flies when you're having fun," I said, then grimaced. "God, that was cheesy. Please forget I said something so profoundly unoriginal. I have a reputation as a witty billionaire to maintain."

"Your secret's safe with me," she promised. "I won't tell anyone you occasionally resort to clichés like a normal person."

We started making our way back toward the marina, but I walked slower than necessary, trying to prolong our time together.

"Let's take a different route," I suggested, gesturing toward a path that followed the beach. "The sunset should be spectacular from there."

She agreed, and we strolled along the water's edge, the dying sun casting long shadows across the sand.

"This is perfect," Anica said softly, watching the play of light on the water. "Thank you for bringing me here."

"My pleasure," I replied, and meant it. "I'm glad you agreed to come. Even with the hangover."

"The hangover was worth it. Though I maintain those drinks of yours should come with a warning label."

"'Caution: May lead to confessions about haunted vaginas'?" I suggested innocently.

She groaned, covering her face with her hands. "Shit, I was hoping you'd forgotten that part."

"I forget nothing. Especially not creative metaphors about female anatomy. That's going in my memoir. Chapter title: 'The Wedding Planner and the Haunted House Between Her Legs.'"

"I will murder you and hide your body where no one will ever find it," she threatened, but she was laughing. "I know at least three wedding vendors who would help me dispose of the evidence, no questions asked."

"It would totally be worth it. Some stories are too good not to share with the world."

We continued along the beach, watching in companionable silence as the sun touched the horizon, sending streams of golden light across the water. It was one of those perfect moments that seem to exist outside of normal time, suspended in a bubble of contentment.

So of course I had to ruin it by checking my watch and realizing I'd made a catastrophic miscalculation.

"Oh, shit," I muttered, stopping abruptly.

"What's wrong?" Anica asked, concern immediately replacing her relaxed expression.

"The boat. The last one back to my island leaves at 6:30. It's 6:45."

"So we missed it. We'll just call for a water taxi or something, right?"

"That would be a great solution. If water taxis operated in this area. Or if there was reliable cell service to call one."

Her eyes widened. "Are you telling me we're stuck here? On this island? Overnight?"

"Unless you're hiding a teleportation device in that very flattering outfit, then yes, that's exactly what I'm telling you."

"But—that's—we can't—" she spluttered, her composure finally cracking, and I couldn't hide my grin behind my hand fast enough. "This isn't funny, Callan!" But a reluctant smile tugged at her lips. "What are we supposed to do?"

"Well, there's a charming little bed-and-breakfast near the marina. We can stay there tonight, catch the first ferry back in the morning. It's not ideal, but it's an adventure."

"An adventure. You and your adventures are going to be the death of me."

"But what a way to go," I said cheerfully, taking her hand and tugging her back toward the town. "Come on, it'll be fun. Like an unplanned sleepover."

"I have no toothbrush," she protested. "No change of clothes. No—anything!"

"The B&B will have toiletries. And I'm sure we can find something for you to sleep in. Worst-case scenario, you can borrow my shirt. Apparently, they're quite comfortable, and you already own my soul according to ancient shirt law, so what's one more? Soon you'll have a complete collection of Callan Burkhardt body parts via clothing acquisition."

She groaned but allowed me to lead her back toward town. "You're enjoying this, aren't you?"

"The opportunity to spend more time with you? Why would I enjoy that? It's not like you're intelligent, funny, beautiful, and capable of making me laugh harder than anyone has in years. Oh wait."

She shot me a look that suggested she wasn't buying my innocent act, but she didn't pull her hand away from mine. I counted that as a win.

The bed-and-breakfast was exactly as I remembered it. A quaint two-story house painted a cheerful yellow, with a wraparound porch dotted with rocking chairs. The proprietor, Mrs. Albury, was a plump, grandmotherly woman with a perpetual smile and an accent that suggested she'd moved here from Cuba decades ago.

"Mr. Burkhardt!" she exclaimed when we walked in. "It's been too long! And you've brought a friend this time!" She looked Anica up and down approvingly. "This one has meat on her bones. Good child-bearing hips."

Anica made a strangled sound beside me as I fought to keep a straight face. "Mrs. Albury, this is Anica. We missed the last ferry and need a place to stay for the night. Please tell me you have a room available."

"For you? Always," she assured me, but her smile faltered slightly as she checked her book. "Although... I only have one room left. The honeymoon suite."

Of course. Because the universe has a sense of humor, and apparently it's twelve years old and raised on sitcom plots.

"That's fine," I said quickly, before Anica could protest. "We'll take it."

Mrs. Albury beamed at us. "You two remind me of me and my Gerold when we were young. So full of life and love. The way you look at each other—" she clasped her hands to her chest, "—it makes my old heart happy."

"Oh, we're not—" Anica began.

"Thank you," I interrupted smoothly. "Anica's a bit shy about public displays of affection. Very professional. Doesn't want people to know she's madly in love with me."

Mrs. Albury patted Anica's hand. "No need to be shy here, dear. Love is beautiful at any age. You hold on to this one. Men who look at women the way he looks at you are rare, like good mangoes in winter."

Anica shot me a look that promised retribution, but she smiled politely at our host. "You're very kind."

After settling the payment and collecting a toothbrush and other necessities from Mrs. Albury's stash for stranded travelers, we were shown to the honeymoon suite. It was charming in that old-fashioned B&B way—floral wallpaper, antique furniture, and a four-poster bed draped with mosquito netting.

One bed. A queen-sized bed that suddenly looked very small for two adults, one of whom was trying very hard not to think about the other one in a non-professional capacity.

"I'll take the floor," I offered immediately once Mrs. Albury had left us alone.

"Don't be ridiculous," Anica sighed, looking exhausted. "We're adults. The bed is plenty big."

"Are you sure?" I asked, giving her an out. "Because I'm perfectly happy to—"

"Callan," she interrupted. "After the day we've had, the last thing I need is to ruin it by feeling guilty about you sleeping on a hardwood floor. We can share the bed. Just... stay on your side."

"Yes, ma'am," I said, saluting. "I shall construct a pillow wall if necessary. Perhaps draw a line down the middle with lipstick. Create a DMZ of blankets. Hire tiny border patrol agents to enforce the boundary."

"Or you could just be a normal person who respects boundaries," she suggested.

"That sounds significantly less fun. But I accept your terms. No crossing the International Date Line of the mattress without proper documentation and approval from border control."

The awkwardness of the situation hit us both as we stared at the room clearly designed for honeymooners, complete with rose petals scattered across the turned-down sheets and what appeared to be massage oils on the nightstand.

"I'm going to take a shower," Anica announced, grabbing the toiletry kit Mrs. Albury had provided. "And pretend this isn't the most uncomfortable situation I've been in since my cousin's wedding where the best man proposed to the maid of honor during the toast and she said no."

"Ouch," I winced. "That's rough."

"He had a backup speech."

I burst out laughing. "No way. That's diabolical."

"True story," she assured me, disappearing into the bathroom.

I heard the shower start and tried very, very hard not to think about Anica naked and wet just a few feet away. Instead, I busied myself removing the rose petals from the bed and turning on the ceiling fan to combat the island's humid night air. I also found and discreetly relocated a book titled "101 Tantric Techniques for Newlyweds" that Mrs. Albury had thoughtfully left on the nightstand.

When Anica emerged twenty minutes later, her hair was damp and she wore a button-down shirt, the hem hitting her mid-thigh. She'd rolled up the sleeves, and the effect was both adorable and unexpectedly sexy.

"Mrs. Albury said I could borrow this," she explained, gesturing to the shirt and a pair of men's boxers just visible beneath the shirt's hem. "Apparently her son leaves clothes here sometimes. They're clean," she added hastily.

"Good to know," I managed, my mouth suddenly dry. "I'll, uh, take my turn now."

I grabbed the remaining toiletries and escaped to the bathroom, where I took the quickest, coldest shower of my adult life. With no alternative, I had to put my shorts back on, deciding to sleep shirtless rather than in my sweaty, salt-crusted button-down.

When I returned to the bedroom, Anica was already in bed, perched as far to one side as physically possible without falling off. She glanced up from examining her phone, which still had no service, and her eyes widened slightly at my bare chest before she very deliberately looked away.

"Sorry," I said, gesturing to my lack of shirt. "It was either this or put back on the shirt that smells like I enjoy marinating in seawater and sunscreen."

"It's fine," she said quickly, looking anywhere but at me. "Just, you know, stay on your side."

"As promised," I agreed, sliding into the opposite side of the bed, careful to leave as much space between us as the queen mattress would allow. "Good night, Anica."

"Good night, Callan," she replied, reaching to turn off the lamp.

The room plunged into darkness, illuminated only by slivers of moonlight filtering through the curtains. I lay on my back, staring at the ceiling, acutely aware of her presence beside me. Her breathing was too measured, too careful, to suggest she was anywhere close to sleep.

"This is ridiculous," she said finally, breaking the silence. "I'm not going to be able to sleep if I'm this tense."

"Want me to tell you a bedtime story?"

179

"I'd rather just... talk. Until I'm tired enough to fall asleep."

"What do you want to talk about?" I asked, turning onto my side to face her, though I could only make out her silhouette in the dim light.

"Anything," she replied. "Tell me something real. Something you don't tell people in board meetings or at galas."

I considered this for a moment. "I'm terrified of ending up alone," I admitted, the darkness making honesty easier somehow. "Not just without a partner, but truly alone. No real connections. Just people who want something from me. Especially when I lose Gram."

She was quiet for a moment. "Is that why you made the bet? To prove you don't need real connection?"

"Maybe. Or maybe to prove I can control it. Keep it on my terms."

"That's not how it works. Real connection, I mean. You can't control it. That's what makes it real."

"Says the woman who controls every single detail of every single day," I teased.

"Touché," she conceded. "We're both control freaks in our own way."

"Match made in heaven," I joked, then immediately regretted it. "Sorry, that was—"

"It's okay. We're good at pretending to be engaged, apparently. Mrs. Albury certainly bought it."

"We should go into business together. Professional fake couple. We could rent ourselves out for awkward family gatherings. 'Want to shut up your nosy aunt? Hire us to pretend we're madly in love and about to elope to Vegas.'"

She laughed, the sound warm in the darkness. "I can see the Craigslist ad now. 'One slightly used billionaire and his wedding planner available for rental. Good at pretending to be in love, terrible at catching ferries.'"

"Hey, missing that ferry was a strategic decision. All part of my master plan."

"To what? Get stranded on an island with your wedding planner?"

"Exactly. Mission accomplished."

She was quiet for a moment, and I worried I'd gone too far. "Callan..." she began hesitantly. "What are we doing?"

180

"Currently? Lying in bed having a conversation."

"You know what I mean," she said, and I could hear the frown in her voice. "This... whatever this is. The island, the boat trip, sharing a bed. It's not normal."

"No. It's not."

"So what is it?"

I took a deep breath. "I like you, Anica. More than I should. More than is professional or convenient or part of the plan. I like the way you laugh when you think no one's watching. I like how you plan for every disaster but still roll with the punches when the unexpected happens. I like that you wear La Perla underwear under those business suits but pretend it doesn't matter how you look. I like that you hate cake but plan weddings anyway."

"You noticed my underwear?" she asked, her voice slightly higher than normal.

"I notice everything about you. It's becoming a problem."

She was silent for so long that I thought I'd completely misread the situation. Then I felt her hand find mine in the darkness, her fingers intertwining with mine.

"I like you too," she whispered. "And it's definitely a problem."

"Because of the contract?" I asked, hardly daring to breathe.

"Because of everything," she said. "The contract, the bride hunt, the bet. You're literally paying me to find you a wife, Callan. That's complicated on a good day. This is... messy."

"I've never been good at staying inside the lines," I admitted, squeezing her hand gently. "Even as a kid. Always coloring outside them, making my own rules."

"Some rules exist for a reason. Professional boundaries protect both of us."

"From what?" I challenged. "From feeling something real?"

She sighed, and she shifted closer. "From getting hurt. I can't go through that again, Callan. Not after Austin."

"I would never—"

"You're planning to marry someone else. That's literally why we met."

I had no good answer for that. She was right, of course. This whole situation was a mess of my own making.

"I don't have to," I said finally. "Go through with it, I mean. The bet. The arrangement. Any of it."

"And lose thirty million dollars? Your friends would never let you live it down."

"Some things are worth more than money or pride," I said quietly. Her hand was still in mine.

"We should probably sleep. It's been a long day."

"Yeah," I agreed, though I made no move to release her hand, and she didn't pull away.

"Good night, Callan," she whispered.

"Good night, darling."

A VERY HANDS-ON CONSULTATION

Chapter 13: Anica

I woke up with my face smooshed against a set of abs that could only have been carved by an ancient deity with a personal vendetta against shirts. For a blissful moment, I thought I'd finally achieved my dream of being transformed into a body pillow for Greek gods, until I realized the abs were attached to my client. My extremely aroused client, judging by the impressive tent pitched in the general vicinity of my thigh.

Holy. Shit.

Somehow during the night, the careful demilitarized zone we'd established in the middle of the bed had been utterly demolished. Not only had I crossed enemy lines, I'd apparently annexed the entire territory, planted a flag, and established permanent settlements. My head was nestled against Callan's chest, one of my legs was thrown over his, and my arm was draped across his stomach like I was protecting the last cupcake at a birthday party.

But the real kicker? His arm was wrapped around me, holding me close, his fingers tangled in my hair like he was afraid I might escape. Which, had I been fully awake and in possession of my faculties, would have been a very legitimate fear.

For a blissful, drowsy moment, I let myself enjoy the sensation. The steady rhythm of his heart beneath my ear. The warm, clean scent of his skin. The way our bodies fit together like puzzle pieces designed by a particularly horny jigsaw manufacturer.

Then reality hit me like a bucket of ice water laced with shame and professional ethics violations.

Oh my god. I was cuddling with my client. My very aroused client with a morning situation that could double as a tentpole for a circus. Who I was supposed to be finding a wife for. Who was not supposed to be pressed against me with what feels like nature's most impressive kickstand.

I carefully extricated myself from our accidental embrace. The last thing I needed was for him to wake up and find me wrapped around him like an octopus with boundary issues.

Too late. As I shifted away, Callan stirred, his eyes fluttering open. For a moment, he looked confused, then a slow, lazy smile spread across his face as he registered our position.

"Good morning," he murmured, his voice deliciously rough with sleep. "I see the border patrol failed spectacularly at their job. Not only did you cross the border, you annexed the territory and established a dictatorship."

"I—I must have moved in my sleep," I stammered, scooting back to my side of the bed. "Sorry about that. I'm not usually a... a cuddler."

"Nothing to apologize for," he replied, stretching in a way that made the sheet slip dangerously low on his hips where his boner still stood tall. "Best night's sleep I've had in months, actually. You make an excellent blanket. Ten out of ten, would be smothered again."

"We should probably get going," I said, desperately changing the subject and ignoring the heat creeping up my neck. "The ferry will be leaving soon."

"Eager to escape, are we?" he asked, raising an eyebrow.

"You seem...um...I'm going to, uh..." I couldn't keep my gaze from dropping to his dick multiple times. Instead of finishing my sentence, I scrambled off the bed, gathered the clothes from the day before, and scurried towards the bathroom. "I'll be out in a minute."

"Wait, Anica," he said, shifting like he was going to get up.

I stared at the ceiling like my life depended on it. "Yes?"

"We should talk about last night."

"Nope. Last night did not happen as of right now."

"Is that what you want?" he asked, his tone switched to something more serious. "To pretend this never happened?"

I paused, my back to him. "I think it's what we need to do."

"Not the same thing," he pointed out.

"No, but it's the sensible thing. And I'm nothing if not sensible. I'm going to shower," I announced, fleeing to the bathroom before he could say anything else. "Maybe deal with your issue before I get back."

"No promises!" He called after me.

Under the spray of lukewarm water (apparently hot water was a luxury the B&B couldn't quite manage), I tried to regain my composure. It was just physical proximity. Just a biological reaction to an attractive man. It didn't mean anything. The fluttering in my stomach when he smiled at me was probably just hunger. Or possibly a tropical parasite. Definitely not feelings. Feelings were for other people.

By the time I emerged, fully dressed and mentally armored, Callan had also dressed and was chatting amiably with Mrs. Albury in the breakfast nook downstairs. The elderly woman beamed at me as I approached.

"Ah! There she is! I was just telling Mr. Burkhardt that you two were the quietest couple we've ever had. Usually, the guests in that room keep the whole house awake!" She winked conspiratorially. "But quality over quantity, yes? Sometimes the quiet ones are the most satisfied. Like my second husband. Silent as a monk in public, but in the bedroom…well, let's just say the neighbors filed noise complaints."

I nearly choked on air. "We didn't…we're not—"

"Darling, Mrs. Albury made us a special breakfast," Callan interrupted smoothly, his eyes dancing with mischief. "Apparently it's her famous 'morning after' spread. Lots of protein. For energy. To replace what was… expended."

"Is that right?" I asked weakly, wondering if it was possible to die from embarrassment. Medical journals would study my case: "Woman Spontaneously Combusts Due to B&B Owner's Sex Assumptions."

"You need to keep your strength up," Mrs. Albury insisted, patting my arm. "Especially with a man like this one. I can tell he has stamina. It's in the shoulders. My third husband had shoulders like that. Once went for six hours straight. Had to ice my—"

"Pancakes!" I interrupted desperately. "Are those pancakes? They look delicious. I love pancakes. Pancakes are great. Let's talk about pancakes and nothing else. Ever."

Callan's shoulders were shaking as I sank into the chair across from him.

"Orange juice?" he offered innocently. "Freshly squeezed. Like your —"

"I hate you," I mouthed silently.

"No, you don't," he mouthed back, winking. "You think my abs were carved by Greek gods."

I froze. "I said that out loud?"

"You mumble when you're sleepy," he informed me cheerfully. "It's adorable. Sort of like when you're drunk."

"Kill me now. Just strike me dead on the spot. I will never recover from this."

Breakfast was a special kind of torture, with Mrs. Albury making increasingly unsubtle comments about our "honeymoon" while Callan played along shamelessly. By the time she started describing a particular technique involving a banana and what she called "the double entendre," I was seriously contemplating swimming back to his island rather than endure the ferry ride with him.

"You two come back anytime," Mrs. Albury said as we prepared to leave. "Next time, ask for the room with the reinforced bedframe. For when you're feeling less... restrained. My fourth husband and I broke three beds and a ceiling fan before we found furniture that could withstand our passion."

"We will definitely keep that in mind," Callan assured her, while I silently calculated the exact amount of alcohol required to permanently erase this conversation from my memory. God, maybe I would drink rum sooner than I thought.

The walk to the dock was mercifully short, though the morning humidity had already turned the air thick. We reached the ferry just as it was preparing to depart, joining a handful of other passengers for the journey back.

"That wasn't so bad, was it?" Callan asked as we found seats near the railing. "Being mistaken for a happily married couple on their sex-filled honeymoon?"

"Speak for yourself," I muttered. "I'm going to need therapy to recover from Mrs. Albury's description of her third husband's stamina techniques. I will never look at kitchen utensils the same way again."

"I thought the part about the bananas was quite educational," he replied, straight-faced. "Though anatomically improbable. At least without significant practice and possibly a physics degree."

Despite myself, I laughed.

"So about my Greek god abs..."

"I'm never going to live that down, am I?"

"Not in this lifetime. I'm having it engraved on my business cards. 'Callan Burkhardt, CEO, Billionaire, Possessor of Deity-Level Abdominal Muscles.'"

We lapsed into a surprisingly comfortable silence as the ferry pulled away from the dock, watching the island recede in the distance. The awkwardness I'd feared didn't materialize; instead, a strange sense of intimacy had settled between us. As if the night we'd spent talking in the darkness, sharing secrets and holding hands, had shifted something fundamental in our relationship.

That was the problem. We weren't supposed to have a relationship beyond the professional. Yet, I was hyperaware of every movement he made, every brush of his arm against mine, every smile that crinkled the corners of his eyes.

Get it together, Anica, I scolded myself. *You are a professional. You have a job to do. A job that specifically involves finding this man a wife who is not you. A job that absolutely does not include thinking about those abs or what might have happened if you'd woken up five minutes earlier and decided to explore the territory south of the border.*

As we approached Callan's island, my phone vibrated in my back pocket; the first sign of service returning. I pulled it out to find a barrage of notifications filling my screen. The first four were from Mari.

MARI: Did you climb him like a tree yet? If not, I'm disowning you as my business partner and best friend.

MARI: Hello? Are you alive or did you die from sexual frustration?

MARI: If you're not responding because you're having wild billionaire sex, I forgive you. DETAILS REQUIRED UPON RETURN.

MARI: Devonna says I should stop texting you, but she also put $20 in the "they didn't do it" pool, so who's the real enabler here?

The next two from Devonna weren't particularly better.

DEVONNA: Hope you're enjoying the island. The Rickter-Bingly wedding has requested a last-minute change to their menu. Also, Mari has started a betting pool about your weekend activities that is highly inappropriate. I put twenty dollars on "mutual pining but no action." Please don't disappoint me.

DEVONNA: P.S. If you did sleep with him, I'll forgive you for making me lose the bet if you provide a detailed rating of his performance. For statistical purposes only.

I quickly shoved my phone back into my pocket before Callan could see the messages, but not before noticing he was frowning at his own screen.

"Everything okay?" I asked.

"Just catching up," he replied vaguely, thumbs flying across his phone. "Angie's sent a few messages."

Right. The perfect candidate. The woman who actually fit his criteria, unlike the wedding planner who was currently fighting an inappropriate attraction to her client and losing badly. Like, surrendering-the-white-flag, waving-it-while-sobbing badly.

"That's good. Is she eager to continue where you left off?" I asked, aiming for a neutral tone and landing somewhere closer to "slightly constipated sea lion."

"Right. Yes," he said, not looking up from his phone.

I hated myself for the disappointment that settled in my stomach like a lead weight. What had I expected? That one night of hand-holding and confessions would make him abandon his plan? That he'd suddenly declare his undying love for me instead of pursuing his arrangement with a woman who actually made sense?

"I should check in with the office." I pulled out my own phone again and pretended to be absorbed in work emails. "Make sure no brides have committed felonies in my absence."

The rest of the ferry ride passed in silence, each of us retreating into our respective digital worlds, the easy camaraderie of the past twenty-four hours evaporating like morning mist under the harsh sun of reality.

By the time we docked at Callan's private marina, I'd recreated my professional walls back to their full height. Bulletproof. Impenetrable.

Definitely not vulnerable to smiles or hand-holding or morning erections that could very well rearrange a woman's insides.

On second thought, poor Angelina.

"I'll have Rhonda prepare your things," Callan said as we walked toward the main house. "The jet can take you back to New York whenever you're ready."

"The sooner the better," I replied, keeping my tone businesslike. "I have client meetings tomorrow."

"Of course." Was it my imagination, or did he sound disappointed? "I'll be back in the city on Tuesday. Should we schedule another bride candidate meeting then? Angie's great, but I'm sure you have others lined up."

"I'll have Devonna set it up," I agreed, the words tasting bitter. "I've narrowed it down to three promising options based on your previous feedback."

"Looking forward to it," he said, though his smile didn't quite reach his eyes.

We parted ways at the main house, Callan heading to his office for what he claimed were urgent business calls, me retreating to the guest bungalow to pack. An hour later, I was alone on his private jet heading back to New York, a strange emptiness settling in my chest that had nothing to do with altitude changes and everything to do with the man I was leaving behind.

"You've checked your phone fifty-four times today."

I looked up from my desk—and yes, my phone—to find Mari leaning in my office doorway, arms crossed and eyebrows raised in an expression of supreme judgment.

"I'm expecting an important email from a vendor," I lied, setting the phone down.

"And does this vendor's name rhyme with 'Fallan'?"

"I don't know any vendors named Fallan," I replied. "Though there is that new florist, Allen, who's been unreliable with his quote for the Luca wedding."

"Cut the shit, Anica," Mari said, dropping into the chair across from me. "You've been moping since you got back from Billionaire Island yesterday. You haven't mentioned Callan once, which is suspicious since you spent an entire weekend alone with him. And Devonna says you've started stress-organizing the emergency kits by category and color, which you only do when you're avoiding your feelings so hard they could file a restraining order."

"I'm not avoiding anything," I insisted, straightening the already perfectly aligned stack of papers on my desk. "I had a professional weekend with a client, came back, and now I'm focused on work. Like a professional. Because that's what I am. Professional."

"You said 'professional' three times in that sentence," Mari pointed out. "Which means you did something extremely unprofessional. Like, 'caught giving a lap dance to the DJ at the reception' unprofessional. Spill."

"There's nothing to spill," I maintained; however, she kept staring at me in that knowing way that I finally threw my head back and sighed. "Fine. We missed the ferry, had to stay overnight in a B&B, shared a bed because there were no other options, and nothing happened."

"You shared a bed?" Mari screeched, loud enough that I was sure the entire building heard her. "And nothing happened? What is wrong with you two? Were you both wearing full body casts? Did you develop a sudden allergy to orgasms? Is his penis purely decorative?"

"We held hands," I admitted in a small voice. "And talked. About real things. Feelings and fears and... stuff."

Mari stared at me in horror. "Oh my god. That's worse than if you'd just slept with him. You're emotionally involved. That's like skipping straight past casual sex to U-Hauling your feelings into his emotional apartment."

"I am not—"

"Save it for someone who hasn't known you since college," she interrupted. "You're into him. Like, really into him. Not just his abs or his billions or his perfect butt, but the actual person. The real Callan, not just the Burkhardt packaging."

I buried my face in my hands. "It doesn't matter. He's still planning to marry someone else. That's literally why he hired us."

"But you said little is working out with the candidates," Mari pointed out.

"He likes Angie."

"The bitch robot with perfect hair and non-bouncy ass?"

"Yeah." The word came out all mopey.

"I doubt he actually likes her." Mari wrinkled her nose. "There is such a thing as too perfect. Maybe this is all a sign."

"A sign of what? That I'm bad at my job?"

"That maybe the right candidate has been standing in front of him this whole time," she suggested gently. "Wearing pencil skirts and organizing chaotic weddings and occasionally drooling on his abs in her sleep."

"Don't," I pleaded. "Don't give me hope where there isn't any. He's meeting with three new candidates this week. One of them will work out. One of them has to."

"And if none of them do?"

"Then I'll find more. We have only a few weeks before his wedding," I pointed out. "That's my job. That's what he's paying me for."

"Is that really all this is to you? Just a job?"

I couldn't answer that. Not honestly. Not without admitting that somewhere between the wedding expo and the island, between blue cocktails and handholding in the dark, Callan Burkhardt had become much more than just a client to me.

"I have work to do," I said instead, turning back to my computer.

Mari sighed but took the hint, rising from her chair. "For what it's worth," she said, pausing at the door, "I think you're making this more complicated than it needs to be. Just tell him how you feel."

"It's not that simple."

"It never is, but sometimes it's worth it anyway."

After she left, I sat staring at my blank computer screen, her words echoing in my head. Just tell him how you feel. As if I could just walk up to Callan Burkhardt, billionaire client who had hired me specifically to find him a wife, and say, "Hey, I think I might be falling for you, despite all my professional boundaries and the fact that you're planning to marry someone else as part of an elaborate bet with your frat boy friends."

Yeah. That would go over great. About as well as suggesting a clown officiate a formal wedding.

My phone buzzed, and I snatched it up embarrassingly fast, my heart doing a little flip when I saw Callan's name on the screen.

CALLAN: Change of plans. Can you come to my penthouse tonight instead of tomorrow? 7pm. Something's come up.

My fingers hovered over the keys as I debated my response. The professional thing would be to reschedule for normal business hours. To maintain boundaries. To not go to his penthouse at night like some booty call disguised as a business meeting.

ANICA: I'll be there.

Professional Anica was apparently on vacation. Possibly still on an island. Drinking something blue and making poor life choices.

CALLAN'S PENTHOUSE WAS exactly as I remembered it from our first meeting. The man himself answered the door looking decidedly less polished than usual, in jeans and a simple t-shirt, his hair slightly rumpled as if he'd been running his hands through it.

"Thanks for coming," he said, stepping back to let me in. "Sorry for the last-minute change."

"Not a problem," I replied, clutching my portfolio of bride candidates in front of me. "I brought the files on the three women we discussed. All of them are available this week for meetings if any catch your interest. I know Angie is the top contender, but like you said, I still have options for you if you'd like."

"About that," Callan said, leading me toward the living area. "There's been a change with her."

"What kind of change?" I asked, taking a seat on the edge of the sofa.

"I broke things off."

"What? With Angie?" I blinked, caught off guard. "But she was perfect. Intelligent, accomplished, beautiful—"

"She asked me to sign a prenup," he interrupted, running a hand through his hair. "Her prenup. An eighty-seven page document her family's lawyers prepared. Before we'd even had a third date."

"Oh," I said, genuinely surprised. "That's... forward."

"It had a clause about scheduled sex," he continued, pacing now.

192

"Twice a week, with provisions for 'reasonable performance expectations' and a section titled 'Allowable Excuses for Non-Compliance.'"

I nearly choked. "You're kidding."

"I wish I were. There was also a detailed breakdown of acceptable vacation destinations categorized by season and a mandatory attendance policy for her family's holiday gatherings, with financial penalties for missing her second cousin's annual Labor Day barbecue."

"That's..."

"Insane? Terrifying? The relationship equivalent of being fitted for a straitjacket while still on the first date?"

"I was going to say 'thorough,'" I offered. "But yes, those too."

"I mean, I appreciate preparation, but this was like she was drafting a corporate merger where my body and time were the assets being acquired." He shuddered visibly. "When I pointed out that it seemed premature, she said, and I quote, 'I like to maximize efficiency in all my endeavors, and this union presents optimal synergies for both our brands.'"

I couldn't help it. I laughed. "She actually said 'synergies'? In a romantic context?"

"While we were having dinner at Per Se. Right after suggesting we should 'align our public personas for maximum market penetration.' I nearly choked on my foie gras."

"Okay, that is legitimately terrible," I admitted. "But that's what you said you wanted, isn't it? A practical arrangement. A business transaction with romantic window dressing."

"There's practical, and then there's treating marriage like a hostile takeover," he countered. "I may be cynical, but even I draw the line at 'performance metrics for bedroom activities.'"

"But you've turned down all of the candidates!" I exclaimed, frustration bubbling up. "Each one was too something. Too serious, too frivolous, too career-focused, too family-oriented. And now too... businesslike? It's like you're deliberately sabotaging this process."

"Maybe I don't know what I want," he admitted, running a hand through his hair.

"Or maybe you don't want to find it," I shot back.

His gaze snapped to mine, something dangerous flickering in their blue depths. "What's that supposed to mean?"

193

"It means," I said, standing up and taking a step toward him, "that you've rejected every qualified candidate for increasingly specific reasons. It means you're running out of time to win your bet. It means I'm beginning to think you hired me under false pretenses."

"False pretenses?" He took a step closer, his voice dropping. "Please, enlighten me."

"Maybe you never intended to go through with this arrangement," I suggested, taking another step forward. "Maybe the whole thing was just a game to you. A way to prove something to your friends, or to yourself."

"You don't know what you're talking about," he said, closing the distance between us even further.

"Don't I? Are you trying to lose this bet? We have only a few weeks left!" I challenged, tilting my head back to look up at him.

"Maybe the bet doesn't matter as much anymore," he replied, his voice low.

"It's thirty million dollars and literally why you hired me!" I was almost shouting now, my professional composure in tatters. "I've spent weeks finding qualified candidates, creating compatibility charts, orchestrating meetings—"

"I don't want any of them!"

"Then what do you want?"

"You," he shouted, and suddenly his hands were cupping my face and his lips were on mine.

For a millisecond, I froze in shock. Then every rational thought fled my brain as I melted into the kiss, my hands flying up to grip his shoulders. The potential bride folder dropped to the floor at our feet, papers scattering everywhere. In that moment, I couldn't have cared less.

This was nothing like the businesslike kisses I'd shared with other men. This was a wildfire, consuming everything in its path. His lips were firm yet gentle, commanding yet questioning, like he'd been thinking about this moment as long as I had. When his tongue traced the seam of my mouth, I opened to him with a soft moan, and the kiss deepened into something that made my knees go weak and my insides turn molten.

My hands slid into his hair, reveling in its softness, while his moved from my face to my waist, pulling me flush against him until every hard plane of his body aligned with mine. The evidence of his desire pressed against my stomach, and a whimper escaped me at the contact.

His mouth left mine to explore my jaw, trailing fire along my skin. When he reached the sensitive spot just below my ear, he paused, his breath hot against me.

"I've been thinking about this since the moment you walked in here the first time," he confessed, his voice a rough whisper that sent shivers through me. "Looking at me like I was a problem to be solved."

"You are a problem," I managed, though it came out breathy as his teeth grazed my earlobe. "A big, arrogant, impossible problem."

"But you like solving problems," he reminded me, his hand sliding down to cup my ass and pull me tighter against him. "It's what you do."

The pressure of his arousal against me sent a bolt of liquid heat straight to my core. I arched into him, seeking more of that delicious friction, and was rewarded with a deep groan that rumbled through his chest.

"Callan," I gasped as his fingers deftly unfastened the first button of my blouse, then the second. "We shouldn't—"

"We absolutely should," he disagreed, pressing a kiss to the newly exposed skin at the base of my throat. "In fact, I can think of at least seventeen reasons why we should, and they all involve making you forget words like 'professional' and 'boundaries' and 'client.'"

The third button popped open, revealing the lacy edge of my bra — the good one, thank god, not the practical beige one I sometimes wore to client meetings.

"La Perla," Callan observed, tracing the lace with a reverent finger. "I knew it."

"You're insufferable," I informed him, even as I arched into his touch.

"And yet, here you are, suffering me quite enthusiastically," he pointed out, lowering his head to press a kiss to the swell of my breast above the lace. "In fact, I'd say you're the opposite of suffering. Unless that little sound you just made was a cry for help." His tongue traced the edge of the lace, and I tangled my fingers in his hair, holding him against me. "Was it?" Callan nipped at my skin. "A cry for help?"

"Fuck, no."

The rational part of my brain, the small portion not currently consumed with sensation, knew we should stop. That this was crossing every professional boundary I'd ever established. That there would be consequences.

But the rest of me, the part currently on fire from his touch, told my rational mind to shut the hell up.

"This is a terrible idea," I whispered, even as I tugged him back up to capture his lips in another searing kiss.

"The best ideas usually are," he murmured against my mouth, walking me backward until my legs hit the sofa. "Like inventing the internet. Or putting pineapple on pizza. Or hiring the world's most uptight wedding planner and then making her lose her mind."

"I'm not uptight," I protested as we tumbled onto the cushions.

"Your emergency kits have emergency kits," he pointed out, settling his weight above me.

"And they've solved plenty of problems," I said, tugging his shirt up to finally, finally get my hands on those abs I'd been dreaming about since day one. "God, you're perfect."

"Speak for yourself, darling," he groaned as my nails raked lightly down his stomach. "You're killing me here."

His mouth found mine again in a kiss that made my toes curl. His hand slid up my thigh, inching the hem of my skirt higher, and I mentally thanked Mari for her insistence that I wear my "good" underwear today instead of my sensible cotton briefs.

I was about to suggest we move this to the bedroom when a chiming sound filled the room, followed by a massive screen on the wall lighting up with an incoming video call. A familiar face filled the display. Vivian Burkhardt, looking elegant as ever.

"Callan, darling, I was just calling to—oh!" Her eyes widened comically as she took in the scene before her; her grandson hovering over a disheveled me on the couch, my blouse half unbuttoned, his shirt rucked up to expose those world-class abs, both of us looking thoroughly debauched.

We sprang apart like teenagers caught by parents, me frantically re-buttoning my blouse while Callan attempted to smooth his hair and appear composed.

"Gram!" he exclaimed, his voice an octave higher than normal. "What a surprise! I wasn't expecting your call."

"Clearly," she replied in a flat tone. "Hello, Anica dear. Lovely to see you again, though perhaps more of you than either of us anticipated."

"Mrs. Burkhardt," I managed, mortification burning through me like acid. "This isn't—we were just—"

"Having a business meeting?" she suggested, her eyes twinkling. "A very hands-on consultation about wedding plans?"

"Something like that," Callan muttered, shooting me an apologetic glance.

"Well, don't let me interrupt," Vivian said in a cheerful voice. "I just wanted to remind you about Sunday dinner this weekend. Anica, you're welcome to join us again. Though perhaps you two should arrive separately to avoid giving my old heart too much excitement. Or wear turtlenecks to hide any... evidence of your business discussions."

"I should go," I blurted, gathering my scattered papers from the floor with shaking hands. "I have an early meeting tomorrow."

"Bad timing, dears?" Vivian asked innocently.

"The worst," Callan muttered, rubbing the back of his neck. "I'll call you tomorrow, Gram," he promised, clearly eager to end the conversation.

"Do that," she agreed. "And Callan? Next time, perhaps consider turning off the auto-answer function on your video system when you're... consulting with your wedding planner. Unless you're interested in producing wedding night videos before the actual wedding."

The screen went black, leaving us in silence.

"Well," Callan said finally. "That was..."

"Humiliating?" I suggested. "Mortifying? The single most embarrassing moment of my professional career? A new entry in my personal 'Top Ten Ways to Die of Shame' list?"

"I was going to say 'memorable,' but those work too."

I groaned, covering my face with my hands. "Your grandmother saw me half-undressed on your couch. I can never face her again. I'll have to move. Change my name. Perhaps enter the witness protection program. Start a new life as a sheep farmer in New Zealand."

"If it helps, she seemed more amused than scandalized," Callan offered, his hand coming to rest on my shoulder. "And for what it's

197

worth, I'm not sorry it happened. Well, not the interruption part. The rest of it."

I lowered my hands to look at him. "This complicates things."

"Understatement of the century," he agreed. "But maybe complicated isn't bad."

"It is when one of us is supposed to be planning the other's wedding to someone else," I pointed out.

Shit. The bet. The arrangement. The professional boundaries I'd just shattered into a million pieces by letting Callan Burkhardt explore my tonsils with his tongue while his hands wandered toward second base.

"Anica," he began, his voice serious. "About the arrangement—"

"I need to go," I interrupted, unable to bear whatever he was about to say. Whatever logical explanation or plan he had for fitting this—whatever this was—into his larger scheme. "I need to think."

"Anica, wait—"

But I was already heading for the door, portfolio clutched to my chest, lips still tingling from his kiss, body still humming with unfulfilled desire. Damn haunted house flooded.

"I'll call you," I said over my shoulder, not looking back at him. "To reschedule. The candidate meetings. We'll... figure this out."

I fled the penthouse before he could respond, my heart pounding and my professional boundaries in tatters. What had I done? More importantly, what was I going to do now?

As the elevator descended, I leaned against the wall and closed my eyes, the memory of Callan's lips on mine still burning.

I am so screwed.

And not even in the fun way.

A WOMAN WITH LITTLE HANDS...

Chapter 14: Callan

I stood, staring at my phone like it might spontaneously transform into a rabid honey badger determined to devour my dignity all because I needed to call a woman who'd seen me with morning wood and knew I was afraid of jellyfish.

Billionaire problems, ladies and gentlemen. Not listed in Forbes, but devastating nonetheless.

It had been exactly twenty-three hours and seventeen minutes since Anica had fled my penthouse, leaving behind the lingering scent of her perfume, the ghost of her lips on mine, and my dignity in tatters. Twenty-three hours and seventeen minutes of replaying our kiss in my mind, each time adding new and increasingly unlikely scenarios where my grandmother *didn't* interrupt us via wall-sized video screen.

I needed to call her. It was the mature, responsible thing to do. We had a business arrangement that had been complicated by the sudden introduction of tongues and wandering hands, and as the gentleman in this scenario, the onus was on me to clear the air.

I picked up my phone, then immediately set it down again. What exactly was I supposed to say?

Hey, remember when we almost had sex on my couch before my grandmother caught us? Good times! Anyway, about those bride candidates...

Or perhaps...

So, that kiss. On a scale from 'career-ending mistake' to 'let's do it again immediately and maybe add some light bondage,' where would you rank it?

The truth was, I had no idea where we stood. She'd run out of my penthouse like it was on fire, which wasn't exactly an encouraging sign. But before that? Before that, she'd been just as eager as I was, her body responding to mine in ways that suggested our mutual attraction wasn't just in my imagination.

I wanted more. A lot more. The kind of more that had nothing to do with our professional relationship and everything to do with the way my dick had gotten hard before she'd moaned against my mouth.

I picked up the phone again, this time forcing myself to dial before I could chicken out. My finger hovered over her name in my contacts.

"Just call her, Burkhardt. You've negotiated multi-million dollar deals. You've testified before Congress. You've explained cryptocurrency to your grandmother. You can handle one conversation with a woman."

I hit dial before I could talk myself out of it again.

She answered on the fourth ring, just as I was composing a casual voicemail in my head.

"Hello, Mr. Burkhardt," she said, her voice so professionally neutral it could have moderated a debate between the Dalai Lama and Satan without taking sides.

"Mr. Burkhardt? Really? After what we... I mean, after yesterday?" I couldn't keep the incredulity from my voice.

"I'm at the office," she replied, her tone softening. "Mari and Devonna are within earshot, and they're already suspicious enough after the island."

"Ah." That made sense. "Can you talk?"

"About business matters, yes."

Business matters. Right. Because that's all this was. Business. Except for the part where I couldn't stop thinking about the little gasp she'd made when I'd kissed that spot just below her ear, a sound that had taken up permanent residence in my spank bank's VIP section.

"I need a date for the Children's Hospital Gala tomorrow night," I blurted, abandoning my carefully planned opening.

There was a pause. "I'm sure Angie would be available."

"I told you, I broke things off." I ran a hand through my hair, pacing across my office like a caged tiger with erectile dysfunction. "I'm not calling her."

"I'm sure I could fix that if you —"

"I'm not asking someone else," I interrupted. "I'm asking you."

Another pause, longer this time. "Is this professional or personal?"

"Does it have to be one or the other?" I countered, then immediately regretted it. "I mean... I'd like you to come. As my date. But I understand if you'd rather keep things strictly professional."

I held my breath, waiting for her answer.

"Okay," she said finally.

"Okay?" I repeated, not quite believing it.

"Yes. I'll go with you to the gala."

"Great!" I winced at my over-enthusiastic tone. "I mean, good. I'll pick you up at seven?"

"Seven works. Text me the details about the dress code."

"Will do. And Anica?"

"Yes?"

"I'm looking forward to it."

There was the briefest hesitation before she said, "Me too," and hung up.

I stared at my phone, an idiotic grin spreading across my face. She'd said yes. She was coming to the gala. With me. As my date.

"You've changed that tie four times now," Erika observed from the doorway of my bedroom. "Should I be concerned you're having some kind of fashion-related breakdown? Or is this early-onset dementia? If so, can I have your yacht when you lose all cognitive function?"

"The blue one looked too corporate. The burgundy one was too much. The gray one was boring. And this one..." I frowned at my reflection, tugging at the green silk tie I'd just knotted. "This one makes me look like I'm trying too hard."

"Heaven forbid you look like you're putting effort into your appearance," my assistant remarked. "The world might stop spinning. Small children would weep. The stock market would crash."

I shot her a look. "So good to have you back, Erika."

"Would it be more helpful if I pointed out that you've never spent this long getting ready for any event, including your TED talk and that time you met the Queen of England? You were less nervous when you testified before Congress about privacy violations. You spent less time preparing for your Harvard commencement speech than you have choosing a tie for this date."

"I'm beginning to regret giving you a key to my penthouse," I muttered, unknotting the green tie and reaching for the blue one again.

"No, you're not. Without me, you'd probably be wearing mismatched socks and that horrible tie your college roommate got you as a joke." Erika stepped into the room, gently pushing my hands aside to take over the tie-knotting process. "The blue one is perfect. It brings out your eyes and complements your suit without being flashy. Trust me."

I sighed, relenting. "Since when do I care about being flashy? Flash is practically my middle name. Callan 'Flash' Burkhardt."

"No, it's not. And you're nervous because this isn't just any date. This is the woman you've been talking about non-stop for weeks."

"I don't talk about her non-stop. You haven't even been here. What do you know?"

"Yesterday you spent thirty minutes telling me about what her hair smells like.'"

"I was making fun of her!"

"You were practically writing sonnets about it." Erika finished with my tie and stepped back to assess her work. "Perfect. Now, are you going to call your grandmother for the pep talk I know you want, or should I dial her for you?"

"How did you—"

"Please. You call her before every major decision or event. It's sweet, actually. One of the few genuinely endearing things about you, along with your secret donations to animal shelters and the fact that you cry during Pixar movies."

"Just for that, I'm cutting your Christmas bonus," I grumbled, but I was already reaching for my phone.

Erika smirked. "No, you're not. You already approved it. In writing. I have copies. In three different secure locations. Plus I've told my mother about it, and she's already planned her cruise. You don't want to disappoint my mother, Mr. Burkhardt. She's still recovering from her non-stroke stroke."

"Get out before I make Gram rate your outfit."

As soon as she left, I dialed Gram's number. She answered on the second ring.

"If you're calling to cancel Sunday dinner again, I'm writing you out of my will and leaving everything to that cat who keeps breaking into my garden to shit in my petunias."

"Hello to you too, Gram. And no, I'm not canceling. I'm calling about... something else."

"The gala with Anica," she said immediately.

"How did you—never mind. Yes. The gala. With Anica."

"You're nervous," she observed. "That's new."

"I'm not nervous," I lied. "I'm just–"

"Callan Anthony Burkhardt, I've known you since you were an overcooked potato in a hospital blanket. Don't try to fool me. You get the same squeaky voice you had when you asked Lia Jennins to the eighth-grade dance and she said yes, then you threw up in the ficus plant."

I sighed, sinking onto the edge of my bed. "Fine. I'm nervous. I don't get nervous. Not about women. Not about anything. But she's different, Gram. She sees through all the noise and she doesn't care about the money at all. She treats me like I'm just a guy, not a bank account with legs."

"That's because you are just a guy," Gram said simply. "A very lucky, very privileged guy with more money than sense sometimes, but still just a man. And from what I've seen—which, may I remind you, was quite a bit more than I anticipated during our last video call—she likes that man."

"She ran out of my penthouse."

"After I caught you two half-undressed on the couch like horny ruffians. Can you blame her? The poor girl was mortified. I saw more of her décolletage than her own doctor probably has."

"She hasn't mentioned it since. The kiss, I mean."

"Have you two talked?"

"Well... no."

"Men," Gram sighed. "You need to talk to her, Cal. Tell her how you feel."

"I don't know how I feel," I admitted. "I just know I want to see her again. I want to spend time with her. I want to kiss her again. A lot. Possibly for hours. Maybe days. In multiple positions and locations."

"Thank you, grandson. That was exactly what I wanted to talk about. Please bury me with white orchids."

"I just mean it's complicated. Really complicated."

"What's complicated about it?" Gram asked. "You love her and she–"

"Love doesn't exist, Gram. I've told you that a thousand times."

"Yes, and I've come to terms that my grandson is a genius in all but that category. When it comes to love, you're a fucking idiot."

"Gee, thanks so much for that." I ran my hand through my hair, instantly regretting the action because I'd used hair gel.

She sighed. "With the examples you were given, I'm not surprised that's your opinion."

"Well, yeah, obviously with Mom and Dad–"

"But," she said, clearly annoyed I'd spoken while she was on some sort of soapbox. "Your opinion on that matter, my dear, is absolute horse shit."

Normally, I'd humor her, but her comment irked me more than it should've.

"Gram, I appreciate the crappy pep talk, but you're wrong and I need to leave or I'll be late picking Anica up."

"You show up on time for her, Cal. That's got to stand for something."

"I love you, Gram."

After hanging up with her, I finished getting ready. Erika's final approval ensured I looked presentable by the time I headed to my car.

By the time I pulled up in front of Anica's building, my palms were sweating. I couldn't remember the last time I'd cared this much about impressing someone. Maybe never.

I texted to let her know I was there, then waited outside my car, using the windows to check my reflection in the rearview mirror one last time. Hair? Perfect. Tie? Straight. Expression? Only mildly terrified, with a hint of "might vomit if rejected" around the edges.

I was just considering whether I should go up to her apartment or wait by the car when the building's front door opened, and there she was.

Holy. Fucking. Hell.

The witty compliment I'd prepared died on my lips as I took in the vision gliding towards me. Anica wore a midnight blue gown that shimmered with every movement, clinging to her curves before flowing gracefully to the ground. The neckline dipped just low enough to be enticing without being obvious, and her hair was swept up in an elegant style that exposed the slender column of her neck. She looked like she'd stepped out of a dream I didn't even know I was having.

I scrambled away from the car, nearly tripping over my own feet in my haste to reach her.

"Hi," I said brilliantly, my extensive vocabulary apparently reduced to monosyllables by the sight of her.

"Hi yourself," she replied, a small smile playing at her lips. God, I'd kissed those perfect lips. I wanted to do it again. Shit, they were moving. "You clean up nicely."

"You... I mean... that dress is..." I gestured helplessly, words failing me entirely. My brain, which had negotiated billion-dollar deals and revolutionized tech industries, was suddenly operating with the processing power of a calculator from 1982.

"Use your words, Burkhardt," she teased, but a faint blush colored her cheeks. "For a man who talks as much as you do, you're surprisingly quiet right now."

"You look incredible," I finally managed. "Absolutely stunning. I'm seriously reconsidering my atheism because you're making a compelling case for the existence of divine beings. Either that, or I've had a stroke and this is a very specific hallucination."

Her blush deepened. "Thank you. You look pretty good yourself."

"Pretty good? I'm wounded. I spent at least forty-five minutes on my hair alone. A small forest died for the products required to achieve this level of casual perfection."

"In that case, you look devastatingly handsome," she amended. "Does that soothe your fragile ego?"

"Immensely," I grinned, opening the passenger door for her. "Your chariot awaits, my lady."

"A Bugatti is hardly a chariot. More like a very expensive missile with leather seats," she observed, sliding gracefully into the seat.

"A missile with excellent handling and zero to sixty in 2.4 seconds," I corrected, closing her door before rounding the car to the driver's side. "I thought about bringing the helicopter, but city ordinances frown on landing in residential areas. Something about noise complaints and 'severe safety hazards.' Bureaucracy at its finest."

She laughed, the sound making my heart do acrobatics in my chest. "I appreciate your restraint."

The drive to the gala was filled with easy conversation, neither of us mentioning the couch incident, though I caught her glancing at my lips more than once. Each time she did, heat pooled in my stomach, memories of our kiss flashing through my mind. It forced me to have to think about other things, like the petunia-pooping cat Gram had mentioned and Norbert the butler in a speedo. When those failed, I shifted my mind to business deals I had coming up. That did the job.

The event planners had transformed the Metropolitan Museum of Art for the evening, its grand entrance flanked by red carpets and photographers. As we pulled up, Anica tensed beside me.

"There are a lot of cameras," she observed, her voice carefully neutral.

"Occupational hazard of these events," I replied, handing my keys to the valet. "Just smile and keep walking. They're vultures, but harmless ones. And if anyone asks, you don't have to answer. That's what publicists are for."

"I don't have a publicist," she pointed out.

"Tonight, you can borrow mine." I came around to her side of the car, offering my hand. "Ready?"

She took a deep breath, then placed her hand in mine. "Nope, let's go."

The moment we stepped onto the red carpet, the flashes began. Photographers called out my name, and occasionally Anica's — apparently someone had done their homework — as we made our way toward the entrance. I kept my hand on the small of her back, a gesture that was partly protective and partly selfish. I liked touching her, liked the subtle reminder that she was here with me.

"Callan! Who's your date?" a reporter called out.

"Anica Marcel," I replied smoothly. "The most talented wedding planner in Manhattan."

"Are those wedding bells we hear?" another shouted.

"The only bells you're hearing are the ones I installed in your head the last time you printed something about my love life," I shot back with a smile that took the sting out of the words. Mostly.

Anica relaxed against my hand as we continued past the press line. By the time we reached the main entrance, she was almost smiling.

"That wasn't so bad," she admitted.

"The night is young," I warned her. "The real sharks are inside, disguised as socialites and philanthropists."

"Way to make me feel better," she deadpanned.

"It's a gift," I agreed. "Along with my devastatingly handsome looks and Greek god abs."

She groaned. "What. An. Ego."

"It's not the only big thing about me," I whispered in her ear as I guided her into the gala. She elbowed me. I couldn't stop grinning.

The Great Hall had been transformed into a glittering wonderland of lights and flowers, with elegantly dressed attendees already mingling over champagne. A string quartet played softly in one corner, and waiters circulated with trays of hors d'oeuvres that probably cost more per bite than most people's weekly grocery budget.

I watched Anica take it all in, her eyes wide. "This is magnificent," she said. "The lighting design alone is incredible."

"Only you would notice the lighting design before the ice sculpture of a cherub riding a dolphin," I teased, nodding toward the elaborate centerpiece.

"Professional hazard," she shrugged. "I'm mentally taking notes for future events."

"Well, feel free to critique anything you like. I'm on the planning committee, so I can pass along feedback."

She looked at me in surprise. "You're on the planning committee? For a children's hospital fundraiser?"

"Did you forget that I also had the Pediatric Cancer event a couple weeks ago? I helped with that one too. Is that so hard to believe?" I asked, feigning offense. "I do occasionally participate in activities that don't involve making money or looking pretty. Sometimes I feed the ducks. Sometimes I pet dogs in the park."

"It's just... unexpected," she admitted.

"I'm full of surprises," I assured her, snagging two glasses of champagne from a passing waiter and handing one to her. "Cheers."

"Cheers," she agreed, touching her glass to mine.

As we mingled, I introduced Anica to various acquaintances and business associates, all of whom seemed fascinated by her. Or, more accurately, fascinated by the fact that I'd brought her as my date. I could practically see the gossip spreading through the room, carried on currents of whispered conversations and meaningful glances.

Strangely, I didn't mind. In fact, part of me, a larger part than I cared to admit, wanted these rumors to be true. Wanted people to think of Anica as mine. Wanted her to be mine.

"What are you thinking about? You've got a strange look on your face." Anica asked, breaking into my thoughts.

"Just contemplating the strange and mysterious workings of the universe. And wondering if the shrimp puffs are worth the inevitable garlic breath."

"Very deep thoughts," she nodded solemnly. "Truly the mark of a philosophical mind."

"I contain multitudes," I agreed. "Speaking of which, would you like to see the pediatric cardiology wing plans? They're on display in the east gallery."

Her eyebrows rose. "You know where the display is?"

"I helped design it. Come on, I'll show you."

Taking her hand, I led her through the crowd to a quieter area where architectural renderings and medical equipment diagrams lined the walls. I stopped in front of a large display showing the proposed new wing of the children's hospital.

"This is the project the gala is funding. A state-of-the-art pediatric cardiology center with the latest diagnostic and treatment technology."

Anica studied the renderings. "This is impressive. The layout is incredibly patient-centered."

"That was the priority. Too many hospitals are designed for the convenience of the staff rather than the comfort of the patients. We worked with child psychologists to create spaces that would feel less intimidating for kids undergoing treatment."

"We?" she questioned, looking at me with new curiosity.

"I've been involved with the hospital for years. My cousin was treated there as a kid. Leukemia. She survived because they had the right technology and the best doctors. Not every family is that lucky."

"I had no idea," Anica said softly.

"It's not something I advertise. Bad for my image as a heartless sexy tech billionaire," I shrugged.

"Heaven forbid people know you actually care about something beyond your stock portfolio," she teased, but her eyes were warm.

"It would ruin me. Next thing you know, I'd be rescuing drowning damsels and helping old people cross streets. My reputation would never recover."

As we continued through the exhibit, I explained various medical technologies with perhaps more enthusiasm than was strictly necessary. But Anica seemed genuinely interested, asking thoughtful questions about the equipment and treatment protocols.

"You know a lot about medical technology for someone who isn't in healthcare," she observed.

"I invest in it. Not just financially, but time-wise. I sit on the hospital's innovation board. We review new technologies, evaluate their potential impact, determine funding priorities."

"That's... actually pretty amazing," she admitted.

"Try not to sound so surprised. I occasionally do things that don't involve being insufferable."

"Only occasionally," she agreed with a smile that took the sting out of her words. "This is clearly your annual good deed."

"Ouch. You wound me."

She laughed, and I found myself inordinately pleased that I'd caused that sound. I wanted to make her laugh more often. I wanted to be the reason for that spark in her eyes, that slight flush in her cheeks.

God, I was in trouble.

As we made our way back to the main hall, the string quartet had been replaced by a small orchestra, and couples were beginning to fill the dance floor. I glanced at Anica, who was watching the dancers with an expression I couldn't quite read.

"Would you like to dance?" I asked, offering my hand.

She hesitated. "I should warn you, I usually don't."

"Consider this research for my wedding, then," I suggested, instantly regretting the reference to our professional relationship. "I mean—"

"Research," she repeated, a small smile playing at her lips. "Of course. Very professional."

She placed her hand in mine, and I led her to the dance floor, my heart beating faster than the situation warranted. As we reached the center of the floor, I drew her into my arms, one hand at the small of her back, the other clasping hers gently.

The orchestra was playing something slow and vaguely familiar, the kind of music that required couples to stand close together. Anica fit against me perfectly, her body warm and soft where it pressed against mine. I was a little too aware of every point of contact between us: my hand on her back, her fingers twined with mine, the occasional brush of her thigh against my leg as we moved.

My body's reaction to her proximity was immediate and embarrassingly obvious. I subtly adjusted our position to maintain a small distance between our lower halves, not wanting to make her uncomfortable. Or more accurately, not wanting her to feel exactly how comfortable she made certain parts of me.

Think unsexy thoughts. Baseball statistics. Tax codes. Jellyfish. Actually, no, not jellyfish. Those floating death bags are too traumatizing. Gram's bunion surgery. The time I walked in on my college roommate naked. Literally anything but the way her breasts press against my chest when she breathes.

"You're a good dancer," Anica observed, looking up at me.

"My grandmother insisted on lessons. Said no grandson of hers was going to shuffle around like, and I quote, 'a drunk toddler on roller skates.'"

"She has a way with words."

"You have no idea. She once described my first girlfriend as having 'all the personality of baby food, but with less nutritional value.'"

Anica laughed. "Harsh."

"The harshest. Gram is not easy to impress. Though she was right. My ex did bear a striking resemblance to mushy baby food."

"And Angie? What did your grandmother think of her?" Anica asked, her tone carefully neutral. "I mean, did you tell her about the prenup from hell?"

"Thankfully, no. Gram would've probably seen through her before I did."

"Smart lady."

"You two are a lot alike in that regard." I spun her around and pulled her closer. "She thinks the bet was stupid too."

"Certainly has more sense than you, then."

"Oh definitely." I pulled back to catch her gaze.

She looked away first, scanning the room. "Everyone's staring at us."

"Let them. I'm only looking at you."

Her gaze snapped back to mine, and for a moment, neither of us spoke. I wanted to kiss her again, right there on the dance floor, regardless of the gossip it would generate.

"Callan," she began, her voice barely audible over the music.

Whatever she was about to say was interrupted by a tap on my shoulder. I turned to find Edward Whitman, the hospital's chief of surgery, smiling apologetically.

"Sorry to interrupt, but the speech is about to begin, and they're asking for you backstage."

I'd completely forgotten I was supposed to introduce the hospital's director. "Right," I nodded. "I'll be right there." Turning back to Anica, I explained, "I have to make a short speech. Will you be okay for a few minutes?"

"I think I can manage not to get lost or kidnapped," she assured me. "Go. Be brilliant."

With reluctance, I released her and followed Edward toward the stage. The speech itself was brief and straightforward—welcome, thanks for coming, introduce the hospital director, exit stage left. I delivered it on autopilot, my mind still on the dance floor with Anica.

By the time I made my way back to her, she was engaged in conversation with a small group that included the mayor and his wife. She looked completely at ease, laughing at something the mayor's wife had said. I paused for a moment, just watching her. She belonged here, in this world of wealth and influence, not because she craved it, but because she was confident enough in herself to navigate it without being overwhelmed.

As if sensing my presence, she glanced up, her gaze finding mine across the room. She smiled, a small, private smile that made my chest tighten. I made my way to her side, sliding a hand to the small of her back in a gesture that was becoming increasingly familiar.

"Nice speech," she murmured as I joined the conversation.

"I'm a man of many talents."

"So I'm discovering."

The rest of the evening passed in a blur of conversations, champagne, and stolen glances. By the time we finally made our exit, it was well past midnight, and I was riding a strange high that had nothing to do with alcohol and everything to do with the woman beside me.

In the car, Anica was looking out the window, but I could feel her awareness of me in the way she held herself, slightly turned toward me despite her outward focus on the passing cityscape.

"Nightcap? I make a mean old-fashioned."

She hesitated, then nodded. "Sure. One drink."

The ride up in the elevator was excruciating. We stood inches apart, both staring at the numbered display as if it held the secrets of the universe. I was hyperaware of her scent, the sound of her breathing, the way her dress rustled softly when she shifted her weight. My palms were sweating, and I was pretty sure I could hear my own heartbeat echoing in the confined space.

By the time we reached my penthouse, I was a bundle of nerves disguised as a functioning adult. I unlocked the door, letting her enter first, then followed, shrugging off my jacket and loosening my tie.

"Make yourself comfortable," I said, gesturing to the living room. "I'll fix those drinks."

"Stay away from the rum."

I chuckled and busied myself at the bar, carefully measuring bourbon and bitters, adding a sugar cube, stirring with perhaps more concentration than the task required. When I turned around, drinks in hand, Anica was standing by the windows, looking out at the city lights.

"Beautiful view," she commented as I approached.

"The best in the city," I agreed, handing her a glass. "Though tonight it has competition."

She rolled her eyes, but a small smile played at her lips. "That was terrible."

"But effective. You're smiling."

"At your expense, not because of your charm."

"I'll take what I can get."

We stood in silence for a moment, sipping our drinks and looking out at the city. Then, simultaneously, we turned to face each other.

"Anica—"

"Callan—"

We both stopped and laughed awkwardly.

"You first," I offered.

She took a deep breath. "What are we doing? Really?"

"Right now? Having a nightcap."

"You know what I mean."

I did. I sighed, setting my glass down on a nearby table. "Honestly? I have no idea. I just know that I want to be around you. I want to talk to you. I want to make you laugh. I want to kiss you again. I want to do a lot more than kiss you, actually, but I'm trying to be gentlemanly about it."

"That's... complicated."

"Because of the arrangement," I acknowledged. "The bet."

"Mainly because you're my client. My very high-profile client who hired me to plan his wedding to someone else."

"What if there was no arrangement?" I asked, stepping closer to her. "No bet. No professional relationship. Just us. What would you want then?"

She looked up at me, her eyes searching mine. "That's not a fair question."

"None of this is fair, but I'm asking anyway."

She was quiet for a long moment, and I held my breath, waiting. Finally, she set her own glass down and closed the distance between us.

"This," she whispered, rising on her toes to press her lips to mine.

This kiss was different from our first. Less frantic, more deliberate. Her lips were soft against mine, tentative at first, then more confident as I responded. My hands grazed her waist, drawing her closer as her arms wound around my neck.

When we broke apart, both slightly breathless, I rested my forehead against hers. "Are you sure about this? Because if you're not, we can stop. No pressure."

"No, I'm not sure. This is probably the worst decision I've ever made. But I'm doing it anyway."

"Gee, thanks, darling."

She rolled her eyes and leaned into me. "I want you, Cal. That's my decision. Right here, right now."

That was all the encouragement I needed. I captured her lips again, deepening the kiss, my tongue exploring her mouth as my hands roamed her back. She made a small sound of pleasure that went straight to my dick.

Our kisses grew more urgent, hands exploring, breaths quickening. When I trailed my lips down her neck, she tilted her head back, giving me better access to the sensitive skin there. I took full advantage, alternating between gentle kisses and light nips that made her gasp.

"Bedroom?" I suggested against her throat.

"God, yes," she agreed breathlessly.

I led her down the hallway, stealing kisses along the way, both of us laughing when I nearly walked us into a wall because I was too distracted by her to watch where we were going. By the time we reached my bedroom, her hair was half down from its elegant updo, and my tie was completely undone.

Standing at the foot of my bed, I paused, suddenly nervous. This wasn't just any woman. This was Anica. Competent, brilliant, maddening Anica, who saw through my bullshit and challenged me at every turn. I didn't want to mess this up.

She must have sensed my hesitation because she reached up to cup my face, her touch gentle. "We don't have to do this," she said softly.

"I want to. God, do I want to. I just... this is different."

"Different how?"

"Different everything," I admitted. "Different you."

Her expression softened, and she rose on her toes to kiss me again, this time slowly, deeply, with an intensity that made my knees weak. As we kissed, her hands moved to the buttons of my shirt, unfastening them one by one until she could push the fabric off my shoulders.

"Greek god abs," she murmured appreciatively, tracing the contours of my chest with her fingers. "I stand by it."

I chuckled as I turned her gently, finding the zipper of her dress and lowering it, my knuckles grazing her spine as I revealed each inch of skin. I followed the zipper's path with my lips, tasting the salt on her skin, relishing the way she shivered under my touch. The dress finally pooled at her feet, leaving her in nothing but a strapless bra and the smallest, laciest excuse for panties I'd ever seen, both in a deep blue that matched her dress.

"Christ, Anica," I breathed, taking in the sight of her. "You're... I don't even have words. And I always have words."

A flush spread across her skin, but she didn't look away. Instead, she reached for my belt, unfastening it. I held my breath. My pants followed her dress to the floor, leaving me in just my boxer briefs, my arousal straining against the fabric with an enthusiasm that bordered on medical concern.

We stood there for a moment, both nearly naked, eyes drinking in the sight of each other. Then, as if by mutual agreement, we came together again, skin against skin, mouths seeking, hands exploring.

I guided her to the bed, laying her down with a gentleness that surprised even me. I wanted to worship her, to learn every curve and hollow of her body, to discover all the places that made her gasp and moan.

Anica paused. "Clean?"

"Yeah," I said, nodding. "You?"

"Yeah."

"Good."

"Good."

Starting at her lips, I worked my way down, kissing her neck, her collarbone, the swell of her breasts above her bra. I reached behind her to unfasten the garment, looking to her for permission. At her nod, I removed it, revealing her to my gaze.

"Perfect," I murmured, cupping one breast as I lowered my mouth to the other. The sound she made when my tongue flicked across her nipple was enough to make my dick throb.

"You know," she said, her voice husky as I lavished attention on her breasts, "for someone who talks as much as you do, your mouth is surprisingly useful for other things."

I grinned against her skin. "You have no idea. This is just the preview."

I continued my exploration, trailing kisses down her stomach, over her hipbones, along the inside of her thighs. When I hooked my fingers in the waistband of her panties, she lifted her hips, allowing me to slide them down her legs.

Looking up the length of her body, I met her eyes, silently asking permission. She nodded, her bottom lip caught between her teeth.

The first taste of her was everything I'd imagined and more. She was warm and wet, her flavor a heady mix of salt and sweetness that made my head spin. I savored her, using my tongue to trace slow circles around her most sensitive spot, careful not to give her too much too soon.

"Callan," she gasped, her hips rising to meet my mouth. "Stop teasing."

I chuckled against her, the vibration making her shudder. "Bossy even in bed. Why am I not surprised?"

Before she could retort, I slid a finger inside her while my tongue focused its attention exactly where she wanted it. Shit she was tight. Her reaction was immediate and gratifying. A sharp intake of breath, followed by a moan that I felt in my bones. If there was any chance I wasn't going to hurt her, I knew I needed to stretch her out a bit first. But fuck, she was already so wet. That, at least, would help.

I watched her as I pleasured her, fascinated by the way her expression changed, the flush that spread across her chest, the way her hands alternated between gripping the sheets and tangling in my hair. She was uninhibited in her pleasure, vocal about what she wanted, and I was more than happy to comply. Adding a second finger, I chuckled against her clit when her hand tugged at my hair. It burned in the best possible way. Her hips bucked up as I sucked and licked.

"Right there," she directed, her voice breathless as I curled my fingers inside her. "God, yes, just like that."

I increased the pressure, the speed, working her body. This woman, no, this goddess was allowing me to worship her with my touch and my tongue. Fuck. If I lasted until she came, it would be a miracle. Her thighs began to tremble, her breathing quickened, and I knew she was close.

"Let go," I murmured against her. "I've got you."

Her release, when it came, was spectacular; her back arching, her inner muscles clenching around my fingers, my name falling from her lips like a benediction. I worked her through it, easing the pressure gradually as she came down from her high.

When I finally made my way back up her body, she was looking at me with a mixture of satisfaction and challenge.

"Your turn," she said, pushing at my shoulders until I rolled onto my back. "I want to taste you too."

Who was I to argue with that? I watched, heart hammering, as she positioned herself between my legs, her hair falling around her face like a curtain. She tugged off my briefs, tossing them over her shoulder to land somewhere on the marble floor.

"Holy shit, Cal," she whispered, her wide eyes meeting mine. I smirked, shrugging as I folded my arms behind me. "Fuck."

"Thank you." I winked at her, and despite her shocked expression, she rolled her eyes.

"How the fuck am I supposed to fit you in my mouth?" She ran a finger up my dick, and my muscles clenched as I held back a groan.

"You're a problem solver. You figure it out." I ran my hand over her knee and up her leg. "I think it'll involve some choking though."

"Fuck you."

"I'm hoping you will."

Anica wiped the smirk right off my face as she gripped me at the base of my dick. I gasped, my lungs forgetting how to work.

"God, fuck." I leaned back against the pillows, closing my eyes to restrain myself. "Anica," I growled.

"Yes?" She grinned at me like a little vixen as she began to stroke me. I nearly lost it when she leaned over and spat on the head, rubbing her saliva and the precum down the shaft.

She took her time, exploring me with her hands first, learning what made me growl and groan. And when she finally took me into her mouth, I nearly lost it then and there. The wet heat of her was perfect, her tongue tracing patterns that had me seeing stars. She was as methodical in this as she was in her work, noting what made me react most strongly and focusing her attention there.

"Fuck, I was right about your hands." I cleared my throat, smiling like an idiot at the ceiling as I tried to distract myself so I didn't explode too soon.

"What?" Pausing, she stared up at me through her eyelashes, licking the head of my cock with her eyebrow raised. "What about my hands?"

"At Rhodes. Little hands, excellent head."

"No one says that."

"Sure they do, they — Fuck!"

The goddess somehow managed to take half of me all the way to the back of her throat before I'd finished speaking. I squeezed my eyes shut, desperately grasping at anything not related to Anica sucking my dick that would keep me from losing it here and now. But I think I'd challenged her with the comment about her hands because she'd picked up speed with her mouth, adding her other hand in tandem with the first.

The sounds she made were ungodly, and I reached for her, wrapping her dark hair around my fist to pull it out of her face. Fuck, I wanted to see her. She was beautiful. Smart. Talented. And stubborn to a fault. She choked, but when she pulled back, she was smiling, gasping for air. She went back down before I could say anything, and she all but decimated any words I'd had right out of my head as she lavished me with her tongue.

"Anica," I warned after a few minutes of exquisite torture. "If you keep that up, this is going to be over embarrassingly quickly."

She grinned up at me, her lips curved in a smile that was pure sin. "Can't have that," she agreed, giving me one last, tortuously slow lick from base to tip before crawling back up my body.

"I have condoms in the bedside table," I said, my voice rougher than it had been a few moments ago. Fuck, she'd undone me.

Anica leaned down to kiss me, her lips wet. A second later, she shifted off of me.

"Wow," she giggled, a flush coloring her cheeks as she leaned over and opened the drawer. "You're certainly prepared for the orgy apocalypse."

When she crawled back over, I wrapped an arm around her waist, rolling us so that she was beneath me once more.

"Nah," I grinned, running my hand up her thigh and snatching the condom from her hand. "That's just enough for a good weekend."

"There are four boxes in there!"

218

"Planning for all contingencies," I teased, tearing the package and tossing it off the bed. I rolled the condom on. Anica's gaze followed my movements. My size had been an issue before with other women, and I paused as I watched her face. Shit. Did I prepare her enough? Maybe I needed to get her off again. I didn't want to hurt her.

"Darling, are you... I don't want–"

"I'm ready," Anica ran her fingers down my arms, pulling me over her. "I can take it."

"I'm sure you can," I leaned down to kiss her, letting my anxieties leak out of me at the taste of me on her lips. I positioned myself above her, bracing my weight on my forearms. "Last chance to back out," I said against her lips, needing her to be absolutely sure.

In answer, she wrapped her legs around my waist and pulled me closer, guiding me to her entrance. Her gaze locked on mine. "Stop talking and fuck me already."

The unexpected directness of her command shot straight to my groin. "Yes, ma'am," I replied, but despite her eagerness, I pressed against her entrance, grinding my jaw as I kept a leash on my restraint.

I eased in slowly until just the head of my dick was inside. Her body tensed at the initial stretch. Every instinct screamed at me to thrust deep, to claim her completely, but I battled against the urge. This wasn't just anyone beneath me. This was Anica.

"Shit," she moaned into the back of her hand.

"You okay?" I murmured, watching her face intently.

She nodded, biting her lower lip. "Just... give me a second."

I stilled completely, lowering my head to kiss her neck, her jaw, her lips; anything to distract from the almost overwhelming need to move. Her hands traced patterns on my back, and gradually she relaxed beneath me.

"More," she whispered against my ear, shifting her hips upwards against me.

I pushed in another inch, then paused again when I felt her tense. "Breathe," I reminded her softly, brushing damp strands of hair from her forehead. The restraint it took not to bury myself inside her was maddening, but her comfort mattered more than my pleasure. I couldn't remember the last time that'd been the case. Maybe never.

Her breathing steadied, and she nodded again. I continued the slow advance, retreating before pressing forward, working my way deeper with each careful thrust. The sensation was torture. Her body gripped me like a silken vise.

"Jesus," I hissed through clenched teeth when I was seated most of the way inside her. I held perfectly still, giving us both time to adjust; her to my size, me to the overwhelming pleasure threatening to shatter my control. "You feel incredible. Fuck, you're incredible."

Her gaze met mine, darkening. "So do you," she replied, her hips shifting experimentally. A soft gasp escaped her lips as the movement changed the angle. "But if you don't move soon, I'm going to flip us over and take matters into my own hands."

"Bossy," I repeated, but obliged, beginning to move within her with shallow, controlled thrusts. Every fiber of my being wanted to take her hard and fast. But something else made me choose gentleness instead.

I watched her face carefully, noting every flutter of her eyelashes, every parting of her lips. When her expression shifted from concentration to pleasure, when her breathing quickened and her nails dug into my shoulders, I increased my pace.

"You want to take more, don't you darling?" I said, voice strained with the effort of holding back. Fuck, I needed her to say yes. I needed to go deeper. Faster.

"God, yes," she breathed, arching beneath me.

I angled my hips, seeking that spot inside her that would make her forget everything but this moment, everything but my name. When I found it, her eyes widened and a moan broken by a gasp escaped her. Satisfaction surged through me that had nothing to do with physical pleasure and everything to do with giving her what she needed.

Her legs tightened around me, urging me deeper, and I complied, gradually increasing both pace and depth until the room filled with the sounds of our pleasure. Gasps, moans, the rhythmic creak of the bed, and Anica shrieking my name along with more profanities than I'd ever heard her use.

"God, Callan, Fuck. Right there," she gasped as I shifted, finding an angle that had her inner muscles clenching around me. "Fuck! Don't stop."

"Wasn't planning on it," I assured her, kissing her hand as she clawed at my arm. I slid a hand between us, my thumb finding her clit, circling it in time with my thrusts. "Come for me."

Her second climax was even more powerful than the first, her entire body tensing as she cried out. The feeling of her pulsing around me, combined with the expression of pure pleasure on her face, pushed me over the edge. My release hit me hard, intense enough that for a moment, everything else disappeared; the room, the bed, even my own name. There was only Anica, and the incredible sensations coursing through my body.

As I came back to myself, I was careful not to collapse on top of her, instead rolling to the side and gathering her against me. We lay in silence for a few minutes, both catching our breath, bodies still humming with pleasure.

"Wow. I've never…It's never been that…" she began, then trailed off.

"Incredible? Mind-blowing? Perfect?" I suggested, unable to keep the smugness from my voice.

She pinched my side. "I was going to say 'good,' but your suggestions work too."

"Good?" I repeated, feigning offense. "I just rocked your world, Marcel. I saw your toes curl. Multiple times."

"Keep telling yourself that," she replied, but her satisfied smile gave her away. "Though I suppose it was... adequate."

"Adequate, she says," I muttered, pulling her closer. "After making sounds that probably got us on a noise complaint watchlist."

She laughed, the sound vibrating against my chest. "Fine. It was amazing. Your ego doesn't need the boost, but yes, it was... memorable."

"I'll take 'memorable,'" I conceded, dropping a kiss on the top of her head. "Though I plan to upgrade that review to 'life-changing' and 'best she's ever had' with a repeat performance later."

"Confident, aren't you?"

"Just goal-oriented," I corrected, my hands beginning to wander again, exploring the dip of her waist, the curve of her hip. "And I always exceed expectations." I grinned, grabbing her by the back of the neck and into a kiss. "How do you feel? Sore?" I murmured against her lips.

"Probably will be tomorrow."

"Want to be extra sore?"

Anica trailed a finger down my chest. "What were you thinking?"

"Well, I'm going to go throw this condom away and when I come back, you better be on your hands and knees."

"Oh? And if I'm not?" She ground against the side of my leg.

"Well," I tapped my chin and made a puzzled expression, "I do have handcuffs I stole off a cop as a teenager. That, and some very nice leather belts."

LOVE DOESN'T EXIST

Chapter 15: Anica

I woke up in a billionaire's bed with sex hair and a full-body ache that suggested I'd been thoroughly railed. Multiple times. Callan had slung his arm possessively across my waist, his morning erection pressing insistently against my thigh. I shifted, weighing my options: sneak out before he woke, or stay and face the exquisitely awkward morning-after conversation.

Callan cut my deliberation short when he tightened his grip, his lips finding the sensitive spot just behind my ear.

"I can hear you overthinking from here," he murmured, his voice morning-rough in a way that had my ovaries doing backflips. "Your brain makes this little whirring sound when it's cataloging situations and planning escape routes."

"It does not," I protested, even as I tilted my head to give him better access. "And my escape routes are planned weeks in advance, not hastily assembled at..." I glanced at the ridiculously expensive watch on his nightstand, "7:36 in the morning."

He chuckled, the vibration traveling through my skin and settling somewhere decidedly south of my navel. "So you're not going to try to slip away from me and pretend last night never happened?"

"First of all, no. Second, also no," I replied, rolling over to face him. "And third, good morning."

He looked unfairly spectacular for someone who'd just woken up. His hair was artfully tousled and he had stubble at the perfect length to be both sexy and irritating. The sheet had slipped to his waist, exposing the chest that had made me forget years of professional ethics last night.

"Morning," he replied, his thumb tracing lazy circles on my hip. "Sleep well?"

"Surprisingly, yes. Though I suspect that has less to do with your thread count and more with being fucked into unconsciousness."

His eyes darkened at my words, pupils expanding like black holes consuming all that blue. "Happy to be of service," he drawled. "Though I'd argue it was mutual."

"Good," I said, grinning. It was dangerously easy to fall into this rhythm with him. The banter, the casual intimacy, the way his hand slid up my side.

"We should talk about this," I said, even as my body arched toward his touch like a cat seeking the sun.

"About what?" he asked, feigning innocence as his fingers traced the underside of my breast.

"About the fact that we just spent the night doing things that would make the Professional Wedding Planners Association revoke my membership, if such a thing existed, which thankfully it doesn't because the annual conferences would be unbearable."

"Ah, that," he said, as if just remembering a minor detail. "Yes, we probably should discuss it. Later." His thumb brushed across my nipple, sending a jolt of electricity straight between my legs.

"Callan," I said, attempting to sound stern but landing somewhere closer to breathless.

"Anica," he mimicked my tone, then his expression grew serious. "Look, I know this complicates things. The arrangement, the bet, all of it. But right now, I don't care. I want you. Not as my wedding planner. Not as part of some business deal. Just you."

It was one thing to have mindless, admittedly spectacular sex with the man. It was another entirely to start believing there might be something real beneath the billionaire playboy facade.

"And what happens when you do care?" I asked quietly. "When the bet deadline approaches and you need to actually find a bride?"

224

His hand stilled on my skin, his gaze searching mine. "I don't know. I just know that right now, the only thing I want is to go another round with the drop dead gorgeous woman lying next to me."

My heart did a dangerous little flip in my chest. "I'd be down for that, but I need to brush my teeth. And my hair. And I need fuel."

"Oh no you don't," he said, catching me before I could pull away.

I didn't have time to argue before he started kissing me. His response was immediate and hungry, his hands tangling in my hair as he rolled me beneath him. The weight of him pressed me into the mattress. There was nothing gentle about this kiss.

"I want you," he growled against my lips, his knee nudging my thighs apart. His erection pressed hard against my hip, already fully aroused.

"Then take me," I challenged, wrapping my legs around his waist.

His eyes flashed. "Don't move," he commanded, reaching across me to yank open the bedside drawer. The muscles in his arm flexed as he grabbed a condom packet, the movement exposing the defined planes of his chest and abdomen.

I watched, transfixed, as he tore the packet open with his teeth and rolled the condom onto his impressive length.

"Ready?" he asked, catching me staring.

"Fuck yes," I said, reaching for him.

He caught my wrists in one large hand, pinning them above my head. "Not yet," he murmured, his lips ghosting along my jaw. "I'm in charge."

In one swift movement, he flipped me onto my stomach, pulling my hips up and back against him. The sudden shift left me breathless, my hands fisting in the sheets as he positioned me exactly how he wanted me. He ran a hand down the curve of my spine. The head of his cock teased at my entrance.

"Fuck, Cal," I gasped, pushing back against him, seeking friction. The emptiness inside me was almost painful, my body already primed and desperate from his touch.

He made a sound of approval, his hand coming down in a sharp smack against my ass that sent shockwaves of pleasure radiating through me. I yelped in surprise, then moaned as he soothed the spot with gentle circles.

"Too much?" he checked, his hand hovering.

"Not enough."

He chuckled darkly. "Careful what you wish for, darling."

Another smack, harder this time, had me burying my face in the pillow to muffle my cry. The sting blossomed into heat that pooled between my legs, my body responding with embarrassing enthusiasm to this new side of Callan.

"You like that. I knew you would. So controlled in your daily life, but here?" His fingers slid between my legs, finding me already slick and swollen. "Here, you want to let go."

"Don't psychoanalyze me during sex," I muttered into the pillow. "It's—fuck!"

His fingers found my clit at the same time he pushed two fingers inside me, stretching me deliciously. God, my muscles were sore. I couldn't find the will to care, though as he circled the sensitive bundle of nerves with his thumb while curling his fingers forward, finding that spot that made my vision blur.

"You were saying?" he asked innocently, continuing his torturous exploration.

I could only respond with a whimper as he worked me with his skilled fingers, my hips rocking back against his hand of their own accord. Just when I thought I might come from his touch alone, he withdrew, leaving me empty and aching.

"Callan," I protested, looking back over my shoulder to find him stroking himself, his jaw tight.

"So impatient," he teased, but the strain in his voice betrayed his own desperation. "Tell me what you want, Anica."

"You," I breathed. "Inside me. Now."

He gripped my hips with both hands, positioning himself at my entrance. "Like this?" he asked, pushing in just enough for me to feel the stretch.

"Yes," I gasped. "All of you."

With one powerful thrust, he buried himself to the hilt, the sudden fullness making me cry out. He was bigger like this, the angle allowing him to reach places that made my entire body tremble.

"Fuck," he groaned, his fingers digging into flesh. "You feel amazing."

He began to move. Shit, he was huge, and my inner walls were already sore from last night. But damn if he didn't feel amazing. One of his hands slid up my back to tangle in my hair, tugging just enough to arch my spine and change the angle.

"Oh god," I cried as he hit that perfect spot inside me. "Right there, don't stop."

"Wouldn't dream of it," he growled, increasing his pace. His free hand snaked around to find my clit again, circling in time with his thrusts. His grip on my hip was bruising, using it to pull me back onto each thrust. The dual sensations of pain and pleasure blurred until I couldn't tell where one ended and the other began, my entire being narrowed to the points where our bodies connected.

"Oh, shit. Fuck, Cal, I'm going to…"

The dual stimulation was too much. I shattered, my inner muscles clamping down around him. I shook, trembling and swearing. He held me steady through it all, his movements never faltering even as my body convulsed around him.

Before I could come down completely, he flipped me onto my back without withdrawing, hooking my legs over his shoulders. The new position drove him impossibly deeper, pulling a strangled cry from my throat.

"I want to see your face when you come this time," he said, his eyes locked on mine as he resumed his relentless pace. God, was he going faster?

"Fuck," I closed my eyes and arched my chest up as he pounded into me. "How are you so fucking good at this?" I gasped, my eyes opening just in time to catch that cocky grin slide across his handsome face.

"Told you. Good at many things," he said, his smirk disappearing as he pulled almost all the way out and slammed back into me.

"Shit!" I held myself with one hand against the headboard. With each thrust, he'd moved me closer to it until I was definitely at risk of smacking my head.

The intensity in his gaze was almost too much to bear, but I couldn't look away. My body started building towards another peak.

"Callan," I panted, clawing at his thighs to pull him closer. If there even was such a thing considering he was balls deep inside me.

He obliged to my nonverbal with a single powerful thrust that buried him to the hilt, the sudden fullness pulling a strangled cry from my throat. He kept up his punishing pace that had the headboard slamming against the wall and obscenities falling from my lips in a continuous stream.

This time, when I came, he followed, his rhythm faltering as he groaned my name. He pulsed inside me, his entire body tensing as he found his release.

We stayed like that for several moments, breathless and tangled together, before he carefully lowered my legs and collapsed beside me. His arm draped possessively across my waist, pulling me against his chest.

"Holy shit," I managed after a moment, my voice hoarse.

"Yeah," he agreed, sounding equally wrecked.

"Yeah," I nodded, no further elaboration needed.

"Still need to brush your teeth?" he murmured against my hair, a smile in his voice. He wove our fingers together as we had at the B&B on the island.

"Shut up," I laughed, too boneless with satisfaction to come up with a better retort.

I wasn't sure how long we lay there. I might've even dipped into a post-orgasm nap. Eventually, though, I stirred, making moves to get up.

"Where are you going?" Callan asked, his hand tightening around mine.

"Shower," I replied. "Then probably home. I have work to do today."

"Stay," he said, and it wasn't a command so much as a request. "Have breakfast with me."

I hesitated, torn between the sensible choice and the temptation of more time with him. "I really should go..."

"I have Belgian waffle batter in the fridge," he said in a singsong voice, his thumb tracing circles on my palm.

Despite myself, I laughed. "Fresh strawberries and whip cream?"

"I'll make sure they're there by the time you're done with your shower," he assured me, bringing my hand to his lips and pressing a kiss to my knuckles that somehow managed to be both courtly and suggestive. "Please?"

"Fine," I conceded. "But just breakfast. Then I really do need to go."

His smile was triumphant. "Deal."

After a shower that took twice as long as it should have due to Callan's insistence on "helping" me wash my back (and other areas that definitely didn't need assistance), I stood in his kitchen, wrapped in a borrowed T-shirt that hung to mid-thigh and boxer shorts that were comically large.

The kitchen was clearly well used. Callan moved through the space, pulling ingredients from the massive refrigerator and heating up the waffle iron.

"I think it's really cool that you cook," I said, watching him whisk the batter. "That you actually seem to know your way around a kitchen."

"Many talents," he replied, pouring batter into the waffle iron. "Some of which you've recently experienced firsthand."

"And yet somehow your ego remains your most impressive feature," I noted, accepting the mug of coffee he handed me, prepared exactly how I liked it.

"I would argue that after this last night and this morning, there is at least one other feature you found more impressive," he countered with a wink.

I rolled my eyes, but couldn't suppress a smile. "Yes. Quite a bit."

There was something disarmingly domestic about the scene; Callan in sweatpants and nothing else, making breakfast in his kitchen while I sat at the island in his clothes, nursing coffee and watching him move. It was the kind of moment that could make a person start thinking dangerous thoughts about futures that had no right to be considered.

"What are you thinking?" he asked, catching me staring.

"That you look unfairly good in sweatpants," I shrugged. It felt wrong to ruin the moment with depressing thoughts.

Callan grinned. "I should bend you over more often. You seem to give out compliments when I do," he said, setting a plate in front of me with a golden waffle, fresh berries, a dusting of powdered sugar, and a dollop of whipped cream.

"I just have to space them out. Can't give them all out at once."

We ate, joking back and forth. The waffles were absolutely delicious, just as promised. I was scraping the last bit of berry from my plate when Callan's phone buzzed. He checked it, then groaned.

"What is it?" I asked.

"My friends," he said, typing a quick response. "The Three Assholes. They're coming over for brunch in an hour."

"Oh," I said, tugging at the hem of the shirt. "I should definitely go, then."

"Or," he suggested, setting down his phone, "you could stay. Meet them properly. Not over the phone like before."

"Really?"

"I'd like you to, yeah."

Part of me wanted to retreat, to maintain the professional distance that had kept me safe for so long. But another part, a growing part, wanted to see where this could go.

"Okay," I agreed, surprising myself. "But I can't meet your friends dressed like this. I need actual clothes."

"I could have some brought over," he offered immediately. "Whatever you need."

"That won't be necessary. I have an emergency outfit in my bag," I assured him, sliding off the barstool.

"Of course you do. Why am I not surprised?"

"Professional preparedness. Never know when you might need to change after a champagne fountain disaster or a drunk groomsman."

"Or after being thoroughly debauched by a billionaire," he added with a smirk that should have been irritating but somehow wasn't.

"That category is a recent addition to my emergency protocols. Still working out the necessary supplies. So far I've listed hair ties, tooth brush, and possibly knee braces."

He laughed. "I apologize for necessitating knee braces. Though not for the activities that led to their requirement."

"Apology not accepted but appreciated," I replied, heading toward where I'd left my bag. "I'll be back looking like a professional human being rather than someone who got railed into next Tuesday and stole her bedmate's clothes."

"Spoilsport," he called after me. "I like you in my clothes. Makes it easier to take them off you again later."

I flipped him off over my shoulder, his laugh following me down the hallway.

True to my word, I emerged in the simple shift dress and flats I kept in my emergency bag, hair neatly styled, looking like someone who hadn't spent the morning engaging in activities that would make a porn star blush.

"You clean up nice," Callan observed, having donned a t-shirt to complement his sweatpants. "Though I preferred the 'thoroughly fucked' look."

"Save that thought for when your friends aren't about to arrive," I suggested, helping him clear the breakfast dishes.

"They'll be here soon," he said, checking the time. "Fair warning: they will absolutely give me shit about this. About us. Just ignore them. It's how they show affection."

"I think I can handle it. I deal with drunk groomsmen and emotional mothers-of-the-bride for a living. Your friends can't be worse than that."

"You say that now," he muttered, but he was smiling.

The doorbell rang, and Callan went to answer it. I took the opportunity to freshen up, heading to the bathroom to check that I looked suitably composed.

On my way back, I heard male voices from the living area. I was about to join them when I caught the sound of my name. I paused, just out of sight of the open doorway.

"So, you and Anica, huh?" a voice I didn't have a name for asked. "Gotta say, didn't see that coming."

"She's hot," another voice commented. "Smart, too. And she clearly doesn't take any of your shit. No wonder you're into her."

"It's more than that," Callan replied, his voice softer than usual. "She's... different."

"Different how?" the first voice asked.

"She sees me," Callan said simply. "Not the money, not the reputation. Just me."

"Damn, Burkhardt," a third voice chimed in, this one with a teasing edge. "You're in love with her."

My heart stuttered at the words, my breath catching in my throat. Was he? Because maybe I was falling for him too and we could find a way to–

231

"Don't be ridiculous," Callan scoffed.

My stomach dropped.

"Come on, man," the second voice prodded. "We've known you forever. You've never talked about any woman like this. You're head over heels in love."

"For the last time, love doesn't fucking exist," Callan snapped, his voice suddenly hard. "What I have with Anica is great, but it's not love. It can't be love because, repeat after me boys, love doesn't exist. Period. Now shut up about it."

My chest constricted as if all the oxygen had been sucked from the room. I was an idiot. An absolute idiot. God, when had I started believing that anything besides us sleeping together could happen.

"Look," Callan continued, his voice lowering, "she knows the score. This is just a good time for both of us. Something fun until I figure out the bet."

I pressed a hand to my mouth, the sting of tears threatening behind my eyes. I'd known, of course. I'd known from the beginning that Callan didn't believe in love. He'd made no secret of his cynicism, his belief that marriage was nothing more than a practical arrangement.

But hearing him dismiss what we'd shared so callously hurt more than I'd expected. More than it should have, given that I'd gone into this with my eyes open.

Vivian's words echoed in my mind: "My Cal has a golden heart." What utter bullshit. His heart wasn't gold; it was carbon. Compressed under pressure, hardened into something beautiful but impenetrable. And I, like every fool who'd ever been dazzled by a diamond, had mistaken its brilliance for warmth.

The worst part? Despite all my professional boundaries, all my promises to myself after Austin, I'd started to fall for him. Started to believe there might be something real beneath the billionaire playboy facade, something that could grow beyond the physical into something meaningful.

What a fucking idiot I was. Anica Marcel, wedding planner extraordinaire, who'd built a career helping other people find their happily-ever-afters while systematically avoiding her own, had let herself believe in the possibility of love with a man who didn't even think it existed.

I backed away from the doorway, moving silently toward the bedroom where I'd left my bag. I needed to get out of here before they realized I'd overheard. Before I had to face Callan and pretend his words hadn't shattered something inside me.

Gathering my things quickly, I shoved my dress into my bag alongside my phone and wallet. I was almost to the elevator when I heard his voice behind me.

"Anica? Where ya going?" Callan asked. "I was about to introduce you to the guys."

I turned slowly, forcing my expression into something I prayed resembled composure. "I just remembered I have a client emergency. I need to go."

He frowned, moving closer. "What emergency? You didn't get any calls."

"It was a text," I said shortly. "Look, I really need to go."

"What's wrong?" he asked, his gaze searching my face. "Did something happen?"

I let out a hollow laugh. "You could say that."

"You heard us talking."

"Enough," I confirmed.

He ran a hand through his hair. "Anica, listen—"

"To what? To more explanations about how this is just 'a good time'? About how love doesn't exist? I've heard enough, Callan."

"That's not—I didn't mean—" He exhaled sharply. "It's complicated."

"No, it's really not," I said, my voice steadier than I felt. "You've been honest from the beginning about not believing in love. I knew that. I just didn't realize how deeply you meant it."

"What do you want from me, Anica? To pretend I believe in something I don't? To lie to you?"

And there it was. The confirmation I didn't want but needed to hear.

"You truly believe love doesn't exist. That what people feel for each other is nothing more than convenient fiction or biological impulse?"

He hesitated, and in that hesitation, I had my answer.

"People build entire lives waiting for something that doesn't exist," he said finally, his voice hard. "I refuse to be one of them."

I nodded, a cold, solid wall erupting from where I'd foolishly let him break it down, brick by brick. "Then there's nothing more to say."

"So that's it? You're just going to leave because I won't parrot some Hallmark card sentiment about love conquering all?"

"I'm leaving because I've spent my life, and more importantly, my career surrounded by love," I said, my voice breaking. "I've watched people sacrifice everything for it. I've seen it transform lives. And I deserve someone who at least acknowledges its existence, even if they haven't experienced it themselves."

"Anica—"

"I'm surrounded by it at work, Ca—Mr. Burkhardt," I continued, refusing to let him interrupt. "I see it daily. And I can't be with someone who looks me in the eye and tells me love is fiction. I won't be someone's 'good time' while they shop for a bride elsewhere. I deserve better than that."

I turned away before he could respond, before the tears threatening to fall could betray me further. The elevator doors opened with a soft chime, and I stepped inside, keeping my back straight, my chin high.

"Don't let this be over," he called after me, a note of desperation in his voice that I'd never heard before. "Please, Anica."

"I'm not *letting* anything happen." I turned, meeting his gaze one last time. "But it is over. Some things can't be fixed with money or power or orgasms, Callan. This is one of them."

The doors closed before he could respond, and only then, alone in the descending elevator, did I allow the first tears to fall. They didn't stop.

FREE FALLING WITHOUT A PARACHUTE

Chapter 16: Callan

Twenty-nine billion dollars in assets, and I couldn't buy back the ten seconds it took for Anica to walk out of my life. I stood frozen in place, staring at the closed elevator doors like the ghost of a man watching his own heart flatline on a hospital monitor.

"Cal? Where's your girl?" Morgan called from the living room.

"She's not—" I stopped, the words sticking in my throat. "She left."

I turned back toward the living room, where my three friends lounged like they owned the place. Kris was already helping himself to my most expensive scotch, Morgan was scrolling through his phone with his feet propped on my coffee table, and Chance was examining the waffle maker with interest.

"Left? Like, to get something from her car?" Chance asked, looking up from the kitchen appliance.

"No," I said flatly. "Like left. Gone. Possibly forever."

That got their attention. Three heads snapped toward me with varying degrees of confusion.

"What the hell did you do?" Kris demanded, setting down his glass. "It's been what, an hour since you slept with her? That's a new record, even for you."

"I didn't do anything," I snapped, stalking to the bar and pouring myself a drink. At ten in the morning. Like the functional adult I clearly was. "She overheard us talking."

Three identical expressions of realization dawned across their faces, followed quickly by winces.

"The 'love doesn't exist' rant?" Morgan guessed.

"And the 'just a good time' comment," I confirmed, downing half my scotch in one go.

"Shit," Kris muttered.

"Yeah. Shit." I dropped into an armchair, scrubbing a hand over my face. "She just... left. Told me she deserves better than someone who thinks love is fiction."

"She's not wrong," Chance pointed out, earning himself a glare from me.

"Whose side are you on?"

"Yours, obviously. Which is why I'm telling you that you fucked up. Badly. Like, textbook 'How to Ruin a Perfectly Good Thing in Ten Seconds' level fucked up."

"I didn't fuck up," I insisted, even as a voice in the back of my head called me a liar. "I was honest. I've always been honest about not believing in love. She knew that going in."

"There's a difference between theoretical skepticism and telling your friends that what you have with someone is 'just a good time,'" Morgan said. "That's like telling someone you're on a diet and then having them catch you behind a dumpster deep-throating a Big Mac."

Kris snorted. "Graphic, but accurate."

"You know what? I don't need this." I stood, pacing across the living room. "I don't need you three idiots analyzing my life. She wants someone who believes in fairy tales? Fine. Good luck finding that in Manhattan. Most men here think 'emotional intimacy' is remembering your Starbucks order the morning after."

"Come on, man," Chance said, his perpetually calm demeanor starting to fray around the edges. "This isn't about fairy tales. It's about basic human connection."

"What would you know about it?" I challenged.

"I've been married for years," he reminded me mildly. "To a woman I love more than anything. And yes, I said the L-word. Try not to have an aneurysm."

"Good for you," I muttered. "Want a fucking medal?"

Kris let out a low whistle. "Wow. You are deep in denial right now. Like, submerged-at-the-bottom-of-the-Mariana-Trench deep."

"I'm not in denial, I'm being realistic. Love, at most, is a chemical reaction designed to ensure the continuation of the species. It's not real, it's just biology. Attachment. Lust. Comfort. Whatever. People dress it up, but it all comes down to the same thing," I insisted, refilling my glass.

"If that's true," Morgan said, watching me carefully, "then why are you this upset that she left?"

I opened my mouth to respond, then closed it again, the scotch bitter on my tongue.

"I'm not upset," I lied. "I'm annoyed. Anica's my wedding planner."

"Bullshit," Kris said bluntly. "You're devastated. I haven't seen you this rattled since your grandmother had that health scare last year."

"Fuck off, Kris."

"He's right," Chance added. "Look at yourself, man. You're pacing. You're drinking scotch before noon. You can't even say her name without looking like someone punched you in the gut."

"You don't know what you're talking about."

"Cal," Morgan said, setting down his phone and leaning forward. "It's us. You don't have to pretend."

Something inside me cracked, just a little. "Fine. I like her. A lot. She's smart and funny and doesn't take my shit, and yes, the sex was mind-blowing. But that doesn't mean—"

"That you love her?" Chance finished for me. "Because from where I'm sitting, it looks a hell of a lot like love."

"It's not. It's... attraction. Compatibility. Chemistry. Whatever you want to call it. But it's not love, because love doesn't—"

"Exist. Yeah, we got it the first fifty times," Kris interrupted, rolling his eyes. "Keep telling yourself that while you drink yourself stupid at ten in the morning over a woman who walked out less than fifteen minutes ago."

I wanted to argue, to defend myself, but the words wouldn't come. Instead, I sank back into the armchair, my drink forgotten in my hand.

"What am I supposed to do? Call her and say, 'Sorry I don't believe in the thing you apparently need me to believe in'? Lie to her?"

"How about," Chance suggested gently, "you start by asking yourself why you're so damn terrified of even considering the possibility that love might be real?"

"I'm not terrified. I'm rational."

"Rational," Morgan repeated skeptically. "Is that why you're clutching that glass like it's a life preserver and you're drowning?"

I looked down, surprised to find my knuckles white around the tumbler. I set it down, flexing my fingers.

"My parents were married for years before they divorced," I said after a moment. "They hated each other. My father cheated constantly. My mother drank. They stayed together for appearances, for business connections, for tax benefits. They never loved each other. Not really. And my grandfather ruined Gram's life when he left her."

"So your sample size for marriage are two shitty examples, and you've decided the whole concept is invalid?" Kris asked. "That's like eating two bad burritos and declaring all Mexican food is poison."

"It's not just my parents. Look around. Half of marriages end in divorce. The other half are just people too stubborn or too scared to admit they made a mistake."

"Or," Chance countered, "they're people who found someone they genuinely want to build a life with. Who choose each other, every day, even when it's hard. Especially when it's hard."

I didn't have a response for that. The certainty in his voice made something twist uncomfortably in my chest.

"I have to call her," I said abruptly, pulling out my phone.

"That's probably not the best idea right now," Morgan cautioned. "You're upset, she's upset. Give it some time."

"How much time?" I demanded. "She thinks I'm a heartless asshole who used her for sex."

"Well, did you?" Kris asked bluntly.

"No! It wasn't like that. It was... good. She's the easiest person to be around. I just... I wasn't using her."

"Well, it sounded like it," Chance said.

I ran a hand through my hair, struggling to find the words. "I mean yes, she's beautiful. And she calls me on my crap and doesn't back down. She makes me laugh. She makes me think. She makes me want to be... better."

The three of them exchanged looks that were far too knowing for my comfort.

"What?" I demanded.

"Nothing," Kris said, poorly suppressing a smile. "Just listening to you not being in love."

"Shut up."

My phone buzzed in my hand, and my heart leapt embarrassingly, hoping it might be Anica. Instead, it was a text from Erika.

ERIKA: *Checking in on the bride hunt. Any progress?*

I stared at my phone for a long moment before taking a deep breath. The bet. The deadline. The whole reason I'd hired Anica in the first place.

"The bet is off," I announced, setting down my phone and picking up the drink again.

"What?" Morgan blinked at me. "You're giving up? Just like that?"

"I'm not giving up," I corrected. "I'm acknowledging that it was a stupid idea from the start. You guys win. Congratulations. I'll transfer the money today."

"Hold on," Chance held up his hand. "This isn't about the money, Cal. It never was."

"Then what was it about?" I challenged.

"It was about trying to prove to us your fucked up notion about love not existing. I think your exact words were that 'love is a sham.' You wanted to prove that it didn't exist and that you could control everything, even something as unpredictable as relationships. That you could approach marriage like a business transaction and avoid getting hurt."

I stared at him. "Yeah well—"

"And now you're walking away because you realized you can't control how you feel about Anica, and it scares the shit out of you because you might actually be falling for her."

"Free falling without a parachute, I'd say," Kris added.

Shit. Were they right? I'd spent my entire adult life building walls, constructing a carefully controlled environment where I could dictate the terms of every interaction. And then Anica had walked in, with her emergency kits and her judgmental eyebrows and her absolute refusal to be impressed by me, and those walls had started to crumble.

"I need to fix this," I said, standing up so abruptly that my drink sloshed over the edge of the glass.

"And how exactly do you plan to do that? You just spent the last ten minutes insisting love doesn't exist, and now you want to, what, convince her you're worth another shot?" Kris asked.

"I don't know," I admitted. "But I have to try."

I grabbed my phone and dialed Anica's number, but it went straight to voicemail. I tried again. Nothing. Undeterred, I tried the office line for her office.

"Knot Your Average Wedding, this is Devonna speaking. How may I assist you today?" The crisp, professional voice of Anica's assistant filled the line.

"Devonna, it's Callan. I need to speak with Anica."

There was a brief pause. "I'm sorry, Mr. Burkhardt, but Ms. Marcel isn't in the office and is unavailable at the moment. Would you like to leave a message?"

"Cut the crap, Devonna. I know she's avoiding my calls. Is she there? Put her on the phone."

"She's not. Would you like to leave a message?" Devonna replied, her tone cooling several degrees.

I blinked, taken aback by the sudden steel in her voice. "When will she be available?"

"Her schedule is fully booked for the rest of today," Devonna informed me, and I could hear her typing on her computer. "And tomorrow. And, in fact, for the foreseeable future. If you'd like to discuss your wedding plans, I'd be happy to assist you, or I can connect you with Ms. Landry."

"I don't want to talk to Mari, I want to talk to Anica."

"I understand, Mr. Burkhardt, but that won't be possible right now. Ms. Marcel has instructed me to handle all communications regarding your wedding. If you have questions or concerns about the arrangements, I'm fully briefed on your file."

"This isn't about the wedding," I said, running a hand through my hair as I tried to keep my growing temper at bay. "This is personal."

"I'm aware and up to date on the situation. I'll relay the message that you called. Is there anything else I can help you with today?"

I was being managed, and I knew it.

"No," I said finally. "Just... tell her I called. Please."

"I'll be sure to do that, Mr. Burkhardt. Have a pleasant day."

The line went dead, and I stared at the wall for far too long after she'd hung up.

"Well? Did you just get shut down by an assistant?" Kris asked, sounding impressed.

"She's a good gatekeeper," I muttered. "I'm starting to see why Anica hired her."

"So what now?" Morgan asked.

"Now..." I sighed, pocketing my phone. "Now I need to talk to my grandmother."

"Bringing out the big guns," Chance nodded approvingly. "Smart move."

"She's the only person I know who's more stubborn than Anica," I explained. "And she seemed to like her. Maybe she can... I don't know, help me figure out how to fix this."

"Or at least tell you what an idiot you're being," Kris suggested helpfully.

"She'll definitely do that. It's her favorite hobby."

"Do you want us to clear out?" Morgan asked, gesturing to the mess we'd made of my living room in the short time they'd been there.

I considered it, then shook my head. "No. Stay. Finish the waffles. I need to do this alone."

"Good luck," Chance called as I headed for the door. "And Cal? For what it's worth, I think she's worth fighting for."

I paused. "Yeah," I mumbled. "I think so too."

WHEN I GOT to my grandmother's house, I used my key, letting myself in without knocking.

"Gram?" I called, setting down the bag of pastries I'd picked up on the way. Peace offerings never hurt with her, especially when she was about to tell me exactly how badly I'd screwed up.

"In the sunroom," her voice called back. "With my feet up and a gin and tonic in hand."

I followed the sound of her voice, finding her exactly as described, reclining on her favorite chaise lounge, a drink in one hand and a romance book in the other. She didn't look up when I entered, turning a page.

"Sit," she commanded, still not looking at me. "And explain to me why you're here instead of with that lovely young woman who actually had the patience to tolerate your nonsense."

I sank into the armchair across from her. "You heard."

"Of course I heard," she sniffed, finally setting down her book to fix me with a piercing stare. "The catering service for my charity lunch is run by Ms. Landry's cousin, who heard from Ms. Landry that you—and I quote—'fucked up royally with Anica and are now on her eternal shit list.'"

I winced. "That was fast."

"Gossip travels at the speed of light, darling. Especially when it involves billionaires making spectacular fools of themselves over intelligent women." She took a sip of her drink. "Now, tell me what happened. Every sordid detail."

"I'm not sure you want the sordid details, Gram," I said, remembering exactly how my morning with Anica had begun.

She waved a dismissive hand. "Skip the bedroom gymnastics. I'm old, not dead. I can fill in those blanks myself. Tell me how you managed to chase away the one woman who's looked at you like you might actually be worth the trouble."

I sighed, then gave her the abbreviated version; Anica staying over, my friends arriving, the overheard conversation, and the devastating aftermath. By the time I finished, Gram was shaking her head slowly, looking equal parts disappointed and exasperated.

"Oh, Cal," she said, and somehow those two words carried the weight of decades of accumulated wisdom and frustration. "You are your father's son in all the worst ways."

The comparison stung. "I'm nothing like him."

"No? The emotional unavailability? The absolute terror of admitting vulnerability? The way you push away anyone who gets too close? That's absolutely my son."

"I'm not scared," I insisted, though we both knew it was a lie.

"Bullshit," Gram snapped. "You're terrified. You have been since you were seven years old and watched your parents tear each other apart while pretending everything was fine."

I looked away, unable to meet her gaze. "Their marriage was a sham."

"Their marriage was a disaster," she corrected. "But that doesn't mean all marriages are. That doesn't mean love isn't real."

"How can you, of all people, still believe in love?" I demanded. "After what Grandpa did to you? After how he hurt you?"

A shadow crossed her face, old pain briefly visible before she masked it with her usual steel. "Your grandfather was a bastard who didn't deserve me," she said matter-of-factly. "But that doesn't mean what I felt for him wasn't real. It doesn't erase the good years before he showed his true colors."

"He cheated on you," I reminded her, anger on her behalf still hot after all these years. "He humiliated you. He nearly bankrupted you."

"Yes," she agreed calmly. "And after I divorced him and took him for everything he was worth, I picked myself up and moved on. Because one failed marriage doesn't invalidate the entire concept of love."

I ran a hand through my hair, frustration building. "It's not just one marriage, Gram. It's everywhere. People cheat, they lie, they fall out of what they call love as easily as they fall into it."

"Some do, but some don't. Some people build lives together based on mutual respect, shared values, and genuine affection. Some people choose each other, every day, not because of some hormonal impulse but because they've found someone who makes life better just by being in it."

Her words hit uncomfortably close to how I felt about Anica.

"I don't know how to fix this," I admitted.

"Yes, you do," she said, setting down her drink and leaning forward. "You're just too stubborn and scared to do it."

"What, tell her I believe in love when I don't? Lie to her?"

"Is it a lie, Cal?" she asked. "Think about how you feel when she walks into a room. Think about how empty your penthouse felt this morning after she left. Think about why you're sitting here in my sunroom instead of at the office making another million dollars. Is that really just 'chemistry' or 'compatibility' or whatever other clinical term you want to use to avoid saying the L-word?"

I didn't answer, couldn't answer. The truth was too terrifying to contemplate.

"You're going to lose her," Gram continued, her voice gentler now. "Because you're too afraid to admit what you feel."

"And what if I do admit it? What if I tell her I... care about her, deeply, and then it falls apart anyway? What if I end up just like them? What if I hurt her?"

"What if you don't? What if it works? What if you build something beautiful together? Are you willing to lose her for certain just to avoid the possibility of future pain?"

Put like that, it seemed ridiculous. And yet, the fear remained, a cold knot in my chest.

"I don't know how to do this, Gram," I confessed, my voice barely audible.

"No one does, darling," she said, reaching out to pat my hand. "That's the terrifying, wonderful truth of it. Love isn't something you can control or predict or manage like one of your tech projects. It's messy and inconvenient and often arrives at the worst possible time, wrapped in the last package you expected."

"Like a judgy wedding planner with plans for every occasion?" I asked, a small smile finally breaking through.

"Exactly like that. And if you let her go without a fight because you're too scared to admit she matters, you'll regret it for the rest of your life."

"I need to see her," I said, standing. "I need to talk to her."

"Yes, you do, but not like this, not half-cocked and desperate. She deserves better than that."

"Then what do I do?"

"First, you figure out what you actually want. Not what you think you should want, or what's safe to want, but what you truly, deeply want." She fixed me with a steady gaze. "And then you find a way to show her that you're serious. Words are easy, Callan, but that woman needs to see you grovel. Preferably on your knees."

I nodded, my mind already racing. "Thank you."

"Don't thank me yet," she warned. "You've still got a mountain to climb, and that girl has every reason to leave you stranded at base camp."

"I'm good at mountains," I assured her. "And I'm very, very motivated."

"Good," she said, picking up her book again. "Now go away. You've interrupted my reading, and just at the part where he's ripping her bodice."

"TMI, Gram."

"Tit for tat."

I chuckled and leaned down to kiss her forehead. "Love you, Gram."

"See?" she said, patting my cheek. "You can say it when it matters."

The next two weeks passed in a blur of frustration and planning. Despite me ending the bet, the wedding was still on. The bride still very much absent, but I fully intended to change that. True to Devonna's word, Anica was completely unavailable. My calls went to voicemail. My texts received polite, professional responses, always signed "A. Marcel" rather than just "Anica."

When I stopped by her office unannounced, Mari intercepted me in the reception area with a sympathetic but firm redirection.

"She doesn't want to see you," she said, crossing her arms. "And I say this as someone who once made a detailed PowerPoint presentation entitled 'Why Callan Burkhardt Should Rail Me Against A Wall.' You need to respect her boundaries right now."

"I just want to talk to her," I insisted.

"And she just wants to not have her heart broken again by a man who publicly declared that love is a fictional construct," Mari countered. "Funny how we don't always get what we want."

I winced. "She told you what happened."

"In excruciating detail. Over several bottles of wine and at least one pint of ice cream eaten directly from the container. It was not pretty."

The image of Anica upset made something twist painfully in my chest. "I need to explain."

"What you need," Mari said, not unkindly, "is to give her space. She's not just angry, Cal. She's hurt. Deeply hurt. And showing up here unannounced isn't helping."

"Then what will help?" I asked, desperation creeping into my voice. "Tell me what to do, Mari. How do I fix this? I *need* to fix this."

She studied me for a moment, her expression softening. "You really care about her, don't you?"

"More than I know how to handle."

Mari sighed, then glanced over my shoulder and gestured for me to follow her into a small conference room. Once the door was closed, she turned to face me.

"Look, I'm going to help you, but only because I believe you genuinely care about her and aren't just trying to salve your wounded ego."

"Thank you."

"Don't thank me yet," she warned, echoing Gram's earlier caution. "If you hurt her again, I will personally ensure that every wedding vendor in the tri-state area knows exactly how to make your life miserable. I'm talking flower arrangements that induce sneezing fits, photographers who only capture your bad side, and DJs who mysteriously only play the Macarena when you're in the room."

"Noted," I said, trying not to smile at her fierce but very strange loyalty. "So what do I do?"

"First, you respect the professional boundaries she's established. The wedding planning continues with Devonna as your point of contact. If Anica wants to be directly involved, she will be. That's her choice."

I nodded, though it pained me to think of continuing the wedding charade when the only woman I wanted was currently refusing to speak to me.

"Second, you figure out what you actually want. Not what your friends want, or what your business interests dictate, or what your parents' screwed-up marriage taught you to expect. What do you, Callan Burkhardt, actually want?"

It was the same question Gram had posed, and it deserved the same careful consideration.

"And third," Mari continued, "when you have an answer to that question, you show her. Don't tell her—show her. Anica has had enough experience with men who broke her trust and her heart. The Douche Who Shall Not Be Named was—"

"Austin? Ow!" I rubbed my shoulder where she punched me in the arm. "You two are violent."

"I said he wasn't to be named, asshole." Mari shook out her hand, eyeing my arm. "What do you have under there? Steel plating? Shit, that hurt." She wrinkled her nose, refocusing on my face. "Anyways. Like I was saying the Dickhead with the microdick was really good at words. He tried to gaslight her into getting back with her after he fucked that client. She nearly did. Thankfully, I'm a good friend and didn't let her, and he ended up sleeping with a different woman while trying to win Anica back."

"What a douche."

"Exactly." Mari nodded once. "My point is, he broke her trust. And her heart. And her faith in men. You had started to fix that until this little fuck up."

I ran my hand through my hair and started to pace the room. "I didn't want to hurt her. I never wanted to hurt her." Facing Mari, I shoved my hands in my pockets and planted my feet. "I'm serious, Mari. You have to believe me."

She gave me a once over. "You need to take action. Words won't mean shit."

"Action," I repeated, an idea beginning to form. "I can do action. But I might need help."

"I'll see what I can do. Anica can't know, though."

"I agree," I said, nodding. "At least for now."

"Good, now get out before Devonna realizes I'm helping you and puts laxatives in my coffee."

"She wouldn't really —"

"Try me," Devonna's voice came from the doorway, making both of us jump. She stood there with her tablet clutched to her chest and a terrifyingly pleasant smile on her face. "Mr. Burkhardt, how lovely to see you in person."

"Devonna," Mari said with a warning look. "Callan and I were just —"

"Conspiring?" Devonna suggested, arching a perfectly shaped eyebrow. "Plotting? Attempting to circumvent my very explicit instructions to keep him away from Ms. Marcel?"

"Something like that," I admitted, deciding honesty might be my best approach. "But not for the reasons you think."

247

Devonna stepped fully into the room and closed the door behind her. "Enlighten me then, Mr. Burkhardt. What exactly are your reasons for lurking in our conference room with Ms. Landry?"

"I want to fix things with Anica. And I need your help to do it."

Devonna laughed, but the sound wasn't exactly reassuring. "That's rich. I thought love didn't exist to you. Why would you possibly care about fixing things with Ms. Marcel when she was just a 'good time'?"

"She really did tell you two everything, didn't she?" I glanced between the two women.

"Everything," Devonna said, nodding once. "So take your big ass ego and your even bigger dick, and get out of the office. She doesn't want to see you."

"D, he–"

"No, Mari. He hurt her." Devonna shook her head. "He doesn't get to waltz back into her life."

Sighing, I leaned against the table. "I deserve that."

"You deserve much worse," she countered, but I noticed she hadn't immediately thrown me out, which I took as a positive sign.

"Look," I said, running my hand down my cheek. I really needed to shave. "I know I fucked up. Monumentally. The bet was stupid and cruel, and I regret ever making it. I called it off when I realized I'd hurt her."

"The bet was stupid, but what concerns me more is how easily you cheapened what you had with Anica because you were scared to be anything more than a playboy."

"You're right." I shrugged. "I was scared. In fact, it still terrifies me even now that I could ever feel this way about another person. But…I…I do. And that's exactly why I need to make this right. Not for my ego, not for the wedding or the stupid ass bet, but for her."

Devonna studied me. "What exactly are you proposing?"

"I need help. I need the wedding at the Rhodes Estate to still happen. Same date, same arrangements, but with some… adjustments."

"Who are you marrying?" Mari asked, leaning forward. "You just said you wanted to win back Anica. How the fuck do you expect us to help you if you're going to–oh… I get it. Never mind."

"What kind of adjustments?" Devonna rolled her eyes at Mari. "Why do you need our help?

"I'm not a wedding planner. And I need to make some adjustments to show I'm not all words." I replied, glancing between the two of them. "Look, I know you both care about Anica. You want to protect her from being hurt again. But I'm not Austin."

"Don't say that name in this office," both women snapped in unison.

"Sorry." I raised my hands in surrender. "I'm not That Guy. I didn't cheat on her. I would *never* cheat on her. I just need to show her how sorry I am and that she's the one I want to be with."

Mari and Devonna exchanged a look.

"He does have that desperate, love-sick puppy vibe. Especially with the scruff," Mari observed. "It's actually kind of pathetic. In a sweet way."

"Hmm," Devonna tapped her finger against her tablet. "And he did come all the way here just to get verbally eviscerated by us."

"I'm standing right here," I reminded them.

"Shh," Devonna said without looking at me. "The adults are talking."

After another moment of silent communication, Devonna turned to face me fully. "If we agree to help you, you need to understand that this isn't a guaranteed success. Anica may still tell you to take a flying leap off the Empire State Building."

"I understand. But I have to try."

"And why, exactly, should we help you?" Devonna asked, crossing her arms. "Give me one good reason that doesn't involve your bank account."

"Or the big ass python you're hiding in your pants," Mari added, eyeing me. "Yes. She told us about that too."

"God, you're weird," I muttered under my breath.

"Not helping, rich boy."

I thought for a moment, wanting to give them the most honest answer possible. "Because I...I love her," I said finally. "Shit. I do. I fucking love her. And I think—I hope—she might love me too. Even if she currently wants to strangle me with my own tie."

"That's a good reason," Devonna said, some of the bite from earlier disappearing as she looked me up and down.

"So you'll help?" I asked, trying not to sound too eager.

"Against my better judgment," she sighed. "But if this blows up, I'm going to have my cousins dismember you piece by piece and dissolve the rest of you in barrels of acid."

249

My eyebrows shot up. "That is… way more dark than Mari's threats."

Next to her, Mari looked at Devonna with a wide grin. "He's right. I like it. Let's go with your option if he fucks this up again."

"Shit," I muttered under my breath. "You guys are terrifying."

"Don't fuck it up then," Mari said, with a shrug.

"Understood," I nodded.

"And," Devonna added, "you should know that we're doing this for Anica, not for you. If at any point we think this will hurt her more than help her, all bets are off."

"I wouldn't have it any other way. She deserves people who look out for her."

"She does," Devonna agreed. "Now, get out. Ms. Marcel is supposed to return soon from a meeting."

The thought that I might be able to see Anica made my heart leap, but I pushed it down. I'd promised I would respect her boundaries, but god I wanted to see her. To hold her. To drop to my knees and beg for forgiveness.

Instead, I nodded once and headed for the door. "Right. Well, I'll call you later to start working out the details."

"Oh, and Callan?" Mari called after me. I turned back to find her grinning wickedly. "When this works and you two eventually have babies, I expect to be godmother to at least one of them."

"Don't get ahead of yourself," Devonna cautioned, but I noticed she didn't dismiss the possibility outright.

As I left the office, I pulled out my phone and Chance's contact, hitting dial.

"Cal?" he answered, sounding surprised. "Everything okay?"

"I need to meet with you and the guys. Tonight. It's important."

"Sure, no problem. Your place?"

"No. Neutral territory. That bar on 25th."

"Should I be worried?"

"No," I assured him. "I'm just going to need your help. All of you."

"Consider it done," Chance said immediately. "Whatever you need."

THE BAR WAS dimly lit and mercifully empty when I arrived that evening. I'd reserved a back booth, ordered a round of drinks, and was halfway through mine when the guys showed up, all three looking unusually serious.

"This feels like an intervention," Kris commented as they slid into the booth. "Are we supposed to tell you how your drinking affects us or something?"

"If anything, I'd be the one staging the intervention," I pointed out. "Especially for you, Kris."

"Fair point," he conceded, reaching for his beer. "So what's the big emergency?"

I took a deep breath, gathering my thoughts. "I called off the bet."

"Yeah, you mentioned that. Quite enjoying the payoff. So is my future bride." Morgan nodded.

"I'm still wondering why," Chance said.

"Because it was stupid," I said bluntly. "Because I don't want to marry some random woman to win a bet. Because..." I hesitated, then pushed forward. "Because the only woman I can actually see myself standing at that altar with wants nothing to do with me right now."

There was a moment of stunned silence, then Kris let out a low whistle. "Holy shit. You're actually admitting it."

"Admitting what?" I asked, playing dumb even as my heart raced.

"That you're in love with Anica," Chance said simply.

I didn't deny it. Couldn't deny it anymore. "Yeah," I said finally, the word barely audible. "I think I am."

Morgan reached across the table to feel my forehead. "Are you feeling okay? Fever? Delusions? Severe head trauma we should know about?"

I batted his hand away. "I'm fine. I'm just... done pretending."

"Pretending that you don't have feelings, or pretending that you don't believe in love?" Chance asked.

"Both," I admitted. "It's exhausting, and it cost me the one person who actually made me happy."

"So what's the plan?" Kris asked, leaning forward with interest. "Grand gesture? Public declaration? Kidnapping? Wait, not that last one. That's illegal. Probably."

"Definitely illegal," Morgan confirmed. "And not romantic, despite what the books suggest."

"I'm not kidnapping anyone," I assured them. "But I am going forward with the wedding."

Three identical expressions of confusion greeted this statement.

"The wedding," Chance repeated slowly. "The one you were planning with Anica? The one that requires a bride, which you no longer have because you want Anica to be the bride, but she's not speaking to you?"

"That's the one. It's actually perfect. Don't you see? This is my chance to show her I'm serious. To prove that I... that I believe in this. In us."

"By... getting married to no one?" Morgan looked skeptical.

"By standing at that altar," I corrected. "Alone if necessary. Showing her that I'm willing to follow through, that I'm committed, that I..."

"Love her?" Chance supplied gently.

I nodded. "I'm going to be there, exactly where I'm supposed to be, hoping she shows up."

"That's either the most romantic thing I've ever heard or the craziest," Kris decided. "I honestly can't tell which."

"Little of both," I acknowledged. "But I need your help."

"Name it," Chance said immediately.

"I need you to be my groomsmen. To stand with me, even if it means looking like idiots when no one walks down the aisle."

"Done," Morgan agreed.

"And I need..." I hesitated. "I need your support. With this whole... feelings thing. It's new territory for me, and I'm not great at it."

"You're terrible at it. Spectacularly bad. Like stuck-your-hand-in-the-garbage-disposal-and-made-a-human-smoothie bad. But we're here for you anyway, because that's what friends do."

I winced. "Thanks, Kris, for that vivid description."

"What Kris is trying to say in his uniquely asshole-ish way," Chance interpreted, "is that we've got your back. No matter what happens."

"Even if she doesn't show?" I asked, voicing my deepest fear.

"Even then," Morgan confirmed. "Though for what it's worth, I think she will. But you need to make sure she knows you're waiting for. She needs to know that you love her."

"How? She won't talk to me and has been avoiding me completely."

"I have some ideas," Chance said. "We can workshop them in a minute, but just to clarify your insane idea, the wedding is still on and you'll be there, at the altar, possibly alone, hoping Anica shows up. And we'll be there with you, looking equally ridiculous if she doesn't."

"Yup, that's the plan," I confirmed.

"I'm in," Kris declared, raising his glass. "To Cal's deranged romantic gesture slash potential public humiliation."

"Thanks,'" I grinned, and clinked my glass against his.

"You know what this means, right?" Morgan asked, a slow grin spreading across his face. "Bachelor party."

"I don't think that's necessary," I said quickly. "Given the circumstances —"

"Oh, it's absolutely necessary," Kris interrupted. "If you're going through with this insane plan, you're doing it properly. All the traditions. Including the one where we get you hammered the night before and make you question all your life choices."

"I'm already questioning all my life choices," I pointed out. "That's how I ended up here."

"Then we'll help you question them with tequila," Morgan declared.

"Fine," I conceded. "Bachelor party. But nothing that will end up on social media or require bail money."

"You take all the fun out of everything. Now, let's talk about how to get your woman to her wedding." Kris slapped my on the back with a wide grin.

I'M FINE:
THE MUSICAL

Chapter 17: Anica

"**I**'ve cataloged twenty-six different ways to commit murder with wedding supplies, and right now the clear winner is strangling someone with fishing line from a bustle repair kit," I announced, viciously stapling a contract with enough force to puncture the desk beneath it. "It's virtually untraceable, available in every emergency kit I own, and I could make it look like a tragic crafting accident."

Mari looked up from her phone, where she'd been scrolling through Instagram wedding photos. "You sound like a deranged Martha Stewart. I'm into it."

"No one's even asked you about him today," Devonna pointed out without looking up from her tablet.

"She did," I pointed out, jabbing an accusatory finger at Mari. "This morning. While I was in the bathroom. You slid a note under the stall that said 'Forgive him yet?' with three heart emojis and a crude drawing of what I can only assume was meant to be his—"

"It was a microphone," Mari interjected innocently. "For karaoke. Which we should go do tonight, by the way. Nothing helps process emotional trauma like screaming 'I Will Survive' while drunk on tequila."

"That was not a microphone," I muttered, attacking another stack of papers with my stapler. "Unless microphones now come with anatomically incorrect veins."

"I'm an artist, not a doctor," Mari shrugged. "And you're avoiding the question, which means the answer is no, he hasn't called, which means you're still pretending you don't check your phone every eight seconds hoping he has just so you can reject the call and cry some more."

"I am not," I insisted, my stapler creating a small crater in a wedding contract. "I made a professional decision to distance myself from a client who crossed boundaries. End of story."

"Uh-huh," Mari nodded, clearly unconvinced. "And that's why you've been wearing the same cardigan for four days straight and I found you crying into a wedding cake sample yesterday."

"I was not crying. I had an allergic reaction to the buttercream."

"You're not allergic to buttercream."

"Maybe I developed a new allergy. People develop new allergies all the time. It's very common."

"Is it common to whisper 'stupid abs' while having these alleged allergic reactions?"

"I did not say 'stupid abs,'" I hissed, my cheeks flaming. "I said 'stupid labs' because the bakery's quality control is clearly subpar."

"Ani, it's okay to admit you're hurt. It's okay to admit you miss him."

"I don't miss him," I lied. "I miss who I thought he was. But that person doesn't exist. The real Callan Burkhardt is a man who doesn't believe in love, who thinks relationships are transactions, who refers to what we shared as 'just a good time.'"

Just a good time. That's all it had been to him. A good fuck.

"You know," Mari said carefully, "there's nothing wrong with 'just a good time' if that's what you both want. Not everything has to be forever to be worthwhile."

"That's not the point," I sighed, setting down the abused stapler before I broke it. "The point is that he doesn't believe love exists. At all. As a concept. How could I possibly build anything with someone who thinks the foundation of what I do—of what I believe in—is fiction?"

"And I've told you that was a fair point the first one hundred times you said it," Mari conceded. "Though to play devil's advocate, which I'm excellent at because I'm basically Satan's more fashionable sister, he did say those things to his bros. Men say all kinds of stupid shit to their bros that they don't actually mean."

"He meant it," I said flatly. "He's been consistent about that from day one. I just... I foolishly thought maybe I could be the exception. That maybe with me, he'd see..."

I trailed off, unable to finish the thought without my voice breaking. That was the humiliating truth I'd been avoiding: despite all my professional boundaries, all my carefully constructed walls, I'd started to hope that Callan might change his mind about love. For me. Because of me.

God, I was pathetic.

"You're not pathetic," Devonna said, making me realize I'd spoken aloud. "You're human. And humans hope. It's what we do."

"Especially when the human in question has abs you could grate cheese on," Mari added helpfully. "And a net worth with more zeroes than my dating history."

"Thank you both for that deeply insightful analysis of my emotional state. Now can we please get back to work? We have the wedding this weekend, and the flower crisis for the one in two weeks, and the cake disaster for the Albertson's wedding to manage."

"Actually," Devonna said, consulting her tablet, "those have all been handled. Mari took care of the wedding details for this weekend, I resolved the flower situation, and the Albertson's cake issue was fixed yesterday when you made the baker cry."

"I did not make her cry," I protested. "I explained, in detail, why five layers of rum-soaked cake at a dry wedding was inappropriate, especially when the bride's father is a recovering alcoholic and the groom's mother is a strict Baptist."

"You made her cry," Mari confirmed. "It was magnificent. You said, and I quote, 'This cake has consumed more alcohol than Lindsay Lohan circa 2007, and unlike Ms. Lohan, it hasn't even had the decency to check into rehab.' I recorded it for my personal collection of 'Anica Destroys People With Facts and Logic.'"

"The point is," Devonna continued, glaring at Mari, "your schedule is clear for the afternoon. We made sure of it."

I frowned, instantly suspicious. "Why would you clear my schedule?"

Mari and Devonna exchanged a look that set off all my internal alarm bells.

"What did you two do?" I demanded.

"Nothing," they replied in unison, which was about as convincing as a groom claiming he didn't notice the stripper at his bachelor party.

Before I could interrogate them further, the office door swung open, and in walked the last person I expected to see: Vivian Burkhardt, resplendent in a sky-blue pantsuit, with Norbert the butler trailing behind her carrying what appeared to be a basket of baked goods.

"Anica, darling," she greeted me like a relative rather than a virtual stranger. "So lovely to see you."

I blinked, momentarily speechless. "Mrs. Burkhardt—"

"Vivian," she corrected, kissing both my cheeks as if we were old friends. "Or Gram, if you prefer. I've decided to adopt you informally, regardless of your current estrangement from my grandson."

"That's... very kind, but unnecessary," I managed, shooting Mari and Devonna accusatory looks over Vivian's shoulder. They both suddenly found various ceiling fixtures fascinating.

"Nonsense," Vivian waved a dismissive hand. "I've been wanting a granddaughter for years, and you're perfect. Smart, capable, and you don't put up with Callan's nonsense. Norbert, the muffins, please."

Norbert stepped forward, presenting the basket. "Blueberry streusel. Madam made them this morning."

"Thank you, Norbert," Vivian said, taking the basket and offering it to me. "Peace offering. I understand my grandson has been spectacularly idiotic, and while I can't apologize for him, he's a grown man who needs to grovel properly on his own, I can at least bring baked goods and sympathy."

"That's... thank you," I said, accepting the basket. The smell of fresh muffins wafted up, making my stomach growl. I hadn't had much of an appetite lately.

"Shall we?" Vivian gestured to my office. "Somewhere private for a chat?"

I nodded, leading her in and closing the door behind us. Vivian settled into the chair across from my desk, smoothing her pantsuit as if it might dare to wrinkle in her presence.

"You look dreadful. Heartbreak doesn't suit you."

"I'm not—"

"Darling, please don't insult my intelligence by claiming you're not heartbroken," Vivian interrupted. "I've lived too long and seen too much to be fooled by brave faces. You're walking around like someone performing a one-woman show called 'I'm Fine: The Musical' with a soundtrack of sad Adele songs playing in your head."

I sank into my chair, too exhausted to maintain the pretense. "It doesn't matter. You know as well as I do that he doesn't believe in love. He made that abundantly clear."

"Ah yes, the 'love doesn't exist' nonsense." Vivian rolled her eyes. "He's been spouting that ridiculous theory since he was a preteen and caught his father with the tennis instructor."

"It's not just a theory to him. It's his worldview. And I can't... I won't be with someone who fundamentally dismisses something I consider essential."

"Very reasonable. Very sensible. And completely miserable, yes?"

I stared at her, caught off guard by her directness. "I... yes. Completely miserable."

"As is he," she assured me. "Though he'd rather gargle glass than admit it to most people. But a grandmother knows. He hasn't been sleeping. Barely eating. Erika says he stares at his phone constantly and has your name programmed into his speed dial even though you won't take his calls."

"He made his feelings clear," I said, trying to ignore the little flutter in my chest at the thought of Callan missing me as much as I missed him. "He told his friends I was 'just a good time.' That our relationship was 'something fun until he figured out the bet.'"

"Men say profoundly stupid things when they're terrified," Vivian replied, reaching into the basket of muffins and selecting one. "Especially men with abandonment issues and commitment phobias the size of small countries."

"That doesn't excuse it."

"No, it doesn't. Nothing excuses hurting someone you care about. But it might explain it, if you're interested."

Despite myself, I was. "I'm listening."

Vivian took a delicate bite of her muffin, chewed thoughtfully, then nodded in approval of her own baking. "My grandson watched his parents' marriage implode spectacularly throughout his most developmental years to the point where he had to come live with me because his parents couldn't parent. My son was a serial philanderer with the emotional intelligence of a turnip. Cal's mother was a social climber who married for money and status, then acted shocked when the marriage was empty. They hated each other but stayed together for appearances until Callan was older, at which point they had the most vicious, public divorce Manhattan had seen in decades."

I'd known the broad strokes of Callan's parents' divorce, but hearing the details from Vivian made my heart hurt for the child who'd witnessed it all.

"And then there was his grandfather," Vivian continued, her voice hardening. "He was charming, handsome, and utterly faithless. We were married for far too long before I discovered he'd been maintaining a second family in Boston."

"That's awful."

"It was. Devastating, actually. I loved that man with everything I had, and he betrayed me in the most fundamental way possible. But do you know what I didn't do?"

"What?"

"I didn't stop believing in love," Vivian said simply. "I was hurt, yes. Furious, absolutely. But I never concluded that love itself was a fiction just because the man I loved was a lying bastard. That's like swearing off oxygen because someone farted in an elevator."

A startled laugh escaped me before I could stop it. Vivian smiled, clearly pleased with her analogy.

"Callan saw two formative examples of marriage fail spectacularly, and being the analytical, pattern-seeking genius that he is, he drew a conclusion: love is not real. It's safer, you see, to believe love doesn't exist than to admit it exists but might not last. One is a philosophical position; the other is a risk."

"And he hates risk," I said, remembering his calculated approach to nearly everything.

"Only in matters of the heart. In business, he's practically reckless. He'll bet millions on a startup with a ten percent chance of success if he believes in the product. But with people? With feelings? He battens down the hatches and prepares for the worst."

"I understand why he believes what he does, but understanding doesn't change anything. He still doesn't believe in love, and I still need someone who does."

"Are you sure about that?"

"Yes, I need that and he said very clearly that–"

"No." Vivian shook her head. "Are you sure he doesn't believe in love, or is he simply terrified of calling it by its name?"

"He explicitly stated—"

"Words," Vivian dismissed with a wave. "Focus on actions, darling. My grandson flew you to his private island, which he's never done for any woman. He left a date with a seemingly perfect candidate to help you in a crisis. And before you say anything, yes, I know about Ms. Angelina. Don't forget that he also brought you to meet me, his only family he still has connections with. Those are not the actions of a man having 'just a good time,' are they?"

Put like that, it did seem like there was more to Callan's feelings than he'd admitted. But still...

"If he felt something real," I argued, "why wouldn't he just say so? Why insist so vehemently that love doesn't exist?"

"Because admitting love exists would mean admitting he's vulnerable to it," Vivian explained patiently. "And vulnerability terrifies him more than bankruptcy ever could. My grandson built an empire on being in control. Love is the ultimate loss of control."

"So what am I supposed to do with this information?" I asked, frustration seeping into my voice. "Wait around hoping he'll eventually overcome decades of emotional baggage? Settle for someone who can't or won't say they love me?"

"Absolutely not. You deserve better than that. You deserve someone who can meet you where you are, who shares your values, who isn't afraid to name what they feel."

"Then why are you here?" I asked, genuinely confused.

"Because," Vivian said, leaning forward, "I like you. And, I believe my grandson might be ready to be that person. Not because he's magically fixed all his issues. God knows that would take several lifetimes and more therapy than Manhattan could provide. But because losing you has forced him to confront what matters most."

"And what's that?"

"You. He's choosing you over his fear. At least, he's trying to. He's a toddler taking their first steps — wobbly and terrified, but desperately wanting to reach what's on the other side."

I swallowed hard, hope and skepticism warring within me. "How do you know?"

"Because he's still going through with the wedding."

I blinked, certain I'd misheard. "Excuse me?"

"The wedding. At Rhodes Estate. Tomorrow at four o'clock. He's going through with it."

"But..." I sputtered. "Who did he choose? Who is he marrying?"

"There's no bride. Just him, standing at the altar. Waiting."

"Waiting for what?" I asked, though I suspected I already knew the answer.

"For you, darling. He's hoping you'll show up."

Shit. Callan was going through with the wedding. The one we'd planned together. And he was, what, going to stand there like an idiot on the off chance that I might come. The man was clearly delusional.

"That's ridiculous," I said, my voice barely above a whisper. "He can't seriously think I'll just... what? Show up and marry him after everything that happened?"

"I don't think he knows what to expect, but he's taking a stand. Literally, at an altar. He's hoping the right person shows up."

"And if she doesn't?"

"Then he looks like a fool in front of two hundred of Manhattan's elite," Vivian shrugged. "Which, between us, might do his ego some good. But I don't think that's what will happen."

"You seem very confident."

"I'm old, darling. At my age, you learn to recognize the real thing when you see it." She reached across the desk to pat my hand. "What you and Callan have, whatever you want to call it, is the real thing. Messy and complicated and terrifying, yes, but real. Sometimes love isn't a pretty gift box with a neat bow on top. Sometimes it's a disaster in a three-piece suit with commitment issues and a god complex. Sometimes it's the man whose been by your side through thick and thin."

I didn't know what to say to that. Part of me wanted to believe her, to rush to Rhodes Estate and find Callan and... what? Forgive everything because he was making a grand, romantic gesture? Another part, the professional, practical part that had protected me since Austin, warned that nothing fundamental had changed. Callan still didn't believe in love. He still saw relationships as transactions. Standing at an altar didn't change that.

"I appreciate you coming here, and the muffins. But I don't think I can do what you're asking."

"I'm not asking you to do anything," Vivian clarified, rising from her chair with the same elegant grace with which she'd sat down. "I'm merely providing information. What you do with it is entirely your choice. The wedding is at four o'clock tomorrow. Rhodes Estate. The staff has instructions to let you in if you decide to come."

She moved toward the door, then paused, turning back to me. "For what it's worth, I think you're exactly what my grandson needs. Not because you'll fix him, no one can do that but himself, but because you make him want to be better. That's rare, Anica. Rarer than you might think."

With that, she swept out of my office, leaving me alone with a basket of delicious-smelling muffins and a head full of confusion.

I spent the rest of the afternoon in a daze, going through the motions of work while my mind replayed Vivian's visit on a loop. Callan was going through with the wedding. He would be standing at the altar tomorrow, alone, all because he hoped I might show up.

It was insane. Irrational. Completely contrary to the calculated, controlled man I thought I knew.

Which was exactly why it kept worming its way into my heart, past all my carefully constructed defenses.

By six o'clock, the office was empty except for me. Mari had left with a suspiciously knowing smile and a "Don't stay too late, boss. Big day tomorrow. Lots of... stuff happening. Wedding stuff. For other people. Not you. Unless..." to which I'd thrown a stress ball at her head with enough force to qualify for a junior varsity javelin team.

Devonna had left too, but not before placing a sealed envelope on my desk that she instructed me not to open until she was gone. Inside, I'd found a detailed schedule for tomorrow, including a 2:00 PM hair appointment at my usual salon that I definitely hadn't booked, with a note in Devonna's handwriting: "Just in case. Wedding planners should always have a plan."

I was gathering my things to leave when the front door chimed, indicating a delivery. Assuming it was the new letterhead I'd ordered last week, I called out, "Come in, just leave it by the front desk!"

"Delivery for Anica Marcel," a voice responded. "A signature required."

Sighing, I made my way to the reception area, where a delivery person waited with a large white box tied with a simple blue ribbon.

"I'm Anica Marcel," I said, accepting the electronic signature pad. "What is this?"

"Special delivery," the woman replied with a shrug. "All I know is I'm supposed to hand it directly to you and no one else. Though the guy who arranged it tipped me five hundred dollars to make sure it got to you tonight, so it must be important."

Curious despite myself, I carried the box to my office and set it on my desk. There was no return address, no identifying information of any kind. Just my name in elegant script on a small card attached to the ribbon.

With trembling fingers, I untied the bow and lifted the lid.

Inside, nestled in layers of tissue paper, was a dress. Not just any dress, but *the* dress — the one I'd tried on weeks ago. The simple, elegant ivory silk gown that had made Callan look at me like I'd punched him in the gut.

Beneath the dress was a small envelope. I opened it with unsteady hands, instantly recognizing Callan's handwriting.

Anica,

This belonged on you from the moment I saw you in it. I'll be waiting at Rhodes Estate tomorrow at 4pm. No expectations, no pressure. But know that there's only one bride I've ever imagined standing across from me, and that's you, Anica Marcel.

Sometimes you have to stand where you're meant to be and hope the right person shows up. I'll be standing there tomorrow, whether you come or not, because it's where I'm supposed to be.

Because I love you.

Yours (if you'll have me), Callan

I sank into my chair, the note clutched in one hand while the other rested on the smooth silk of the dress. Tears filled my eyes, blurring the words.

With shaking hands, I lifted the dress from the box and held it against myself, moving to stand before the full-length mirror I kept in my office for last-minute client adjustments.

The woman who stared back at me looked nothing like the controlled, professional Anica Marcel who planned other people's happy endings while keeping her own heart safely locked away. This woman looked raw, vulnerable, full of hope and fear in equal measure. She looked like someone on the verge of the biggest decision of her life.

"The thing about love," I whispered to my reflection, echoing something I'd told countless brides but never fully believed for myself, "is that it's a verb. A choice. One you have to make every day."

I had less than twenty-four hours to decide if I would be at that altar tomorrow. Less than twenty-four hours to decide if I believed what Vivian had told me. That Callan was trying, in his own flawed way, to show me that he'd changed.

Less than twenty-four hours to decide if I was brave enough to risk my heart again.

To make that choice.

JUST FIVE MORE MINUTES...

Chapter 18: Callan

"The road to hell is paved with asymmetrical flower arrangements and people who don't understand the difference between eggshell and ivory," I snapped, adjusting a centerpiece that had dared to exist approximately 0.3 inches off-center. "If one more thing is out of place, I will personally ensure the responsible party spends eternity planning budget weddings for bridezillas with Pinterest boards the size of the national debt."

My apparent descent into wedding planner psychosis—a condition I'd clearly contracted from spending too much time with Anica—drew concerned glances from the Rhodes Estate staff. Three months ago, I wouldn't have noticed if the flowers were not quite right, let alone if they were 0.3 inches off center. Now I was channeling my inner Anica, seeing all the tiny imperfections she would have spotted instantly. It was both terrifying and comforting, like carrying a piece of her with me while the staff politely avoided the elephant in the room. Or rather, the missing bride in the venue.

"Mr. Burkhardt," Ms. Windsor approached, clipboard in hand and frown lines permanently carved into her face. "While everything looks absolutely exquisite, there is the small matter of... well..." She cleared her throat. "The bride? Or rather, the lack thereof?"

"Ms. Marcel will be here," I said, adjusting my cufflinks for the fourteenth time. "Or she won't. Either way, the wedding proceeds as planned."

Ms. Windsor blinked, as if trying to process this information through her proper British sensibilities. "I... see. It's just that in my many, *many* years managing this venue, we've never had a... solo wedding before. It's not like you can marry no one."

"If she doesn't show, then obviously I won't be married by the end of the day," I replied, spotting another imperfection, a chair with a slightly looser bow than its neighbors. I strode over to fix it, ignoring the whispers from the catering staff.

"But sir, the—"

"Everything has been handled. Besides, this estate has been paid in more than full already. I don't know why you're complaining considering the other sizable donation I made."

Ms. Windsor looked like she wanted to say more but thought better of it, retreating with her clipboard and wrinkles.

I couldn't blame her. This whole situation was certifiably insane.

All because I tripped and tumbled straight into that stupid L-word.

Love. The word I'd spent my entire adult life avoiding, dismissing, and thoroughly denying.

I pulled out the folded paper from my pocket. My vows, rewritten seventeen times since last night. The current version still felt inadequate.

"Those better not be stock market predictions," a familiar voice said from behind me.

I turned to find Chance, adjusting his bowtie.

"Vows," I corrected, tucking the paper back into my pocket. "For when she shows up."

"When," Chance repeated with a small smile. "*When* she shows up. Not *if*. That's progress."

"Where are the other two assholes?" I asked, glancing around for Kris and Morgan.

"Checking on the bar situation. And by 'checking on' I mean 'depleting.' Kris said something about needing liquid courage to stand next to you while you potentially humiliate yourself in front of New York's elite."

"Good to know my groomsmen have such faith in me."

"Actually," Chance said, his expression growing serious, "we do. Have faith in you, I mean. This is... it's brave, Cal. Possibly insane, definitely dramatic, but brave."

"Or desperate," I muttered, spotting another imperfection in the floral arrangements and resisting the urge to fix it. "I'm not convinced there's much difference."

"How are you feeling? After everything?"

I stared out at the assembled chairs, the flower-draped archway, the string quartet warming up in the corner. Everything perfect, everything planned down to the last detail by the woman who might or might not walk down that aisle minus a few adjustments from me.

"I don't know. Terrified may be the best way to explain it."

"Are you excited?"

"Of course," I said simply. "I want, no, I *need* to see her again. And shit, if it's in that dress, I may need you to find the nearest AED to bring me back when I inevitably keel over."

My phone buzzed in my pocket. Gram.

"How's my boy doing?" she asked without preamble when I answered.

"Depends on your definition of 'doing,'" I replied. "If you mean 'micromanaging floral arrangements while sweating through an extremely expensive suit,' then I'm doing spectacularly."

"Nerves are good," Gram said. "Shows you care. How's the venue? I'll be there soon enough if Norbert would step on the gas instead of the brakes every five seconds." In the background, Norbert muttered an apology.

"Don't worry. It's not four yet. And the venue is perfect. Exactly as we planned. Everything's ready except—"

"The bride," she finished for me. "I spoke to her yesterday."

My heart stuttered. "And?"

"And I did my part. The rest is up to her... and you."

"What does that mean? Did she seem receptive? Angry? Did she mention me? The dress?"

"Patience, Cal. Some things can't be rushed, controlled, or bought. This is one of them."

"That's not helpful."

"It wasn't meant to be. It was meant to be true." A pause, then: "Are you ready to tell her you love her."

"Yes, because I do."

"Good boy."

"I just hope I get the chance to tell her if she shows up."

"*When* she shows up," Gram corrected, echoing Chance beside me. "See you at the altar, darling."

She hung up before I could respond.

"Everything okay?" Chance asked, watching me carefully.

"Gram talked to Anica yesterday. But she won't tell me what was said."

"Probably for the best. You're already one floral adjustment away from a complete nervous breakdown."

"I am perfectly calm," I insisted, while simultaneously straightening my already straight tie.

"Sure you are. How about we get you a drink?"

Before I could respond, Kris and Morgan appeared, both looking suspiciously more relaxed than when they'd arrived.

"That's an awesome idea! The bar is excellent," Kris announced, clapping me on the shoulder. "And fully stocked for either celebration or consolation, depending on how this circus plays out."

"Have a little faith," Morgan chided, though he too seemed to have fortified himself with liquid courage. "Our boy's about to make romantic history."

"Or tragic history," Kris countered. "Either way, I'm just glad I'm here to witness it. This story's going to be legendary regardless of the outcome."

"Thanks for the vote of confidence," I said as I ran a hand down the side of my face.

"Anytime," Kris grinned. "Now, is there a protocol for this? Do we still stand up there with you if it's just you? Is this more of a performance art piece or an actual wedding at this point?"

"We stand with him," Chance said.

"Of course we do," Morgan agreed, suddenly serious. "We're just giving him shit because that's how we show love."

"Don't use the L-word around Cal," Kris stage-whispered. "He's still building up immunity to it."

Despite everything, I laughed. "You three are the worst groomsmen in history."

"But we're yours," Morgan said, straightening his boutonniere. "So what's the plan, boss? How long do we wait if..." He trailed off, but the unspoken question hung in the air between us. How long would I stand there, alone at the altar, before admitting defeat?

"As long as it takes. Five minutes. Then five more after that. And then another five."

An uncomfortable silence fell between us, broken only when Ms. Windsor reappeared, looking even more pinched than before.

"Mr. Burkhardt, the guests are arriving. We really should—"

"Everything proceeds as planned. Start seating them."

She looked like she wanted to argue but nodded stiffly before walking away, murmuring into her headset.

"I should go check on... something," I said vaguely, needing a moment alone. "Make sure the guys don't drink all the champagne before the ceremony," I added to Chance, who nodded.

I went to a small antechamber off the main pavilion, a room traditionally used by grooms for last-minute preparations. The mirror on the wall reflected a man I barely recognized—still me, but somehow different. Less certain. More vulnerable. Terrified, yes, but somehow more alive than I'd felt in years. In fact, he sort of reminded me of the kid in the bathtub wearing a DIY merman tail. There was hope there standing alongside fear. I hadn't seen that kid in a long time.

Shaking my head, I pulled out the vows again, scanning the words I'd written. They felt simultaneously too much and not enough. How did you compress a complete worldview shift into a few sentences? How did you explain to someone that they'd fundamentally changed the way you wanted to live your life?

"If love exists anywhere in this world," I whispered to my reflection, folding the paper carefully, "what I feel for Anica is it. And if I'm wrong about everything else, I'm right about her."

A sharp knock on the door interrupted my thoughts.

"It's time," Chance called. "Everyone's seated."

God, how long had I been in that room? It felt like seconds. Had it really been twenty minutes? The nerves I'd felt before tripled in a heartbeat, and I struggled to swallow. What if she didn't show? What if I really had lost her for good? I didn't even care that I was going to look like an idiot. I just...

I just wanted her.

The woman I loved.

I took a deep breath, straightened my jacket one last time, and stepped out.

The Rhodes Estate garden pavilion had been transformed into something from a dream. White chairs lined either side of a center aisle, adorned with small bouquets of blue and white flowers. An archway of twisted branches and more flowers stood at the far end, overlooking the lake that shimmered in the late afternoon sun. The string quartet played softly in the background, and two hundred of New York's elite sat in expectant silence, their curious glances following me as I took my place at the altar.

Standing there, I nodded to Gram, who sat in the front row. Beside her sat Norbert. What the hell? Why was my grandmother's butler holding her hand? I raised an eyebrow and she winked at me. On Gram's other side, Erika sat with her husband and their two kids. She gave me a thumbs up, leaning in to whisper something to her husband.

On the opposite side of the aisle sat people I'd only met that morning. Anica's family. Mainly her parents. That in itself had been a very, *very* awkward encounter. But as I nodded to her father and smiled at her mother, they both gave me reassuring nods, holding each other's hands. Mari had helped me get in touch with them, and had been there to help introduce me, for which I would be forever grateful, even if she had mentioned I'd railed their daughter with my "extra large package" and stolen her heart. On second thought, maybe it would've been better if it had been Devonna making the introductions.

Either way, her father had given me a stern talking to before shaking my hand and pulling me into a bear hug. Someone was supposed to get him and take him around behind the wall of hedges so that he could walk Anica down the aisle when she arrived. I just hoped he got the chance.

The officiant, a judge I knew from charity functions, had agreed to the unconventional ceremony with minimal explanation. He leaned in close.

270

"At what point do we begin?" he whispered.

"When she walks in. Until then, we're waiting," I said firmly, glancing at my watch. Four o'clock exactly.

"Alright then. We wait." He nodded.

The minutes ticked by with excruciating slowness. Four-oh-five. Four-ten. The whispers from the assembled guests grew louder, more concerned. I could feel the weight of their stares, their curiosity, their growing certainty that they were witnessing a very public humiliation.

I may as well have brought in the medieval stocks so they could throw rotten food at me. That would've been better than standing there.

Four-fifteen.

"Mr. Burkhardt," the officiant murmured, "perhaps we should —"

"Five more minutes," I said, my voice steady despite the growing knot in my stomach. "Then five more after that."

Chance shifted beside me, placing a supportive hand briefly on my shoulder. Kris and Morgan exchanged glances but remained steadfast, standing behind like guards.

Four-twenty.

The whispers had evolved into open conversations. Someone in the back row stood, perhaps preparing to make a discreet exit. I couldn't blame them. This was rapidly becoming the social car crash of the season.

Four twenty-five.

"Cal," Chance said softly. "Maybe —"

"She'll be here," I insisted, though the conviction in my voice had waned. "She has to be."

But even as I said it, doubt crept in. I had hurt her. Deeply. Why would she forgive that? Why would she take a chance on someone who had dismissed something she found fundamental? Why would she show up for someone who had called what we shared "just a good time"?

Four thirty.

I really was an idiot.

The string quartet had cycled through their repertoire and were now repeating selections, their glances toward me growing increasingly uncomfortable. Ms. Windsor hovered at the periphery, clearly contemplating some kind of intervention. I tried to keep my chin tall as my attention remained glued to the wall of hedges at the back. But it was clear at that point.

Anica wasn't coming.

I really had lost her for good.

"I think," I said finally, my voice cracking as I struggled to keep the hurt contained, "we should —"

The music changed.

It happened so suddenly that at first I thought I'd imagined it. The quartet shifted seamlessly into the processional we'd selected months ago. A collective rustle passed through the guests as heads turned toward the back.

Mari and Devonna, both in simple blue dresses, walked down the aisle arm in arm looking equal parts surprised and delighted to be there. Devonna gave me a look that clearly communicated "hurt her and they'll never find your body," while Mari winked at me.

But I couldn't focus on them, couldn't focus on anything but the woman who'd just appeared at the end of the aisle.

Anica stood beneath a second archway, illuminated by the golden late-afternoon sun, wearing the dress that had stolen my breath the first time I saw her in it. It did it again. I couldn't breathe. My lungs had completely rejected the notion that they were supposed to work. I choked and made what was definitely one of the most pathetic sounds I'd ever made.

But, fuck, she was the most beautiful thing I'd ever been lucky enough to lay eyes on.

The simple, elegant ivory silk that followed the curves of her body before flowed gracefully to the ground. Her dark hair had been swept up, a few tendrils framing her face. She looked nervous, determined, and so stunning it physically hurt to look at her.

Next to her, Anica's father patted her arm–when had he slipped away without me noticing? The sneaky bastard. They began their walk down the aisle. Each step she took toward me felt like a miracle, a gift I didn't deserve.

Shit. A tear escaped down my cheek, and I wiped it away with the back of my hand hoping no one noticed. All eyes better be on Anica. How could they not be? My goddess was radiant.

When she reached me, our gazes locked, and the rest of the world faded away. I thought that was just a cliché lovesick fools talked about. But no. There were no guests, no friends, no string quartet.

Just us, standing face to face after everything that had happened.

God, I'd missed her.

"Sorry I'm late. There were ducks."

"Fucking ducks." I choked on something between a laugh and a whimper.

Her father passed her over to me, kissing her cheek and placing her hand in mine. I nodded once to him, watching as he went to sit back down by her mother, who was crying silent tears with a wide smile. He kissed her forehead and wrapped an arm around her.

Anica followed my gaze and squeezed my hand. "Thank you for that. For them."

I squeezed her hand back. "You came," I said, my voice barely above a whisper.

"I didn't want to waste a good dress," she replied, smoothing the fabric with her other trembling hand. "And Mari said if I didn't show up after all this drama, she'd repost my college karaoke video where I massacred 'Total Eclipse of the Heart' while wearing a feather boa and a criminal amount of body glitter."

Another laugh bubbled up from somewhere deep inside me, relief and joy mingling into something that felt dangerously close to uncontrollable tears. "I would pay good money to see that video."

"You can't afford it," she quipped, her eyes shining. "Besides, you look like you've been standing here for days."

"I would have waited longer," I admitted. "As long as it took."

"Now you know how I felt every time you showed up late." She raised an eyebrow, flashing a grin.

Lifting her hand, I pressed my lips to her knuckles. "I vow to never be late for you again. Ever."

"Is that an official vow? Because I will hold you to that." Anica squeezed my hand, and the world returned to normal.

The officiant cleared his throat, clearly trying to make sense of what was happening. "Shall we... proceed?"

Anica glanced at me, a question in her eyes. "Are you sure about this? Because once we start, there's no backing out. Not ever. Divorce is not an option for me. If you're mine, you're mine. Forever."

"I've never been more sure of anything in my life," I said, taking her other hand in my free one. "But you should know what you're getting into. I'm stubborn, a workaholic, and occasionally believe I'm right about everything."

"Occasionally?" she raised an eyebrow.

"Fine. Frequently." I ran my thumbs over the backs of her soft hands. "But I'm working on it. On all of it. For you. Because of you."

"I'm not here to fix you, Cal. I'm here because, against my better judgment and all professional boundaries, I love you. God help me."

Her words, her confession, stole my breath. She loved me. Despite everything, she loved me.

"I love you, Anica Marcel. You are the woman who proved me wrong. Love does exist. You taught me that. And I love you." Despite the tears that threatened to fall, I looked her up and down. "God, I love you."

"Well then," the officiant said, a smile finally breaking through his confusion, "let's make this official."

The ceremony started and a collective sigh of relief and delight came from the assembled guests when they realized they were witnessing a real wedding and not an elaborate mental breakdown.

Then came the moment for vows. I pulled out my carefully prepared notes, took one look at Anica's face, and promptly tucked them back into my pocket.

"I had something written," I began, "seventeen versions, actually. But I think they need another revision."

I took a deep breath, forcing myself to maintain eye contact despite the vulnerability coursing through me.

"Anica Marcel, I've spent my entire adult life convinced that love was fiction. A chemical reaction. A convenient myth we tell ourselves to explain basic biological impulses. I built walls, theories, entire philosophies around this belief because I didn't have the experiences with love that other people had. I didn't have parents who loved each other. I experienced broken marriages, unfaithful spouses, and too

274

much hurt to ever believe that love existed. "But," I said, glancing at Gram, "I was absolutely, categorically wrong."

A murmur rippled through the crowd, but I ignored it, returning my focus to the woman before me.

"Love was there all along. I just was too stupid to see it. It was there in the way my grandmother cared for me unconditionally despite my weird phases." In the audience, Gram beamed at me and blew a kiss. "It was there in the way my asshole friends supported me and called me out on my bullshit through the years." Behind me, Callan clapped me on the shoulder and Kris and Morgan chuckled. "And most of all, it was there from the moment you refused to work with me without a bride present for a wedding based on a bet with the aforementioned assholes."

Anica looked confused, but I continued. "You demonstrated love for me before you even loved me. You were willing to walk away from a million-dollar contract because you believed I deserved better than a loveless marriage. You showed me that love isn't just romantic feelings. It's integrity, it's boundaries, it's demanding the best from someone even when they're determined to settle for less.

"I know this because I love you," I continued, the words still new but increasingly natural on my tongue. "Not in the theoretical sense. Not as a concept or a hypothesis. But as a fact, as fundamental to my existence as breathing. I love your meticulous organization and your emergency kits. I love how you call me on my bullshit like my friends and you care about me like my grandmother. I love that you refuse to be impressed by my money and you want me despite seeing that godforsaken merman photo. I love that despite your ridiculously busy schedule, you agreed to drop everything to come on an adventure with me. I love that you aren't afraid to be honest, even when that vulnerability hurts you. You are brave, smart, and beautiful and I know I need to spend the rest of my life trying to deserve you."

Anica cried quietly as I spoke, and I continued to rub soft circles onto the backs of her hands with my thumbs.

"I spent my whole life convinced love didn't exist, until I met you. You didn't just plan my wedding, Anica. You taught me what love actually is. Not a fantasy or a delusion, but a choice. A daily, hourly, minute-by-minute choice to put someone else's happiness in front of your own. To be vulnerable when every instinct screams for self-protection. To stand at an altar, terrified and hopeful, because the alternative, a life without you, is unthinkable.

"I can't promise to never be an idiot again," I admitted. "In fact, I can promise I will absolutely be an idiot on probably a weekly basis." Both of us chuckled. "And I can't promise I won't occasionally revert to old habits or say the wrong thing at the wrong time. But I can promise to choose you, every day, for the rest of my life. Only you. To love you in action, not just in words. To be worthy of the trust you're placing in me by standing here today."

I reached up to brush away a tear that had escaped down her cheek.

"So on this day, our wedding day—the one you planned impeccably despite my constant meddling—I promise you this: I will never take for granted the miracle of finding you. I promise to be the kind of partner who deserves your trust and your heart. I promise that on our fiftieth anniversary, I'll still be looking at you the way I am right now, like you're the most extraordinary person I've ever met. Because you are, darling." I tilted my head, grinning. "And I solemnly swear to arrive on time to every important event for the rest of our lives; a vow that might be harder for me to keep than 'till death do us part,' but one I make with complete sincerity. Because you are absolutely worth being punctual for."

I paused, taking a deep breath before I spoke next. "With all that being said, there's something I didn't do." I let go of her hands and dropped to one knee. "I am so sorry for hurting, Anica. I hope you can forgive me."

She nodded. "I do forgive you, but I thought that was kind of obvious." Anita gestured first to her dress, then to the rest of the venue. "I'm here, after all."

"Right. Good. Great. It still needed to be said though. And in that case…" I glanced at Chance, who nodded and pulled out a small blue velvet box. Her face transformed from surprise to more tears to a slightly crazy looking grin. "Anica Marcel, will you marry me? Today. Like, right now?"

A collective gasp rose from the assembled guests, followed immediately by delighted laughter and scattered applause. Behind me, Kris let out a wolf whistle. Gram dabbed at her eyes with a handkerchief while simultaneously giving me a thumbs up. Even Ms. Windsor, who had been hovering anxiously at the periphery of the ceremony, looked relieved that her venue was finally hosting something resembling a normal wedding.

Anica laughed and nodded with tears trailing down her cheeks. "Yes. I will marry you."

More applause erupted as I slid the ring onto her finger and rose to my feet. The officiant, who had somehow maintained composure throughout the unconventional ceremony, cleared his throat.

"I believe it's time for the bride's vows," he prompted.

Anica took a shaky breath, clearly collecting herself before speaking. Her gaze locked with mine.

"I didn't prepare anything," she began, "because until about an hour ago, I wasn't entirely sure I was coming."

That earned a ripple of laughter from the guests.

"Callan Burkhardt, you are without a doubt the most infuriating man I have ever met. You steamroll through careful plans, you show up late to everything almost all the time, and you have the audacity to make me fall in love with you while supposedly planning your wedding to someone else."

She shook her head, a smile playing at the corners of her mouth.

"I've spent years helping others find their perfect day, never believing I'd have my own," she said, her voice growing softer. "I was afraid to trust again, afraid to believe. But some things are worth the risk. You're worth the risk. For someone who didn't believe in love, you somehow managed to make me believe in it again when I half considered that part of me was dead."

Her hands tightened around mine.

"I love you," she said simply. "The man who flew me to his island, who helped save a wedding disaster in the middle of a date with someone else, who stood at this altar alone rather than give up on us. Not the billionaire or the tech genius or the eligible bachelor, but just... you. Cal. The man who bakes with his grandmother and is absolutely terrified of jellyfish."

I groaned as laughter erupted from the guests, particularly from the three traitors standing beside me.

Anica continued once the laughter had subsided. "Things will not always be easy, but relationships take effort, and I will put in everything I have. Everything I am for this. For you. I promise to choose you, every day, even when it's hard. Especially when it's hard. To build something real with you. I love you, Cal. I will love you for the rest of my life."

"Well then, by the power vested in me," the officiant said after a moment of perfect silence, "I now pronounce you husband and wife. You may—"

I didn't wait for him to finish before pulling Anica into a kiss that probably bordered on inappropriate for the setting. But after waiting for her, after thinking I'd lost her, I couldn't help myself. I poured everything I couldn't say into that kiss. My gratitude, my joy, my love.

Thankfully, she responded in kind.

When we finally broke apart, breathless and grinning, the guests' applause sounded like thunder. I kept her hand firmly in mine as we turned to face them, officially husband and wife in a ceremony that had gone from potentially disastrous to the best day of my life.

"Well," Gram said as she approached us at the reception, champagne in hand and satisfaction written all over her face. "That was quite the spectacle. Cutting it rather close, weren't you, Anica dear?"

"I wanted to make an entrance," Anica replied with a smile. "And honestly, I was still debating in the car. Mari threatened to push me out if I didn't walk in voluntarily."

"It's true," Mari confirmed, appearing beside us with a champagne glass in each hand. "I had the door unlocked and was ready to roll. My exact words were 'either you walk down that aisle like a goddamn queen or I'm shoving you into those rosebushes and claiming it was a squirrel attack.'"

"What changed your mind?" I asked.

Anica glanced at me, her expression softening. "Your note. 'Sometimes you have to stand where you're meant to be and hope the right person shows up.' It made me realize that's exactly what I've been doing for years—standing in the wrong place, planning other people's happiness while convinced I didn't deserve my own."

"And now?" I asked softly.

"Now I'm standing exactly where I'm meant to be," she replied, squeezing my hand. "Scary as that is."

"Terrifying," I agreed. "Come on, there are oatmeal chocolate chip cookies with your name on them. And maybe a piece of cake for me."

"Cookies?" She asked, her eyes growing wider like a kid in a candy store.

"Your mom's recipe." I said with a wink, pulling her hand up to my mouth to kiss her knuckles. "She said she'd teach me how to make them with the secret recipe after we get back from the honeymoon. In the meantime, though, she made a special batch just for you."

As we signed the marriage certificate later that evening, making it all official, Anica glanced at me with a hint of mischief in her eyes.

"So," she said casually, "what does my husband want to do tonight?"

"Honestly?" I finished my signature and wrapped my arms around her, kissing her forehead.

"Of course."

Leaning down, I whispered in her ear so no one nearby could hear. "I want to make love to my wife. And then I want to fuck her."

She pulled back just enough to meet my gaze, her eyes darkening in a way that made my heart race and my dick hard. "Well," she murmured, her voice dropping to a sexy tone, "I've been planning this wedding for months." Her fingers trailed up my lapel as she leaned up on her tiptoes to whisper back, "And I always save the best part for last."

My jaw actually dropped, and she laughed, the sound both delighted and wicked. "What?" she asked innocently. "You thought I was just good at planning the ceremony?" She bit her lip in a way that nearly undid me on the spot. "That was just the warm-up act."

"You," I managed once I'd recovered, "are the best decision I've ever made."

"I know," she agreed, taking my hand and leading me toward the exit. "Now let's go."

I'd never moved so fast in my life.

EPILOGUE:
ONE YEAR LATER

Anica

The Chicago Wedding Expo was everything I'd hoped for and more. A booth with beautiful decorations, a cross-country expansion, and a husband who somehow managed to show up on time despite a 5 AM conference call with Tokyo.

"Your wedding sounds like it's going to be magical," I said, shaking hands with the beaming bride-to-be. "My assistant will email you our availability for consultations by the end of day."

As the couple walked away, I checked our growing list of potential Chicago clients. Twenty-seven solid leads in just a couple hours. Not bad for our first Midwest expansion event.

"Your business partner seems... intense."

I glanced up to find Mrs. Sullivan, the expo coordinator, surveying our booth. Her gaze was fixed on Mari, who was currently rebuilding a toppled display of sample centerpieces while muttering what sounded suspiciously like death threats.

"Mari's just excited about our Chicago launch," I offered with a smile.

"And your booth neighbor, Mr. Gable, seems equally... enthusiastic about the expo."

I followed her gaze to Perfect Day Planning's immaculate booth. Hudson Gable had introduced himself this morning as a transplant from some high-end LA company who'd decided Chicago needed his particular brand of wedding expertise. I'd only spoken to him briefly during setup, but he seemed to know what he was doing. He was tall, impeccably dressed, with a very familiar kind of smile to my husband's, in that he seemed to know exactly how handsome he was without needing to mention it.

What had seemed like professional courtesy at 10 AM had devolved into something far more sinister by noon.

"Did she actually move his sample books?" Mrs. Sullivan asked, nodding to Mari, who stuck her tongue out at Mr. Gable when she thought no one was looking.

"She told me he moved ours first," I explained. "While Mari was in the bathroom, she said he completely rearranged the books. There was a sticky note that just said 'Fixed it' with a smiley face. Although, between the two of us, I didn't see the sticky note. She also claimed he stole our consultation with the young couple by telling them our 'vintage aesthetic' was code for 'outdated techniques.'"

Mrs. Sullivan's eyes widened. "I've coordinated this expo for eleven years, and I've never seen two vendors develop such an intense rivalry in less than two hours."

"And I've known Mari since college, and I've never seen her this fixated on someone she just met," I said, glancing at my best friend. "I apologize for any... disruptions she's caused."

"Just keep it professional," Mrs. Sullivan warned before marching away.

I turned to find Mari at our backdrop, aggressively straightening a banner. "Any chance you could dial it back a notch with the neighbor? We're trying to make a good first impression in Chicago."

"He started it," Mari hissed, not looking away from Mr. Gable's booth, where he was calmly explaining something to a potential client. "Did you see what he did to our brochure display while you were helping that other couple? He switched them all with his own materials! Three couples picked up *his* brochures from *our* display!"

"That's actually pretty clever," I said, then immediately regretted it when Mari shot me a look that promised she's spit in my coffee for a week.

"He's not clever. He's a pretentious saboteur with product in his hair." She squinted suspiciously. "Look at it. No one's hair naturally does that. It's unnatural."

Mr. Gable did have great hair, I'd give her that. The kind that belonged in a men's grooming commercial, dark and artfully styled in a way that looked effortless but definitely wasn't. His booth was also objectively gorgeous; sleek and modern with a striking black and gold color scheme that made our blue and silver look almost quaint by comparison.

"Have you considered that maybe—"

"If you say I'm attracted to him, I will superglue your emergency kit shut and replace all your protein bars with those disgusting keto ones Callan likes," Mari threatened, pointing a finger at my face. "I have never been less attracted to anyone in my life. He's a snake in Italian leather shoes who thinks he can just waltz into our territory with his stupid holographic display boards and his ridiculous custom scent diffusers."

"His booth does smell amazing," I murmured before I could stop myself.

Mari's eye twitched. "I'm going to get coffee. Don't fraternize with the enemy while I'm gone."

As she stomped away, I caught Mr. Gable watching her retreat, his expression unreadable except for a slight quirk at the corner of his mouth; not quite a smile, more like the look of someone who'd just moved a chess piece exactly where he wanted it. When he noticed me looking, he gave a polite nod before turning back to his client.

I was so distracted by the strange tension between our booths that I didn't notice Callan until he was right in front of me, looking unfairly handsome in my favorite charcoal suit that made his blue eyes even more striking.

"There she is," he said, leaning across the display table to peck me on the lips. "The most successful wedding planner in two cities."

"Three if you count the pop-up in Boston," I corrected, unable to prevent the smile spreading across my face. After a year of marriage, he still had that effect on me. One look and I was twenty degrees warmer and significantly wetter in places that had no business responding during business hours.

"How's the expo going?" he asked, glancing around at our setup. "You guys did a great job, even without my help." He put his hands in his pockets. "Sorry about that. I had that call with–"

"I know. Don't worry about it," I said, smiling. "Mari and I kicked ass at this long before you came around to haul heavy boxes." I beckoned him inside the booth. "And to answer your question, twenty-seven potential clients, two booking deposits, and only one vendor rivalry threatening to escalate into physical violence."

Callan raised an eyebrow. "Mari?"

"Who else? She's developed a pathological hatred for the wedding planner next door." I nodded toward Mr. Gable's booth. "They've been passive-aggressively sabotaging each other all morning."

"Ah, the guy with the hair." Callan studied Mr. Gable and shrugged. "Mari mentioned him in approximately fourteen furious texts in the group message. Something about 'symmetrical features that belong on Mount Rushmore but with the personality of a shark in Gucci loafers.'"

"That's the one." I finished arranging a display of sample invitations. "Though I have to admit, his setup is impressive. Those holographic displays showing venue transformations? Genius."

"Should I be jealous that you're admiring another man's... displays?" Callan's voice dropped to that low register that made my stomach flip and my thighs clench.

"Depends. Are you here to just visit, or did you come with a purpose?"

His eyes darkened as he leaned closer, his breath warm against my ear. "I missed my wife. And I was thinking about what happened the last time we were at a wedding expo together."

"Cal," I warned, glancing around to make sure no one could hear us. "We're working."

"You know what else we could be doing?" His eyes held that mischievous glint that never failed to short-circuit my professional boundaries. "I saw a supply closet by the south entrance. Locked, but I happen to know how to get a key for fifteen minutes using a hundred dollar bill."

"Of course you do." I rolled my eyes even as my pulse quickened.

"So is that a yes? Or a hell yes?"

"I can't just leave the booth unattended." I gestured to the displays we'd spent hours perfecting. "And Mari's getting coffee."

"What about me?" Mari appeared beside us, clutching a coffee cup and shooting at least three scathing glares at Mr. Gable.

283

"Callan was just leaving," I said quickly, ignoring the heat crawling up my neck.

"No, he wasn't." Mari's gaze darted between us, a knowing smirk spreading across her face. She dropped her voice to a whisper. "Oh my god, you two were about to sneak off for wedding expo sex. Seriously? It's been a year. Aren't you supposed to be in the 'comfortable Netflix and sweatpants' phase by now?"

"Some of us don't believe in phases," Callan replied. "And some of us appreciate taking breaks to properly... reconnect with our spouses."

Mari made a gagging noise. "Get out of here before you contaminate our booth with your marital bliss. I've got this covered." She glanced toward Mr. Gable's booth and narrowed her eyes. "Besides, I need to keep an eye on Lucifer over there."

"Be the bigger person," I advised, even as I gathered my purse.

"Impossible. I'm only five-foot-three and spite is my primary personality trait." She waved us away. "Go. Fifteen minutes. Any longer and I'll assume you've been kidnapped and call security."

"Twenty minutes," I countered.

"Seventeen and I want details later," Mari bargained.

"No details, and I'll bring you a real coffee tomorrow morning from that place across the street from the hotel," I offered.

"Deal. Now scram before I change my mind."

Callan didn't need to be told twice. He placed his hand on the small of my back as he guided me through the crowded expo hall, the heat of his palm burning through my dress in a way that made it difficult to walk normally.

The supply closet was exactly where the janitor Callan had paid said it would be, tucked away in a quiet corridor far from the main expo floor. The door swung open to reveal a cramped space filled with cleaning supplies and folded tables.

"Very romantic," I deadpanned as he pulled me inside and locked the door behind us. "Nothing says 'I love you' like the smell of heavy-duty industrial floor cleaner and the ambiance of fluorescent lighting."

"Would you prefer rose petals and string quartets, Mrs. Burkhardt?" He grabbed my waist, drawing me hard against him so

I could feel exactly how much he'd missed me. "Because I can have those here in thirty minutes if you're feeling under appreciated."

"Shut up," I murmured, rising on my toes to kiss him, my fingers already working on his tie. "And stop calling me that when you know what it does to me."

His laugh vibrated against my lips. "That's precisely why I do it, Mrs. Burkhardt."

My retort was lost as his mouth claimed mine again, the kiss deeper, hungrier than before. For all our teasing, there was nothing funny about the way his hands skimmed down my sides, bunching the fabric of my dress until he could grip my bare thighs above my stockings.

"We have seventeen minutes," I reminded him, already breathless as he lifted me onto a stack of folded tablecloths. "Probably closer to fifteen now."

"Then we better not waste time," he growled, pushing my dress up to my waist.

The sound I made when his fingers found me through my underwear was embarrassingly needy, but I was past caring. He groaned against my neck when he discovered how wet I already was, the thin silk of my panties soaked through.

"Still glad you married me?" he asked, his fingers slipping beneath the fabric to stroke me.

"Ask me again in five minutes," I gasped, fumbling with his belt.

"I'm insulted you don't think I can last longer, darling." He bit my earlobe as he pushed a finger inside me. I moaned against his shoulder.

"Oh I know you can, but this is more about efficiency."

What followed was a desperate, frantic collision of hands and lips and whispered instructions. The confined space meant we knocked over a mop and nearly toppled a shelf of paper towels, but neither of us could be bothered to care as I wrapped my legs around his waist. Callan braced one hand against the wall behind me, the other gripping my hip as he drove into me hard enough to make me bite my lip to keep from crying out.

"God, I missed you," he panted against my neck, his rhythm building as my nails dug into his shoulders through his shirt. "Three days is too long."

"Yes. Definitely too long." The words dissolved into a moan as he hit that perfect spot inside me. "Oh god, right there."

Callan's grip on my hips tightened, his thrusts growing harder, more insistent. He held me against the cold wall of the supply closet, the contrast of heat and chill sending electric shocks through my body. My legs wrapped tighter around his waist, heels digging into his lower back, urging him on.

"Don't hold back," I breathed into his ear, my voice barely a whisper. "We don't have time for gentle."

A low growl rumbled in his chest, and he captured my mouth in a fierce kiss, teeth grazing my lower lip. The shelves behind us rattled with each movement, the sound of our bodies colliding echoing in the small space. His fingers dug into my flesh, holding me in place as he drove into me again and again.

He swore under his breath, his pace increasing until the world around us blurred. The scent of sex and sweat filled the air. My heart pounded in my chest, my breath coming in short gasps as pleasure coiled tight within me.

"Close," I managed to choke out, my body tensing as the first waves of orgasm began to crest. "So close."

Callan's hand slid between us, his fingers finding my clit. He stroked me in time with his thrusts, the dual sensation pushing me over the edge. I bit down on his shoulder to muffle my cry as I came, my body convulsing around him.

"Fuck, Anica," he groaned, his movements growing erratic as he chased his own release. His body stiffened, and he buried his face in my neck, a low groan escaping him as he climaxed.

For a moment, we stayed locked together, breathless and trembling in the aftermath. Then he raised his head to look at me, his eyes soft with a tenderness that still took me by surprise sometimes.

"I love you," he murmured, pressing his forehead to mine. "Even in supply closets that smell like bleach."

"How romantic," I laughed, but my heart swelled with the same ridiculous happiness I felt every time he looked at me like that. "I love you too. Now put me down before someone comes looking for cleaning supplies and finds the CEO of Burkhardt Industries with his pants around his ankles."

"Mm-hmm," he agreed chuckling, making no move to pull away. "Just give me a second to recover. You wrecked me."

I laughed softly, pressing a kiss to his jaw. "I think that's my line. You're the one who did all the work."

He pulled back just enough to meet my gaze, a wicked grin spreading across his face. "Trust me, darling, that was anything but work."

With a sigh, I unwound my legs from his waist, my feet touching the ground for the first time in what felt like hours. Callan stepped back, tucking himself away and straightening his clothes.

"We need to get back," I said, checking my reflection in the compact mirror from my purse. "Mari's going to know exactly what we were doing."

"She already knew before we left," Callan pointed out, fixing his tie. "Besides, it's not like we haven't done this before."

"True. I suppose we've turned it into an expo tradition."

"I quite enjoy this tradition." Callan grinned at me, smoothing a strand of hair back into place. "We should make it an every event tradition."

"We go to at least a hundred events each year."

"Exactly." He winked at me.

"You're ridiculous," I said as I smacked him on the chest, but I couldn't stop the smile spreading across my face.

"That's not what you were saying five minutes ago," he teased, capturing my hand and bringing it to his lips. "In fact, I distinctly remember you calling me a 'god' at one point."

"Temporary insanity," I replied, checking my watch. "We've been gone twenty-four minutes. Mari's going to be —"

A piercing alarm cut through the air, making us both jump.

"What the hell is that?" Callan asked, wincing at the sound.

"Fire alarm." I grabbed my purse and yanked open the door. "We need to go. Now."

We hurried through the corridors, joining the stream of confused vendors and attendees heading toward the exits. The smell of smoke grew stronger as we approached the main exhibition hall.

"It's coming from our section," I realized with growing horror, quickening my pace.

"I'm sure it's nothing —" Callan began, but stopped short as we rounded the corner into the hall.

287

Both our booth and Mr. Gable's were partially engulfed in flames. Fire extinguisher foam covered what wasn't burning, creating white mountains across the displays. In the center of this apocalyptic tableau stood Mari and Mr. Gable, both covered in foam and what appeared to be gold glitter, locked in what could only be described as a wrestling match. Mr. Gable had Mari in a headlock while she seemed to be attempting to bite his forearm, both of them shouting incoherently as security guards tried to separate them.

I gaped at them. "What the actual—"

"Fuck." Callan finished for me. He recovered faster. "Well," he said with inappropriate cheerfulness, "at least we know it wasn't our fault."

I shot him a glare before rushing forward, my wedding planner crisis mode activating instantly. "Mari! What happened?"

At the sound of my voice, Mari stopped trying to bite Hudson and looked up, her expression morphing from rage to casual greeting so quickly it was almost comical.

"Oh, hey! You're back." She shook her foam-covered hair out of her eyes. "How was your 'inventory check'?"

"What. Happened." I repeated through clenched teeth.

"This psychopath set our booth on fire!" Mari twisted in Mr. Gable's grip, still trying to bite him. "He sabotaged us!"

"I did nothing of the sort," Mr. Gable snapped, though his cool demeanor from earlier had clearly cracked. His perfect hair stood on end, covered in white foam and what looked like ash and gold glitter. His immaculate suit was torn at the shoulder, and a scratch ran down one cheek. "This woman is deranged. She attacked me with a cake serving knife!"

"It was a spatula, you dramatic asshole!" Mari shot back. "And you started the fire when you planted those trick candles in our display that wouldn't blow out!"

"I did no such thing," Mr. Gable replied, his voice cold but his eyes blazing. "Though I can't say I'm surprised your tacky decorations went up in flames. That much polyester in one place was practically begging for combustion."

"Oh, so now you're a fashion critic and an arsonist?"

"I am a professional wedding planner with standards, not a circus ringleader with a glue gun and a death wish!"

I stared at them in disbelief. "You've known each other for *two hours*."

"Two hours too long," they said in unison, then glared at each other with renewed hatred.

Security finally managed to separate them completely, though both looked ready to lunge again given the slightest opportunity. A small crowd had gathered, several people filming on their phones despite the expo staff's attempts to move everyone along.

"This is completely unacceptable," a security guard growled, keeping a firm grip on Mr. Gable's arm. "Both of you are facing removal from the premises and possible legal action for damages."

I stepped forward, slipping into the calm, reasonable persona that had defused countless wedding disasters. "I understand this looks... bad," I began.

"They set two booths on fire and destroyed a third with the sprinkler system," the guard said flatly.

I glanced at the adjacent booth, now soaked beyond recognition. "We will, of course, cover all damages," I assured him, silently thanking the wedding gods that I'd married a man with a good lawyer. "This was clearly an unfortunate accident —"

"She's the accident. A walking breathing accident," Mr. Gable interrupted, attempting to straighten his ruined suit with his free hand. "I want her arrested for assault and arson!"

"That is my best friend you're insulting, Mr. Gable." I lifted my chin, narrowing my eyes. "Be careful what you say."

He opened his mouth and quickly closed it, wisely choosing not to respond.

"You're the man who weaseled his way into my conversation with a couple and told them our centerpieces looked like something a drunk toddler would make at summer camp!" Mari shot back.

"I was merely offering an expert opinion," Mr. Gable replied. "One they clearly appreciated, given how quickly they signed with me."

"You snake! You corporate vulture! You —"

"Enough!" I rarely raised my voice, but when I did, people tended to listen. Both Mari and Mr. Gable fell silent, though they continued to glare at each other. "This is ridiculous. You're both adults, not children fighting over toys in a sandbox."

"Tell that to the woman who tackled me," Mr. Gable muttered. "She started it."

"I don't care who started it." I turned to the security guard. "We'll pay for the damages and remove ourselves from the premises immediately. No need for further escalation."

The guard looked skeptical but nodded. "Get them out of here before I change my mind."

As the guard released Mr. Gable, Callan appeared beside me, looking suspiciously entertained by the whole situation. "I've already called our insurance," he murmured. "And offered to make a donation to the expo's rebuilding fund that should smooth things over."

"My hero," I sighed, leaning against him momentarily before turning back to the warring planners. "Both of you, outside. Now."

To my surprise, they complied, though they maintained a careful distance from each other as we made our way through the now-emptying exhibition hall. Once outside in the parking lot, I rounded on them both.

"I don't know what happened in there, and honestly, I don't care. Mari, we're driving back to the hotel. Mr. Gable, I apologize for whatever part we played in this... catastrophe."

Mr. Gable straightened to his full height, somehow managing to look dignified despite being covered in foam and glitter. "It appears we got off on the wrong foot, Mrs. Burkhardt. I assure you, I don't normally resort to such... primitive tactics in business competition."

"Could have fooled me, Fire Starter," Mari muttered. "What's next, slashing our tires? Poisoning our coffee?"

A muscle twitched in Mr. Gable's jaw. "Your she-devil of a friend seems to bring out the worst in me."

"Feeling's mutual, asshole."

I noticed something then that I'd missed in the chaos. The way Mr. Gable's eyes never left Mari's face even as he spoke to me, the slight flush on his cheeks that couldn't be attributed entirely to their physical struggle, the way his hands clenched and unclenched at his sides as if he was physically restraining himself from reaching for her.

Oh shit.

Glancing at Mari, I noticed the same intensity mirrored in her expression, though she'd disguise it as hatred if questioned.

Callan must've noticed it too. "Fascinating," he murmured in my ear quietly enough that neither of them would hear. "A thousand bucks says they're sleeping together within a month."

"Two weeks," I whispered back. "Mari doesn't do slow burns."

"What are you two whispering about?" Mari snapped, finally tearing her gaze away from Mr. Gable. "I don't like that look in your eyes, Burkhardts. Fix it, or I'll fix it for you." She glared at Callan and me before whirling on Mr. Gable. "And you. If I ever see you again, I will skin you alive and feed you to the piranhas in the Chicago River."

"There aren't any piranhas in the Chicago River."

"Well lucky for you, dickhead, my best friend married a billionaire and he can get his hands on piranhas so that I can carry out my plan."

"I actually could," Callan whispered to me, and when I glared at him he shrugged his shoulders. "Just saying."

"I'd sooner date a piranha than see you again, Missus..."

"Oh hell no. I am not giving you my–"

"Her name is Mari Landry," my husband said, holding his hand out for Mr. Gable to shake. "And you've met my wife, Anica Burkhardt. I'm Callan. It's nice to meet you."

Mari looked ready to start threatening Callan, and I decided to step in.

"Time to go!" I grabbed Mari's arm before round two could commence in the parking lot. "Mr. Gable, I'm sure we'll see you at future events. Preferably with a fire extinguisher on standby."

"Mrs. Burkhardt." He gave a stiff nod. "Mr. Burkhardt." His gaze slid to Mari, hardening again. "Ms. Landry, I look forward to never working near you again."

"Feeling's mutual, dickweed," she spat.

As we walked toward our car, I glanced back. Mr. Gable was still standing there, foam-covered and disheveled, looking at Mari with an expression I couldn't quite read, but it fell somewhere between fury and fascination.

"I cannot believe you," I hissed once we were out of earshot. "Our first Chicago expo, and you nearly burn the place down!"

"He deserved it," Mari muttered, attempting to brush glitter from her ruined blouse. "You should have seen what he did to our consultations. He kept sliding in with his stupid face and dropping

291

lines like 'Oh, have I shown you our 3D venue projections yet?' as if we were offering finger paintings compared to his tech."

"So you set his booth on fire?"

"I didn't set anything on fire! I was just swapped his fancy little business cards for some I grabbed while getting coffee. They were for a sketchy spa downtown. The fire started when I found those weird candles hidden in our display. They wouldn't go out when I tried to blow them out, and then suddenly everything was in flames!"

I rubbed my temples, a headache building there. "This is going to cost us thousands in damages. Not to mention our reputation."

"Actually," Callan interjected, checking his phone, "we're trending on Twitter. #WeddingWars. The videos are getting serious traction. I just got a text from my marketing director asking if this was a planned publicity stunt because our website traffic has quadrupled in the last half hour."

Mari brightened. "See? Silver lining!"

"We are not spinning an act of arson into a marketing opportunity," I said firmly, despite the small voice in my head calculating exactly how many new clients we might get from the viral exposure.

"Of course not," Callan agreed. "Though it is kind of hilarious and definitely something I'd watch on television. Could make a fun reality TV show."

"Absolutely not."

"Obviously." He paused. "But I did just get a message from Erika. A producer wants to speak with us. They made a compelling offer."

"You're kidding me. This soon?" I stared at him with my mouth open. He nodded. "No. Absolutely not."

"It would be strictly exploratory," he assured me, wrapping an arm around my waist and pressing a kiss to my temple. "Besides, don't you think 'Wedding Wars' has a certain ring to it? Mari versus Mr. Gable in a battle of event planning titans?"

"I'd crush him," Mari declared.

"Hell yeah you would," Callan said, giving her a high five over my head.

"I'm surrounded by lunatics," I muttered, leaning into Callan's embrace despite my exasperation. "And I'm married to the ringleader."

"I just need the fun top hat."

As we reached the car, Mari suddenly stopped. "Shit, I left my phone in what's left of our booth. I'll be right back."

Before I could protest, she jogged back toward the building. Through the glass doors, I could see Mr. Gable had apparently had the same idea, returning to salvage what he could from the wreckage. They collided just inside the entrance.

Even from a distance, I could see the spark as they started arguing again, gesturing wildly at each other.

"They're definitely sleeping together within the month," Callan declared, watching the scene with amusement.

"Week," I corrected. "Did you see the way he looked at her? That's not just hatred."

"Reminds me of someone else I know." He turned me to face him, his expression softening. "Someone who looked at me like she wanted to either kill me or kiss me, with very little middle ground."

"I never looked at you like that," I protested.

"You absolutely did. Usually right before threatening me."

"Well, you deserved it."

"I was in love," he corrected, pulling me closer. "Just too stubborn to admit it."

Read the First Chapter in

Mari's Book

EXPO–NENTIALLY BAD DECISIONS

Chapter 1: Mari

Two weeks ago, I had the best sex of my life with a man who turned out to be my professional nemesis. The universe didn't just fuck me. It fucked me, filmed it, and is now selling tickets to the show.

"Call me when you land," I said, hugging my best friend Anica at the airport security line. She'd pulled her dark hair into its usual perfect bun, not a strand out of place despite our mad dash through O'Hare. "And if Callan tries to convince you that letting him fly the plane would be more fun, please remind him that billionaires who die in private aircraft accidents become cautionary TED Talks with titles like 'How One Man's Ego Created a New Crater.'"

Anica rolled her eyes. "I'll keep him in coach class with the rest of the peasants, I promise."

Callan, her obscenely rich and irritatingly handsome husband of one year, raised an eyebrow. "Ladies, I'm standing right here."

I squealed, opening my mouth and grinning. "Oh my god, hi Cal! I didn't see you there." As if I could miss the tall, broad-shouldered Apollo wannabe. "We were just talking about you," I said, patting his cheek. "Now go back to Manhattan and make more money while I expand your wife's empire. Try not to buy any small countries while I'm gone unless you're going to give them to me for Christmas."

"If I find any countries looking for psychotic blond dictators, I'll make sure to put in a bid," he promised, slipping his arm around Anica's waist in that casually possessive way that made my ovaries simultaneously sigh and tell my brain to shut up about my perpetually single status.

"You're going to do amazing, Mar," Anica said, squeezing my hands. "You've got this. I wouldn't trust anyone else with our Chicago office."

My stomach twisted like I'd swallowed a live squid that was now attempting to escape through my bellybutton. Knot Your Average Wedding had been our baby since college. Well, Anica's baby that I'd enthusiastically co-parented by adding equal parts creativity and chaos. It was weird to think that she trusted me enough to fly solo with the new expansion. Just me, alone in Chicago, responsible for making or breaking our Midwest presence.

God, she was an idiot.

"Text me about the celebrity meeting tomorrow," Anica called over her shoulder as they headed toward security. "I want every detail! No improvising without running it by me first!"

"Yeah, yeah, I'll be a perfect little Anica-clone!" I shouted back, making a face that she couldn't see but definitely knew I was making.

Aw, shit. I was going to miss her. Damn it.

I watched until they disappeared into the TSA line, Callan's arm around Anica. They were disgustingly perfect together, like someone had designed them in a laboratory where they grew ideal couples from celebrity DNA and fairy tales. I was only slightly jealous. Okay, moderately jealous. Fine. Watching them made my uterus do the entire floor routine from the national women's gymnastics team, but I'd rather lick the bottom of a groom's shoe after an outdoor farm wedding reception in the middle of a shitstorm than admit that out loud.

I tugged my blonde waves into a messy bun. As I headed to my car, I was already mentally preparing for tomorrow's meeting with celebrity chef Manny Kussikov and his film director fiancée Lia Martin. Landing their wedding would be like shooting the Chicago expansion directly into wedding planners' heaven, complete with gold-plated harps and champagne waterfalls.

Our Chicago office was a converted industrial loft in the West Loop that made me feel like I was starring in my own romcom montage every time I walked in. Exposed brick walls. Massive windows. The kind of hardwood floors that had definitely witnessed at least three murders back in prohibition days.

I spread my materials across the reclaimed wood conference table that Anica had shipped from some sustainable forest collective in Oregon. Tomorrow's meeting needed to be perfect. Not Anica-perfect, which was impossible without surgically removing my personality, but Mari-perfect. Creative, memorable, and the perfect amount of holy-shit-did-she-really-just-say-that.

My phone rang from an unknown number. I answered with my Professional Voice™, which was just my regular voice minus the swearing and sexual innuendos.

"Mari Landry, Knot Your Average Wedding, how can I help you?"

"Ms. Landry, this is Mr. Radfordt from First Chicago Bank."

My stomach dropped. Banking calls were never good news. They were the equivalent of your gynecologist calling you personally instead of having a nurse do it.

"I'm calling about your business loan application for the Chicago expansion."

I perched on the edge of the conference table, needing something solid under me. This loan was everything. The difference between Knot Your Average Wedding: Midwest Empire and Mari Landry: Crawling Back to New York with Her Tail Between Her Legs.

"Yes! I was just reviewing our projections, and —"

"We have some concerns about the viability of the expansion without more substantial assets or existing Chicago clients."

Condescension dripped through the phone. Translation: We don't think you can hack it in the big city, little girl with the funny ideas and ridiculous blonde hair.

"I understand your concerns, Mr. Radfordt, but I actually have a meeting tomorrow with Chef Manny Kussikov and Lia Martin. You know, the Oscar-nominated director? They're looking for someone to plan their wedding here in Chicago." I forced brightness into my voice. "Their wedding would immediately establish our reputation in the Midwest market."

"Celebrities are notoriously fickle, Ms. Landry," he replied in a tone that suggested he found my prospects about as promising as a cash bar at a Kardashian wedding. "Send over the details if you secure the contract, and we can reassess. Until then, I'm afraid we'll need to put your application on hold."

I hung up and resisted the urge to throw my phone into the Chicago River. Instead, I did what any mature professional would do. I grabbed the emergency tequila from my desk drawer and took a swig straight from the bottle. The good tequila, too.

The burn hit my throat, and I coughed. I missed Anica. She's spent the last four years trying to break me of my emergency alcohol habit. She called it "problematic coping." I called it "cheaper than therapy and faster than meditation."

This celebrity wedding wasn't just important anymore; it was the lifeline our Chicago dream needed. Without it, Anica's faith in me would crumble, and I'd officially become the family disappointment my parents always predicted I'd be.

As I sorted through my presentation materials, a white napkin fluttered to the floor from between my portfolio pages. I bent to pick it up, and the sight of the scrawled room number, *805*, sent a rush of heat straight to places that had no business heating.

"Damn it," I whispered, staring at those three digits like they were an incantation that could summon the devil himself. Or in this case, the devil's hotter, better-in-bed cousin.

Two weeks ago. The hotel bar. The night before the expo disaster.

I'd been doing a final check for the next day, and more importantly, avoiding Anica and Callan after they made their icky bedroom eyes at each other, when I decided one drink wouldn't hurt. Just something to take the edge off my pre-expo jitters.

One drink turned into three, and three drinks turned into making eye contact with the most fuckable man I'd ever seen, sitting alone at the end of the bar.

Tall, with dark brown hair that looked like he'd been running his hands through it all day. A jawline that could cut glass. Eyes so intensely green they should be illegal. And hands. Jesus Christ, his hands. The kind of hands that made you imagine them gripping your thighs, your hair, your —

I'd never done the one-night stand thing before. I was more of a three-date-minimum kind of girl, partly because I had trust issues the size of Texas, and partly because my work schedule meant dates usually ended with me taking emergency calls about missing boutonnieres and drunk groomsmen.

But something about this man — the way he looked at me like I was the highlight of his day, the slight curve of his mouth when I made him laugh, the way he listened to me — had me writing my room number on a napkin before my better judgment could tackle my libido to the ground and put it in a chokehold.

What followed was a night that should be classified as a national security risk because I'd probably give up state secrets if someone promised me a repeat performance. His mouth should have a PhD in female anatomy. His hands knew exactly how much pressure to apply and where. And the way he'd looked at me while he was inside me had broken something open in me that I hadn't known was closed.

And then morning came, and with it, the harsh reality that we'd never exchanged names or numbers, just body fluids. He was gone when I woke up, leaving nothing but the lingering scent of his cologne and muscles I'd forgotten I had screaming in delicious protest.

I'd rushed to the expo, running on caffeine, endorphins, and the lingering high of multiple orgasms, ready to conquer the Chicago wedding world. I'd been arranging our display when I heard a familiar voice behind me.

"You must be from Knot Your Average Wedding. I'm Hudson Gable, of Perfect Day Planning."

I'd turned, coffee in hand, to find myself face-to-face with my anonymous hotel bar sex god. Only now he wasn't anonymous, and he wasn't looking at me like I was the answer to every question. He was looking at me with what I assumed was the same look of utter shock.

I blacked out, but I'm pretty sure I swore.

Yeah, I probably swore.

The recognition in his eyes had been instant, followed by something that looked like panic, quickly masked by professional detachment. "I look forward to some friendly competition," he'd said, extending his hand like we hadn't spent the previous night with his head between my thighs.

I'd shaken his hand on autopilot, too stunned to speak. I'd watched in horror as he turned to a potential client and said, "You might want to check out my booth instead. Some companies"—his eyes flicked meaningfully to our vintage-inspired display—"rely on outdated techniques because they lack innovation."

The rest of the day had spiraled into increasingly hostile territory. He'd rearranged our display and left a sticky note saying, "Fixed it." I'd replaced his business cards with a sketchy spa place down the street. He'd told another client that my color schemes were "so 2019." I'd started spreading rumors that his business was being investigated for price gouging.

By afternoon, we were in a full-blown war that culminated in me knocking over a candle display that set fire to his ridiculous foam photo backdrop (not that I'd told Anica that. I may have spun a teeny-tiny little lie that the fire was his fault...). The sprinkler system had activated, someone had found a fire extinguisher, and in the end, three booths were ruined. Thanks to Anica's smooth-talking, we were only ejected from the expo and not arrested.

I hadn't seen him since, but that didn't mean I hadn't thought about him. Constantly. Infuriatingly. My brain kept serving up highlights from our night together at the most inappropriate moments, like during client consultations or while brushing my teeth.

I stuffed the napkin into my desk drawer and slammed it shut. I hadn't told Anica about the one-night stand part of the expo disaster. As far as she knew, Hudson and I had taken an instant, professional dislike to each other. Which was true. I disliked him. Professionally.

Other parts of me had different opinions, but they didn't get a vote. Especially not my lady parts, which apparently had the decision-making skills of a toddler in a candy store, grabbing the shiniest, most appealing thing without considering the consequences.

My phone pinged with a text from Devonna, Anica's assistant, who'd been assigned to help me remotely from New York:

Finalizing materials for tomorrow. Need anything else?

I typed back, but didn't hit send right away. *Just a personality transplant that makes me less likely to sleep with the enemy or commit felony arson. But I'll settle for extra copies of the proposal.*

I deleted it and rewrote the message.

All good. Thanks.

The office felt too quiet without Anica. She'd always been the steady one, the planner, the voice of reason to my creative chaos. I was the emotional one, the one who once threatened a DJ with garden shears when he tried to play the Chicken Dance after the bride specifically banned it. ("It wasn't a threat," I'd explained later to Anica. "It was a promise. With visual aids.")

My phone rang again. It was a bride calling about an emergency cake crisis for her wedding this weekend. This I could handle. Wedding emergencies were my jam, my specialty, the thing that made Anica keep me around despite my tendency to say "fuck" in front of grandmothers and accidentally set things on fire.

"What's wrong with the cake?" I asked, already reaching for my emergency vendor contact list.

"The bakery just called. Their refrigeration system broke down overnight, and my cake is ruined!" Her voice had reached a particular pitch that only dogs and wedding planners could hear.

"Okay, first, take a deep breath," I said, using my Calm The Fuck Down Voice. "Second, cancel your plans for the next hour. I'll pick you up in twenty minutes."

"Where are we going?" She asked, the panic in her voice dialing back from 'imminent meltdown' to 'manageable crisis.'

"We're going to visit the three best bakeries in Chicago, and by the time we're done, you'll have a cake that makes your original look like something from a gas station vending machine."

"But my cake had hand-painted sugar flowers that took weeks to—"

"Trust me," I interrupted. "I got a replacement cake once with six hours' notice during a flour shortage. This is practically luxury timing."

By seven that evening, I'd secured a last-minute cake from Chicago's most exclusive bakery, confirmed all the details for tomorrow's celebrity meeting, and stress-eaten half a pizza while going through our presentation one more time.

The bank's rejection still stung, but I was Mari Fucking Landry. I'd built a career out of making the impossible happen on deadlines that would give normal people aneurysms. One snooty banker wasn't going to stop me.

I gathered my materials and headed out. Tomorrow's meeting needed me at my absolute best.

Which meant I had approximately twelve hours to exorcise both the ghost of sex past and the nightmare of professional disaster from my brain before I faced the clients who could save our Chicago dream.

Maybe I needed to stop at the liquor store first...

Read the rest of

Mari and Hudson's story

in the next book...

RIVALS
NOT
WELCOME

SCAN THE CODE BELOW TO FIND BOOK 2 ON AMAZON!

Acknowledgments

I'd like to first thank my husband, who deserves a medal for not divorcing me after I kept waking him up at 1 AM to ask questions like, "Is it believable that someone could have sex in a supply closet without knocking over at least one mop?" Your patience, your input on male anatomy descriptions, and your willingness to "help with research" are the reasons this book exists, and possibly why our neighbors no longer make eye contact when we walk the dogs.

Speaking of the pups. To my babies, who somehow understand that Momma staring at a laptop isn't her ignoring them. Instead, she's mentally wrestling fictional people into submission. Your placement of toys on my keyboard and insistence that the middle of explicit sex scenes is the perfect time for dinner kept me grounded in reality, even when I preferred fictional worlds.

My eternal gratitude goes to my grandmother, the inspiration for Gram, who once told me, "Love isn't something you can control or predict or manage. It's messy and inconvenient and often arrives at the worst possible time." She was talking about her third husband, but the wisdom applies universally. Thanks for teaching me that love exists, even when it's wrapped in outrageous stories and inappropriate comments.

This book wouldn't exist without my incredible beta readers who weren't afraid to write "WTF IS THIS?" in all caps in the margins. To Lily M., Rachel H., Dani T., Sam P., Brittany B., and to Tyler K., who bravely read this as the token male perspective and responded with simply, "Men really are this dumb sometimes." Your honesty made this book better, and your friendship made the process bearable.

And finally, to you, the reader who has followed Anica and Callan to their happily ever after. You invited these characters into your life, possibly stayed up too late with them, and maybe even fell a little in love alongside them.

If you found yourself laughing in public places, frantically turning pages in the bathtub, or sending screenshots to friends with excessive exclamation points, would you consider leaving a rating or review? Not because algorithms demand them (though they do, the hungry beasts), but because somewhere, another reader is wondering if they should pick up this book, and your words might convince them to take a chance on a story about a billionaire who doesn't believe in love, a wedding planner with emergency kits for every occasion, and the incredible chemistry they had from the moment she stepped out of that elevator.

I mean… Mari would probably review the book… *Shrugs*

About the Author

Carina Walsh lives for three things: perfectly timed banter, the sound of readers gasping at plot twists, and telling stories where the guy gets the girl (or the other way around). She is so excited for her debut novel, *Bride Not Included*, to be out in the world for readers to devour. When she's not writing steamy romcoms, she can be found reading in her favorite chair, testing TikTok recipes in the middle of the night, or testing specific scenes from other spicy romcoms with her husband (for science). Carina currently resides in Boston with her husband and their two dogs, and is excited to continue writing sexy books with laugh out loud moments.

www.ingramcontent.com/pod-product-compliance
Lightning Source LLC
Chambersburg PA
CBHW020226260626
47156CB00002B/560